PRODIGY

Dave Kalstein

PRODIGY

Thomas Dunne Books ⚜ St. Martin's Press | New York

THOMAS DUNNE BOOKS.
An imprint of St. Martin's Press.

www.stmartins.com

Book design by Irene Vallye

ISBN 0-312-34096-6
EAN 978-0-312-34096-4

First Edition: January 2006

10   9   8   7   6   5   4   3   2   1

For my parents. The first—and finest—teachers I've ever had.

And for the real Cooley and Goldsmith, wherever they may be.

ACKNOWLEDGMENTS

I was born standing up and talking back. I knew everything there was to know about life by the age of thirteen. Luckily for me, there always happened to be those along the way who begged to differ, those who knew how wrong I was but were patient enough to believe in me anyway. They're the people who made this book possible and to whom I am forever indebted with my thanks. . . .

To Kate Lee, my friend and agent who always just *knew*. Kate, from the very beginning the warrior inside you inspired me. To Sean Desmond, my editor, who took a chance, grabbed hold of a boy's daydream, and turned it into a reality. To Josh Beane, the best friend who watches my back, pulls me up after those nasty tumbles, and always reminds me of what it is to be a man. To Thor Halvorssen, who taught me how to fight and, more important, how to be inspired. To Jonathan Kalstein, my brother, who has the kindness and conscience to which I aspire. To Mike Paris, Todd Bishop, Zachary Knight, Brooke Cucinella, Carlos Suarez, Anna Nordberg, Erin Fitzpatrick, Marc Kushner, Doree Shafrir, Ellen Killoran, Jennifer Rubell, Nora Zehetner, Ian

Somerhalder, Cy Carter, Courtney Murphy, Katherine Cunningham-Eves, and Andrew Feltenstein: All friends who never whined about it being too early in the day for cocktails or doubted the dreams that spilled out over them—for this I will always love you.

And to all my teachers: The ones who embraced me, the ones who censored me, the ones who kicked me out, the ones who promised me that one day school would let out forever and I'd find myself finally, impossibly, grown up. . . . This one's for you.

PRODIGY / ˈprä-də-jē / noun:

Middle English, from Latin *prodigium*: a monster, an omen.

1. **a**: a portentous event. **b**: something inexplicable.
2. **a**: an extraordinary, marvelous, or unusual accomplishment, deed, or event. **b**: a highly talented child or youth.

—*Merriam-Webster's Collegiate Dictionary*
(11th Edition, circa 2004)

In me school destroyed a great deal...All I learned there was Latin and lying.

—Hermann Hesse, *Reflections*, 257:
"Education and Schools"

Soap and education are not as sudden as a massacre, but they are more deadly in the long run.

—Mark Twain, *A Curious Dream*:
"The Facts Concerning the Recent Resignation"

PRODIGY

PROLOGUE

Mr. Daniel Ford Smith.

There were so many things he hated about that school, but that—the way they stretched out each specimen's name (first, middle, and last all lined up together as if it were not a name but an exotic, complex mathematics equation) and stuck a formal "Mr." or "Miss" at the front—was not one of them. He liked it. Not that he'd ever have admitted this, but Mr. Daniel Ford Smith secretly loved hearing it uttered by the adults who ran the place, the professors who taught the progressions. Even the sound of his full name squeaked out by one of the many younger, smaller specimens he bullied over the years gave him satisfaction every time. He relished hearing it turned into a digitized phrase by the InterAct system in his old dorm room (*Good morning, Mr. Daniel Ford Smith*, the alarm intoned each day for twelve years at 6:30 A.M. and it gave him a small surge of pride, as if he'd seen his name in print).

It had been almost three years since he graduated at the bottom of the Stansbury School's Class of 2033 and not a day passed without him thinking of the one place he swore—they all swore—he'd never think of again. Granted, the place had its way with you, but it sure made a kid feel regal while he was there; from the anointed (and cursed, in Smith's opinion) valedictorians to the rank-and-file honors kids to the merely average ones headed to Ivy League schools (sans scholarships) all the way down to the unbalanced specimens like him. Mr. Daniel Ford Smith. Had a nice ring to it. A certain dignity.

A dignity that was motivating him to run for his life.

In midsprint, Smith scanned the streets of San Angeles. Shabby, vintage twentieth-century buildings seemed to morph into gleaming towers, peeling paint giving way to hundred-story stretches of titanium, glass, and steel. Like a brilliantly eccentric but unlicensed urban planner had become a plastic surgeon and performed an improvisational back-room procedure, grafting experimental, avant-garde implants to this old, faithful matron of a metropolis. The megacity's blocks were packed tightly, filled with an amalgam of high- and low-value real estate bunched together like giant, gleaming haystacks. Above, gyromobiles ferried people through the maze of floating traffic signals on New Sunset Boulevard, which hung a couple of thousand feet in the air. Below the hazy airways, the occasional jalopy with an old-school gas engine chugged along, sputtering, as if unsure of what to do with all the empty space ahead of it on this neglected stretch of Old Sunset.

The rubber-Teflon blend in the soles of Smith's work boots (soles guaranteed by Nike to last seventy-five years, although he would have been happy with the next seventy-five seconds) gripped the slick pavement as he pivoted into an alley off 3rd Street on Avenue R. He leaned against a crumbling, greasy brick wall, heaved panicked breaths in and out, and listened for their footsteps. The morning sky was white and wet. A selection of sounds: the hiss of a monorail's doors as they slid closed on the tracks a few feet away in the street; crisply screeching whistles from the city wranglers guiding non-Stansbury-related citizens from one side of the street to another. Nothing out of the ordinary.

Nothing except that four other ex-specimens, alumni of the same school he hated and helplessly revered simultaneously, had been killed at the rate of one per month for the past four months. There were six of them when everything began, improbably, six months before that day. And then they were all gone except for him and his old accomplice. The delinquent duo. Mr. Daniel Ford Smith and Mr. Jonathan Clark Riley. Unlike the others, Misters Smith and Riley were pals back in school, so when they heard about them disappearing one by one, they kept in touch. They spoke just two weeks ago, knowing the whole time but never saying out loud that they were the only ones left and that hence, the next to go would be one of them. After hanging up the phone, Smith remembered hoping that Riley would go before him. Simple, basic, animalistic self-preservation. But now that he was running and the soft, inevitable roar of the footsteps behind him weren't stopping, weren't ever going to stop, Smith was thankful that it was his turn. Maybe Riley would hear the news and play it safe. Maybe he'd get out of town and disappear, forget about their impossible plans, and start a new life somewhere, anywhere.

Standing there in the alley, drenched in the polluted, yellowing rain, he decided to keep running, because the least Smith could do was give his old buddy a few more minutes of a head start before the footsteps came after him.

The patter of the rain drummed a beat on his shoulders. Shoulders grown thick, riddled with pipes of tendons that trailed down into a network of shivering muscles in his arms. Muscles courtesy of Stansbury School. Unfortunately, the school's famous med cycle didn't work the same magic on his cerebral cortex: he barely graduated. His parents wouldn't pay for community college; twelve years of Stansbury tapped them out. He wasn't finding a job. As if the odds weren't poor enough, given his lack of credentials, the release of the first wave of gyromobiles corresponded with his year of birth. The floating vehicles replaced conventional automobiles—virtually eliminating traffic accidents—and gave way to the Population Boom of 2015. Just in time for those babies to grow up and compete with him for minimum-wage labor. Sure, he was a Stansbury specimen and all, but competing in a job market with twelve billion other people was no cakewalk. Then one day the Stansbury Alumni Relations Board called Smith up out of the blue and offered him a job shifting units of packaged intravenous cafeteria foodstuffs around the school's plant in the outskirts of San Angeles. He accepted graciously. The offer made him think the school wasn't so bad, after all. They took care of their own. No one called him "Mister" at the plant though, just a spat-out "Smith," like it was a four-letter word, but a job was a job, and he was determined to tough through it and make an honest living. His mom and dad were proud. Relatively speaking. Families that forked out the $500,000 Stansbury tuition each year tended to expect a bit more out of their children than rigorous manual labor six days a week, but their hopes for him dimmed long ago.

If only he could've stretched this thing out a bit longer, and lasted till the end. If Mom and Pops saw what he and Riley and the other alumni were going to pull off, they would've taken back everything. The plan formed six months ago, when Miss Stella No-Middle-Name Saltzman called him up and broke the news: the school only gave him the work to keep tabs on his whereabouts. Because he mattered. And then she told him everything else.

Smith leaned his head toward the street and listened: raindrops curled down his neck, a single set of leather soles scraped against the pavement, just a bit too cautious to be casual. An anomaly. At this hour, there wasn't enough room to walk alone on the sidewalk; there should have been too many people packing the street, unless . . . He crouched down and waited. The anomalous set of feet approached, complete with a familiar head and eyes up top, looking for a shoulder-level target and not finding him anywhere. Still squatting, Smith threw out his rippled arms, grabbed the ankles and yanked the figure to the ground, dragging the squirming body into the alley like he wasn't Mr. Daniel Ford Smith, Class of '33, but like the crazed, scared misfit he had been told his whole life he was.

A quick glance at the face: meaty jowls, a lazy brown eye. Officer Jamison, Stansbury security detail, trying to fly under the radar in civilian's clothing.

"Mr. . . . Mr. Smith . . . stop and . . . ," Jamison sputtered. Three years after graduation and Jamison still looked the same: a sneering grown-up drunk on authority and a title, just another bully who never matured. Smith slammed one of his huge, labor-deformed fists into Jamison's face and smashed his head into the pavement with the other. Smith had wanted to do that the entire twelve years spanning first grade to senior year, but he never had the excuse or the balls.

Jamison went limp. Smith stayed close to the ground and, much to his chagrin, started trembling.

Slow down and put it together: Stella told him to run, to meet Riley on Avenue R and hide out somewhere. She'd find them when it was time, she never said how. Ever since she reappeared in his life six months ago (the first time he'd seen her since commencement day back at the tower when she gave a speech he slept through) he always did what she told him because of this thing about her, this warm look in her eye that said she believed in him unconditionally. She didn't treat him like just another burned-out, unbalanced specimen teetering on the verge of unemployment. Miss Stella No-Middle-Name Saltzman smiled and touched his cheek and still called him Mr. Daniel Ford Smith like that name actually meant something to her.

Standing over Jamison's body, Smith made a promise to himself: He was going to run faster than them. Hit harder than them. He was going to make it out of this mess because he always loved the way that name sounded all stretched out and regal, but for the first time in his twenty-one years he wanted to know what it meant. He was betting good old Mr. Jonathan Clark Riley was feeling the same way. He'd find him. It would be like they were freshmen once more, but in . . . life. They'd watch out for each other and learn and maybe one day they'd graduate all over again. For real this time. Smith made one more promise. After he got himself out of this jam, he was going to find each kid he smacked around, every one of the runts he put the fear of God in, look them in the eyes, and apologize. Repent. Because he was Mr. Daniel Ford Smith and, although he was not sure what he was going to grow up to be one day, he was certain that he was a man.

"There!" Smith heard a man's voice call out. On the opposite end of the alley, three figures in black approached him. He squinted, checking out their ordnance, and saw the standard gear: Hawkeye Tac IX utility vests weighed down by pouches holding flex cuffs, magazines of ammo, and flash/bang kits. Shock sticks swung from their belts, a mere button-flip away from humming to life. Black, fire-resistant Nomex balaclavas concealed their faces and protected their scalps and ears. Their eyes were hidden behind shatterproof silver ballistic polycarbonate goggle lenses. Standard-issue assault boots covered the distance between them and Smith with a cautious but efficient pace. The lead man reached a gloved hand into a holster on his Tac IX and came out with a Colt M-8 pistol.

And then, instantaneously, the sight of that metallic barrel aimed at him from fifty feet triggered something in Smith, an eerie but familiar sensation he hadn't felt in years began coursing through his veins and immediately he placed it. His breathing automatically slowed from frantic gasps to a deliberate, measured pace. He felt his muscles loosen and relax, limbering up. It was the Normalcin from Stansbury's med cycle. The chemical stayed in a specimen's body permanently, kicking in when adrenaline flow reached fight-or-flight levels. Smith's fingers and toes stopped shaking. Years of Stansbury Phys-D progressions flashed before his eyes. The barrel of the Colt M-8 was closer now. He watched the three men as they carefully followed the protocols of their training. He stifled a grin. The trio's leader was ten feet away. Smith saw four ways of disarming him nonlethally.

"Hold steady," murmured the leader to his men. He was now seven feet away. Smith saw eighteen ways of disarming him. All of that high-tech gear made the group seem as if they were approaching a wild, perhaps infectious animal. The other two circled around, surrounding him. "Specimens aren't faster than bullets, now are they?" grinned the leader. He held Smith at gunpoint from three feet away. Smith saw twenty-nine ways. He chose number twelve and let his conditioning take over.

With impossible quickness, he swung up an open palm, easily batting away the Colt M-8 into a high airborne arc. The squad leader froze, his body language contorted into a hieroglyphic flash of shock and confusion. Smith brought his foot down on the man's knee, feeling the patella shatter beneath his Nike sole, grabbed the shock stick from the man's belt, activated it, and cracked him in the back of the head. Concluding that single, fluid motion, Smith hurled the humming, electric weapon directly at the guy to his left, catching him flush in the mouth. Smith glanced down at the two would-be assailants on the ground, their bodies clenched with the helplessness of severe pain. Smith heard the steel body of the M-8 hit a brick wall and clatter to the pavement. Technique number twelve had taken roughly three seconds. His eyes moved to the last man standing and knew his lips were trembling beneath the balaclava.

"Jesus Chr—," he blurted, reaching for his own pistol. Smith grabbed the collar of his Tac IX vest with both hands and yanked, head-butting him, driving his forehead into soft nose cartilage, feeling it rupture and explode. The man crumpled. Smith saw blood soak the inside of the balaclava and seep through the Nomex as the fallen foe writhed on the ground. Upon graduation, every specimen had to register themselves with the police department in their place of residence. Their training and physiques classified them as potentially lethal weapons in the eyes of the law. During their time at school, a daily dose of beta blockers in the med cycle made it virtually impossible for a specimen to get worked up enough to maim someone else in a pique of fury. By graduation, they all knew their skills were only meant to be used in self-defense, that their Stansbury education foisted a huge responsibility upon them, the kind of responsibility that comes with power. Well, that was the theory anyway, and no one could really begrudge law enforcement agencies from taking the proper precautions.

But my God, Smith thought, did it feel good to cut loose and raise some Hell.

He grabbed the stray Colt M-8 from the pavement and took off running, pulling his iPro Industries Tabula 5600 from his jacket, hitting speed dial as he headed for another alley. A weary old woman's voice answered.

"Senator Bloom's office," she said.

"Stella. I need to talk to Stella right now . . . Christ, I—"

"Ready for code."

"3328 dash Charlie dash 44. Come on, I'm—," Smith heard a series of beeps before he could finish.

"Yes?" Stella's voice was calming, easy, warm molasses rolling down a scoop of ice cream. The same way since they were little kids.

"I'm out. They just came after me. You tell the Senator that I'm out and—"

"Slow down. If they've come for you, it's too late to stop now." She paused and he somehow knew which question was coming next.

"Did you kill them?" He glanced up at the airway above and swore he saw an unmarked gyro pull out of the flow of traffic and begin a descent toward him. He started moving faster. "Mr. Smith, did you—"

"No. I know I'm useless to you guys if I'm a murderer."

"But that's not why you let them live." Despite his awful predicament, he could picture that beatific, knowing smile on her lips. "It was because of the good inside of you. The good that they told you didn't exist. You remembered the oath . . ."

Smith's brain flashed back, twelve years of a daily pledge coming back verbatim, echoing in the chorus of four thousand children speaking in obedient unison: *By virtue of the Gifts bestowed upon me, I swear my Eternal Duty to all those without such Gifts. For Power may point the way, but only Honor can lead it.* Good old Doc Stansbury—R.I.P.— meant well enough, but Smith and Riley always thought it was a crock. That gyro sank closer to the street. It was headed for him. He jacked a bullet into the Colt's chamber.

"You're going to make it," Stella said. "Now think about how you can—"

"I'm not good at that! You picked us because we're not as smart as you, goddamn it! And now we're all dying, one by one."

"Are you armed?"

"Yes."

"Get to the northwest corner of 6th Street in Sector D. Stay in the crowds. I'll meet you there."

Smith got goosebumps. "You're . . . you're in San Angeles?"

"Just go, Mr. Smith."

He hung up and ran for the street at the end of the alley.

"You can't escape this, Mr. Smith," called out a voice from above.

He glanced up and saw Captain Gibson looking out the driver's side window of that unmarked gyro floating thirty feet above him in the narrow gap between tenement buildings. Gibson's hair was wet and thin. Smith could make out the white of his scalp from where he stood down below.

The fifteen-year-old in him thought: if Gibson's off campus, getting soaked like the rest of us, that means I'm in *really* deep shit this time. But the adult in him knew: yeah, it really is gonna end. Right here. Twenty-one years old. Just like this.

The sight of Gibson made him panic. His heart started racing again, a young man's fear overriding his conditioning. Smith emptied the M-8's clip in the direction of the gyro. It swerved, easily dodging the bullets. Several figures in black sailed down from above, macabre, human-sized raindrops with arms and legs and guns. Three more gyros descended. Officers approached Smith on both sides. He looked around at the alley: debris and puddles, empty cartons from McDonald's, foul hand-and-mouth food none of the Stansbury specimens would've tolerated. Then he remembered another time he was in this part of town, the corner of Avenue R and Third. He and Riley snuck off campus, both of them flat broke and craving the hand-and-mouth stuff, so they traded a dog-eared September 2030 issue of *Young Buns* magazine for two super-sized orders of salty, steamy French fries. They held onto the cardboard containers for weeks afterward, smelling the treasure of the grease and fat like it was ambrosia inside the school's walls.

Brown brick buildings surrounded him on the left and right. The masked officers aiming those gleaming black guns made their steady advance. One of them pulled off his Nomex balaclava and tossed it to the side. Smith caught a glance at his face. Officer Jackson: he busted Smith for stealing a biology exam from an unlocked progression room sometime back in his junior year. Jackson smiled ruefully and raised a gun with slightly jagged edges and an angular body that required a two-handed grip to heft the large scope up to his eye. Smith didn't recognize the model and figured it was another in a long line of experimental prototypes that some team of Stansbury ballistics experts created with the intention of hawking to the military. Jackson flipped a switch and the weapon beeped slowly, methodically. Then faster. Smith had no idea the ThermaGun prototype was locking onto the heat patterns of his body, triggering Stansbury's new patent-pending "Fire-and-Forget" technology.

What would Riley do, Smith wondered. Come to think of it, just what the hell is Riley going to do if . . . when they come after him?

He threw his shoulder into the boarded-up wooden planks to his right and tumbled through the remnants of a doorway, landing in a darkened hall amid piles of wood and scrap metal. Smith felt a loose iron pipe grinding into his back and grabbed it, running through the abandoned building's catacombs. No footsteps behind him. He slid around a corner into what used to be an office. It still smelled like instant coffee, menthol cigarettes, and linoleum. The pipe in his hand was about the size of a baseball bat and easy to swing. He tried it out a few times, iron whooshing through air, and got ready, twirling it like a toothpick in his caveman hands. Silence. His stomach fluttered. He couldn't even hear the rain anymore. He picked a prime spot: no other points of entry, no windows, tucked away in a corner. They might get him eventually, but the first guy through that door would get his head knocked for a line drive off the back wall. Run, Riley— start running now, man.

A gunshot echoed. What were they shooting at? There was no point of entry here and . . . A .45-caliber bullet flew around the corner, defying every law of physics he never bothered to learn, and Smith went down hard, his skull cracking against the floor, his feet flying up toward the water-stained ceiling before slamming down to the ground. His hand reflexively went to his chest. It was warm and wet, going on soaked. His fingers got covered in a sticky, shock-inducing shade of red. He started to gasp and found he could not.

His iron bat rolled away, bumping against a wall and lying still. What's up with these big leaguers throwing the heat high and inside, he wondered. The edges of the dingy office started to go black on him.

Through the pain, he heard footsteps getting closer and squinted, tensing his biceps just in case they were somehow connected to his weakening eyes and brain. The shapes weren't unfamiliar, given that he was a lifer at the school: a sleek laser-tipped syringe (just like the kind they had back in the tower) moving in, a specimen—male, maybe seventeen or eighteen (why aren't you in class young man)— he was wearing a crisply pressed dark blue blazer with a golden patch bearing *that* tower and stitched-in words: ESTABLISHED 2009 STANSBURY SCHOOL *NOVUS ORDO SECLORUM*. The truant specimen leaned closer and closer, his face still in the shadows, that laser syringe's beam pulsating in his hand, getting closer and closer.

Stansbury School. *A New Order of the Ages.*

Smith felt the cold steel of the syringe's barrel against his neck. Then came the light burn of the laser's pinch as it passed through the skin and into his bloodstream. He thought of Riley. He already missed him. They never got the chance to catch up over cold beers and fill in the years since all of the insanity that began with Miss Stella No-Middle-Name Saltzman's phone call months ago. Riley and his fringes of permanently matted hair. Smith always wondered how he got it to stick up like that. It was hard to breathe now, verging on impossible.

Ah, Mr. Riley. The stories we could've told.

1

From a distance, Stansbury Tower seemed proud.
Expensive and proud. It jutted up 125 stories—1,353 feet—from the
flat desert floor, a windowless, silvery monolith that glinted like jew-
lery when the sun hit it just right. Ask the school's prim, purse-
lipped professors and they would have likened it to a glorious
mirage, an oasis of knowledge and progress providing a beacon of
hope in the wasteland of a spoiled world sown with the seeds of
mediocrity.

But if you asked the kids—sorry, the specimens—they'd have told
you the tower was a big, shiny penis. The kind you'd find in a
Tiffany's catalog from Spring 2036, if they'd commissioned Frank
Lloyd Wright to craft the world's priciest dildo.

This observation was not childishly perverted. Childishly precocious, perhaps, but not perverted. They were specimens, after all. By
the age of ten, they had all been conditioned to analyze the symbolic
imagery—implicit or explicit—in any source of stimuli, including a
glaringly obvious phallic substitute that even the non-Freudian

would have spotted a mile away. But they'd never share this insight with an outsider. It would ruin their mystique. They were bred—all four thousand of the current student body, from the ages of six to eighteen—for top-of-the-line performance. Flagship editions of youth. And leaders, so they were taught, needed to maintain an aura about them, exist in a world where there were no vulgar temptations, curse words, or 125-story penises.

But the penis thing didn't come up very much, because the view from inside the school was much different. And since the specimens were only permitted to leave the tower's walls twice a year (two weeks for the winter holidays, two weeks for summer—with the rare exception of a daylong field trip), time spent viewing Stansbury from a distance was too precious to waste making dick jokes. It was a complex thing, observing the way a specimen treated his or her return to school after vacation. It always happened the same way: the long gyrobus floated smoothly on a bed of air high above the desert floor, carrying its load of one hundred specimens per trip (males on the right side, females on the left), and when the tower rose up on the horizon maybe twenty miles away, a hush fell. The younger ones stopped making wet farting noises with their lips and hands and wept silently, already missing Mom and Dad. The romantics mourned the end of brief affairs with carefree, nonuniformed outsiders. The academics unconsciously nodded with pride at their return to duty. And you could always count on one of the unbalanced specimens to make a crack.

"Looks like it's giving us the middle finger," said Mr. William Winston Cooley upon his return, following the winter holiday in 2036. "A bright, shiny fuck-off for coming back when we could've ran for the hills." He smirked at his roommate, Mr. Thaddeus Bunson. Bunson was preoccupied with his electric razor, shaving off the last of his Christmas stubble lest he get caught with it on campus and disciplined.

"They'd find us," he replied, his mouth angled to the side, stretching the skin on his cheek taut for the humming blade. "They always find the ones who run." Bunson brushed stray stubble spikes from the sterile white leather of the seat, resignation in the swipe of his hand.

Toward the end of each return trip, when the bus slowed down for its descent, all of the specimens would go silent. In a routine as reliable as it was instinctual, each boy and girl turned his or her head in the same direction at the same time for that final, lingering glance at the setting sun. They soaked up every detail: the seared orange it happened to be at that time of the day; whether it felt warm or cool on their faces through the windows; the way its reflection in the metal of the bus walls burned the corners of their squinting eyes. The specimens then deposited the information into a special part of their well-developed cerebrums, a specific area that was not perpetually firing with efficiency and goal-directed action. It was the secret brain compartment that each of them developed unwittingly, a place where they stored the imaginary postcards bearing memories taken from the world outside the tower's windowless walls: a sunset, a cartoon, the taste of melted caramel on the lips.

Mr. Thomas Oliver Goldsmith went through this ritual one final time in January 2036. The bus started its descent and the hush fell. As a senior, this was the twelfth time he had returned from winter holiday, so he made an effort to watch the other specimens that day rather than the sun itself. He wanted to understand the occurrence objectively, the way an outsider might. The desert was cloudy that day, the sun wrapped inside a hard, unyielding gray. Goldsmith noticed something: all of them still turned toward the direction where the sun *should've* been (displaying tropism like the plants stretching toward light he learned about in advanced biology so many years ago) and, as if by reflex, squinted despite the presence of the shadows. It was then that Goldsmith realized the specimens never took that final gaze at the sun out of some nostalgia for nature. They did it to keep themselves sane.

This is what a quick flip through a few of Goldsmith's mental postcards would have revealed: natural, golden light poured into a home in perfect geometric shapes through a venetian blind while a young woman sang a lullaby with his name; the soft hands of that same woman, probably his mother, and they felt warm on his scalp. And then he remembered the stale sheets of the cot he slept in back at San Angeles Municipal Orphanage. Before Stansbury rescued him.

A shaft of white light hit Goldsmith squarely on the eyes, but he was already awake. How did the InterAct light alarm know that he was standing by his mirror tying on his navy blue silk tie and not lying in bed?

Good morning, Mr. Thomas Oliver Goldsmith! The time is now 6:30 A.M., said an automated voice. Some automated voices these days sound so natural you wouldn't know they're fake, but not Mrs. InterAct. The school kept her nice and robotic so you wouldn't forget everything was official, regimented, that there was a job that needed to be done.

Goldsmith finished with his tie and pulled a blazer on over a crisp white dress shirt. The gold on the blazer's emblem matched his hair, which matched the metal glint of the wire rims on his glasses. He was one of the academics—the kind that nodded in silent obligation when the tower approached on the horizon—but not just any straight-A specimen. Stansbury had plenty of those. He was valedictorian. There was a medal hanging on his wall that said so. Placed in between the certificate affirming his place as President of the Specimen Council and his acceptance letter to Harvard (which, incidentally, was a formality—the dean of admissions extended an under-the-table offer through Stansbury's president shortly after the first semester of Goldsmith's junior year) was a palm-sized medal of solid twenty-four karat gold with raised letters that read VALEDICTORIAN, CLASS OF 2036.

The school's philosophy on valedictorians went like this: Too many specimens got top marks to appoint just one. However, appointing several would have defeated the purpose of the position in the first place—to denote the top specimen in the senior class—and watered down a goal that required twelve years of rigorous schooling to accomplish. So the faculty devised a plan. Right before the beginning of the fall semester of their final year, all of the senior specimens with perfect grades over their careers (usually between ten and twelve out of roughly three hundred and fifty) underwent the Selmer-Dubonnet Aptitude Test.

Selmer and Dubonnet were part of the group of educators who founded Stansbury back in 2009 under the direction of Dr. Raymond Stansbury himself. These educators—mostly the top teachers from the country's best elementary, middle, and high schools, along with some administration types—were fed up with the control and power the nation's teachers' unions exerted over the world of schooling at the start of the twenty-first century. The state of public schooling had become increasingly dire. Reading and comprehension levels were at an all-time low, despite the fact that the flow of information and knowledge were more readily available than at any other time in history. The problem was not the students' access or social skills. It was the teachers. They were being paid more than ever before (a famous case in New York City was an eleventh-grade math teacher who earned $211,498 in salary and overtime in 2008 while his seventeen-year-old students were functioning at a fourth grade level) working without accountability for their students' performance.

Due to union labor laws, it had become virtually impossible to fire the teachers. Teachers who did not want to join the unions were physically assaulted and ostracized. The situation seemed hopeless until Dr. Raymond Stansbury, then a high school principal, organized a coalition of the best teachers from across the country—a select group of forty-five men and women from all disciplines—who promptly quit their jobs, all tendering their resignation letters on the same day. Using funds donated from private philanthropists, they founded the Charter School, based out of Dr. Stansbury's California ranch estate.

There were forty specimens (Dr. Stansbury himself coined the term) in the school's first graduating class in 2009. Seventy-eight percent of them were admitted to first-tier Ivy League universities. Word spread quickly. Any parent who could afford the formidable $100,000 tuition sent their children. The following year's senior class numbered one hundred. The year after that one hundred and fifty. The numbers kept increasing without a decline in attention to individual specimen needs. Dr. Stansbury—a world-renowned expert in the field of organic chemistry and pharmaceutical science—began to develop nutritional supplements that lengthened specimens' attention spans and increased their endurance.

Soon, Charter School specimens were requested on the research teams of major drug companies and world-class universities. They published novels before they were able to get behind the wheel of a car. Alumni were being elected to national office. Currently eight United States senators are former specimens, along with two cabinet members and the president's head of the Joint Chiefs of Staff. Fifty-nine alumni are serving terms as judges in federal courts across the nation, including the two who are justices of the Supreme Court (one a strict constructionist, the other a loose constructionist, as the Senate successfully convinced the Executive branch that providing a former Stansbury specimen to only one side of the debate might permanently slant the ideology of the highest court in the land). Currently, twenty-two of the top thirty Forbes 500 corporations had CEOs who counted Stansbury as their alma mater. Five years ago, motion picture director Charles Packard (*the* Charles Packard—Class of '21) became the school's first Academy Award winner. Sure enough, civil rights groups, often with the support of teachers' unions, took to the media to protest the Charter School, calling it an elitist, racist institution, despite the fact that it boasted a population more ethnically diverse than most colleges and workplaces. In response, Dr. Stansbury and his new school president, Judith Lang—a politically shrewd young woman who looked great on television—announced the first official Charter School Lottery Fund in 2017: full-ride, twelve-year tuitions to be given to ten randomly selected orphans from across the United States each year. Goldsmith was one of the winners in 2024.

The Charter School's prestige went international in 2019, when Dr. Frederick Hester, a school professor, and a team of fifteen hand-picked specimens, constructed the chemical combinations that were the basis for the world's first affordable, effective AIDS vaccine. By the time Dr. Stansbury died of old age in 2020, he left behind a healthy private donor fund and a nearly-completed Stansbury Tower: a state-of-the-art educational complex designed by Rikka-Salvi & Partners, the famed architecture firm responsible for the postmodern-style high-rises that have come to define the skylines in megacities such as Tokyo, Hong Kong, and Kuala Lumpur. It was intended to be a self-contained world made specifically for nurturing the elite young minds destined to be this nation's future. The Charter School was renamed for its founder in a memorial service following his funeral. The late doctor also left behind a mission statement of sorts, and what began as a short, idealistic pledge he had posted on the wall of each progression room in the school is now known as the Stansbury Oath: *By virtue of the Gifts bestowed upon me, I swear my Eternal Duty to all those without such Gifts. For Power may point the way, but only Honor can lead it.*

Since the doctor's passing, the entire specimen body has recited this passage in unison—right hands placed over their hearts, many with their eyes closed, as if they are performing a mass séance to the spirit of Raymond Stansbury himself—as the opening ritual to the school's daily assembly held each morning in the coliseum.

Hence, with such an extraordinary pedigree, Stansbury School required an extraordinary valedictorian. Which is where Doctors Edwin Selmer and Francine Dubonnet came in. Selmer was an authority in the field of child and early adult psychology (his book, *Discipline Without Guilt,* was a national bestseller). Dubonnet was a mathematician-turned-behavioral sociologist who made a name for herself when she created the multimedia personal aptitude examination, colloquially referred to as "the Dub Test," that is now administered to all candidates up for promotion to the highest levels of authority in the fields of law enforcement and military intelligence.

From the outset, Dr. Stansbury realized that his school's valedictorian needed more than just top scores. He or she also required an inherent understanding of the philosophical principles upon which the school was based and, just as important, a value system in accordance with his own. In other words, he or she must understand that the success of the school—and, by extension, American society—depended on the specimens' acceptance of their elite status and the responsibilities entailed. The top specimen must be the very embodiment of the Stansbury Oath's principles. His valedictorian couldn't just be a showpiece to parade in a dog and pony show for the universities and the press. He or she had to be an active ally of the faculty in maintaining order and morale within the school's walls. After all, the doctor reasoned, who had more to gain from the status quo than the specimen whom it benefited most?

The Selmer-Dubonnet test was an examination wherein the select group of top senior specimens was confronted with situation upon situation, nonstop, over a grueling four-hour period. Some samples of these test situations: the specimens' physiological responses to video footage of violent behavior; lengthy essay questions on the nature of right and wrong; timed logic puzzles; and recordings of actual courtroom cross-examinations broadcast with critical sections missing so that the specimens were expected to argue the relevant point through intuition. The final stage? Goldsmith had been trying to forget that one since the moment it ended, but despite his wondrous intellectual gifts, he could not. Each year, the senior class's straight-A specimens had one shot at the test. Everything that occurred during the test was kept strictly confidential, except for the only thing that mattered: who won. Goldsmith was the first full-ride scholarship orphan to be appointed valedictorian. Captain Gibson, the school's head of security, observed Goldsmith's entire four-hour Selmer-Dubonnet session and promptly anointed him "the natural."

He heard the footsteps of specimens on their way to first hour progressions through the door of his personal bedroom suite. Another perk: the school gave the valedictorian his own separate space, too, no roommates allowed. Like they knew he'd be long on prestige and short on friends. He glanced at the long, flat plasma screen Nature & Co. window hanging on his wall. There was one hanging in every dorm room in lieu of actual windows. The window broadcasted a lush green forest underneath a yellow sun. A bird of indiscernible species flew past. Looked pretty close to real. Except that it was not.

He checked the screen of his late-model iPro Tabula 7000 (everything was in order: no unread e-mails, homework data was ready for upload, his vital signs were normal and healthy, and there were no voice mails waiting because he was and had always been, as previously mentioned, short on friends) and slid it into his breast pocket, then checked his hair in the mirror one final time before heading for the hallway outside. The door handle was cold in his grip. One thought got him through the days: he was graduating next week.

2

"Good morning, Mr. William Winston Cooley and Mr.
Thaddeus Bunson . . ."

"Hey lady! Nag him, not me! I'm up and running."

". . . the time is 6:45 A.M."

"No shit. It's fifteen fucking minutes later than the last time
you . . ."

Bunson's voice trailed off as he ran through the bedroom suite to
the bathroom, his standard-issue black wing tip loafers pounding
heavily against the white marble floor. Still curled up underneath his
blanket, Cooley heard the sink running and an electric hum. His
roommate was shaving, even though he shaved before lights-out last
night. Good old Bunson. A man's man with a five o'clock shadow by
two o'clock, twice daily. Cooley opened his eyes and could see the InterAct light alarm's beam casting its glow through the wool quilt, exactly where his eyes would be if they weren't strategically shielded.
This was his version of the snooze button, circa 2036.

Suddenly, the quilt was yanked off his body and sailed across the room. Cooley lay there in his boxer shorts, looking up at Bunson in full uniform. Bunson—all six feet, nine inches, and 250 pounds of him—was staring at their Nature & Co. window, shooting nervous glances Cooley's way once every ten seconds. They'd rigged it to broadcast grainy camera footage from a strip club somewhere in one of the grimier parts of San Angeles. It beat the fake mountains and rainbows, or whatever idyllic rerun the school had playing that week. A skinny brunette doffed her top. An arm from an unseen man in the audience slipped a dollar bill into her G-string. Bunson's hulking frame blocked most of the plasma screen. Cooley was certain the guy would've been a big fella even without the school's med cycle beefing him up for the past twelve years.

"Switch the sequence back to the school broadcast," Cooley said.

"No."

"Do it."

"Get dressed," Bunson snapped.

"When I'm ready."

Bunson flipped off the strip show, replacing it with an ocean scene. Palm trees on an island in the distance. "Fact number one," said Bunson. "Last night's dopazone hits were engineered to be hangover-free. Fact number two: we're almost done with our senior year."

"Your point?"

"You don't have any excuse. You're just a miserable bastard."

Cooley rolled over. "Wake me on commencement day."

Bunson headed for the door. "Hurry up." The door opened and closed behind him. He stomped his way down the hall with the rest of the specimens.

Cooley sprang up and headed for his desk. He activated his network terminal and glanced over at Bunson's workspace while the system warmed up. Photos abounded. Bunson came from a big, rich family. They made a killing on West Coast real estate when San Angeles was formed in response to the E-Bomb blast back in 2016. Back then, the United States had spent years of research and trillions of dollars building up its defenses against what everyone believed would be the inevitable, all-out strike by a hostile nation or cadre of terrorists. Huge death toll forecasts of a possible weapon of mass destruction—mainly of the conventional nuclear, dirty, and chemical varieties—kept the general paranoia fresh and political careers flourishing. And then, at 4:34 P.M. EST on May 9, 2016, a crudely improvised version of an electromagnetic pulse bomb—an E-Bomb, or flux compression generator—was assembled by an unknown source for an unknown group of hostiles for an estimated $400 (the total cost of the required tubing, copper coils, and plastic explosives) and detonated on a two-passenger plane two thousand feet above the Cape Cod coastline. The only direct casualty from the blast was that of the pilot, but estimates of the indirect casualties have ranged from anywhere between 100,000 to 250,000 people. The electric grids powering the entire Eastern seaboard were hit by the magnetic fields from the explosion, and channeled that huge, crippling pulse to every machine with a wire, microchip, or spark inside of it. There were no cameras left functioning to capture the sight of hundreds of gyromobiles that fell from the skies, the dozens of commercial airliners circling airports that crashed, the stories of people who died because hospitals were left without power, or the chaos of mass riots that spread like viruses in every East Coast town and city. Life was suddenly plunged back into the nineteenth century. Economic devastation, lack of communication, supply shortages, and weeks of virtually uncontained anarchy sent all of America running West for space, safety, and power sources. With its state of the art missile defense system crippled, the government braced its people for a nuclear or chemical attack piggybacked to the initial damage of the E-Bomb. It never came. Every terrorist organization on the planet took credit for the EMP, which was just as helpful as none of them doing so. And now, twenty years and scores of modernized electrical grids later, it seemed as if the entire nation was still tensed up, readying itself for that crippling blow that could still arrive at any moment.

Meanwhile, the new pilgrimage West had caused Los Angeles and San Francisco to burst at the seams with overpopulation (average life span following the advent of the gyromobile and the AIDS vaccine: ninety-four years of age; average number of children per family: 2.78), so the federal and state governments, along with some savvy developers, broke in all the land between Southern and Northern California, creating the world's most sprawling metropolis. Bunson's family owned a chunk of something like a million acres that were targeted for the San Angeles Development Project, and they sold it for a pretty penny. Not that the huge addition of space eased the crowding for the people now known as San Angelenos. Over the years, the new, affordable, and easily dispensed disease vaccinations were such a boon to Third World and developing nations that the populations of India, Africa, and Asia skyrocketed. Simultaneously, globalization and free trade had opened up borders and kept U.S. immigration offices very busy: the influx of cheap labor, after all, is what helped the country's economy rise up again from what was supposed to be a fatal blow.

Cooley looked at a silver frame on his roommate's desk: Bunson and his three hefty sisters. A gold frame: Bunson and his dog, a yellow Lab named Trigger. A big wooden frame: Bunson with his toothy mom and dad. Dad had one satisfied hand resting on the kind of paunch meant to be a sign of wealth. Bunson *pere* was a Princeton man. He made it clear to Bunson *fils* that his access to the family fortune and goodwill depended solely on whether he would be a Princeton son.

Stansbury's most recent senior class—the already legendary class of 2035—saw a record-breaking 84 percent get in to Harvard, Yale, or Princeton. However, since Bunson occupied the bottom 10 percent of Stansbury's Class of 2036, the odds were not exactly on his side. Still, he applied and waited it out, knowing the whole time that the grades on his transcript were lacking. He watched the mail and gave himself an ulcer. The school's med technicians upped his daily dosage from the specimen's average of 100 milligrams to 400 milligrams of Equimode anti-anxiety capsules. A thin letter bearing Princeton's colors arrived last month. He got wait-listed when he should have been rejected outright. Forty-nine other specimens were accepted. Bunson figured his Stansbury diploma, his dad's alumni pull, and decent final semester scores might be enough to make him number fifty. The big guy started waking up on time. He hit the med tech bay in the atrium each day and popped his four hundred milligrams. He relaxed only occasionally, letting himself do dopazone once a week to stay sane, and on the other days he came home near dawn after closing down the study hall. He was getting edgy, irritable, but Cooley understood. Suddenly giving a shit about one's future tended to do that to people.

Cooley's computer gave the ready signal and he turned back to his side of the room. No photos or fancy frames. No father with high expectations. No mother to make proud. No point in wondering whether having them would have made things turn out differently. He opened a drawer and grabbed a black cuff with a cord attached to it. He pulled the cord taut, plugged it into the back of the computer, and strapped the cuff to his wrist, carefully matching up the red grid network on its surface with the veins in his wrist. Cooley navigated through a series of screens on his monitor, cracked through the Stansbury network wall and arrived at a spare page that read Dopazone Domain. He typed in his user name and password. A new screen popped up with a graph indicating the reserves left in his account. Not much there—the Stansbury monthly allowance to scholarship orphans didn't factor in many personal expenses—but enough for one hit to get him through the morning. After tightening the wrist cuff, he hit the button labeled Return.

That's right, he thought. Return. Bring me back. Some place that's not a plasma screen broadcast. Somewhere the light isn't engineered.

The dopazone molecules transferred digitally from the site's mainframe server to Cooley's terminal by bouncing in between thirty-eight separate destinations, all of which were decoys designed to throw off Stansbury's built-in security system. It was a crude technique that wouldn't work for someone trying to bootleg real data or private files, but dopazone (a genetically engineered chemical made up of designer neurotransmitters that simultaneously mimicked the effects of dopamine reuptake inhibitors *and* the phenethylamines found in pure MDMA) was simple enough to pass through undetected. It was Bunson's trick. He learned it from a dealer over winter holiday—he'd just sent in his Princeton application and was feeling daring—and added his own technical expertise for their on-campus benefit. Figures, Cooley thought. The only outsiders smart enough to beat the school were drug dealers after money. Bunson described the science behind the whole dopazone concept better, though. His grades stunk, but he still drank the Kool-Aid. He still took his meds. They made him smart. Specimen smart. Too bad they couldn't make him care. But that, Cooley knew, was the fundamental problem behind the whole goddamned system running this . . .

He went light-headed and his eyes drifted shut involuntarily. The artificial sun and the dorm room's sterile, glaring lamps faded away. The dopazone molecules rode the electric currents and shot through the wrist cuff, transferring past the skin and into his bloodstream. His capillaries bloomed wide open, neurotransmitters passed into his brain and triggered channels with a counterfeit physiological command to release huge natural supplies of dopamine, the body's own personal pleasure juice. Cooley slid back into his chair and let the trip take him to a familiar place.

The heavy haze gave way to an image in the distance: a long, one-level imitation Neutra house (one of the cheaper prefabs that became popular around 2013), thin glass walls blending into sliding doors of tinny faux steel. The garden outside had daisies trampled by a man's big footsteps, the man without a face in the living room who stood above a woman bleeding from the mouth, two lips split open in different places. Cooley cowered in the corner and the woman never took her eyes from him, even when she went cross-eyed from another left hook to the jaw. The man stepped in between them, cutting off her line of sight, throwing her to the side. Red drops fell from her head, staining the soft white fur of the Flokati rug. But she told the man that she loved him. Outside, the sun started to sink.

"Go and play outside, William!" echoed her voice. "I'll leave a light on for you."

The man picked up a folding chair. Cooley had been on this trip before and knew he was not big or strong enough to stop him, so he tried to catch a glimpse of the woman. He always heard her voice but missed her face. The chair went airborne, skimming her head and shattering the glass door behind her like it was made of clear, smooth rock candy and—

Wait. Rewind that. Cooley's dopazone tolerance had gotten to the point where he could half-wake himself just enough to pause the narcotic trip into his subconscious midstride and scroll backward through the images. The chair traced its ellipse back in through the door, the glass showering upward in reverse like a choreographed flock of birds swarming to the same point. Back inside the living room. Red stains on the Flokati rug went from dry back to wet, zinging up into his mother's broken mouth like macabre raindrops arcing back up to heaven. Through the high, Cooley could feel his fingers trembling against the steel arm of his chair and tried to get back into the haze. There. His mom. She was right there, just a little blurry, but there: maybe twenty-five, a birthmark near her mouth on the left side, right where her upper and lower lips met. Sandy brown hair that would look mousy on any other strange lady, but on her looked . . .

And then she was gone. Disappeared into a sheet of black, like someone pulled the plug on the television of his memory. Cooley's eyes snapped open. The computer screen sent him a message: *Account Empty/Insufficient Funds.*

He threw off the wrist cuff and jumped up, catching a glimpse of himself in the mirror. Six feet tall, 175 pounds, maybe a little scrawny in his boxer shorts. A normal kid anywhere else, but among the Stansbury specimens he was a runt. In the outside world, adults cautioned children to avoid the myriad perils that would stunt one's growth: coffee, masturbation, a lack of vegetables in the diet, too much television, et cetera. Inside the tower, adults warned specimens against being average, and the primary way to avoid this misfortune was a rigorous observance of Dr. Stansbury's hallowed med cycle. And, as was the case most of the time (far too often for Cooley's taste, anyway), the Stansbury people knew what they were talking about.

Cooley never liked pills. Even as a six year old he found himself freaked out by the ghoulish, far-off stares on the faces of the older specimens. He stashed his meds in his pockets and dumped them in the trash when he was alone, like a kid avoiding Mom's asparagus. He figured no one would know the difference, but pretty soon Cooley realized that there was a reason he fell behind in rudimentary-level progressions after the first day of school each year. Taking notes from the teacher's lecture was like trying to count bullets as they left the barrel of a machine gun. He'd catch colds and miss classes, slowly grasping the reason he was the only one lying around in the school infirmary. Routine three-hour exams left him exhausted; the black filled-in bubbles on his Scantron sheet went blurry eighty minutes in. Cooley would watch in disbelief at the sight of specimens polishing off five hundred pages of Dostoyevsky in one sitting, prior to banging out corresponding essays the same night. He tried everything, the tutors and study groups, but no one had the patience or time to slow down for him.

In the beginning, the school paid special attention to him, never suspecting that he'd skirted the med cycle. The cycle, after all, made the hard stuff—studying, comprehension, producing results—that much easier. What specimen wouldn't accept the advantage? By the time the physical effects of shirking the cycle became obvious—the school's tailors had to custom-make his uniforms because Stansbury's patented IGF-1 (insulin growth factor-1) protein never got the chance to boost his muscle growth and immune systems to average specimen levels—the administration decided Cooley was better off being ignored. No one would notice the sight of one student in approximately four thousand falling through the cracks. And after all, he was just an orphan without a tuition-paying family expecting a better return for their investment.

Cooley knotted up his tie while running out the door. The hallway was empty. An elevator pod beeped around the corner, ready to make its journey up 120-odd floors to the Stansbury atrium and the morning's progressions. He had seven seconds before the doors slid closed. Seven seconds before he lost another five minutes waiting for another elevator during rush hour. Seven seconds before this absurd world left him behind once again. Cooley counted down the time while breaking into a sprint, as thoughts and numbers flew through his head.

Seven seconds . . .

Ninety-eight percent: the odds that a specimen on the med cycle would be on time.

Twelve percent: the odds a random candidate would be accepted at Princeton University.

Five seconds . . .

Fifty percent: the odds a Stansbury specimen would be accepted at Princeton University.

Thirty-four: the amount of dollars Cooley had in the bank.

Six million: the amount of dollars his twelve-year, full-ride Stansbury scholarship was worth.

Three seconds . . .

(Couldn't they have just given him a check instead?)

One: the average number of Stansbury Lottery–winning orphans per year that didn't end up going to college. The Class of 2036's lucky guy? Yours truly.

One second . . .

Four: the number of days until Cooley was let out of this big metal dick of a prison forever, thereby getting on with the rest of his life.

Fifty-fifty (and maybe the only numbers that mattered): the odds he'd be able to convince Sadie to push back her first year of college to spend it with him.

Cooley slowed to a leisurely stroll upon seeing that Bunson was propping open the elevator doors, keeping the pod in place. Seven other specimens stood behind him, checking their watches and glaring helplessly. Cooley grinned and stepped inside. The pissed-off looks evaporated. No one said a word. The pills might've gotten them better scores, he thought, but they couldn't teach these kids about being The Man. It wasn't in the grades. It was in the way you walked.

The doors slid closed and Cooley considered what he might be when he grew up. Bunson had Princeton. Cooley had been wait-listed by this riddle in his head: whatever happened to Mom? One rumor: she dropped him at the orphanage after meeting some rich guy who didn't want kids. Another: he ended up with the rest of the motherless children after his own mother took yet another beating. One she would not wake up from. Cooley didn't hold it against her. He just hoped she went down swinging.

Graduation. Fuck the speeches and fancy writing on sheepskin, fuck all the specimens ready for another four years of servitude at some college. He rehearsed his own commencement day speech: Dear Mom . . . You never wrote. You never called. Are you dead or what? Hope you kept that light on, though, 'cause next week I'm coming home.

3

The elevator dinged and stopped on Level 19. Misters
Nathan Donald Oates, Robert Ryu Sugiyama, and Miles Boyd Mancuso stepped in. The seven geek specimens already inside the pod
took a few steps toward the back, making room. Cooley and Bunson
nodded. The doors slid closed. Oates, Sugiyama, and Mancuso started
giggling. Cooley and Bunson cracked smiles.

"Blew my fucking mind," grinned Oates.

"Tripping on the dopazone," said Sugiyama. "Nice."

"You're gonna hook us up, right, Cooley?" asked Mancuso. The
geeks in the back exchanged glances, rolling their eyes and straightening already straight ties. Oates stared them down.

"What're you looking at?"

They stopped straightening and commenced with studying the elevator pod's gray carpeting.

"Clean piss," said Cooley. "Yeah, I'll hook it up." Out of habit, he
glanced up at one of the tiny fiber optic camera/surveillance mic
holes that the tower had installed in the top left-hand corner of every

elevator pod. Similarly discreet monitoring apparatuses dotted all of the public spaces in the school, but had not been active since 2019, when a group of seniors successfully petitioned Doc Stansbury to allow the specimen body a larger degree of civil liberties. Far from being reincarnations of the radicalized student protestors of years past, the petitioners made their case—based on arguments hearkening back to philosophers such as John Stuart Mill and Voltaire, among others—rationally, patiently presenting their logic to the board of trustees without any threats of boycotting classes, agitating their peers, chaining themselves to furniture, or worst of all, going to the media. Stansbury and the board decided their tower of prodigies had earned their trust, and besides, so their thinking went, the med cycle had successfully eradicated the more serious delinquent urges. Since then, as professors are fond of telling their specimens, Stansbury Tower has felt less like a police state and more like organized civil society. Still, Cooley eyed those camera and microphone implants each day. To him, their continued (albeit inactive) presence despite the 2019 ruling loomed as a constant, subtle reminder that the school could change its mind on a whim.

"Word is, the piss man's coming this week," murmured Sugiyama. "If we want to test clean, we'll need the samples by—" Bunson glowered down at him. Sugiyama shut up.

"The piss man's coming *tomorrow*," Bunson said.

"Says who?" asked Mancuso, posing the question more to show that he wasn't intimidated than out of genuine skepticism.

"Harvey. Works the reception desk downstairs. Piss man's logged in on the visitor list."

Sugiyama went pale. Cooley looked at Bunson.

"When did Harvey tell you that?" he asked.

"Last night. We were tripping. I forgot to tell you."

"What if he doesn't let me out today?"

"He'll let you out."

"Easy for you to say," Sugiyama cut in.

"He's gotta let you out," Bunson resumed. "He's not gonna let us take a fall like this four days before graduation. He can't. And Mr. Riley likes you, he'll—"

"He's not a fuckin' specimen anymore." Cooley snapped. "Just call him Riley. Christ." The geeks in the back gave each other looks. Man- suppressed a smile. Cooley took two steps in Bunson's direction, jamming him into the back corner of the pod, lowering his voice to a whisper. "You're telling me that I've got to get off campus to San An-geles, track down Riley, and convince him to produce fourteen urine samples, all within four hours?"

"Well, yeah . . . I guess so," stammered Bunson. He reached into his pocket, pulled out a wad of cash, and handed it to Cooley. "This is enough for all of us. Man . . . I feel bad about this, but—"

"It's fine."

"Uh . . . Cooley," stammered Oates, "so you're gonna—"

"I've got it under control."

"But that means you've got to cut class and go like, right now if you're gonna . . ." Sugiyama glanced at Bunson. Bunson laid a huge hand on Sugiyama's shoulder.

"He said he's got it under control."

The elevator dinged and stopped on Level 21. The pod went silent. Miss Shannon Louise Evans, Miss Katherine Mary Lewis, and Miss Sadie Sarah Chapman strolled through the doors. The guys checked them out: navy blue cardigans with gold Stansbury emblems over white button-down shirts, charcoal gray skirts that gave way to three long pairs of legs in navy blue knee socks and black flats. Sadie stood in front of Cooley, her back to him. He leaned in and got a whiff of her familiar scent: hair that smelled like fruit from some tropical is-land he'd never visited but had seen on the school's plasma screens plenty of times.

"Come here often?" he asked. The girls cracked up. The doors started to slide closed. Sadie did a quick 180-degree twist of the hips and pecked Cooley on the cheek. Then a hand shot in between the sliding doors: five long, thin fingers with precisely manicured nails in a deep red shade. The color made Cooley think of blood dripping from the fangs of a particularly civilized but deadly predator, the kind that feasted on the carcass of its fallen prey. The motion sensors beeped and the doors slid open again. In walked Miss Camilla Moore II. Her dark brown hair was pulled back against her scalp into an efficient ponytail against pale, china-doll skin that had never seen a day of makeup. Her cold eyes shimmered behind the tortoiseshell frames of her glasses. Cooley remembered Camilla's handwriting when they were eight years old: it was compact, elegant. Dignified. It resembled the looping black cursive on display in the laminated copy of the Declaration of Independence that hung on their progression room's wall. Like every word she put to paper would be permanent, fit for study for the next three hundred years. (*We hold these truths to be self-evident, that all men are created equal* . . . What a fuckin' joke, thought Cooley.)

Even when they were all merely children, Camilla looked like an adult, just on a smaller scale. Most of the specimens' faces and bodies went through the normally clumsy physical tug-of-war over the years before their skin and bones finally settled on a true identity, but not her. Her template was set from the beginning. When they studied Homer's *Iliad* back in second grade, the Trojan War myth inspired one of the more artistic specimens to paint a sprawling mural on the progression room's ceiling. When he finished, everyone noticed the same thing: Pallas Athena, the hard-hearted goddess of war and wisdom who sprang from the head of Zeus fully formed, was a dead ringer for Camilla. That is, if she switched her uniform for a golden battle helmet, flowing white gown and spear. Cooley recalled trying to think of an appropriately sarcastic crack for the benefit of his peers but came up with blanks. He always imagined her whenever Homer spoke of "gray-eyed Athena," too. A hush fell over the elevator. The doors slid closed.

Cooley looked at Camilla out of the corner of his eye, knowing that everyone was thinking the same thing: grab a complimentary gawk at one of Stansbury's first purebred specimens while you can. Her parents (Mr. Robert Cavil Moore and Miss Camilla Peterson) graduated back around 2010. Mr. Moore went on to invent the compressed gyroscopic engine—the basis for the gyromobile—in 2013. *Time* stuck a photo of him on the cover in between images of Thomas Edison and Henry Ford. Old Doc Stansbury would have loved Mr. Moore's and Miss Peterson's only child. He would have drunk in her distinguished pedigree, her lack of wasted words, the proud absence of girlish giggles, and blushed, a modern-day Pygmalion seeing a masterpiece he once dreamed up come to life.

The other girls teased her when she was little with a nickname that stuck: Camilla Moore 2.0. Like she was some kind of upgrade on an earlier version. And according to school legend, this new model came complete with a photographic memory, supposedly the result of having two parents brought up on the med cycle; the human race ascending to the next level in the evolutionary stratosphere, so the story went. From the first day of her enrollment, she was the hot choice for valedictorian of 2036. All of Stansbury agreed. Each year, some guys in the junior class organized an underground gambling pool so the specimens (and, some say, the faculty) throughout the school could wager on the Selmer-Dubonnet winner, and this purebred girl was considered a virtual lock at 3 to 2 odds, the highest in recent memory. But then the impossible happened. She didn't win. The title went to the dark horse, Mr. Goldsmith, and that was that. Even though Miss Moore never had any friends, the rest of the specimens took care not to mention the word "valedictorian" in her presence again, like she had become some kind of phantom who would awaken to wreak havoc if anyone dared to invoke that fateful term in her presence.

After Camilla 2.0 came up short, nobody looked at her in the same way. Her name didn't sound quite as aristocratic coming from the mouths of teachers. She became less of an idol and more of a curiosity to the younger specimens; still respected, but not revered. Lately, unbalanced types like Misters Oates, Sugiyama, and Mancuso wondered if she was any good in bed and joked about whether they'd be able to get Miss Moore drunk enough to give her a go before graduation. Over this past winter holiday, Sadie and her family flew Cooley out to New York City for Christmas. They went on a tour of the Metropolitan Museum of Art for kicks, wearing blue jeans and sneakers like they were normal eighteen-year-old kids. In the Ancient Greek and Roman wing, the guide brought them by an elegant twelve-foot-tall statue. It was missing an arm and half of its helmeted head, but the rest of the cracked white marble kept its proud posture, the remaining arm clutching a spear snapped in half countless years ago.

"For some reason it reminds me of Camilla 2.0," whispered Sadie. "Weird." She shivered and headed off with the crowd toward the Egyptian wing's Temple of Dendur. Cooley glanced at the tag near the statue's feet. It read: "Athena, 2nd-Century Roman, marble." He looked around to tell Sadie about the coincidence, but she was gone.

All he saw around him were more white marble statues with jagged edges where arms, shoulders, legs, and heads should have been. There were hundreds of them. Maybe enough to match one up with every specimen who ever enrolled at Stansbury School.

Cooley glanced at the gold emblem on Miss Moore's navy blue cardigan, silently reading the school's familiar Latin motto. *NOVUS ORDO SECLORUM.* A new order for the ages. Maybe. Camilla made him think of another Latin cliché, the only other one he could recall from memory: *Sic Transit Gloria.* Glory fades. Even for someone like her.

Level 22. The doors slid open. The first thing he saw was the blond hair and the calm eyes behind wire-rimmed glasses. Spare me, Cooley thought. Good morning, Mr. Thomas Fucking Goldsmith.

4

Goldsmith entered the pod, dutifully avoiding eye contact with everyone, lest his gaze be interpreted to mean that his duties to the school were performed with anything less than strict impartiality. He stood next to Camilla. They exchanged curt nods like diplomats of enemy nations.

"How's it goin, *Tommy?*" sneered Mr. Mancuso. Goldsmith stood just in front of him, back straight, shoulders held high. He felt his jaw clench involuntarily and hoped no one else noticed. "You narc on anyone yet today?" Mancuso jabbed him in the lower back with his index finger.

"No, Mr. Mancuso," said Goldsmith, not turning around to face him. "I have not."

"Don't look so bummed, Tommy," said Cooley. Goldsmith felt his jaw tighten again. "It's early yet." Goldsmith looked over at him: the punk had his eyes pinned back, pupils dilated, probably coming down from dopazone, and the sun was barely up in the sky. Goldsmith wondered what the smug bastards would think if they knew how close the school was to busting all of them for drug possession, expelling them less than a week before graduation. He also wondered if any of these burnouts had enough brain cells left to figure out— thanks to a confidential order last semester from President Judith Lang—the security detail secretly reactivated the school's surveillance technology on two randomly selected days each week of the year. Today happened to be one of them.

It's funny, Goldsmith thought, Cooley's reputation made you forget what a shrimp he was. All the guys towered over him by five inches, at least, and he stood just about eye level with most of the girls. Goldsmith was six feet five inches tall, the male average for the Class of 2036. Ten years ago, the school had to install new doorways and elevators because the specimens were getting so big. The combination of the med cycle's IGF-1 protein gene therapy that promoted accelerated muscle growth and repair, regular hand-eye coordination drills, Phys-D progressions, and the cafeteria's nutrient formulas had given Stansbury's bookish young men the build and gait of NBA point guards. The girls got lithe, healthy bodies that were the fetish of just about every red-blooded male in the outside world. The ones in this elevator alone—Sadie, Katherine, Shannon, and Camilla—would render even the most jaded of lotharios in the outside world a stuttering wreck. What with their sleek five-eleven frames, their round, firm D-cup breasts straining at the thin cashmere of their matching cardigans, their long, elegant fingers, and flowing waves of hair, they looked like a team of superheroines working undercover as students. Like they had just stepped out of the pages of a beautifully illustrated comic book and into real life. The specimens all got to live forever or somewhere close to it. Projected life span for that year's seniors was up to 117 years of age.

And then there was Mr. William Winston Cooley, who probably wouldn't live to see fifty, because he liked keeping the angst-ridden, unbalanced specimen routine going just to prove some point that no one else knew or cared about. Goldsmith's feelings regarding Cooley were different than those the valedictorian held for the rest of the usual crowd of unbalanced specimens. He and Cooley were both orphans who won full rides to Stansbury; both started out as average boys with sad stories. But the med cycle changed everything. Like a self-contained lab experiment, Cooley and Goldsmith existed side by side in the same environment, but one chose to buy into the system while the other rejected it. And now, twelve years later, the results spoke for themselves. Goldsmith was number one. Cooley was number 350. It didn't just reinforce the effectiveness of the school's methods, it confirmed one fundamental premise for Goldsmith: he owed Stansbury everything.

But despite the obvious failure of Cooley as a specimen, Goldsmith was powerless to do anything about it. The administration appointed him valedictorian to enforce the school's code of conduct, to help them show through example that, unlike the chaos of the outside world, within this tower's walls there were clear-cut, absolute standards of right and wrong. And yet, when it came to Cooley all bets were off.

Goldsmith spent the majority of his time here in anonymity. He lacked the privileged upbringing of Bunson or Sadie and didn't have the natural mystique of specimens like Camilla, so he made up for it with a blue-collar work ethic and indomitable will. From his first days at the school, Goldsmith knew if he could keep his grades perfect and eventually end up in that elite group that underwent the Selmer-Dubonnet test, he'd win. It was a mystery environment that discounted all of the socio-economic benefits he never had, and his rivals simply *wanted* to emerge victorious. Goldsmith *needed* to.

After he defied the odds and won (he heard afterward that the 3 specimens out of 779 who bet on him in the gambling pool came away with small fortunes), he started his final year at the tower with his legend firmly established. But Cooley had a legend of his own, and it was sealed long before his. Goldsmith remembered the day it happened like it was an hour ago. They all did. One simple word summed it up: Guernica.

Their class was on a field trip to a Picasso retrospective way back during freshman year. Stansbury field trips tended to be few and far between, mainly because those on the outside world had no problems bringing noteworthy exhibits, performances and lectures to the tower, if for nothing else to take the tour and get a glimpse of life inside the walls. But when the San Angeles Metropolitan Museum of Art refused (understandably, perhaps) to lug $200 million worth of Picassos to the desert, the specimens had to go to them.

They went on a warm, muggy Wednesday afternoon in June. After viewing the Picassos, their class was waiting on the street for the fleet of gyrobuses to whisk them back to campus when a group of three rough-looking teenagers decided to cruise the female specimens in their short skirts and knee socks. One of them grabbed Shannon Louise Evans by the arm—the same Shannon who was standing right there in the elevator behind Goldsmith, actually—and yanked her into the street toward their old brown minivan. His buddies got in between her and her fellow specimens, daring someone to stop them. There wasn't a policeman around: a five-alarm fire on the West Side was blazing and had most of them occupied. It was a surreal sight outside the museum, three dozen larger-than-life guys in blazers standing there calmly, watching these thugs in ripped, baggy jeans gesticulating and swearing, Shannon crying and petrified, looking like a fragile, exotic bird who'd gotten lost and fallen from the skies above, down onto this crumbling, filthy San Angeles street. But despite their years of training in physical defense progressions, nobody was doing anything.

Goldsmith was one of those three dozen frozen male specimens, and he knew the reason why: the med cycle incorporated Tenormen, a beta blocker that slowed down the specimens' heart rates, thereby making them less excitable and more calm and malleable without sedating them (nervous politicians in the twentieth century often popped Tenormen before delivering speeches to large audiences). Also, Dr. Stansbury tweaked these beta blockers to eliminate psychological urges for violence and the type of anger hot enough to cause a brawl. Goldsmith remembered the sight of big, scary Bunson getting shoved repeatedly by one of the much smaller thugs in the street, passively staring off into the distance the whole time. Despite their skills and physical gifts, the meds had put a pharmaceutical leash on all of them.

And then Cooley swung a fist, smashed the thug's nose into a red, pulpy mess and sent a knee into the guy's kidneys before his body hit pavement. Goldsmith himself recognized the technique; it was a fairly standard opening combination of blows the specimens were taught in the "Multiple Assailants: Armed/Unarmed" seminar of eighth grade Phys-D. And Cooley moved fast—too fast. Thought and motion had become one. Unlike everyone else, there was not an ounce of hesitation in his eyes, no careful calculation of the possible consequences of his actions. And hence, no way, Goldsmith knew, that Cooley was following the med cycle. Which meant that he had all the knowledge and training of Stansbury's Phys-D program without the self-control or maturity to handle it responsibly: he was literally a walking, insubordinate, fourteen-year-old deadly weapon. Cooley's white dress shirt went untucked as he kicked the thug's buddy into unconsciousness. The last one remaining finally let go of Miss Evans and came at Cooley with a knife, opening up a gash on his left side before Cooley wrestled him to the ground while everyone else stood around and watched. Cooley choked him out with one hand and took the bloody knife in his other fist, raising it above his head. Goldsmith was sure he was going to kill him. But the blade fell from his hand and clattered to the street. Shannon stopped crying and, as if on cue, the rest of the female specimens started. Professor Smart ran over and pulled Cooley away, stitching him up with the first aid kit on the bus. Stansbury security smoothed things over with the police. Captain Gibson paid off the punks' families so they wouldn't press charges. President Lang made sure the newspapers wouldn't write a word about it. The school erased all traces of the incident, except for the very astute memories of the specimens who witnessed it.

Even now, Goldsmith wished he had the will to somehow override those med cycle beta blockers, that he were the one who jumped in first, or at least joined in the fight right after Cooley did, and he knew for certain the rest of the guys felt the same way. Within two hours of the incident, the whole school had heard the story. Goldsmith figured that enshrining Cooley in the school's pantheon of unofficial folk heroes was the specimens' way of repenting. After what was now referred to in Stansbury lore as Guernica, Cooley had won their respect and, perhaps more significant, more or less laissez-faire treatment from the administration. Saving Shannon (who came from a full tuition-paying family and had two younger brothers enrolled as well) seemed to be enough to convince the headmaster and President Lang that the least they could do was allow him to flunk the rest of his classes in peace. Despite his obvious transgressions of school policy, Goldsmith had yet to see Cooley called to the disciplinary level. He almost never saw him waiting in line with everyone else for the regular physical and chemical examinations all the specimens went through. And he never forgot the way Cooley moved, back at Guernica. That speed, that grace, that confidence. After that, Goldsmith and everyone else understood that no other specimen—no matter what his age or size—would stand a chance against him in a fight and accorded him the proper blend of fear and respect.

The flat-screen monitor on the elevator pod's wall lit up with the seven A.M. broadcast. A news anchor addressed her audience, bright and chipper.

"Good morning to you on this very wet and rainy March 29, 2036 . . . ," she began.

"It's raining outside," Cooley said.

"Say it ain't so," said Bunson.

"It ain't so. Every day's a sunny one inside Stansbury, isn't that right Tommy Goldsmith?"

". . . And now," continued the anchor, "the biggest headline of the year, and perhaps of the generation. Late last night, the federal Food and Drug Administration officially gave its stamp of approval to Panacetix, better known as the antidote to more than ninety-five percent of all the cancerous tumors that afflict mankind." The monitor cut to a shot of Professor Partridge (Goldsmith's fifth-hour Biochemical Compounds and Analysis progression instructor). He was working in one of the tower's 39th floor labs, surrounded by specimens in white lab coats bearing the school's emblem. You could always tell a specimen when you saw one on television: they had the type of serene poker faces most commonly seen on chess masters thinking three moves ahead of everyone else. The news anchor cut in again:

"Panacetix—a hybrid of engineered proteins and amino acids that selectively target and eradicate the mitochondria of cancerous tissues, effectively destroying the binary fissure and karyokinetic ability of eukaryotic cells—was developed three years ago by Prof. Alan Partridge, a biochemist who works exclusively with the elite students at Stansbury School . . ." The news broadcast ran the standard Stansbury lead-in graphic. The school's crest on a flag elegantly blew in the breeze, a young woman's voice-over breathlessly cooed the expensive, focus-grouped catchphrase: *"Stansbury Labs—Because you deserve to live in the future perfect."*

"Go team," said Oates.

"Like we need any more pressure," said Sugiyama.

"This is huge," said Shannon. "Bigger than Hester's AIDS vaccine back in 2019."

A series of thin, sickly chemotherapy patients flashed past on the screen. "This . . . this is just a miracle," said one. "I thought I had two weeks to live . . . ," said another.

"The Panacetix approval bodes well not just for these terminally ill patients, but for Stansbury School itself. Soon the United States Senate will be voting on the controversial proposal to allocate one trillion dollars annually to the prep school, so that they may continue their research and studies in fields ranging from pharmaceuticals to national security technology, free from the time-consuming practice of fund-raising from private donors . . ."

The elevator dinged and the doors slid open. Level 125. The atrium. The specimens in the pod parted ways like the Red Sea, letting Cooley and Sadie out first. That's the thing about Cooley, thought Goldsmith. Everyone talked up Guernica, that brutal brawl outside the museum, like it was some once-in-a-lifetime moment of truth. But for Cooley it was not. For burnouts like he, Guernica was every day of his sorry life.

5

Sadie, along with Shannon and Katherine Mary Lewis, walked into the girls' restroom on Level 125 just before the entrance to the atrium. Five or six younger female specimens moved about inside, copying homework at the last minute, gossiping, and applying one final dab of makeup for that special male specimen in their first-hour progression. Sadie entered and, as usual, voices dropped to whispers and the freshmen girls spent just a little less time in the mirror, lest her clique notice and deem the behavior overly vain or, worse, competitive. Sadie, Shannon, and Katherine ("Katie" to those in the clique, the more refined and mature "Kate" to particularly cute boys like Nathan Donald Oates, the monosyllabic and mildly erotic "Kat" to the older boys she met during her rare trips to the outside world) were used to the deferential behavior. They were, after all, widely regarded as the most attractive girls in the entire tower. That is, attractive in the context of the flesh, as opposed to on paper as candidates for admission to top-tier Ivy League universities.

Last winter holiday they were shuttled into San Angeles along with the rest of their peers, so that they could be transferred to airports and train stations and begin their respective trips home for vacation. The girls had just read *Breakfast at Tiffany's* for a Twentieth-Century American Literature progression and, on a whim, Sadie, Shannon, and Katie secretly decided to push back their flights twenty-four hours (Sadie didn't even tell Cooley about this) and paint the town red like Holly Golightly. Since specimens were not permitted to wear anything other than the standard uniforms each day, none of them had the slinky designer armor and expensive high heels that most girls possessed—those girls they would be competing with for attention in the city's bars and clubs that evening. They had no pocket money to purchase any of these accoutrements. Stansbury gave the specimens' parents strict orders to provide them with only enough cash for the trip home and a few dollars for "emergencies," so the girls pooled their meager funds for a budget-rate hotel room and settled on wearing their boring school uniforms for their big night out. It was on that night that Sadie realized the effect that three Stansbury girls who—thanks to a potent combination of good genes and the med cycle—filled out the regulation knee socks, cardigans, and pleated skirts could have not only upon men but on the very fabric of society itself. Gyrocabbies refused their money. Packs of pedestrians in the city streets parted ways for them and stared, openmouthed. Bouncers and doormen standing behind velvet ropes at the most exclusive clubs not only allowed them inside for free, but chased them down the street with promises of immediate and complimentary admission when they saw the girls take note of the immensely long lines down the block and opt to move elsewhere. Although they were initially concerned about the prospect of feminine rivals, it soon became obvious that there was no contest whatsoever. Sadie was shocked by the slouching, sloppy posture of young outsider women in garish metallic shirts that bared far too much skin to leave anything to the imagination. The outsiders' makeup—she remembered a preponderance of glittery lips and blue eye shadow—looked more like war paint than anything else. These desperate women poured sugary pink drinks down their throats and shouted small talk over the pounding music at men who kept glancing over their bared, artificially tanned shoulders to see if anyone better was available.

Sadie, Shannon, and Katie contented themselves with leaning against the bar smoking cigarettes and sipping crystal-clear gin martinis (like Miss Golightly herself), never once raising their crisp, articulate voices above a normal volume, despite the throbbing sound track. Men, they quickly realized, didn't mind leaning in and tuning out everything else in the world when they were presented with superior—well—specimens.

Sadie fielded no fewer than eight proposals of marriage that evening from complete strangers. Historically shy Shannon befriended a group of wealthy European bankers who seemed to command an endless supply of Champagne. A man old enough to be their father offered $500 in cash to Kat—she had left both Katie and Kate at home that evening and brought out this salacious alter ego for her big city debut—if she provided him with a lap dance right there in the club. And he didn't even want her to take off her uniform—in fact, he demanded she leave it on in its entirety. Kat, the forward-thinking, liberated specimen readily obliged and it occurred to Sadie that girls lost inhibitions with every vowel and consonant they dropped from their given names. As amusing as it was watching her friends cavort around, flirting (and flirting herself, she privately admitted), she found herself happy that she'd never fall victim to the abbreviations that seemed to steal away Katie's innocence. After all, the only option for a nickname she had would be paring down Sadie to the somewhat sobering moniker of Sad.

Standing there in the bathroom, Sadie watched as Katie glared at Shannon while Shannon attempted to casually avoid eye contact.

"What are you waiting for?" Katie asked.

"I did it yesterday," Shannon responded, finally looking at her. "I do it like, all the time."

"But you said if I got the Camels this month you'd do it one extra time per week. Didn't she, Sadie?"

"You did, babe," said Sadie. She pulled out her birth control pills and swallowed one dry, remembering when she was a young specimen and saw the older girls taking them, thinking that the unfamiliar white pills in those strange circular cases were the reason the seniors had the graceful curves to their legs, hips, and chests that she and her friends so clearly lacked. It wasn't until her mother took her to the doctor years ago that she realized the pills were actually solutions to the inevitable problems those curves posed rather than the cause of them.

"They don't even use those things anymore," whined Shannon, looking up at the camera lens implant jutting out of a hole in the ceiling above the sinks.

Katie rolled her eyes and cut loose with the kind of specifically feminine guttural growl that communicates annoyance and hopeless frustration. "C'mon. That's what they *want* us to think." She glanced at her reflection in the mirror, deciding to unbutton her white shirt a little more before giving her bosom a decisive shove upward. Satisfied with the additional cleavage effect, she turned back to Shannon. "I'm just telling you what Cooley told me, okay? He says you can't trust the security detail."

Shannon responded with a guttural growl of her own, striking the specifically feminine stance of leaning back on one heel while defiantly thrusting up the hip on the same side and crossing the arms across the chest. "Well, maybe I think Cooley's paranoid."

"Oooh," cooed Katie. "Struck a nerve, did I? I shouldn't have mentioned Cooley. Sorry, sweetie."

"Bitch," said Shannon, flushing bright red before looking over at Sadie. Sadie just smiled.

"Don't be such a bully, Katie," she said, playing her usual role of restroom diplomat.

"You're not looking at a bully. You're looking at a nicotine fiend." Katie took another quick glance in the mirror. "A nicotine fiend with unbelievable tits, if I do say so myself. And we've only got a few minutes before assembly starts. If I have to say that fucking oath without my fix, I'm gonna—"

"Fine," Shannon said with a huff as she slipped off her polished black shoes and climbed up on the porcelain sink directly below the bathroom's security camera. She swiveled the small lens so it aimed at the corner of the mirror, which reflected a harmless view of the stalls rather than the prime real estate in front of the sinks and before the mirror itself. Sadie caught a view up Shannon's skirt. She was wearing a white G-string underneath her uniform and . . .

"Oh my God!" blurted Sadie. "Did you give yourself a Brazilian wax?"

"Slut!" giggled Katie. The younger girls standing around them looked down in embarrassment.

Still perched up top, Shannon also unplugged the electronic smoke detector. "The things I do for my friends," she mumbled.

"Friends," said Sadie, "are God's way of apologizing for our families."

"I get by with a little help from my friends," said Katie.

"I get high with a little help from my friends," grinned Shannon as she hopped down to the floor. They looked at Sadie expectantly.

"Gonna try with a little help from my friends," she deadpanned.

"Why so sad, Sadie?" Katie asked as she passed out Camel Lights. "Must be tough being such a hot little number, hmmm?" She spoke up so the whole bathroom could hear: "Don't any one of you in here feel sorry for Sadie Sarah Chapman or any girls like her, okay? Oh, don't worry little ones. You'll know them when you see them. The boys may think you're sweet, but girls like Sadie? They're the ones they humiliate themselves for, the ones they fight over. The rest of us make do with compliments like 'she's got a great ass' or 'hey, decent set of tits,' while the Miss Chapmans of the world get the nervous stammers and dinner invitations. You know, the kind in the outside world where the guys actually pay for you? But that's just fine with me, Sadie, because the rest of us don't mind having to hang out around the bar until closing time so some hammered guy can offer to take us home and grope us on the doorstep. And then we finally invite him in before giving him the 'I normally don't do this' serenade before proceeding to do whatever 'this' is, like it's the most normal thing in the world. No, I don't mind it at all that the whole time you were tucked away in bed with your Prince Charming way before last call. At the day's end, all of this song and dance," she waved the hand holding her smoldering cigarette in Sadie's direction, "your perfect face and body, those impeccable Chapman manners of yours—they only get you home maybe two hours before the rest of us on a night out. That's it girls. Hear me? Two hours of extra sleep. So don't go and give yourself an eating disorder over her, or whoever ends up being the Sadie Sarah Chapman of your class."

"Actually, the med cycle makes it physically impossible for us to get eating disorders," pointed out Shannon.

"I meant figuratively, not literally."

"When did you get to be such an expert on the real world?" asked Sadie. "You've only been to like three bars in your life, *Kat.*"

"Hey, I'm a specimen. Which means I'm a quick study."

"I am *so* going to miss you girls next year," said Shannon. "There's no way the girls at college are gonna understand us the same way, you know? It's almost unfair that we've got to leave this place and—"

"Slum around with sorority sisters and outsider guys with nuclear-grade acne?" asked Katie.

"Yeah."

After a few puffs, they were engulfed in a cloud of blue smoke. Sadie noticed that the younger girls were sticking around, not at all worried about the possibility that they might reek of tobacco afterward and get in trouble. Most of them were too young to really know that the security detail should scare the daylights out of them. Still, history showed they went easy on girls, and while by-the-book Goldsmith probably would not, they were safe because the valedictorian only craved the real challenges, the big fish, older guys like Cooley and his friends. Cooley spent his whole career at Stansbury analyzing the comings and goings of Captain Gibson and the detail, and as a result had gotten away with more than anyone ever thought was possible. Between Guernica and his hotly anticipated returns from illicit trips to the outside world loaded up with coveted black-market swag like cigarettes, candy, and music files, her boyfriend had become something of a local celebrity. He had told her the scary stories about peer reviews and solitary confinement and electroshock treatments, but after Goldsmith won the Selmer-Dubonnet exam that fall, he reasoned that she would never have to see that side of Stansbury. Cooley kept a close eye on the short list of candidates who could be his bête noire for the coming academic year, and out of concern for his girlfriend he had been particularly worried that Camilla 2.0 was going to win. Girls, he explained (with a savvy that she found endearing in a then-seventeen-year-old boy), were always harder on other girls than they were on guys. Cooley—bless his sweet, scrappy heart—didn't know the half of it.

The younger specimens were still dawdling around, filing their nails and waiting for something to happen, not worried about being tardy or coming off as rude. They probably reasoned that getting a glimpse inside the glamorous world of upperclassmen was worth it. And hey, if the security detail came calling, they could always blame Katie for corrupting their fragile innocence. Sadie might have done the same if hers hadn't been ruined long ago.

She wasn't meant to end up at Stansbury. Sadie grew up in the Chapman family townhouse on 61st Street and Fifth Avenue in New York City, the only daughter of Margaret and Martin. While her father was busy making his fortune investing in pharmaceutical companies on Wall Street, her mother raised her to become the next in the family's long line of blue-blooded debutantes. Unfortunately, Sadie's fast track to a life of lunching with ladies and sensible marriage took a turn for the worse following nursery school. Her parents placed her name on the waiting list for the prestigious Saint Cecelia's Elementary School at the right time (that is, six years before she was even born) and Martin Chapman was a known philanthropist who could be relied upon to generously donate to the school's endowment fund for many years. Sadie's admissions test scores were even above average, but still the unthinkable occurred. At the tender age of five, she was rejected for the first time. The Chapmans made numerous phone calls and appointments to demand explanations from Saint Cecilia's admissions officers and even the school's headmistress, but no one had a single answer that was deemed acceptable. Her father decided that, since they had covered all of the other bases in applying, it must have been her admissions interview.

"Not good in a room," he fumed to Sadie's mother over dinner. "Doesn't matter how pretty the dress was, Madge. The girl's just not good in a goddamned room."

"Shhh . . . Marty! She's sitting right here! Just because they didn't accept her doesn't mean she's deaf."

If Sadie was possibly not good in a room during her Saint Cecelia's interview, she was certainly awful afterward. Her mother got some strings pulled at the Westerly School, where she herself had attended many years ago, and Sadie remembers very well even today that the interview portion of her application was doomed from the start. She spilled orange juice down the front of her Laura Ashley dress with blue flowers (to bring out the color in her eyes, her mother said) at the breakfast table and was so mortified that she neglected to inform

Mommy because, at the time, having to change out of her special out-
fit seemed more terrifying than walking into the biggest meeting of
her young life looking and smelling like she was bleeding citrus. Sadie
was well aware that her tiny palm was cold and clammy when she
shook the interviewer's hand. It was an older, gray-haired woman
named Mrs. Styne who was very thin and wore a tightly pulled back
bun. Mrs. Styne discreetly wiped her hand off on her dress after they
greeted each other. Young Sadie thought she looked like a pretty lady
who had the misfortune of being born into a family of witches. When
Sadie sat down in the big leather chair, the cushions hissed and
groaned, making an embarrassing farting noise.

"Is something wrong, Miss Chapman?" asked Mrs. Styne. She gave
Sadie a thin, dry smile.

"No, ma'am."

"Well, let's get started, shall we? What would you say is your most
distinguishing characteristic?"

"I'm bad in a room," she blurted, not wanting to seem as nervous
as she really was. "No matter how pretty the dresses Daddy buys me
are, I'm just really bad in a room."

Silence ensued. Mrs. Styne went through the rest of the interview,
asking the perfunctory questions and taking up another twenty minutes, but Sadie knew she was doomed. When the rejection became a
reality, her father went on a lengthy tirade about the city's private
schools, raving about how he would spend five times the tuition on
the famous (and famously high priced) Stansbury School, just so
none of the ornery sons of bitches who ran the academic institutions
so popular with his colleagues' children would benefit. He made a
single phone call to the head of the corporation that licensed Stansbury's AIDS vaccine. Martin Chapman had become something of a fi-
nance industry legend back in 2020 when he famously worked his
team of twenty-three men for two days straight in an effort to beat
out his competitors for the deal. The vaccine was licensed for $2 bil-
lion and everyone came away happy and rich. Chapman himself was
rumored to have come away with a 3 percent commission and secured Stansbury twice that sum. Three days after he made that phone
call, Sadie was packing her bags for the long journey out to the California desert. The prospect of boarding school—even the most elite

one on the planet—did not sit well with her. She felt that she had not only been rejected from Saint Cecelia's and Westerly, but from her own home as well. In fact, her five-year-old brain had already reasoned that Daddy was so ashamed he was willing to spend *five times* the money on a school just to get rid of her. Sadie privately decided never to get rejected again, in the hopes that one day she could reclaim her rightful place at the dinner table inside the Chapman household at 2 East 61st Street.

It was as if with that resolution her body responded to the challenge. Eventually, anyway. Sadie was not always beautiful. For the majority of her early years she was plagued with so much baby pudge—from the ages of one to approximately eleven, and in spite of the Stansbury cafeteria's intravenous nutrient diet and the med cycle—that she started to suspect she was simply and unavoidably fat. Then the chubbiness started to melt away and, like a science experiment gone wrong, her legs and arms would just not stop growing, until she started to resemble a bird with a frame elongated to such ludicrous proportions that flying wasn't really worth the effort anyway. Then her vintage hit its ripe phase: sixteen years and eight months. It was February, and it was the eleventh grade. Less than two years to go at Stansbury and suddenly light started hitting her cheekbones differently. The black and white image of her senior page in the 2036 edition of the yearbook spoke most eloquently: A tousled, tangled sea of honey brown waves pulled back, restrained by some unseen rubber band, resting atop a long forehead with a single brown freckle a half-inch above her clean right eyebrow, off-center but somehow essential. Her blue eyes addressed the camera with the sort of earnest clarity and attention one would offer a lost tourist in a strange land. An army of tan freckles dotted her small nose and cheeks, barely perceptible but obvious; she had never and would never use makeup to cover them, and as a result they rewarded her, always making her seem amused and grave all at once. Like she had seen things in her day, given them the proper names and definitions and, most important, was not scared to see them again. Her lips were also small, but full, the top one just slightly curled upward more than the lower. It was a mouth that said—in this picture anyway—*Oh yeah? Just try me. I'm begging you. I dare you.* But, really, it was the way the light hit her cheekbones and gathered before rolling downward into two smooth, steep slopes shaped like a V with a barely rounded tip. People in real life, much less high school seniors—even Stansbury specimens—simply did not look this way.

During that same fateful February, Sadie found that when she donned her normal pair of black pumps and knee socks, her legs and feet looked just like the pictures in magazines (she didn't even have to tighten her muscles and hold them just so). She also learned that she no longer had to contort her body in order to have the mouth-watering figure that became legendary in the halls and boys' dorm rooms inside the tower. After all the years lived in fear of another round of rejections, the various crushes plagued by unrequited love, failed friendships, and generalized nonacknowledgment of existence on the planet Earth that accompanied aesthetic mediocrity (even by Shannon and Katie, girls who were always pretty, and didn't allow her into their clique until her looks eclipsed theirs, as if their social lives were governed by the perverse Darwinian notion that if they were not the fairest of them all, they had better stick close to the girl who was, and pray for her leftovers), Sadie had adolescence at her feet. She didn't quite trust the results of her overnight metamorphosis, half-suspected that it was a temporary state before regression to her old, familiar self; or worse, a step closer on the inevitable journey that ended with adulthood and her mother's looks.

But that didn't stop her from systematically rejecting all the guys who sought to win her heart, slowly (but surely, of this she was certain) piecing together something that she—if she had had any prior experience with it—would have recognized as a sense of pride. She knew it seemed like a terrible cliché, the ugly-duckling-turned-swan gleefully relishing the rejection of so many who richly deserved it; but that was not what it was at all. The only thing Sadie despised more than being overlooked—and constantly living in fear of rejection at the hands of another Saint Cecelia's or Westerly, because everyone and everything had a bit of those schools in them, as far as she was concerned—was the sight of spoiled specimen boys scrambling to cling onto a bandwagon when it rolled through town. She was satisfied with the feeling of all of those new, accepting eyes upon her in progressions, with her freshly minted girlfriends saving a place for her at their table in the cafeteria, with the way that dozens of heads would turn during a casual stroll through the atrium. Although this didn't completely erase the memory of the previous rejection that plagued her early years, it did make her feel more prepared for the next time she might have to undergo the rigors of application for acceptance from any person, place, or thing.

And then she met William Winston Cooley. Actually made his acquaintance as opposed to merely having some random run-in inside an elevator pod or meds line. Sadie, like everyone else, knew of him. She was one of the specimens present during the Guernica incident freshman year. This was before she had become beautiful and had been quite used to being just another face in the crowd. Cooley had long been something of a phenomenon among the Class of 2036. The older specimens took him under their wings and included him in their inside jokes. He was quiet in progressions but always ready with a sarcastic quip if the occasion arose, and no one else had the spine to spit it out, lending the impression that every time he opened his mouth something charming or witty would spill forth. Even before Guernica, Cooley made waves. Like the time he brought an antiquated game called Spin the Bottle to this repressed school of theirs, a game that was, as everyone knew even back then, just a protracted excuse to provide himself, Bunson, and the rest of the guys the opportunity to say that they'd kissed girls for real, and likewise allowed the girls in question to make the same boasts about them. Spin the Bottle caught on like wildfire, and for about two weeks it seemed as if every specimen in the school was spending more time tracking down bottles and practicing kisses (with tongue, even!) than doing homework. As strange as it sounded, this delinquent orphan somehow ushered in the era of puberty and hormones for a large number of specimens who otherwise would've ignored their natural urges entirely. Predictably, the security detail found out about this and outlawed the games, and the headmaster probably gave Cooley the cursory slap on the wrist. But, nonetheless, his peers loved him for shaking things up a bit. And stories like this were what made all of the girls (except for maybe frigid little Camilla 2.0) hang on his every word and move.

When Cooley rescued Shannon by taking on those thugs outside the museum singlehandedly, Sadie, as well as the rest of the girls, silently reasoned that he did it because he had a crush on her. And although she never said it out loud, it was obvious that Shannon hoped this was true. She started wearing makeup around the tower and encouraged her circle of friends to spend more time with Bunson, Oates, Mancuso and the rest of Cooley's loyal entourage. It was impossible for Cooley not to have known this, but he never treated her any differently than before, smiling in a friendly manner whenever Shannon tried to initiate eye contact in progressions, politely making small talk in the event that their friends just happened to leave them alone together near the digitized river in the atrium, discreetly excusing himself after a suitable amount of time.

Sadie first spoke with Cooley a few months into the new, physically stunning stage of her existence, around May of 2035 to be precise. She sat alone at a table in the cafeteria doing homework after dinner when he set his tray of food jars and laser syringe down next to her.

"You mind?" he asked, sitting down before she could even answer.

"No," she replied, feeling a bit nervous. More nervous, anyway, than when any number of other prominent male specimens made similar overtures. His eyes were dark and calm, almost unnervingly so. He sat down in the steel chair and immediately started leaning back on its two rear legs, balancing his weight precariously against the slippery marble tile. The fact that at any moment it could slide out from under him created an aura of spontaneity that was very exotic inside the controlled environs of the tower. Still, she had an aura of her own to maintain, namely that of the unapproachable sort. It was, after all, easier to preempt rejection by enacting it rather than dawdling around waiting for it to find you. "There's a seat open at Shannon's table," she said with a hint of sarcasm, gambling that he might get up and leave, but knowing the chances of him doing so were slim. (At this point Shannon and Katie were still in the process of recruiting her for their social circle.)

"Oh yeah?"

"Yeah."

"Why would I want to sit over there?"

"I heard she's got a thing for you."

"How would you know?"

"Because she only cakes on that lipstick before the progressions that you're in."

"That field trip's ancient history," he said, leaning over the table toward her.

"I don't know Mr. Cooley . . . normally, schoolgirl crushes die hard."

"Miss Chapman, the schoolgirls around this place aren't any more normal than the school itself."

"So why'd you save her then?" Sadie asked. "You know at . . ." She faltered, not wanting to call it Guernica in front of him because she didn't want him to think she was like everyone else.

"She was with us. Someone's got to look after our own. God knows the meds aren't teaching anyone to do it."

"Our own? I thought you hated this place."

"I do. But it's the only place any of us have at the moment."

"So you'd have thrown yourself into the street at those guys for anyone?" At that moment, Goldsmith—at the time just an anonymous junior specimen—walked past their table.

"Sure," he said, nodding in Goldsmith's direction. "Probably even for that kid." It was then that Sadie distinctly remembered giving him the first consciously seductive smile of her life. It made him blink and he looked down, bashful, like he just lost a high-stakes staring contest.

"Would you do it for me?" she asked, knowing what an indulgent, loaded question it was. "You know, if I needed protecting." Then she felt his hand on hers—it was warm and surprisingly soft—right there out in the open on the tabletop for anyone to see.

"I can't wait to do it for you," he grinned. Suddenly Sadie felt dangerous and safe all at once. She was not sure what sort of fine, upstanding young men she would have met in the years that followed Saint Cecelia's or Westerly, but was certain that none of them would've been like William Cooley.

Sadie finished off her cigarette and tossed it into a toilet, listening to the satisfying sizzle. Shannon and Katie tossed theirs as well and began to primp their hair in the mirror. Shannon, to her credit, never held the Cooley matter against Sadie. Every now and then Sadie would catch her sending forlorn gazes his way but was never too concerned, for rejection was a thing of her past. After all, at that particular stage in her young life even Daddy would have admitted it: she was nothing if not spectacular in a room.

6

While the conventional use of the word *atrium*
evokes images of a soaring, wide-open space filled with sunlight, the
one located on the 125th floor of Stansbury Tower was—as one might
expect by this point—anything but conventional. The walls indeed
stretched up several hundred feet toward a domed ceiling that did, in
fact, soar. The surface stretched far and wide enough to allow every
specimen, professor, administrator and security guard in the school to
traverse the space comfortably at once. The hum of seventy-eight
strategically placed holographic projectors was muffled by sound experts. All that was left was the smell of freshly cut green lawns and
the sweet wetness of flowers in March melting into the air. It was
enough to make a kid forget what kind of place he really lived in.

Scores of specimens stepped out of their elevator pods and into the
space, greeted with a sight that was nothing short of breathtaking: a
golden sun hanging in a blue morning sky delicately frosted with
wisps of clouds. They moved onto an expanse of lush grass with carefully manicured paths that intertwined into minimalist, elegant loops

and curves. Oak trees reached upward with their huge, newborn
leaves still wet with dew. The sound of a stream twinkled around a
bend and into the forest. The atrium was Nature & Co.'s crowning
achievement, a multimillion-dollar work of interactive art that the
San Angeles Times described as "more natural than nature."

Even after twelve years it took Goldsmith's breath away on a daily
basis. He surveyed the land ahead of him: hundreds of uniformed
specimens carrying their books to progressions across the greatest
campus in the world. Just look at the group of juniors quizzing each
other with flash cards before Calculus 4. And there was Professor
Schultz leading the second graders across the bridge over the river to
the med tech bay. They held hands in a perfectly straight line, quietly
pointing out a deer grazing over yonder through the trees. And there
was Mr. Charles Edgar Shapiro up on the hill, his easel out, the paint-
brush a blur in his hand, getting in some inspiration before the day began. Goldsmith strode down the path leading toward the med tech bay,
catching the glances of Misters Nathaniel DeShawn Green, Howard
John Spencer, and Gerald Michael Simmons—fellow Stansbury lifers
who were scheduled to graduate along with him.

"Good morning, gentlemen," said Goldsmith.

"Whatever," said Green.

The rest glanced around and averted their eyes. Goldsmith had
gotten used to it: no one wanted to be seen getting friendly with the
valedictorian. It still gnawed at him. After eleven years of anonymity,
he thought that being officially named as the top specimen would finally turn him into one of the faces of the Class of 2036, a well-
known character like Cooley, Camilla, Sadie, or Mr. Shapiro (even if
Shapiro was, in Goldsmith's opinion, a little on the artsy-fartsy side).
But winning the Selmer-Dubonnet test did the opposite. Whereas
before the specimens looked through him, now they looked away, at-
tempting to hide any traces of guilt in their eyes.

The headmaster warned him from the start that no valedictorian
was ever loved by his peers, but Goldsmith honestly believed he'd be
the exception. He tried being chummy. He played up his humble ori-
gins. And yet, his entrance into a roomful of specimens never failed to
cast a chill over the natural joking and flirting of high school life. Just
once, Goldsmith thought, he'd like to be invisible. He only wanted to

know what the room was like before he came in and spoiled every-thing. He'd be happy to go back to being ignored, unnoticed, if only to hear one or two of the punch lines he always missed. And if he was invisible, he could smile as big as he wanted and not worry about anyone thinking he was playing an angle or being unfair. For all the knowledge in Goldsmith's head, he was never able to get the joke in time to laugh with the kids who were supposed to be his friends.

"*Good morning, specimens,*" chirped Mrs. InterAct with her morning announcements. "*Final exams begin tomorrow and round-the-clock study halls commence after today's progressions. After you've picked up your meds, don't forget to stop by the tech bay for your Stimulum injection.*"

A cloud sailed past the sun, then abruptly disappeared. Then it ap-peared again, passing the sun like it did before, but this time freezing in midair before disappearing and reappearing. It zinged back and forth, right to left over the sun again and again. And then a flock of birds froze in midflight. A herd of deer started to flicker. Nature went several shades off color, grays and browns where whites and oranges should have been.

"Oh my God," shouted Cooley, loud enough for everyone to whip their heads over in his direction. "We're not *really* outdoors! I had no idea!" The specimens chuckled and continued on their paths. Cooley looked over at two big security detail officers in their Tac IX vests, their Nomex balaclavas hanging from their belt loops. He'd gotten ac-customed to feeling their eyes on him. One of them had slapped a bandage over his swelled, obviously broken nose to go with a lazy eye sporting a wicked shiner. Cooley wondered which specimen decided not to go down without a fight.

"I'm going on eleven years now and these kids still give me the creeps," said Officer Jamison.

"You've just got hard feelings because your face got rearranged," said Officer Jackson. "Or maybe you're just jealous because they're smarter than you'll ever be?"

Jamison chuckled. His hand instinctively touched the Colt M-8 on his belt. "Shhhh," he said. "School's probably got 'em reading minds by now."

A chubby silhouette strolled in front of Officers Jamison and Jack-son. Pudgy Mr. Hurley, the yearbook professor, unknowingly blocked

Cooley's view. As usual, he had that old-fashioned camera around his neck and was kissing specimen ass. He cornered a group of sophomores by the stream.

"Last minute call for yearbook photos," Hurley said. "I don't want you to be left out and you don't want to be forgotten! Smile!" The specimens stood there, stone-faced, as the flash went off one, two, three, four times.

"*Hurleee!*" shouted Mr. Bunson. "You're a rock star!"

"*Hurleeeeeee!*" shouted specimens all over the atrium. Hurley saw Bunson and rushed over to him, Cooley, and Sadie, panting from the exertion.

"Miss Chapman, don't you look lovely today! Mind if I take a photo?"

Sadie hid her face behind her hands. "No . . . I was up late studying and . . ."

"Please? Just take a second . . ." She dropped her hands and gave him that smile. Cooley watched the way her face lit up with that up-from-under-the-lashes look and felt his stomach get all soft and queasy. The flash blinked brightly. "Gorgeous! Gorgeous!" Hurley cooed. "Mr. Cooley? A shot of the Class of 2036's most popular couple?" He aimed the camera at Cooley, who covered the lens with his hand. Undaunted, Hurley whirled around just in time to see Goldsmith pass by. "Mr. Goldsmith, sir! A candid of the class of 2036's valedictorian?" Goldsmith turned his face to the camera while walking, giving the lens his best side. The flash went off. "Beautiful! Get this kid to Capitol Hill! Get him an agent! Get him . . ."

Hurley's voice disappeared into the crowd as Goldsmith got in line at the med table along with the rest of the specimens. One by one, they stepped up to the stainless steel counter where two overseers clad in sterilized white jumpsuits distributed individually customized pill packs. Goldsmith stepped up and was handed the pack with his name printed on it. Eight pills: two multinutrient/hormone capsules, two of the standard Stansbury blend, one antianxiety tablet, and three antidepressants. Weird. Up until last week Goldsmith was only taking one of those. Someone high up must have thought he needed extra help easing his conscience. He swallowed four pills at a time, washing them down at the counter's built-in water fountain.

Cooley stepped up to the counter as Goldsmith walked off. An overseer handed Cooley his med pack and watched him stick it in his blazer pocket.

"Never seen you take your meds, Cooley," he said. "You save them for later or what?"

"I feed 'em to the birds." On cue, a holographic blue jay sailed down from the atrium's engineered sky and flew through Bunson like a ghost.

"There's no birds around here," said the overseer. "Not real ones, anyway." Bunson took his pack and washed his pills down.

"Meds make you smarter, partner," he said. "And they're so tasty."

"I'm on a diet," Cooley said. "They go straight to my thighs."

Sadie glanced over at Camilla 2.0 as she washed down her meds. She remembered that Katie was the one who came up with that cruel yet perfect nickname for her during second grade. For a good week or two Katie encouraged everyone in their progressions to speak in a dull, robotic monotone that was an extreme caricature of Camilla's uniquely controlled manner of speaking. It was quite funny, actually, listening to a room of twenty little specimens droning out routine conversations like miniature versions of Mrs. InterAct. When it became clear that Camilla was not about to burst into tears or even acknowledge the phenomenon, Katie and her friends took the abuse to the next level and began moving around her in exaggerated herky-jerky motions as if they were stiff automatons that needed a good dose of oil. But it was all for naught, as young Camilla's steely gaze just seemed to cut right through them. It was as if she knew even then that the antics of mean children relied upon an appropriately hysteric reaction from the victims in order to perpetuate themselves with any effectiveness, and she had resolved to deprive Katie of the satisfaction. Soon, the robot routine petered out and the only option left to Camilla's antagonists was to shun her with a collective cold shoulder. But even back then, Sadie remembered, she knew that they were playing right into her hands, that that was how she wanted it from the beginning. No shoulder in the entire tower, after all, was colder than Camilla 2.0's.

The only time that Sadie saw her betray anything remotely close to a moment of weakness was in eighth grade. They were using the communal showers in the girls' locker room on Level 42 following their Core Cross-Training B progression—approximately twenty-five fourteen-year-old girls self-consciously scrubbing themselves clean as quickly as possible, their haste due to the unforgiving, roving eyes of their peers—when a stream of bright red blood appeared on the white porcelain tile directly underneath Camilla's showerhead. Sadie remembered being the first one to see it only seconds after Camilla noticed it, and how she quickly but calmly examined herself for cuts or injuries, clearly a bit confused about what was happening to her. Soon enough, the sound of whispers and giggles mixed in with the pattering of water against the floor until, one by one, each showerhead was turned off. The only one that remained on was Camilla's, probably because she preferred to wash the blood away as soon as it emerged.

"What's the matter with you, Camilla?" a girl asked.

"What are you, stupid?" asked Katie, her loud, high voice echoing against the tile. "It means you're pregnant!" She started laughing. "You're gonna have a baby!" Other girls started to laugh, too.

"Camilla 3.0 is on the way!" someone else cried as the girls began to file out into the locker room to get dressed. Sadie wrapped herself in her white towel and walked over to her. They were the only ones left. Camilla finally turned off her own showerhead and cinched a towel around her small frame.

"I'll walk with you to the infirmary if you want," offered Sadie.

"I'll be fine, thank you."

"Are you sure?"

"Yes."

"But what if you're—"

"The only problem I have, Miss Chapman, is the absurd similarity of my life to a Stephen King novel." Sadie blinked. Later, she figured out that King was a famous horror author of the late twentieth century. Even today Sadie wishes she would have laughed at what passed for Camilla's attempt at sarcastic humor, showing her that she wasn't as dense as the other girls. Sadie, Katie, Shannon, and the rest all experienced their own periods for the first time in the months that followed. As would become more and more apparent over the proceeding years, Camilla never had any fear or apprehension about coming in first place, far ahead of the timid little children that surrounded her.

Camilla bent down to sip from the med table's water fountain and Sadie tried not to be intimidated. "Um, hi," she stammered. "Miss Moore?" Camilla leaned up from the fountain and looked her in the eye. Sadie found it difficult to return her gaze and focused on the three-dimensional, replicated grass at her feet instead. "Look . . . you know I'd never ask you this but . . . well, we've both got Harking's first-hour progression and I was swamped last night and didn't—"

"Have a chance to do your work for today?"

"I just need one answer. Come on, help me out. You're the smartest one in this whole place and—"

"Actually, I'm not."

"Number two in our class is a lot higher than I ever was."

"Which one, Miss Chapman?"

"What?"

"Which answer do you need?"

"Number four. The long-form essay." Sadie pulled out her iPro Tabula and flipped it on, the blue light from the small monitor matching the color of her eyes. She extended the antenna and got ready to type.

"Question number four," began Camilla. "The Puritanical notion of the Elect was based in the concept of a select, inherently elite few who would save the human race from itself, primarily . . ."

"So it's true." Sadie couldn't help but stare.

"What?"

"You really do have a photographic memory. I guess I always thought it was one of those urban legends."

"Type faster, Miss Chapman. I don't do reruns." Sadie started typing as Miss Moore recited the question's answer at a slow, deliberate pace so she could keep up. While she spoke, her eyes followed Goldsmith as he walked down the more-natural-than-nature path through the grass toward the med tech bay. Camilla saw the look on his face and placed it, wondering if he still felt guilty about what happened during the Selmer-Dubonnet exam and if he'd still want to hold her hand if she was the one who won. She watched the way Goldsmith moved: a boy in a man's armor.

Goldsmith got in line at the med tech bay. A tech in a blue jump-suit tapped a set of laser syringes. The line moved forward, one by one. One of the specimens in front of Goldsmith rolled up his sleeve and didn't bat an eye at the sight of the red pulsing laser beam. He, like everyone else, had gotten used to it. There was that quick burn-ing sensation followed by a series of cool blips, almost like water drip-ping onto the skin, as the serum's molecules transferred their payload into the physiology. No blood, no needles, no nasty welts or bruising left from daily injections.

"What's on the menu today?" he asked the med tech.

"Stimulum," he said. "The perfect cocktail of stimulants and nutri-ents to keep you up—and most important—coherent for sixty-eight to seventy-two hours, depending on your body weight. Fortified with subtle neutralizers, so it won't interfere with the med cycle's calming agents. The ultimate study aid. Only the best for you kids. Just like the commercials say: 'Because you deserve to live in a future perfect.' "

"Is this the stuff they give to the marines during long missions?"

"It's what *we* give the marines. Stimulum was developed in Stans-bury labs," he said. He pulled the laser out of the specimen's arm with ease. "Like taking a hot knife from butter."

"What?" asked the young man. "I'm not familiar with that idiom."

"Just a saying. Late twentieth century. Guess I just dated myself, didn't I?"

Goldsmith walked to the front of the line. The tech bowed his head.

"Good morning, Mr. Goldsmith," he said.

"Good morning, Dr. Wilson."

"Some of the specimens don't like staying up all night. Say it drives them nuts."

"I don't mind it."

"Oh? Why's that?"

Because of the bad dreams I get, thought Goldsmith. I'm nailing other specimens to wooden crosses in the atrium, their blood leaves spatters on my pressed white shirt. The mother I never met is every person in the crowd, and she's cheering me on. "Because I'm here to get the job done," he said out loud.

Dr. Wilson nodded. Goldsmith walked off, rolling his sleeve back over his arm. In the corner of his eye, he saw Camilla step up for her injection. She extended her bare arm. Her skin was the precious white of a frozen pond in winter, subtle blue veins extending beneath. She didn't wear perfume but still smelled fresh.

"Miss Camilla Moore II," drawled Dr. Wilson. "Why wasn't it Camilla Moore Junior?" She glanced up from the sight of the laser pumping the serum into her bloodstream and looked past him. "Right . . . ," he smirked. "Bet you were a real hit with the boys at prom time."

"Two minutes until assembly. Please gather in the coliseum on Level 125 for announcements from Headmaster Latimer and President Lang," said Mrs. InterAct.

Cooley saw the flow of specimens merge and gather, heading toward the coliseum in a single-file line. From where he stood, they looked just like critters in an ant farm he saw back in a third grade Earth Science progression. Now was his chance. He looked over at the elevator bank: Jamison and Jackson were standing guard, making sure no one ditched assembly. Cooley headed for the usual stairwell off a side corridor, away from the light of the atrium. He opened the door and smelled the thick scent of damp concrete and ammonia, normal for the innards of the school where no specimens dared to tread. He looked over the railing and saw hundreds of steps spiraling down into darkness. As he began the long descent, it occurred to him that the smell of fire and brimstone would have been more appropriate.

Meanwhile, the coliseum was packed with specimens numbering four thousand strong. It was a vast, elliptical space, based on the design of the ancient Coliseum in Rome: long stretches of white levels rose up and up, but with row upon row of beige Eames chairs in the place of the hard marble benches of old. All eyes were on the circular stage placed front and center, waiting for their cue. Two figures— President Judith Lang and Headmaster Lloyd Latimer—rose from their seats simultaneously. The entire specimen body followed their lead, rising in perfectly timed unison. Right hands were solemnly placed over hearts. Eyes went to the huge white marble slab that appeared to be suspended several hundred feet in midair, high above their heads near the coliseum's ceiling. Everyone had memorized the slab's large, black Roman-font lettering, thanks to this daily invocation each morning since their arrival in the tower, so the collective gaze upward was really for effect, as if Doc Stansbury's soul were perched somewhere in the rafters, wistfully watching over the children he left behind.

"By virtue of the Gifts bestowed upon me," recited this grand chorus of prodigies, *"I swear my Eternal Duty to all those without such Gifts. For Power may point the way, but only Honor can lead it."* Goldsmith finished and let the standard ceremonial moment of silence pass through the space and evaporate. With the Stansbury Oath affirmed, everyone sat back down, except for President Lang, who took the podium and began to speak. The stage began its slow rotation, so that she could address the entire specimen body without any section of the audience feeling left out.

Goldsmith studied her. Lang always looked as if she were being broadcast on television even when she stood before you in the flesh; a soft glow seemed to surround her at all times, lending her an ethereal quality that would be mesmerizing if it weren't for her hair. It was a dyed shade of brown concealing what was clearly a natural blonde hue. He wasn't the only one to notice this strange mishap in her appearance: Stansbury rumor had it that President Lang grew up a sunny, bright-eyed knockout of a girl, but she toned down the look during her early tour of duty in Washington, D.C., so the men that ran the town would accord her a respect that, even in this day and age, most ambitious women did not receive. Capitol Hill did good things for her: the microphone projected her voice up into the rumbling tenor of authority and unimpeachable moral righteousness. As she spoke, her finger jabbed the air like she was the second coming of Hillary Rodham Clinton.

"... And I'm sure you've all heard the good news about Prof. Alan Partridge's crowning achievement," echoed her voice. Her dark, somber eyes took in the crowd, drawing out the moment for maximum effect. "Specimens, it is also *your* achievement. Tomorrow the United States Senate Select Committee on Education is voting on the Stansbury grant proposal, and it will pass. It will then move quickly from Congress to the office of the president himself. Stansbury School is on the verge of a glorious victory."

Four thousand faces nodded silently back at her, the shine in the stitched emblems on their uniforms glinting against the bright lights. Lang sat down. Headmaster Latimer rose and stood at the microphone, his gray hair adding to a personal history that each specimen was well aware of: he was the first administrator Dr. Stansbury asked to join him in the founding of this school. He grabbed the sides of the wooden podium like a grizzled captain guiding a weathered seaborne vessel in a storm, and he smiled at his loyal crew.

"Specimens, the eyes of the world are upon us," he said. Goldsmith knew what was coming next: a meaningfully inspirational aphorism to send them on their way. "I leave you now with the words of George Bernard Shaw. 'The reasonable man adapts himself to the world; the unreasonable one persists in trying to adapt the world to himself. Therefore all progress depends on the unreasonable man.' I ask each and every one of you to be as unreasonable as humanly possible. Forever. And do so with the honor of our oath, the honor that Dr. Stansbury held so dear." The specimens burst into applause. Goldsmith's ears pounded from the reverberations as he stood up and began to file out of the coliseum with the rest of them.

A hand grabbed him by the arm. He whirled around and saw an outsider slouching, the way all outsiders do, inside of a brown linen suit. He smoothed out the guest pass stuck to his lapel. It read VISITOR in large red letters underneath a tag bearing the school's emblem.

"Mr. Goldsmith?" he asked.

"Can I help you?"

"I doubt it, but you've got potential. What am I gonna do with the head Boy Scout?" The visitor felt the valedictorian's cold gaze on his face and felt his guts twitter. "John Pietropaolo. I'm with the *San Angeles Times*. But everyone calls me Pete." He handed a business card to Goldsmith. Goldsmith glanced down and handed it back like there was a fungus festering on the paper stock. Pete voyeuristically looked around at the specimens passing them and caught a glimpse of Mr. Frederick Grady Jr. himself. The seasoned reporter was surprised to feel a twinge of starstruck adrenaline flow through him. Grady Jr. in the flesh—no shit! The kid didn't look so big the last time Pete saw him on TV, in a football stadium surrounded by grown men twice his size. Just that past autumn, Grady, the eighteen-year-old son of NFL Hall of Fame running back Freddie Grady Sr., became the youngest person ever to play in a professional football game. And boy did he make the most of it, Pete remembered, seeing the replay in his mind all over again.

It was the last game of the 2035 season for the cellar-dwelling San Angeles Raiders. After riding the bench for the entire season, through fifteen games (and fifteen straight losses) the coaching staff called Grady's number with one minute and four seconds left in the fourth quarter against Cleveland. Sixty-four seconds of game time for what Pete and every other skeptic out there deemed a cheap marketing ploy by a dead-end franchise.

The landmark *Bright v. National Football League* case was overturned by the United States Supreme Court back in 2014, deeming it unconstitutional for any professional sports league practicing age discrimination to deprive a citizen of the opportunity to make a living. (Even back then, Pete, at the time just a cub reporter, considered the dynamics of the ruling interesting: the case was the only one to date in which the two famously opposed former specimens sitting on the Court—the loose/strict constructionist duo—were in agreement, like they knew something about young prospects that no one else did.) The ruling was a ho-hum deal for most leagues. They had already been drafting kids out of high school for years, but the case did, however, deal a mortal blow to the traditions of the last holdout: the National Football League. Current and former NFL types always maintained that what happened on the gridiron was strictly a grown man's game, that even the most talented high school All-American could suffer permanent injury or worse against the biggest, fastest, most brutal athletes on the planet. Not to mention the players' union didn't want any veterans getting cut from their teams to make room for the new kids. However, for twenty-one years after the ruling came down, not one franchise drafted a single prep phenom. It was the free market speaking: no general managers or coaches were willing to waste even a late-round pick on a kid, when they could get a more developed prospect with potential from the college ranks. Then, in 2035, the Raiders selected Stansbury eleventh grader Frederick Grady

Jr. with the final pick of the final round of the draft. It was a choice that shook up the sports world. A freshly graduated high school senior making the jump to the NFL was radical in itself, but an eleventh grader? Freddie Jr. was Stansbury's starting quarterback, a six-foot-six, 240-pound stud with 4.3 speed and a howitzer of an arm, the kid who had led the school to three of its last seven consecutive state *and* national championships. The California High School Athletics Association regularly tested all players for banned substances such as steroids, always paying the closest attention to members of Stansbury teams, but (much to opposing coaches' chagrin) no specimen ever came up positive. The med cycle incorporated no illicit ingredients, and the patented formulas were readily available to anyone who could pay the lab's prices, but very few high school jocks or schools could afford a six-figure supplement budget or the additional cost of a trained med tech to administer dosages on a regular basis. The CHSAA determined that the cycle was no different than a regular trainer's "secret" herbal ointment to cure an ailment: a bit hard to pin down, but wholly legal. Needless to say, there were many championship banners hanging from the rafters of the tower's gymnasium.

Which brings us back to Freddie Grady Jr., Class of '36, the most heralded jock in the school. The Raiders said he'd been drafted as a pure athlete rather than a quarterback, that they'd move him around when he got to training camp, and he might end up a wide receiver. The pundits all called it a PR stunt that stunk of desperation. The kid wasn't going to see playing time, even if he did defy the odds by making the regular season roster. He'd ride the bench and be a circus freak show, good for a few weeks of media hype if he didn't get his head blasted off his shoulders by the opposition in practice. He was sure to end up a cautionary tale for young athletes everywhere. Nobody could get an interview with Freddie on the day he was drafted, because he was busy studying for his final exams at Stansbury. The *Times* tracked down his Hall of Famer dad. Freddie Sr. said he was giving his consent and allowing his son to train, play, and travel with the team while maintaining his senior year course load. Another reporter got a hold of President Lang and asked her if the school didn't think the distraction of an NFL season would be too much for even a specimen, and wasn't Stansbury concerned?

"The only concern we have," she responded, "is finding a new quarterback before summer practice sessions begin."

The 2035 NFL season followed. Freddie Jr. made the roster but didn't see a moment of playing time in any of the team's fifteen consecutive losses, losses that just about broke the hearts of Pete and the millions of other die-hard Raider fans in San Angeles. Then, during the last game of the season, at the tail end of a 14–0 beating at the hands of a mediocre visiting Browns squad, it happened. Pete witnessed it while standing on 89th Street in B Sector, watching the game clock wind down on a plasma screen in the display window of an electronics store. A few dozen others were huddled around, angling for a view, any view to take their minds off the surging unemployment and sidewalks packed to bursting. They caught some audio as it echoed out from the bar next door: the blare of a color commentator mixed in with a cacophony of anguished laments from disconsolate Raider fans inside. There was one minute and four seconds left in the fourth quarter and San Angeles had possession of the ball. On the sideline, Coach Hudler barked something into his headset. A hush fell over the stadium. Grady Jr. got up from the bench, nodded at his coach, and started fastening his helmet straps. The kid wore number 80 and jogged toward the huddle on the field.

"Finally!" mused a grizzled, tired old man standing to Pete's right. "But I reckon if they had sent that boy in to get himself killed earlier in the season, we all probably would've given up on watching right then and there."

"It's a conspiracy," said someone else. "The TV network knows everyone's giving up on those overpaid bums, and they ordered the league to stick Junior in now to keep the advertisers happy. And I'm bettin' the network is sliding a fat cash kickback to Stansbury for helping them boost ratings." Pete rolled his eyes and watched Grady Jr. line up as the flanker. The Raiders' over-the-hill quarterback barked out audibles. The offense was on its own thirty-yard line. Second and ten, but everyone—despite everything they knew about this pitiful team, its shattered season, the mediocrity, its proverbial snowball's chance in hell—was hoping for something special. The clock started ticking.

Pete caught some commentary from the TV inside the bar: *"Grady*

Jr. looks simply out of his league. Are we witnessing a coming out party or an execution?" The crowd—in the stadium, in the bar, in the street around Pete (more and more San Angelenos had surrounded the store window, all wanting to catch a glimpse)—held their breaths, doing what they knew best in that day and age: faintly hoping for a pleasant surprise, but publicly expecting yet another letdown, the latest in a long line that started when all of America descended upon this city in the aftermath of the EMP, looking for an escape from a nuclear apocalypse that never came when they expected it, but could always be right around the corner.

The play started. Junior sprinted ten yards downfield. Pete saw a Cleveland cornerback level the kid, knocking him to the turf. The QB watched it happen and got dropped for an eight-yard loss. The crowd gasped, but Junior bounced back up. Forty-four seconds left on the clock. He retook his flanker position. The ball was snapped. This time that wily cornerback jammed him, locking his hugely muscled, long arms around Junior's, pinning his hands down and preventing him from even turning around in time to see the pass sail over his head. The guys standing around Pete started to boo the overhyped Stansbury specimen. So did the 150,000 fans in the stadium. As the jeers rained down, Junior lined up again, seemingly unaffected by the wave of taunts being hurled in his direction.

Ball on the San Angeles twenty-two-yard line. Fourth down and forever to go. Last play of the game. Last play of the season. Down 14–0. Touchdown or no, the Raiders were still losing this one. But everyone kept watching anyway. They booed, threw down empty beer cups, and watched. They still had one last play before going back to their lives. The ball was snapped. The QB dropped back, helpless in the face of a furious pass rush. And then the damnedest thing happened. Junior drove his shoulder into his defender and swung his inside arm up, freeing himself for a split second with a textbook rip move. It created a flash of space, just long enough for him to use his med cycle–enhanced physique to create a sliver of separation between him and everyone else. He flew down the field. The QB heaved a prayer in Junior's general direction. And then Pete felt it: that sudden hush that descends in slow motion when a stadium, a street— hell, even a city packed full of people—shuts up to gaze at a spiraling football soar through the air, up into the heavens, and arc back down to earth. Instinctively, people watching from chairs rose to their feet and those standing rolled up to the tips of their toes for a better view, their mouths all unconsciously formed into dumbstruck O's, each of them rendered silent by the electricity of the moment.

Two defenders who dropped back into prevent-scheme coverage converged on the ball. One of them leaped for it. Junior leaped higher. They collided in midair. Junior came down with it, kept his balance, hurdled Cleveland's lunging free safety, and ran for the end zone forty yards downfield. The weak-side cornerback sprinted after him, closing the gap. Junior glanced over his shoulder, saw him coming, and then hit his sixth gear. Off to the races. The crowd was suddenly rabid now, screaming an unintelligible roar, jumping up and down like this game still meant something. Pete stood there on the street and just plain watched as guys around him bounced around, complete strangers grabbing him by the jacket, yanking that fanatic *are-you-fucking-watching-this* Morse code into his body. Pete watched. That weak-side corner caught up to Grady Jr. ten yards from the end zone, grabbing him from behind. Junior's knees buckled for just a moment, and then the kid threw himself forward with his opponent hanging on his back. Just as his body crashed to the turf, he reached that football across the goal line. Touchdown.

The game clock expired. The Raiders never kicked the extra point. Final score: 14–6, Cleveland over San Angeles. But you wouldn't have known it from the ecstasy in the stadium and beyond. The sad, wet, packed streets were filled with whoops of joy. Pete was as skeptical as the next guy, but he felt it, too. A game starts. It's called life. You get knocked down. You get held up by some dirty trick. No one's there to help you. Everyone's waiting for you to stay down. But you don't give up. You adapt and you run fast, fast enough to get a moment of breathing room and reach down past your heart and into your gut to do something no one's ever seen before, something that nobody ever thought possible. Something that makes a tough-luck city, filled with millions of miserable people, rise up in awe. Something that makes a touchdown worth a great deal more than six points. Call it six points and good helping of hope. Hope that next season (and, really, next season started the moment the last game ended, so next season was right at that moment) would be a brighter one, a time not too far off that could herald a return to greatness or not, but for now, everything was filled with this ripe, pregnant possibility.

Pete watched the on-field postgame interview with Freddie Grady Jr. He didn't look elated. He wasn't pumped up. Like all of the specimens, he had a look of confident calm that seemed so incongruous with the emotions of a football field. The reporter held a microphone up to Junior's face.

"Freddie, the whole season, people have been saying—myself included—that you weren't ready for this level, that you'd get injured, that you were in way over your head. You've got the physical gifts, but on paper, there's no way you should've been able to—"

"That," cut in Junior with his Stansbury monotone, "is why they play the games."

The men around Pete heard this and cheered, raising their fists in the air. *"That's why they play the games!"* they chanted together. *"That's why they play the games!"* Pete walked off. Some boys in the street were tossing around their own football, replaying Grady Jr.'s impossible catch, run, and reach for the end zone.

"I'm open!" Pete called to the ten-year-old quarterback. The kid dropped back, checked off his imaginary receivers and then hefted a wobbly pass in his direction. Pete leaped up and caught it, feeling the leather smack against his palms, and landed, briefly juking out unseen defenders. For a moment he was Freddie Grady Jr. too: young again, bursting with potential, ready to rise to the occasion and defy the odds. And so was all of San Angeles. He tossed the ball back and heard his Tabula ring. "Yeah?" he answered.

"Tell me you just saw that game!" said Len Kinsley, the *San Angeles Times*'s editor-in-chief.

"You mean that final loss in an 0-16 season?"

"You just wait till next year! Junior'll be starting and—"

"I've got to get inside that school, Len. Talk with those specimens. Find out what really goes on in that tower."

"You and that school. Why don't you trust them? They've only been saving the world for the past twenty years. And now they're saving our Raiders!"

"I'm gonna get inside. I know some people who can pull strings."

"Fat chance. You think they're actually gonna let you talk to specimens? No way."

"Hey, lighten up boss," Pete grinned, watching the little boys reenact Junior's score for the umpteenth time, "that's why they play the games." And for the record, President Lang found her new quarterback. Just one month before Mr. Frederick Grady Jr.'s NFL debut, Stansbury won its eighth consecutive state football championship.

Junior brushed by them on his way out of the coliseum, oblivious to the nod of acknowledgment that Pete directed at him. Goldsmith grabbed him by the arm, snapping him out of his reverential awe.

"I said, are you authorized to be here, Mr. Pietropaolo?" Goldsmith asked.

"It's just Pete. And yes, I'm authorized by none other than President Judith Lang. She told me to find you and stick real close."

"Why me?"

"She probably figures it's good PR before the Senate committee's vote tomorrow. Don't mind me, kiddo." Pete gave him a smile. "C'mon, don't look at me like that. I'm just an ink-stained wretch."

Goldsmith felt the crush of his fellow specimens as they pushed past him through the crowd, and suddenly became protective of his home. "I know who you are," he said. "You wrote that hatchet job on the mayor right after the election."

"Oh, that?" Pete's expression broke into a grin best described as that of the shit-eating variety. "His opponent wakes up in a motel room with a hooker and a hangover and doesn't remember how he got there? Twenty-four hours before the polls open? A photographer just happened to be on the premises? I wasn't the only one who thought it reeked of setup." Pete's smile shifted genres to the kind meant to make a man feel like a child. "Or maybe you're defensive because the mayor's an alumnus of this place?" Goldsmith looked away. Pete took it as a signal to continue, maybe twist the knife just a tad. "Funny how things always work out for you Stansbury people, isn't it?"

"There are no scandals around here."

"Then don't look so nervous. I'm merely a humble servant of that patron saint of journalism, the Truth. Headmaster's a big fan of

George Bernard Shaw. So am I." Pete winked. "Shaw had some bang-up one-liners. Here's another one for you: 'All great truths . . .'"

Goldsmith racked his brain just to shut Pete up. He came up with the rest of the quotation in the blink of an eye, just like the school taught him. ". . . begin as blasphemies," Goldsmith said, staring him down.

"Bingo, Mr. Valedictorian."

Goldsmith headed through the atrium, Pete two steps behind. He could feel the eyes of the specimens on him and sped up the pace toward the privacy of an elevator pod. "Stansbury Tower was completed by the world renowned Rikka-Salvi & Partners architectural firm in 2020," said Goldsmith, launching into some standard tour guide schtick, wondering if he could literally bore Pete to death. "It stands 125 stories high. The lowest levels are used as storage facilities and floors four through twenty-five, generally speaking, are residential. Twenty-six through forty contain faculty offices and conference rooms, forty-one through seventy-five are progression rooms, seventy-six to ninety house research labs, and—"

"Yeah, yeah, Goldsmith. You're not telling me anything I haven't found on the school's Web site. How about some gossip? The headmaster take a liking to President Lang's little skirts? Who's banging their math teacher? Come to think of it, who are *you* banging?" Pete got a wicked glare in return for his inquiry. They arrived at an elevator pod and Goldsmith hit a button that read "49." Harking's progression beckoned. Pete glanced at the rows of buttons and pointed at an unmarked one that looked to be somewhere in the fifties or sixties.

"Where does that one take you?"

"Just some storage level, I think."

"An unmarked storage level? I'd love to check it out." Before Goldsmith could answer, Pete jabbed the button with his thumb. It would not light up.

"Must be out of service," said Goldsmith. "Sorry."

The pod whisked them to 49. The hallway was lined with progression rooms. Some professors had already started their lectures. A triad of detail officers passed, sizing Pete up.

"Don't those goons freak the kids out?" he asked.

"I'll assume by 'kids' you mean specimens. Those goons, Pete, are here for our safety. And the security detail only hires the most experienced professionals, former police officers, former military personnel, even some former Special Forces soldiers. Each and every one of them is highly trained. Frankly, you pose more of a threat to me than they do."

"Hey, I don't have any qualms with cops or soldiers, but let me suggest there might be a reason all of the guys you mention have 'former' in their descriptions."

"What are you implying?"

"Nothing, I just—" Pete glanced inside an open progression room and froze, catching a long look at a hi-def image of what looked like grisly roadkill broadcasted on an extralarge plasma screen above the chalkboard. "What in God's name *is* that?" Goldsmith took a peek inside the room and recognized the shot immediately.

"A cluster of herpes simplex B sores festering on male genitalia. Magnified approximately three hundred times."

"Ugh . . . why?" asked Pete, looking nauseous.

"For Professor Brighton's tenth grade Sexual Education progression, of course," said Goldsmith, lowering his voice so as not to interrupt Brighton's lecture.

". . . albeit necessary, but yet more proof as to why you are strongly advised not to engage in sexual intercourse," said the professor to his specimens. "Nor was this cross-section taken from a San Angeles prostitute, let me assure you! It was taken in the infirmary just last week, found on a male specimen who is currently enrolled at Stansbury." The professor looked at the terrified young faces before him, their eyes wild with speculation as to who the poor guy could be. "A specimen who contrived to have a torrid affair with . . . an outsider!" The specimens looked at each other, aghast at the possibility. Goldsmith grinned, leaning over to Pete.

"Here's some gossip," he whispered conspiratorially. "Brighton gives his specimens the same line every year. That image is at least ten years old."

Pete looked over the specimens behind their desks, taking in the girls' healthy, tanned legs as they practically glowed against the dark fabric of their knee socks. The boys sat there, chisel-jawed mannequins in uniform staring at Brighton's screen and taking careful notes.

"Oral sex is a healthy alternative to actual penetration," continued Brighton. He switched the STD image to that of two anonymous, featureless, virtually androgynous animated forms miming a blowjob. "The stimulus is of sufficient quality to attain orgasm, but the probability of disease transmittal and unwanted pregnancy is greatly diminished." One of the girls glanced from the X-rated animation over to Pete, who could tell she was completely oblivious to any kind of sexual tension. Her hair was pulled back in a tight blonde bun. She crossed her arms across her chest and applied balm to her supple lips, returning her eyes to the screen without so much as a glimmer of interest in him.

"But remember that *this* fate," said Brighton, flipping back to the herpes image and magnifying it even more so the sores seemed to glisten and breathe, "is what could await you, should you choose to act irresponsibly. A small number of your fellow specimens are purebreds from the egg and sperm of happily married alumni, and these offspring have the gifts to prove it. You are all familiar with Miss Camilla Moore II and her incredible sense of recall. But there is also Mr. Charles Edgar Shapiro, the artistic prodigy who is now the youngest person ever to have a painting added to San Angeles Modern Museum's permanent collection. And don't forget Anna Bryce Johnson, the tenth grader who is currently the third-ranked tennis player on the planet. These are merely the high-profile ones. The most recent purebred specimen to exhibit extraordinary gifts is only a second grader, one whose name I am not yet at liberty to reveal. But suffice it to say that Stansbury's psychiatrists have determined that she may in fact possess a sixth sense that enables her to read minds." Brighton looked at his progression. "I hope you understand what I am driving at, children. Proletarian outsiders are free to have their foul orgies, at liberty to spread their diseases amongst each other. But as far as each of you is concerned, sexual intercourse—nay, love itself—comes with a great responsibility. It is within you, within your bodies, within your hearts, to carry our race to the next stage of evolution."

A hush came over the room. Pete looked at Goldsmith. The kid was nodding like Brighton was preaching the gospel. Then he glanced at two mischievous-looking male specimens in the back row. One of them just passed something to his buddy. A photo. Pete squinted. It was a full-color, eight-by-eleven shot of some gorgeous girl specimen in a locker room wearing skimpy panties and nothing on top. She had no idea there was a camera present, was caught totally unaware, candid. She had this creamy skin and the best rack Pete had ever seen on any woman, anywhere, movie stars included. It was actually the Platonic rack of perfection. Full, firm, practically gravity-defying. And as if that wasn't enough, her legs went on forever. She was a gourmet three-course meal, if Pete had ever seen one. The kid gawking at the photo looked like he could now die happy.

"Sadie Sarah Chapman," he breathed, soaking up every pixel. "Cooley's gonna mash your face into inside-out hamburger if he finds out."

"Shut up and give it back," hissed his buddy. "It's mine!"

Pete laughed, comforted to see that some things in high schools would never change. He looked over at Goldsmith to see if he had caught the whole thing, but the valedictorian was already ten feet down the hall. Pete jogged after him, half-wishing he could enter some alternate dimension, one where he was young enough to enroll in school at this tower and his parents had enough dough to send him. Yeah, right. Keep on dreaming. No chance. But he'd settle for the next best thing: some deep, dark, Stansbury secret exposed on the front page, his name underneath the sixteen-point-type headline. Sniffing those stories out was *his* sixth sense. And it was only a matter of time before he found one.

Down on Level 1, Cooley exited the stairwell, his forehead glistening with sweat from the trip all the way to the tower's base. It was quiet. The soles of his shoes echoed as they clicked along in calm, even beats. He made his way to the registration and reception wing, deftly avoiding the security cameras panning above. Over at the desk, Harvey sat in his chair, love handles stretching his guard's uniform at the seams. Now *this* guy could've used the med cycle, Cooley thought as he walked over.

"Harvey."

Harvey flinched, snapping the graphite point of his pencil. "Mr. Cooley . . . trick or treat?"

"Treat." Cooley tossed his pack of meds onto the desk. Harvey opened it up and peeked inside, smiling. He whistled.

"Jesus. Sedatives. A pile of them. The med techs must really think you need some doping up," Harvey said.

"I'll be gone soon," Cooley said. "Got a new supplier lined up?"

"Don't you worry about me." He punched some keys on the simulcast terminal behind his desk. "Cab's on the way. Now go and get us all some clean piss before the test tomorrow. Do I get a bonus for being your travel agent, too?"

"They're still testing staff?"

"Routine. They don't want us dipping into the stash." Harvey grinned, looked at Cooley and saw years of shared secrets flash past his eyes. "You've been good to me, Cooley. Maybe I'll let you out once more after this before you graduate. For old times' sake. A romantic, two-hour getaway for you and sexy Sadie?"

"Deal." Cooley smiled and walked over to the electromagnetically sealed sliding door at the school's entrance. Harvey pressed a button underneath his desk. The thick metal hissed, exhaling purified Stansbury air into the warm dust of the desert outside. Cooley looked at the cracked surface outside the tower. It was dark brown and muddy from the rain pouring down. Slippery. Don't forget to wash off the shoes before stepping back inside, he reminded himself. It's a dead giveaway. Real, live dirt and the atrium didn't mix. The door slid shut behind him, hissing goodbye in his wake.

Fifteen minutes later, a light shined on Cooley from above. The hot air of a gyroengine blew exhaust. The door of the cab read: Universal Taxi. Cooley got inside and gagged: Stansbury could cure cancer and AIDS, but cabbies still smelled like barnyard animals.

"San Angeles," Cooley said. "West Side. D Sector." The cabbie glanced at him in the rearview mirror. The gyro also reeked of mint-flavored chewing tobacco and the grime from a brass spittoon affixed onto the dashboard.

"Last I heard, specimens aren't supposed to go off campus," he said. "I could lose my license."

"I've got two hundred dollars for you. That's double the meter rate."

"Two hundred and fifty."

Cooley grabbed the door handle. "Then let me out."

"Fine! Two hundred plus tip!" The gyro rose up into the sky. Cooley watched the ground get farther and farther away. He looked over his shoulder through the window, watching the tower get smaller in the distance. He thought about Sadie and Bunson back there, sitting somewhere in a safe little progression room way up high, and wondered whether this was really who he was, whether he was always going to be the guy ditching class. But the cabbie threw the gyro into another gear and Cooley's head snapped back against the seat, cutting his thoughts off before his med-free brain could formulate an answer.

Back inside the tower, the first hour Philosophy: Theory and Practice course had commenced in Progression Room 9 located on Level 49. Fifteen specimens and one newspaper reporter sat in two-person rows as the glow of a large plasma screen television broadcasted the eccentric, tweedy likeness of their instructor, Prof. Harold Harking, who was delivering his lecture while in the midst of a sabbatical in England. Goldsmith sat in a row next to Pete and his jaw clenched over and over again, this man at his side a physical reminder of his social leprosy.

Camilla sat across the row from Pete, dutifully taking notes, even though everyone knew she was only doing it for their benefit, as Harking's words were downloaded straight into her brain the moment they left the plasma screen's stereo speakers. Bunson and Sadie sat near the back row. Bunson leaned his large frame into various contortions every time Harking glanced over, so the old man wouldn't notice that Cooley's seat was empty. Sadie watched Harking's lips move for a moment before her eyes drifted toward the French windows behind him on the screen. It was a sunny day in Great Britain.

". . . and the Puritans' concept of the Elect," Harking said with just a touch of that pretentious faux English accent familiar to many starry-eyed Americans abroad creeping in, "the elite few who would rescue the human race from itself, from the evil of its own sins, rings true even today." Harking spotted Mr. Stuart Brian Richey raising his hand. "Yes, Mr. Richey?"

"But sir, doesn't the notion of the elite contradict everything America is about? How all men are equal?"

"Men are equal in the eyes of the law, certainly. But those of you in Stansbury Tower are held to higher standards because, like it or not, you *are* elite. John Winthrop, one of the original Puritans, spoke words in 1639 that still resonate today." Harking cleared his throat and donned his reading glasses. He glanced down, fumbling for a loose paper, and began. "'We must consider that we shall be a city upon a hill. The eyes of all people are upon us. So that if we shall deal falsely with our God in this work we have undertaken, and so cause Him to withdraw His present help from us, we shall be made a by-word and story throughout the world.'"

Goldsmith looked over at Pete, who was jotting down God knows what in his notepad. Goldsmith craned his neck for a peek, but the man's handwriting was sloppy, unformed. He finally gave up and wondered why Bunson was thrusting one shoulder forward while stretching the other upward and leaning his torso to the left, watching Harking's line of sight the whole time.

The gyrocab started its descent into San Angeles. Cooley looked down at the city streets. They twisted and turned. Gyro and pedestrian traffic pulsated like fluid through the veins of a breathing beast. It was all gridlock, all the time on the sidewalks. People just pressed their shoulders against each other and relied on the flow of momentum to take them to where they needed to be. A few years ago, some bright San Angeleno entrepreneurs decided they were fed up with getting the grime of their fellow citizens all over their clothes from the continual physical contact, so they started selling long, shiny ponchos that could be tossed out after one use. It was easy to spot the rich people: they upgraded from the billowing, clumsy ponchos to multiuse waterproof jumpsuits. They made the wearers look like nuclear scientists inspecting a contamination site, but were effective and therefore popular; businessmen took them off when they reached their offices, spiffy three-piece suits clean underneath.

Throughout the streets, whistles chirped repeatedly. The wranglers. The city got the idea from that original bastion of overpopulation,

Tokyo. The wranglers were easy to spot—they directed and facilitated the flow of traffic with brightly lit batons, usually in fluorescent white, for the masses to follow. The wranglers were big, tough guys who weren't quite sharp enough to get hired as minimum-wage rent-a-cops like Harvey. Their sole purpose was to force you to go with the flow. If you didn't follow their batons, you got jabbed in the ribs with them.

"Look at that clusterfuck down there," said the cabbie. "Thank you, AIDS vaccine! Thank you, cancer cure! Thanks a lot, gyrotechnology! Life's so cushy now that no one dies and we all get to climb over each other like rats."

"I'll get out right over there, thanks," said Cooley. The gyro descended, floating down the remaining few hundred feet to a street in D Sector. He handed the cabbie some of Bunson's money and stepped out into the rain. Yellow drops hit his face and trickled down under the collar of his shirt. Sure, it was polluted and supposedly harmless acid rain, but inside a school where it never got cloudy, it felt like a decently refreshing, exotic treat.

An arm reached out from the passing throng of human bodies, grabbing Cooley by the elbow.

"Excuse me," came a stranger's voice. Cooley glanced over at him, a working-class guy on his way to whatever shit job he had this week. There was a little boy and a lady who must have been his wife next to him. The lines in their faces were deep, even on the kid. Cooley wished he had some meds left to slip the man; they might have gotten rid of the cold that was making him hack and cough. He followed their eyes: all three of them were staring at the emblem on his blazer. Cooley pulled his arm back from the man's grasp.

"Are you . . . really one of . . . them?" the man was saying.

"What?" said Cooley.

"Daddy, he is!" said the little boy. "Look at the patch on his jacket!" Even though Cooley got to the outside world more than most of the specimens, routine tasks still slipped his mind from time to time. He sighed and took off his blazer, wrapping it up into a ball and tucking it under his arm.

"I'm sorry, young man," said the boy's mother. "He's never seen one of you Stansbury kids before. In person. None of us have, actually." She looked up at him, desperation in her eyes. Cooley had seen it before on previous trips outside the tower. She was waiting. Waiting for him to say something memorable, something quotable and reassuring, something that would help her get through the long days in the rain, knowing that there was this bunch of genius kids working around the clock on making the world a more perfect place. He hated these looks. They made him feel like a fraud, a charlatan wearing the robes of a mystical healer ready to sell the townies snake oil in the name of a higher power. The wide eyes of the mother and father standing there kept darting from him to the skies, like they were expecting another EMP blast or worse at any moment and were certain that he, a specimen, would be able to do something about it.

"Excuse me, ma'am. But I've got to go." The traffic light changed. Whistles rang out, echoing through the tall canyons of buildings down the city block. The wave of pedestrians rolled forward toward the white batons in the distance, sweeping Cooley along. He looked back at the family. The mother and father were still watching him go, soaking up every last detail so they could recount it to their skeptical friends. Cooley saw the little boy wave good-bye. He tried to wave back but could not. His arms were pinned to his sides by the crossing crowd. The hives of people in this town didn't allow the space necessary for such gestures.

The specimens affixed Professor Harking with their characteristically focused gazes. They were unlike anything he'd seen anywhere else, even at Oxford. If he looked closely enough, he thought, he could probably see the little gears and synapses firing and turning over inside their brains.

"And now," he said to the progression room on the other side of the plasma screen, "observe the following interaction." The specimens watched as the screen cut to footage taken from a cable news talk show. It was dated March 28, 2036. Just the day before. President Lang sat on a small stage, glowing and calm as usual, across from a bearded man with long, stringy hair who could not seem to get his upper lip to stop trembling from anger.

". . . and what you're doing, Dr. Lang," he said, his voice slowly rising to a screech, "you and the rest of your brainwashers cooped-up inside the ivory tower that is Stansbury—is creating a new elite of doped-up rich kids to take over the country!"

The show's host leaned forward and smiled. "Whoa," he said. "Now let's slow down here for a minute and—"

"Actually, Stansbury gives away ten full-ride scholarships to underprivileged orphans each year," said Lang, her voice smooth and sure. "And Stansbury's contributions to the arts and sciences are not limited to any specific economic class. They elevate the quality of life for all Americans."

"You're turning kids into *zombies!*" said the bearded man.

There was a polite, unmistakably official knock at the progression room door. The footage froze and cut back to Harking. His on-screen image glanced over. "Come in," he said. The door swung open and Captain Gibson entered. All of the specimens instinctively looked away except for Goldsmith. He started to gather his belongings because he knew what would come next.

"Good morning, Professor Harking," said Gibson. "Sorry for the interruption. Mr. Goldsmith, would you mind coming with me?" Goldsmith stood up and headed for the door. Pete grabbed his notebook, but before he could rise, Gibson placed a hand on his shoulder. He gave Pete a cold, professional smile.

"Mr., uh, Pietrop—"

"Call me Pete, big fella. I guess just 'cause the kids are smart enough to get my name right doesn't mean *you* are, does it?"

"Please stay seated. Miss Camilla Moore II will be your guide until Mr. Goldsmith is finished with his business."

"But—"

"Your cooperation is appreciated."

Pete sat back in his chair, shaking his head and smiling. "Bet you kids pick up the underlying themes in Kafka *reeeeeal* quick, right?"

Goldsmith glanced back at the other specimens before he stepped through the door. They all shared the same simultaneous look of contempt and paranoia. Who was on the hot seat now? Was it their turn next? Or maybe their best friend's? He caught Camilla's eye and for the first time thought she might have been more worthy of the title. True valedictorians did not hesitate. They were above reproach and the judgment of lesser specimens. Perhaps his victory was a fluke, a flaw in an imperfect method of evaluation. I'm sorry, Camilla, he thought. Sorry for the things I did to you that day. I'm sorry, everyone, for trying way too hard to impress you so much. I was hoping you'd forget I'm a poor kid on scholarship without anyone at home waiting for report cards and acceptance letters.

And despite this internal reverie (the emotion of which shocked even Goldsmith himself), as the door shut behind him and he followed Captain Gibson into the hallway one final image sat frozen inside his mind: Harking's progression room, fourteen specimens other than himself, Bunson not quite big enough to conceal that one conspicuously empty seat.

Where are you, Cooley? Run fast. It's only a matter of time before we find you.

7

The water started popping into a boil, causing the kettle on the old-fashioned gas stove to rattle and click. Tin clattered against iron over and over again. The sound matched the patter of raindrops against the dormant air conditioner lodged in one of the two windows inside the five-hundred-square-foot studio apartment that Mr. Jonathan Clark Riley—Class of 2033—had lived in since graduation. Riley sat on the sofa and watched the muted television. The ring on his index finger tapped against the remote control, the third in a trio of loud stuttering sounds that was doing nothing to calm the most troubling stuttering of all: the incessant throbbing of his pulse.

Riley wanted to stand up and turn down the flame on the stove so the kettle did not succeed in driving him the rest of the distance from paranoia to total nervous breakdown, but he did not. Since the stove was near the window and through the window, people—well, let's be more specific, not just people, but *they*—might catch a glimpse of him. This did not occur to Riley when he lit the stove's flame only ten minutes ago, but he was nothing if not perceptive. So what if he had two post-Stansbury jobs: sobering himself up from the life of a drug addict and, as soon as it was physiologically feasible, selling black-market samples of his sober urine to other drug addicts who were not as fortunate as he in their battles with addiction. He still had his diploma, and that made him better than most of the people in this town, anyway.

Smith never called. They were supposed to get in touch just a few days ago, but now it looked like Danny Ford Smith had disappeared. Like the rest of them. But Danny was different. He was Riley's friend, after all. The others were just names to go with faces that passed through the atrium in between progressions. He looked at their faces gazing up at him from the pages on his coffee table: four black-and-white yearbook photos on four separate pages, each with a thick red X drawn through them. He ripped them from the 2033 yearbook, spread the documents out along the center of the table, and placed the rest of the thick yearbooks he still owned (twelve total) around them in a semicircle of four-inch stacks. Riley's own personal remembrance.

He looked at Smith's picture on the page and could not bring himself to reach for the red marker used to do the deed. After all, what if Danny wasn't gone? Maybe he was just . . . Riley racked his brain for possible scenarios, explanations for the end of his pal's biweekly calls just to check in and confirm that they were both still intact and breathing. That was the way it ought to have been, after all. Smith and Riley weren't going to go quietly like the rest did. (Admittedly, Riley had no idea how the rest ended up going, willingly or by force. All he knew was that they were gone.) And then he realized it was useless creating hopeful, against-all-odds situations to explain Smith's sudden absence. The first disappearance was strange. The second, a coincidence. The third, a pattern. The fourth, a ruthless, unrelenting, and undoubtedly disturbing pattern. Old epistemological habits die hard, Riley thought: Smith's disappearance would merely follow the logic of events as dictated by inductive reasoning and concrete evidence. To posit otherwise was a contradiction of irrefutable physical phenomena based on tendentious assumptions. His parents got what they paid for. Stansbury was so good at teaching him how to think that, even today, his brain instantly ruled out all possibilities of sentimentality and optimism in the face of what was most likely hopelessness. So he picked up the marker and, although he hated himself for it, marked a large (and he hoped, dignified) X through the face of his former best friend.

The kettle started rattling. Riley leaned back, looking at the last unmarked yearbook page on the coffee table. The one with his face on it. His Tabula rang. Got to be her. At eight A.M.? Who else could it be? He grabbed the trilling device. The silent television broadcasted a female news anchor with pancake makeup. The graphic banner in the top right-hand corner read: NEWS ALERT! STANSBURY SCHOOL SUCCESS!

"You call earlier than my parole officer," said Riley.

"Our debut's in twenty-four hours," she said. Her voice was, as always, calm. No rattling kettles or tap-tap-tapping wherever she was calling from.

"It's still on?" he asked.

"Of course. Unfortunately, Mr. Smith won't be joining us, as I'm sure you've already realized."

"I . . . I know."

"I'm sorry, Mr. Riley. I hope you see how much more important this makes you. And how much is at stake."

"I know."

"Do you still have what I gave you?" she asked.

Riley reached under the blanket on the sofa next to him and felt the rubber-and-steel angle of a loaded Glock 12's grip. "Yeah."

"Good. Just stay inside and don't open the door for anyone. You know where and when to meet me tomorrow morning."

"Right, right."

"Everyone else is dead, Mr. Riley. You're too crucial to let yourself—"

"Well, there's this specimen who might come by and—"

"Not for anyone."

"He's harmless. Comes around once a month."

"You trust him?"

"Well . . ."

"Don't open the door for anyone. Especially one of the specimens."

She hung up. Riley stared at the Tabula's blank screen and set it down. His yearbook photo looked pretty lonely on the table. He reached over to the 2033 edition and found her name. There it was, on page 434—Miss Stella Saltzman. Valedictorian. Round face, the kind of girl you just knew would be a kind mother some day, the type that baked kick-ass chocolate-chip cookies. He tried to imagine anyone wanting to hurt someone so harmless and could not, but since he now accepted that they got Danny Smith, he was not feeling so good about any of their odds. Even her. Riley ripped Miss Saltzman's page from the yearbook and placed it next to his. He looked at the two of them together, their pages side by side. The way she looked you in the eye made him think she had a beef with Stansbury, one that gnawed at her gut and kept her up nights. He never had the nerve to ask her what it might have been.

The Tabula rang again. Riley answered.

"Look, you don't have to keep checking up on me, I—"

"Riley." A male voice. Come on, place it. "Riley, relax. It's me."

"Cooley. What is it?"

"I need a favor. Piss man's coming tomorrow. We need samples. I've got money."

"It's a bad time."

"It'll take a second, man. Come on. I need fourteen vials. That's a decent pay day for you."

"Sorry. I'm on my way out."

"So I caught you just in time—"

"What? Where are you?"

"On my Tabula. Right outside your building. I'm coming up." Riley heard a click and then footsteps coming up the stairwell. They entered the hallway—his hallway—slowly, methodically getting closer. He grabbed the Glock 12, flipped off the safety, and rushed over to the door. He jammed his ear against it, listening. *Ladies and gentlemen, the Class of 2033!* rang out the voice of some cheeky game show host in his head. *Where are they now?*

Between the approaching footsteps and the pounding of his own heart, Riley did not even hear the kettle on the stove blow out its high, sharp whistle. It sounded just like a train about to leave the station for some far-off place.

8

Captain Gibson's strides were long, powered by a sense of purpose as he walked down the hallway toward the elevator bank at the far wall. Goldsmith kept up easily, his long specimen legs pumping along at half the speed, but covering just as much ground. Gibson was tall, too—for someone who didn't grow up on the med cycle, that is—and he was light on his feet, with the well-proportioned frame of an athlete growing old.

"President Lang apologizes for the news reporter," the captain said in midstride, his gaze still fixed on his destination. "The guy called her and threatened to stir up trouble if we didn't give him access. The school can't afford that, with the big vote coming up tomorrow. You're the best we've got. She knows you can handle him."

The reporter? Goldsmith thought. You think I don't know where we're headed right now? You think Pete's a fucking blip on my radar at the moment? Shut up and let me get my game face on, for Christ's sake. "Who've we got downstairs?" he asked aloud.

"Eleven specimens. Male. We popped a test on them a day early.

They've all got dopazone traces in their bloodstreams." Gibson looked at Goldsmith and smiled. "Piece of cake for you."

They arrived at the elevator bank. A pod slid open. Gibson held the door for Goldsmith and he stepped inside. Gibson followed and swiped his key card against the sensor pad above the rows of buttons. It beeped and he hit that unmarked button, which lit up.

"What's with the cold-feet look?" asked Gibson. "Come on. You're the best. It's the same with every valedictorian, trust me. They all want the glory, but when it comes down to it—"

"Nobody wants to be the bad guy."

"Except for you. Number-one status, plus this . . . ," Gibson said, jabbing the emblem on Goldsmith's blazer, ". . . equals a first-class ticket to whatever future you can dream up. You know the rules. Big dog has the most to gain by keeping the yard nice and orderly. As is."

Goldsmith looked over, game face finally complete, eyes focused, brimming with unwavering rectitude. Works on the specimens every time. It would work on Gibson. Build up the voice, let the air come up from the lungs and out of the mouth and just say it. "This is my last trip to the disciplinary level, Captain."

Gibson didn't even try stifling a snort. "What? With four days to go?"

"I'm resigning."

"Come on. You're the rags-to-riches poster child. Don't blow it now."

"Rags to riches and no friends in between or ever."

"Hey. Look at me. It's goddamned lonely at the top. Everyone knows that. Come graduation day, the world's at your feet. You got the rest of your life for friends." The pod beeped, sliding to a halt. The doors slid open. "Cowboy up, son. It's show time."

They walked into the hallway. It had the same structure and dimensions of any other hallway in the tower but there was concrete on the floor in the place of white marble. The walls were cloaked in shadows by intermittently placed spotlights shooting upward in the place of the school's whitish-blue regulation Xenon lights. There was a lone door at the end of the corridor labeled: DISCIPLINARY LEVEL. It was three inches of thick steel and hinges, but to Goldsmith it always looked like a soft, red velvet curtain placed onstage to separate him from his soon to be captive audience. The sight of it never failed to make him forget about everything else.

"Who's in the box?" he asked Gibson. Gibson handed him a summary sheet.

"Fiber optic surveillance picked up their chat in an elevator pod this morning. They were talking about recent dopazone trips."

Goldsmith scanned the sheet. Misters Nathan Donald Oates, Robert Ryu Sugiyama, Miles Boyd Mancuso . . . Eleven names total, all members of the Class of 2036. Four days till graduation. Tough luck guys, you were close. Eleven of the usual suspects and two glaring omissions.

"Is there a problem, Mr. Valedictorian?"

Goldsmith remembered Cooley's pinned-back, dopazone-laced pupils in the elevator pod, and Bunson, his obedient goon. They couldn't possibly have tested clean if the rest of their gang's samples were tainted. "Two problems, actually," he answered. "Mr. William Winston Cooley and Mr. Thaddeus Bunson. Why aren't their names on here? They're known associates of the others on this sheet. They were in the elevator pod with the rest. Were they tested?" He studied Gibson's face: his eyes twitched slightly upward and to the right (an involuntary muscle reaction produced when the brain is *creating* facts as opposed to *recalling* them, according to the valedictorian's manual, 2035 edition) before they refocused on him; a smile appeared maybe one half-second too fast.

"Ah, yes. The baddest apples in the bunch," said the captain. "And the proverbial fish that got away. Cooley never discussed getting high with his pals this morning. Kid's too smart for that. Only thing he mentioned was sneaking off campus to pick up clean urine samples. My men are following up on that right now. And everything Bunson said got garbled somehow in playback . . . a technical glitch. Headmaster Latimer doesn't want to spring tests without more concrete evidence than blind suspicion. Maybe next time you'll nail them. Because there *will* be a next time, won't there?"

"No. Enjoy the performance while you can, Captain. It's the finale."

"We'll see," Gibson smirked.

Now. One last deep breath and dive in, no hesitation. Goldsmith pulled open the steel door, took two steps inside yet another corridor and stopped, sizing everything up the way they taught him. Eleven specimens: six against the left wall, five against the right. Their heads were covered with eyeless hoods, just the way he liked it. The hoods, thickly woven woolen sacks, were thrown over the specimens' heads as they were apprehended by the security detail. The purpose was not discomfort (although they were very hot and uncomfortable), but sensory deprivation. Keeping them unbalanced and unaware of location, time, and other sensory stimuli facilitated his task. The captive specimens were already slouching, shifting their weight from one leg to the other—one was keeping himself limber by bouncing his back against the brick wall—and most likely, sweating profusely. Goldsmith took two steps forward. All of them cocked their heads in his direction, listening for any clue as to what might come next. Goldsmith swallowed down the deep, tenor sternness he threw at Captain Gibson and brought up just the right tone: an octave higher; dumb down the vocabulary to their level, add a dash of uncertainty.

"Look guys," he started, standing still at the front of the corridor. "I don't like this any more than you do." Silence. "I'm only human and I hate the school for giving me this job, all right? I . . . I've just started to feel this way and . . ." There. Bring in just the right amount of introspective-sounding hesitation. Layer in a coating of conspiracy. Easy does it. "Help me out and I'll help you guys out, okay? I've known you for twelve years. We've grown up together. We've come too far. I'm not letting them expel any of you. That's a promise. Just be honest. All I need is one of you—just one—to talk to me, and I'll make everything right." Pause. Let the words sink in. "Who's in?"

Silence. Not one specimen raised his hand or stepped forward. Goldsmith got that familiar twinge: adrenaline surging as his thoughts raced far ahead of the psyches inside each name on that summary sheet. He ran through each specimen's profile in his mind and forecasted every behavioral permutation in the time it took to crack a smile of pity for his prey.

"That's great. Six of you. Thanks guys, you're doing the right thing." Predictably, eleven pairs of feet started to shuffle nervously. Goldsmith stepped in between the lineup and grabbed two arms, one from the right and one from the left. He walked them down the corridor toward the examination room. He sat one specimen down on the bench outside and Gibson walked over, taking a seat next to him. Goldsmith dragged the other one inside the room, shutting the door behind him.

Inside the spare space was a table bolted down to the floor and two chairs, one on each side. He placed the specimen down in the chair and sat across from him before glancing at the mirrored wall and looking at his reflection for just a moment. He smoothed down his hair. Good. Now reach over, pull off that wool hood.

Goldsmith sat back and watched Mr. Nathan Donald Oates as he blinked a dozen times before opening his mouth into a variation of contorted shapes, stretching out his face's overheated flesh, letting it breathe.

"Hello, Mr. Oates."

Oates got his bearings, instinctively looking for a wall clock that was not there (the suspects always looked for a clock) because he wanted to figure out how long he'd been detained. He gave up and fixed Goldsmith with a defiant glare.

"Come on," Goldsmith said. "We're both Class of '36. We've had progressions together since we were six. You've got four days left. Don't blow it now. I know you, Nathan. You're not behind the dopazone that's being passed around our school." Lean over the table just a tiny bit, reel him in. Watch his body, reflect his posture back at him, making him feel at ease, understood. Reach out and create empathy where none exists. Oates leaned back in his chair. He crossed his legs. Goldsmith leaned back, too—just hanging out buddy, just one of the guys—and crossed his legs. "Someone else offered you the stuff," he continued. "You were just experimenting. Nothing serious. You got roped in. I know. Who hooked you up? Give me a name and you walk." Just when Mr. Oates's blank face looked like it was starting to thaw . . .

"Fuck you," he hissed. Goldsmith did not move or flinch. Water off my back, pal. "You sold your soul for a goddamned medal and a title. Put the fucking hood back on me, 'cause I can't stand the sight of a whore."

Goldsmith glanced over at the mirror. Easy there, son. He worked up a convincing sigh of resignation.

"Points taken. I'm letting you go back to today's progressions."

"You . . . you are?"

"Yes." Oates did not let himself smile with relief because he didn't want to jinx his good fortune. "Just answer a few questions for me," Goldsmith said. "Routine stuff. Simple yesses and noes will suffice." Goldsmith glanced down at the summary sheet on the table. "Is your name Nathan Donald Oates?" He pretended to hit a red button marked *record* that was built into the table.

"Yes."

"Louder, please. For that speaker over by the door. We've got to get this part on tape for the school's records. Thanks."

"Yes!"

"Good. Is your birthday November 6, 2018?"

"Yes!"

"Damn. I don't think the speaker's picking it up. One more time, but even louder, please?"

"Yes!"

Mr. Oates's shouts were audible outside the examination room.

"Yes!"

The hooded suspect who was still waiting on the bench outside sat up ramrod straight, his head leaning toward the door. Captain Gibson cracked a thin smile.

"Yes! I said 'yes'! Are you deaf?" A few moments passed. The door opened. Goldsmith steered Oates—hooded once again—into the hallway. Gibson stood up, leading him by the arm. Now, Goldsmith thought. Stick the knife in and twist. He grabbed the other suspect, taking his arm in the pinching grip of an angry father before dragging him inside the examination room and tossing him into the chair. It almost tipped over from the weight, but the specimen righted himself just in time, breathing heavier, faster.

Goldsmith ignored the chair and table this time, opting to circle the stationary suspect methodically, and his heels clicked against the floor. After two slow orbits, he reached down and yanked off the hood so quickly that he could see strings of drool stuck to the wool as it pulled away from the suspect's mouth. There went the routine: the blinking, the breathing, the reorienting. But there was no glare this time. Just a child's dread of what came next.

"Hello, Mr. Mancuso." Goldsmith snapped back to the elevator pod this morning and wished everyone who was there had a front-row seat. "You were half right. There is, in fact, a narc in our midst. But it's not me." Mancuso's lips started to tremble. Goldsmith moved in front him and squatted down, leaning his face just a few inches away. He inhaled: shampoo, sweat, morning breath. So that's what fear smelled like. "I couldn't shut Mr. Oates up." Tough guy Miles Boyd Mancuso's eyes filled with tears. Goldsmith was tempted to crack a smile but choked it back.

On the other side of the examination room's mirrored wall, his audience was impressed as usual. Through the one-way glass, Captain Gibson, Headmaster Latimer, and President Judith Lang watched as Mancuso's lips started moving, slowly at first, then faster. The best confessions always started with a trickle and ended with a pouring rain of verbiage.

". . . Yes, Oates and Sugiyama gave me the money . . . ," came Mancuso's voice through the observation room's speaker system. The headmaster stepped forward and slid a switch on a wall pane to ease down the volume.

"Last year it would've taken us three hours to crack these unbalanced specimens," said the headmaster. Gibson caught his eye and nodded in Goldsmith's direction.

"Says it's his last session."

"They all say that," said Lang, never taking her eyes from Goldsmith as he stood behind Mancuso on the other side of the glass. "He'll be fine."

"Great kid," said Gibson.

"A natural," agreed the headmaster.

"Wonder who he gets it from?"

"He's an orphan," said Lang. "Keep on wondering." The room's door was opened. Lang's assistant entered holding her personal Tabula.

"It's Senator Mathers, ma'am," he said. Lang stood up, took it, and headed for the exit. Gibson watched her go.

"I reckon these days you're the most popular lady in all of D.C."

"Pay attention to Mr. Goldsmith, Captain," she said. "You could learn something."

Through the window and back inside the examination room, Goldsmith watched Mancuso as he lapsed into silence.

"And?" he asked him.

"And . . . that's it. That's everyone who did it. Look . . . you're not gonna kick us out, are you?"

"Confirm something for me. Is it true that Misters Bunson and Cooley were involved in the dopazone ring?"

"I already told you that we—"

"A yes or no is more than adequate."

"Yes." Goldsmith glanced at the one-way and wondered when the administration was going to bring Bunson and Cooley down here. Sooner rather than later, he hoped. Goldsmith, after all, had exams to study for. No. He was retiring. After all, he just gave his notice a few minutes ago. Right? "Are they gonna kick us out?" Mancuso whined. "You said if we cooperated you wouldn't let—"

"The outcome of this session is not within my control. I'm just a specimen. A middleman."

"But you're gonna . . ."

Goldsmith got that familiar poking feeling that descended from his throat into his stomach. It bounced back up with a jolt. C'mon, hold it down just for a . . . He calmly walked through the door before breaking into a sprint for the examination room across the hall. He stumbled inside, slammed the door behind him and found his favorite trash bin in the corner. He grabbed it, raised the white plastic container up and let a salvo of vomit fly. It splattered. The force of his choking brought Goldsmith to his knees. The poking started again and another barrage shot from his mouth into the bin. It left behind a calm sensation. He pushed the smelly can to the side and sat on the floor, leaned against the wall and waited for his breath to return.

"Never gets any easier, does it?" asked the headmaster. Goldsmith looked up. He was standing in the doorway in his usual slim, black suit. The combination of the clothes and the combed-back white hair made him look like a mayor who just stepped out of some movie from the Silent Era.

"They're all goners, aren't they?"

"It could be four days till commencement or four years. Violation of policy—drug use, no less—cannot be tolerated."

"I heard the yearbook's voting me Most Likely to Join the Secret

Police," he said, slowly rising from the floor. The headmaster chuck-led and handed him a glass of ice water. Goldsmith sipped.

"Captain Gibson tells me that you're throwing in the towel."

"I love being valedictorian. Setting an example. Working with you and President Lang. But this part of the job . . ."

"A braver man than I would suggest that you relish this part of the job more than you care to admit, but that, as they say, is neither here nor there. Tell me, why did you wait until now to resign?"

Goldsmith smiled and looked him in the eye. "Maybe it's a last-minute expiation of guilt. Or maybe I know it's too late in the year for you to appoint Camilla Moore II as my replacement." The headmaster smiled back. "Sir?" Goldsmith began, "Mr. Bunson and Mr. Cooley weren't called here today. Am I correct in assuming they'll suffer the same fate as the rest?" The headmaster's smile disappeared.

"Captain Gibson has informed the president and myself that there is a lack of evidence against them. We have never and will never ex-pel a specimen solely based on allegations by other specimens, much less specimens who, in this case, are not reliable witnesses." Gold-smith nodded. "What is your next progression?" asked the headmas-ter, not leaving any room for a debate on finer points of Stansbury law.

"Principles of Game Theory."

"Come then. I'll walk you."

The headmaster and Mr. Goldsmith strolled through the atrium. It was quiet and empty between progressions. Goldsmith looked up at the "sky": the clouds were still dancing and vibrating from glitches, the sun had gone from a distorted gray to a translucent white.

"I'm an orphan too, in a way," said the headmaster. "I lost my wife and little girl in a car wreck close to twenty years ago."

"I know, sir. If only they had gyrotechnology back when—"

"And if only Professor Partridge had discovered Panacetix in time to beat your father's brain cancer." He walked off the path toward a wall broadcasting an illusory hologram that made it appear as if there was no wall at all, only a meadow that went on for miles. Goldsmith watched as Headmaster Latimer waved his hand over a switch. A hidden panel and miniature screen revealed themselves. Goldsmith studied the headmaster's movements as he hit some buttons. Instantly, the atrium's environment reverted to normal. The mutant clouds disappeared into a morning mist and the sun went gold, a bright flame against immaculate blue. Goldsmith detected the trickle of a flowing river getting louder and louder. "Hear that?" asked the headmaster. "The sound of water running under the bridge. Our lives are now defined by progress." The panel disappeared into digitized air. They resumed walking along the path.

"Yes, sir."

"Your mother left you in an orphanage where you were assigned a random number. Your number was one of ten selected that year in our lottery. Finally, you saw a light glimmering at the tunnel's end." He stopped, setting his hand on Goldsmith's shoulder. Goldsmith looked down at him: the headmaster stood barely six feet but, like Lang, had always seemed taller. "Remember that light, son. Because when you leave this tower in a few days, it becomes you. You'll burn so brightly. And never forget the incredible gifts that have been bestowed upon you."

" 'For Power may point the way,' " he recited, " 'but only Honor can lead it.' I'll make you proud, sir."

"I'll be watching." He turned. Goldsmith understood that this was as far as their walk would go. "And so will President Lang." The headmaster started down the path in the direction from which they came. A flock of geese shot by, their large bodies skimming the ground. After they passed, he was gone. Scattered voices—real voices—began to echo around the atrium. They built into a cacophony that brought with it a tide of specimens.

"He's all yours, Mr. Goldsmith," came Camilla's crisp voice behind him. He didn't even hear her approach. He whirled around and saw her standing with Pete. She gave Goldsmith a blatant roll of the eyes and walked off, disappearing into the crowd. Pete watched her go and jabbed Goldsmith in the ribs.

"Man," he said, checking her out as she walked off. "You've gotta tell me girls around this place are legal. But then again, if there's grass on the field, play ball, right?"

Goldsmith walked off wordlessly (not quite feeling as unburdened by his early retirement as he had hoped he would) and wondered if it were possible to find some friends—best, childhood, lifelong, any shape or size would do, really—in fewer than four days. He glanced around at the specimens. What do you think, guys? Their response was silent: grave, focused face upon grave, focused face; hundreds of pairs of cold, unflinching eyes set on some ideal and invisible point off in a bright, glorious future—their own.

9

"Come on, Riley. It's me. Open up." Cooley banged on the dented iron door marked 5c one more time. A shadow passed the light behind the peephole and disappeared downward. His guess: Riley was squatting, leaning his ear against the door and listening for something. Cooley was hoping he'd be able to make it back to the tower by lunch hour if everything went smoothly. Unfortunately for his schedule, "smoothly" did not include Riley treating a routine visit from a familiar face like a bad cop show rerun on late-night television. Cooley had never actually seen late-night television since he left the orphanage for Stansbury at the age of six, but in any case, he had not heard good things about those cop shows.

Come on, Riley. He was an unbalanced specimen Cooley met when Cooley was just a freshman. Riley dug Stansbury's injections a bit too much, traded them in for heroin shortly after graduation. He tried to kick the habit and ended up with a nasty methadone interlude, before stopping off at alcoholism on his way back to sobriety.

"You alone?" Riley shouted through the door.

"Of course."

"Take five steps back until you hit the wall. Reach your arms out, flatten your palms, and don't move until I say so. Got it?"

Jesus Christ, Cooley thought. Does this cops-and-robbers shit mean that he's off the wagon? If so, I'm dealing with a guy who's not only psycho but worthless. What good is his piss if it's tainted? Cooley considered saving himself the trouble and possible bodily harm and wondered why he just didn't cut his losses and leave right then, before remembering his twelve buddies who'd all go down in flames if they didn't have the stuff to pass that test tomorrow. And what about him? What if he was not as invincible as everyone thought? Guernica wasn't yesterday. Chances were, kicking the asses of a few outsiders four years ago and rescuing Shannon Evans wouldn't cancel out drug use on the scales of Stansbury justice. And as much as Cooley hated to admit it, without the school he had nowhere to go, except for some hovel, probably in this part of town, probably located next door to Riley. Not getting this job done meant that he skated the vicious circle back to exactly where he was standing right now. But it always returned to the bottom line: Sadie. Sadie and the look on her face as he'd be packing his bags with the rest of the guys. See you when I see you, okay babe? Cooley thought about the two inches of iron that separated him from Mr. Jonathan High-on-God-Knows-What Riley. Really, there wasn't any decision to make in the first place.

He took five steps back, felt the wall, and spread his arms out. "All right," he called out. "I did it. Just get this over with, man."

The door swung open. Riley was standing just inside the apartment and his eyes scanned the areas to Cooley's left and right. He was aiming a gun. "Come in," he said, as he gestured for Cooley to enter with the weapon, as if he were conducting a symphony. Cooley walked inside and felt like he was entering some alternate reality.

"Riley, what—" Riley grabbed the scruff of his neck and slammed him against the wall next to the front door. Cooley felt a hand tracing the line of his leg, another grabbed his crotch and he stifled the urge to snap his foot up into Riley's ribcage. "You think I'm fucking *armed?*" he asked, incredulous.

"She said don't trust anyone, don't trust—"

"It's me," Cooley said. "Relax." The teakettle on the stove rattled and sent up a long whistle, as if in warning. Cooley watched sweat roll down Riley's neck.

Riley stood up and frisked Cooley's torso, patting down his blazer. "How's our alma mater?" he asked.

"I'm graduating in four days," said Cooley, grateful for the small talk.

"Mom and Dad proud?"

"Never knew Dad. And Mom's probably dead."

"Christmas must be a blast."

"Specimens are nondenominational, remember?"

"You're one of the full-ride orphans, now I remember. Lucky guy."

"Anything I can look forward to after Stansbury? You miss it at all?"

"No and no. But seeing the sun on a regular basis is nice. When was your last glimpse?"

"Just about six weeks ago."

"All right," said Riley, stepping back. Cooley turned around and saw him gaze at the television as if in a trance: pretty anchor lady, Panacetix, Stansbury miracle-workers, blah, blah, blah. Cooley sat down on the old couch and propped his feet up on the cluttered coffee table. "Hear the good news?" Riley said, pointing to the muted TV with his gun.

"How could I have missed it?"

"Cancer was a tough one . . . but good old Stansbury licked it." Riley walked over and sat down next to Cooley. His spine stayed straight and his shoulders were tensed like he was shell-shocked, waiting for someone to smack him upside the head. "Just the latest in a long line of conquests, right? Guys like us, Mr. Cooley? We're not what was intended."

"I take that as a compliment."

"Me too, kid."

Cooley's eyes darted around the room. They came to a stop on the coffee table. Weird: ripped-out yearbook pages with red X's all over the place behind a fort of other yearbooks. "What's with the yearbooks?" he asked. "You feeling nostalgic?"

"It's nothing, man," said Riley, suddenly grabbing them from the table. "I was just messing around." He kneeled down and pulled up a rug, removing what appeared to be a fake wooden plank from the flooring. He slipped the sheaf of yearbook pages inside and replaced the elements of his hiding spot.

What's wrong with this freak? Cooley wondered. His heart started to pound and he felt something odd—call it bad vibes, mojo, juju, whatever. He glanced at a digital clock on the wall and started to get antsy. "Just get me the stuff," he said. "I'm behind schedule and I can't get caught off campus again."

"How many samples?"

"Are you still clean?"

Riley nodded his head at Cooley and smiled eerily. "Of course," he said. "These days, I only wish my problems were the kind that came in a syringe."

"Fourteen samples. Thanks." Cooley watched as Riley stood up, stuck the gun into his waistband and walked into the bathroom, closing the door behind him. Minutes sludged past. There was something stale in the air that made him want to take a shower and disinfect himself immediately. He glanced curiously at the rug covering Riley's hiding spot in the floor. What was with the top-secret routine and those stupid yearbook pages? God only knows what else the dude has stashed down in there. Is there any way this guy is still on the wagon? And why doesn't he do something about that goddamned rattling kettle over there? It's enough to drive a guy . . . "Riley! You fall in?" Silence.

Cooley got up and looked at the bathroom door. The white paint was dusty and cracked, baring slivers of a previous incarnation in pink from years before. He looked at the line of yellow light at the foot of the door and waited for movement, noise, anything. He tiptoed up and played the Riley game: he crouched down, pressed his ear against the door's surface, and listened for clues before he decided that he didn't have the time and banged his fist against it. "Hey . . . What's up?" Silence. He grabbed the small brass knob and felt it twist in his grip, unlocked. Cooley gingerly pulled the door open a few inches before it flew straight back at him and pushed him two steps backward into the hall.

Riley collapsed on top of him. They tumbled to the floor together, Cooley's hands on Riley's torso: it was vibrating, muscles humming and jerking like he swallowed a beehive. Cooley felt something wet on his face and realized what it was when he pulled back and got a look at Riley, the guy's eyes rolled back into his head, white foam bubbled from his mouth, blood poured from his nostrils and lips, his teeth grinded against a meaty, gashed stub that could only be the remnants of his tongue before it was bitten off. Cooley saw maroon drops stain his white shirt, felt the blood and drool on his face, on his neck, and started to gag. He stifled back a scream, grabbed Riley, and got his footing before he dragged him into the bathroom and laid him prone.

"Riley! Can you hear me?" Riley started choking and sounded like he was losing air. Veins bulged in his neck. Cooley saw a laser syringe hanging out of Riley's arm. He yanked it out and tossed it to the side. He finally stopped convulsing and everything got quiet. Cooley leaned against the bathtub and tried to catch his breath as he wondered what to do next.

Through the half-closed bathroom door, he heard something thump against the floor out in the living room. His eyes went to the mirror on the wall, checking for moving shadows against the reflection of the light. He looked at Riley's waistband: Where was the gun? Cooley glanced around but did not find it. Still sitting on the floor, he slowly nudged the door open with his foot, half-inch by half-inch, until his impatience got the best of him and he kicked it open. He found himself looking down the barrel of six guns, all of which were much bigger than the one Riley pointed at him just a few minutes before. Cooley counted six Stansbury security detail jarheads on the other side of the doorway.

"Stay right there, Mr. Cooley," said Officer Jamison. He lowered his gun to waist level and stepped inside the room.

"Show your hands," ordered another officer in his regulation black jackboots, black pants, and black utility vest. Cooley looked up at them from the floor and raised his hands. From the doorway, another one—a young guy Cooley didn't recognize—saw Riley and didn't bother hiding the look on his face.

"Jesus . . ."

"I don't know what happened," said Cooley.

"Why are you off campus?" asked Jamison, his gun still aimed.

"Take a guess," said the young guy, suddenly a hard-boiled prick.

"I know him . . . ," murmured another detail goon as he looked down at the body. "That's Mr. Riley, Class of 2033."

"That *was* Mr. Riley," said another.

"You're in a lot of trouble, Mr. Cooley," said Jamison. He was slowly inching closer. Cooley drew an imaginary line across the white tile floor stained red from spilled blood. Riley's body spasmed and convulsed one more time. Everyone flinched. Jamison looked over and then stepped across that line. Cooley sprung up to a crouch and grabbed Jamison, pulling him close to block the detail's line of fire, and shoved him through the big glass window above the toilet. Jamison crashed through and landed on the rusted fire escape outside. The rain poured down on him while he blinked his eyes and tried to pick glass shards from his face.

Cooley leaped through the window frame, landed on top of Jamison, and rolled. He hit an iron hook and watched the fire escape ladder shoot down to the pavement five floors below. He grabbed the rails—nice and slick from the rain—braced his smooth leather soles against them and slid down, feeling the chipped paint on the ladder scrape his hands along the way.

Jamison stood up, his face wet from blood, rain and sweat. "Jackson! He's moving!" he barked into his wrist microphone. "You locked?"

Jackson stood in the living room, one eye closed, the other looking through a large metallic scope mounted on his ThermaGun. He saw the computer's reproduction of the entire apartment: the sofa, the television, and the hallway toward the bathroom all white lines on a black screen. The image zoomed in past the bathroom door where he saw five digitally rendered bodies in red and one on the floor in blue—R.I.P. Mr. Jonathan Clark Riley, he thought—and another red one that stood on the fire escape outside who looked like he was trying to pull tiny glass pieces from his cheek with fingers too meaty for the task. Jackson hit the zoom button on the ThermaGun one more time and it brought him down the outline of the fire escape, where he saw yet another red body as it flew down the ladder, fast. There. Jackson's thumb hit a button on the gun's grip. It beeped.

"We're locked," he said into his microphone. "Coolant vests." The six red bodies in the bathroom and the one on the fire escape turned blue. Past them and below, that last red body was just about to hit the sidewalk. The beeping got faster. The ThermaGun started humming. "Good night, Mr. Cooley," said Jackson. He pulled the trigger. A white ceramic bullet flew from the barrel before curving around through the bathroom door faster than the speed of sound. It weaved around the detail officers' legs and torsos with engineered precision and sailed through the broken window frame into the rain, missing Jamison's ear lobe by less than half an inch before it traced an arc downward.

Five floors below, Cooley's feet hit the pavement. At the end of the alley, he saw a monorail slide to a halt. The wranglers' batons glowed like white fluorescent buoys in the rainy distance. Fifteen seconds before the doors closed . . . Cooley broke into a sprint. Three steps in and he hit the damp, slimy pavement face-first, the bullet lodged in the back of his neck, half of its shell sticking out from his skin as the rest of its white surface dissolved into an engineered chemical tranquilizer that filtered into his bloodstream.

The security detail crowded into Riley's bathroom. Jamison opened up a small steel strongbox and flipped on the coroner. The green sensors on the silver crab lit up and gears inside its shell began to whir and hum. He set it on the floor and it climbed on top of Riley as six pincer legs felt their way around and gathered samples. The rain tapped a tinny pulse against the fire escape. Feet started to shuffle out into the hallway. More footsteps: dress shoes, not boots. Jamison looked up and saw Captain Gibson enter.

"Mr. Cooley is secured," Gibson said. The coroner unit slid down Riley's forehead and reentered its strongbox. Jamison closed it and waited for the LCD display.

"Preliminary results indicate an overdose of an unspecified chemical," Jamison said as his eyes followed the readout. "Probably a street drug, Class A. Laser syringe is present. My bet's heroin. Mr. Riley has a history of addiction. He was treated less than two years ago." He pressed a button and watched the report print out from the side of the strongbox. "I'll take the results to district police and—"

"Give me the results," said Gibson.

"Sir, I'm more than happy to—"

Gibson stepped up and got in Jamison's face. Jamison handed it to him. "Yes, sir." The captain slipped it into his jacket pocket and turned to go. He grinded the heel of his leather brogan into Riley's limp hand and pushed off. Jamison heard the bones inside Riley's fingers snap. He watched the other detail officers part for Gibson as he disappeared through the doorway and into the living room.

Officer Jamison zipped up his Tac IX utility vest and snapped shut the holster of his gun. He checked his reflection in the mirror and wondered if the fresh slices caused by his Cooley-sponsored trip through the window would leave permanent scars. Probably. He started to get pissed, but then remembered the sight of Cooley lying on the street in the rain and realized the dark places that little punk had been were nothing compared to where he was headed now. Given his choice of scars, Jamison always preferred the ones on the outside.

10

President Judith Lang leaned back in the ergonomic chair behind the long Le Corbusier desk nestled inside the Level 119 executive suite and felt more than a little exultant. Professor Partridge had finally done it, and with such graceful timing! Dr. Lang had spent the better part of two years drumming up support for the Stansbury grant proposal and now it was finally a reality, coming to a vote in the Senate Select Committee on Education a mere twenty-four hours from now. Her close ally, committee chairwoman Senator Frieda Mark, had promised her she would end debate and hasten the parliamentary process of getting it to the Senate floor, where Lang knew she had a majority on her side. She had run herself ragged shuttling between the tower and the corridors of power in Washington, D.C., meeting with varied and influential special interest groups, promising favors (an exclusive computer network contract with Apple, a $134-million microchip pact with Intel, a gyrodevelopment contract with Ford Motors, nutrient ingredient contracts with farmer magnates across the Plains states, billion-dollar deals with Dupont and GE for pending Stansbury patents for the next hundred years, not to mention the eventual agreement with the Pentagon to equip soldiers with ThermaGun technology) so that they would in turn apply pressure to the recipients of their campaign dollars to cast a vote in Stansbury's favor. And the brilliant financial minds who controlled Stansbury's endowment fund—former specimens who retired early from Wall Street with nine-figure portfolios and wanted to give something back to their alma mater—had just completed their biggest coup yet: in anticipation of Partridge's cancer cure, over the past eleven months they quietly bought up a huge chunk of publicly traded Stansbury stock, all of which the fund then discreetly spread out through dozens of dummy corporations, virtually undetectable. Now it was only a matter of time before the school (after a $56-billion IPO eight years prior) could position itself as a wholly autonomous, effectively private corporation once again.

Lang knew how much it irritated Headmaster Latimer, all of this flesh-pressing and compromising, the bending of the rules to suit their school's needs and assorted backroom deals, but she was simply working within the reality that existed outside of the cloistered walls in which the old man had become so comfortable. That was why, after all, the trustees had hired her in the first place. The distinguished academics could live in their little Garden of Eden while she built up its protective gates and foundations so that they could continue educating their specimens without concern for the dreaded real world.

President Lang examined herself in her pocket mirror: masterfully colored brown hair (not a trace of that foolishly bright blondeness with which she was born), a strong jawline, the perfect set of capped and laser-whitened teeth that have been de rigueur in political circles for some time now. It was the face of a breadwinner, the master of the house, the Hector who would defend the walls of Dr. Stansbury's mythical Troy until all of their foes were sprawled before them in defeat. This school was her castle. She wore the pants, both literally and figuratively, keeping the place safe for those prissy little professors to continue teaching their impossibly gifted specimens in a state of perpetually blissful ignorance of the machinations that went on behind the scenes. And yet she adored each and every one of them and would not have had it any other way.

Alan Partridge, however, did not deserve President Lang's friendly condescension, at least not on that particular day, arguably the greatest since the school's founding back in 2009. The man—with help, of course, from the elite of Stansbury's elite—actually discovered a one-in-several-billion combination of amino acids and proteins that would destroy virtually every cancerous tumor known to mankind. Panacetix was his brilliant name for it, a new name derived from the word panacea: the cure of all cures. The only thing that exceeded Partridge's scientific and medical genius was his marvelous sense of timing. Certainly, Lang had a much more than adequate curriculum vitae to parade before the Senate committee, one packed full of revolutionary advances in the arts and sciences produced over the years by scores of child prodigies who would give Mozart himself a run for his money. But the cure for cancer! It was a challenge to mankind so great that it had become proverbial in its impossibility. Panacetix. She had the right to feel exultant. It was the final, most splendorous feather in the school's cap, one that virtually guaranteed a successful vote to allot $1 trillion to Stansbury, thereby freeing it from the tedious chains of annual fundraising drives and the arduous process of dragging distinguished professors and the occasional specimen across the country to parade before potential donors. Most important, that vote would provide the one thing that Dr. Stansbury, the headmaster, and everyone else inside the tower had always craved: a permanent legitimacy in the eyes of the nation. With the government's stamp of approval, the school would no longer be regarded as the genius—and possibly insane—stepchild of American education. The Senate's validation would render all of the debate about Stansbury's methods moot. The special interest dinosaurs could picket all they wanted, the underachieving thugs who ran the teachers unions would be—to use their kind of language, Lang smiled to herself—pissing in the wind. All she needed to do was make certain committee chairwoman Frieda Mark stayed focused, keep those fifty-one carefully selected and lobbied senators in her pocket, and Stansbury would become part of the American lexicon, along with the founding fathers, the Industrial Revolution, Wall Street, and the War on Terror. It would be a synonym for excellence. Progress. Ambition.

There was only one thing that prevented her from lighting up a celebratory cigar in the privacy of her own office at that very moment. It was a person, actually, more than a thing. The man who could sink the future prospects of Stansbury, Panacetix, and everything else; an anachronistic voice from a bygone era, the relic of all civil rights relics: Senator Arthur Milford Bloom (R-California). Indeed, the thought of him made President Lang's carefully applied facial features cringe, but alas, that thought was not all with which she had to contend that morning. Bloom had logged a last-minute request that she provide testimony before the Senate Select Committee on Education, on which he sat. It was a ploy to stir up the waters and make the Stansbury grant proposal seem more controversial than it really was: if he could cloud the issues and start playing his standard game of fear politics, he reasoned that he might attract some last-minute defectors to his side of the aisle in the debate. She refused to obey his beck and call to travel to Capitol Hill in person, so the old coot had to settle for a simulcast. Lang's terminal trilled.

"Madam President?" asked her assistant, Mr. Samuel Matthias Toll, Class of 2029.

"I gather it's time, Samuel?"

"It is."

"Tell me, is the old man simulcasting to us from a shuffleboard court at his rest home in Palm Springs?" She heard him chortle over the speakerphone.

"The committee's office in Washington, D.C., I believe."

"Very well then. Let's go live." The plasma screen on her desk lit up. She saw the Senator's face: skin tanned leathery like a cowboy clad in a television-friendly suit, a smirk that said he'd like to have known Judith Lang back in the good ol' days when he could give her ass a nice love tap after a four-martini lunch at the Army-Navy Club.

"Mornin', Madam Judith," he drawled. Bloom grew up in Tennessee before moving out to Hollywood in the pre-San Angeles days, where he made a fortune producing blockbuster action films, all of which featured lantern-jawed heroes shooting, stabbing, and blowing up whichever brown-skinned ethnicity happened to be the most sinister that year. He styled himself a Reaganite idealist for the twenty-first century, but found his success trading on the *aw-shucks* modus operandum of big-stick diplomacy made popular by the Bush dynasty. He was an outspoken proponent of archaic curriculums that were still mired in the perpetual extolling of Western Civilization's virtues, complete with faith in a patriarchal, Eurocentric society, God, apple pie, and any and all words scribbled down by the Dead White Men from which he no doubt descended. Cowboys like Bloom routinely called for an erosion of civil liberties, never failing to wrap their soft bigotry in the flag of "tradition" and "family values."

"That's Madam President, Senator."

"You can call me Artie if I can call you Judy."

"Senator Bloom," came the impatient voice of her friend and chairwoman Frieda Mark (D-New York).

"Right then, my friends," said Bloom. "Let's get down to brass tacks, shall we? Now, Madam President, in the committee's discussions regarding the imminent vote involving your fine educational institution, the topic of standardized testing arose, leaving us sharply divided."

"By standardized testing," answered President Lang, "I take it you mean the vastly flawed, biased, and overemphasized means of evaluating student progress and achievement? The tests that have beholden schools of all levels to the corporations who create and distribute them? The tests whose proponents readily admit only provide evidence of the students' ability to take that particular test—and of course, pay the test-taking fee—and nothing more?"

"If you mean the only feasible means to determine the general aptitude of an impossibly large body of students, the least imperfect of all the imperfect methods of evaluating academic potential, then yes, I do," he countered.

"What my distinguished colleague is driving at," said Senator Mark, "is his belief that Stansbury provides its students with an unfair advantage when it comes to taking the standardized tests required for college entrance, such as the SAT or Stansbury's own Eaves exam, which, thanks to your school's considerable marketing efforts, is rapidly being adopted as the new certification accepted by elite academic institutions."

"The only advantages we provide our specimens are quiet rooms in which to study, round-the-clock tutors, and a nice breakfast on the morning of the testing day," said Lang. "And these benefits are extended to each and every one of the children at Stansbury, regardless of race, gender, or economic background."

"Beg your pardon, ma'am," smirked Bloom, "but it isn't your tower's windowless rooms or fancy little croissants in liquid form that gives a reasonable man such as myself pause." His mangling of the English language caused Lang to return his gaze with a smirk of her own: *your tow-ah . . . croy-sants . . . mah-self . . .* "I was speaking of all the drugs that your people are shootin' into those young boys' and girls' bodies. The bookworm's version of steroids . . ." *Bookwum's vuh-shun of steeeroyds . . .*

"Stansbury's med cycle has been vetted by multiple studies in the labs of major universities," she responded. "The chemical combinations involved are safe and legal. The med cycle is no different than responsible parents seeing to it that their children eat healthy, get plenty of rest, and follow a light exercise routine on a daily basis."

"Let's say the Eaves exam is a horse race, why don't we? Are you gonna wager on the pony that's been eatin' healthy and joggin' each day? Or the stud that's been shot up with stuff that buries anxiety attacks and keeps him up studying for three days at a time? Specimens," snorted Bloom. "You raise 'em, stick 'em in uniforms, give 'em pills, keep 'em inside for months at a time . . . frankly, ma'am, I'm surprised you people don't take the ones who don't get into Harvard, Yale, or Princeton out behind the woodshed and put 'em down right on the spot."

"There is a flaw in your premise, Senator," said Lang, as the syrupy, insouciant drawl in his voice seemed to turn hers harder and crisper. "You operate under the assumption that all children are raised under conditions of equality, that they enter that testing room coming from identical backgrounds across the board. But even you must know this is not the case. I've seen tens of thousands of children over my career, and know very well that the son of a lawyer—or a big-time Hollywood producer, for that matter—has a huge advantage over the son of a mechanic in the inner city. But economics are not where it ends. Some are born with mental disabilities while others are quick studies. Some girls may not succeed because of subtle sexual discrimination within the classroom. What we at Stansbury are doing, ladies and gentlemen of the committee, is merely evening out the playing field.

In our school, all specimens, no matter what their histories, undergo the same med cycle, and the benefits are not exclusive to those whose parents are particularly generous donors. In fact, the valedictorian of the Class of 2036 is an orphan who won a full-ride scholarship in our annual lottery. He overcame the odds presented by poverty, a dead father, and an absentee mother, worked within our system for twelve years, and is now bound for Harvard in the fall. Are you, Senator Bloom, going to tell this young man that he won his achievements by cheating? By taking the easy road?" Of course you won't, she thought. Because men like you are all the same: fat cats who love dictating right and wrong from the comfort of your country clubs, surrounded by nodding, glad-handing mirror images of yourself. And when someone like Dr. Stansbury comes along and starts leveling the playing field, all they are left to do is start crying foul and wistfully reminisce about the high times when everyone knew their place and no feisty young'uns got uppity.

President Lang knew this all too well. Uppity should have been her middle name growing up in a working-class town outside Detroit. Around the age of twelve, she realized that distance from Flint, Michigan, was directly proportional to her chances of success in life and decided that she would like to attend a school as far away as possible. A boarding school, like the kind she read about in *A Separate Peace*. Mr. Meyers, her seventh-grade guidance counselor, laughed it off at first, but upon seeing the earnest look on her face, he printed out some information downloaded from various Web sites of famous prep schools like Griffin, Harrowton, and Parkinson. They were all, predictably, beautiful to young, blonde-haired Judith: big white buildings covered with ivy and dotted with red brick, paths winding through carefully manicured green lawns, and, of course, the fresh-faced students in gloriously crisp, distinguished uniforms bearing brightly colored coats of arms. She distinctly remembered those proud emblems because she always thought only those who were born into aristocracy were allowed to take them as their own. But no! Not outside Flint, anyway. All you had to be was a student on one of those pristine campuses and you got to wear one yourself. It was like being part of a club.

"I'd like to get a scholarship to the Griffin School," Judith decided.

She was already thinking about how good she would look in one of those dark green blazers, how the color would be a pretty contrast to the yellow of her mane.

"But only boys are allowed to go there."

"Mr. Meyers," she said, invoking that soon-to-be familiar tone of precocity for the first time in her life. "There are things I can do better than everyone else, including boys."

"Like what, Judy?"

"Lots of things."

"You should pick one of them and stick with that."

Judith thought about gym class that morning. They played tennis on a cracked, uneven asphalt court behind the school. She won all of the matches she played, even against the boys. Her mother had a racquet at home she could practice with. Tennis balls were probably cheap, and if they weren't, she could steal them from the school. "In that case, I think I'll pick tennis," she decided.

And so it went. Even sitting there in her executive suite while simulcasting before the Senate Select Committee on Education, she remembered the details. Later that day she watched the older girls on the high school varsity team play, and heard their coach berate them for their poor backhands, which usually ended up in the net or far out of bounds. In gym class, Judith saw that girls her own age were also bad at backhands, so she tried to hit the balls to that side of the court as much as possible. And then a new strategy struck her: initially, she played right-handed, but if she could teach herself to hit left-handed, she could not only hit more balls to her opponents' weak side, but she could also switch hands in the middle of the match—in the middle of a point, even—making it almost impossible for the girl on the opposite side of the net to adjust her game properly or strategize her shot selection. For several weeks, that racquet never left her hand, right or left. Other kids made fun of her at first, watching Judith's clumsy attempts at hitting balls with her off hand. But then her shots started landing in the court. Soon after, they weren't just plopping inside the service box. They became fluorescent yellow blurs that just barely skimmed the white lines of the court, snapping against the green surface with the torque of a vicious topspin. And always to her opponents' weak side. If she (or he, by this point; the school's tennis coach found it simply too demoralizing for other girls to get mauled by Judith Lang on a daily basis, and he began matching her up against boys) had a decent backhand, she'd pummel her with ground strokes. If they could keep up, she'd move to volleys, attacking the net, finessing drop shots, and pounding overhead smashes. And if all else failed, she'd end it quickly with a killer serve. Soon she was playing against the high school men's team while in eighth grade, and Mr. Meyers did his part by calling the Griffin athletics director and raving about this budding tennis prodigy from Flint, Michigan. It just so happened that the following year the distinguished old school in Maine was going coed and they needed to start filling out the rosters of their women's sports teams.

College—Amherst—followed Griffin. The coach who gave her the scholarship put his hand up her skirt after the team's first practice and she promptly quit the team. At first she thought it might be hard, giving up this game she had come to master and love over the years, but it was not in the least. She always controlled her skill more than it controlled her: it was simply the means to her end of getting away from Flint, shortening the distance to a better station in life. She taught herself to play ambidextrously, not because she viewed it as an innovation within the sport, but because it simply got her where she needed to be in a more efficient manner, as quickly as possible.

With her schedule considerably more flexible, she double-majored in political science and education. A summer internship with a teachers union lobbyist on Capitol Hill taught her two things: a man named Dr. Stansbury was about to set the world on fire with his new way of teaching and she had to lose the blonde hair. No matter how late she worked, how powerful the men she lunched with were, her trademark golden locks became a virtual signal to influential people of both genders that she was more of a cute little go-getter, rather than an ambitious woman with gravitas. Judith ate ham sandwiches for dinner for two months (it was just like practicing left-handed, actually) and got her hair dyed brown professionally with the money she had saved. Soon afterward she went in for an interview with Raymond Stansbury himself, and he hired her as his special assistant. She watched, learned, and served with complete loyalty. He taught her the intricacies of understanding the specimens, how every action from authority produces a reaction from the flock, how creating a specific, carefully controlled environment fostered an atmosphere that was the perfect balance of comfort and pressure. She kept the private lab records as the old man tested his new, performance-enhancing chemical blends on himself and, upon seeing his formerly fuzzy mind get twenty years younger right before her eyes, she requested to start the med cycle as well. After her first few doses, the pills turned the buzz of the world and constant onslaught of information that formerly bombarded her senses into a harmonic song. With Stansbury's increasingly high profile came the need for an extensive public relations program and a forceful presence both in the media and in Washington, D.C., power circles. Dr. Stansbury tapped his apprentice as the perfect candidate to run that crucial end of the business while he and Headmaster Latimer looked after the schooling of their children.

And now that apprentice would sooner slit her own wrists than watch Arthur Milford Bloom stop the progress of her school. President Lang knew that she had him on the ropes. She watched him on the simulcast screen, huffing and puffing about moral standards, family values, and hallowed traditions. He was coming up short, sounding just like the style-over-substance reactionaries who opposed suffrage for women, integration of schools and the military, open immigration, and gay marriage in years past. She caught a glimpse of Senator Frieda Mark on her screen and could see from the look on her face that Mark had already tuned him out. It was right there, clear as day: they were going to win the vote because Senator Bloom was simply on the wrong side of history. She felt her morning cocktail of 300 milligrams of Equimode, an antioxidant nutrient blend, and Stimulum, surge through her body. Senator Bloom looked at her on the screen, saying something or other. President Lang glanced at the clock on her desk: roughly thirty hours before the vote and all was going according to her carefully laid plans. She glanced at the wheezing gasbag and realized she had only one thing she wanted to say:

You're done, old boy. Game, set, and match, if I do say so *mah-self.*

11

The plasma ions on Goldsmith's Nature & Co. window broadcasted a dark blue sky dotted with white stars. The moon hung in the corner, so ivory and bright that it hurt the eyes to look at it, as if this lunar body were just another ambitious young planet that dreamed of one day giving the constellations themselves a run for their celestial money. The display was artificially digitized, but Goldsmith was grateful for it nonetheless: staying awake for a Stimulum-enhanced seventy-two hours could drive a specimen batty if he didn't keep himself anchored in something resembling a reliable time frame. Morning, noon, and night must still exist, even if they had no effect on you or your productivity. The Stimulum formula managed to transform debilitating exhaustion and fatigue into a mild case of jet lag wherein time itself became an imaginary friend, an apparition that helped one keep his bearings. Sleep, of course, was not necessary, but it always helped to be aware of the fact that yes, it was in fact one o'clock in the morning and no, you were not the least bit tired.

"Ready?" asked Camilla, who was seated on the opposite side of the table in Goldsmith's dorm room. Placed in between them was a black octagonal flash card projector.

"Sure," said Goldsmith. She pointed a small remote control and hit a button. The octagon produced a hologram of a protein structure with seven prongs extending from a diamond-shaped bulb. It glimmered and rotated in midair. Through its hazy gray body, he looked at her. She looked at the timer on the remote control, waiting for him to identify the projection. Camilla was headed to Yale next year, having won a spot in its prestigious creative writing program. He wanted to join her. Not in the program—Goldsmith was more of a science-and-numbers guy—but at the college itself. He casually floated the idea back in autumn, but she went cold on him as usual.

"Another four years of being number two to you?" she'd said through a thin smile. "No thank you." Then she went back to her homework, mumbling something about visiting him in Cambridge before the winter chill set in. Goldsmith smiled good-naturedly, made a crack about Yale being a safety school for Harvard, and wondered if that line about being number two was sarcasm or the real thing.

"Five seconds," said Camilla, her eyes still fixed on the flash card apparatus's timer.

"Minocycline and iron five," said Goldsmith, focusing on the protein. She didn't look up, but hit the remote control's button once again and it created a new hologram. This one looked like four oak trees sans leaves in November sprouting out of a twenty-sided pyramid.

Last August—the night before the Selmer-Dubonnet test—they ran into each other up in the atrium along a path by the river. The other finalists isolated themselves around the tower to gear up for whatever myriad horrors awaited them the following morning: rumors about the test always ran wild and tended to be more than a little absurd, touching on everything from no-holds-barred kickboxing matches to lying in a coffin full of live snakes. Camilla and Goldsmith never had much to say to each other before that evening, but she asked him to join her for a stroll anyway—she was polite, saying she was fretting the coming morning, couldn't sleep, and just wanted some company

to pass the time. He was jumpy too, and grateful for any kind of ca-
maraderie. He walked silently by her side as the reputed purebred ice
princess of Stanbury nervously rambled on and on about everything:
her absentee father, her mother who was having an affair with another former specimen, how Camilla always wanted a big brother to
protect her, how the tiny goldfish she bought for twenty-five cents
somehow stayed alive for seven years and grew to be the size of her
hand, how her roommate Miss Eliza Anne Petersmarck farted relent-
lessly in her sleep. They stopped to take in the view near a digitized
wooden fence that overlooked an illusory cornfield and a computer-
generated red barn in the distance.

"I should probably shut up," Camilla suddenly said. "I can be such
a . . . dork sometimes, you know?"

No, Goldsmith remembered thinking, Stansbury's very own gray-
eyed Athena a dork? Never. "I'm nervous about tomorrow, too," he
said out loud. "You're going to win. Everyone thinks so."

She turned to him. A single lock of long brown hair fell loose,
lightly clinging to the outline of her face. Camilla looked down and
tucked it behind her ear. "Well, what if I don't?"

"I . . ."

"And what if you don't win, Mr. Goldsmith?"

"Then someone else will. Probably you."

"If that happens, will you think of yourself as a failure?"

"No."

"Would you think of me as a failure if I don't win?" she asked. Her
eyes moved quickly back and forth, scanning his face. Goldsmith
knew he wanted to say no but faltered: being valedictorian was, as far
as the school's specimens (himself included) were concerned, an inte-
gral part of the legend of Miss Camilla Moore II. She read his thoughts
immediately. "It's okay," she said. "You're not the only one."

"No, Miss Moore," he said. "Really. I wouldn't think of you as a
failure." Then she smiled, raised herself up on the balls of her feet like
a ballerina and kissed him on the cheek. Goldsmith glanced around
quickly, wondering if anyone saw and if they'd get in trouble, maybe
even somehow get disqualified from the test the following day. Her
lips lingered for a moment and lightly drifted down the side of his face
as she pulled away. They smelled like cherries and made him think he

could handle disqualification just fine, eleven years of hard work notwithstanding.

"I'm holding you to that," she said.

"Go ahead."

Camilla then looked up at the artificial moon and blushed. "God," she giggled. "I am *such* a dork." And then she headed down the path, one foot kicking the heel of the other and a light, fairy-like sashay in her step brushing up a cloud of digital dust.

Somehow, watching her go, he already knew that it would be a long time before he and Camilla ever got back to this place they discovered in the atrium, just a guy and a girl talking, getting to know each other like they were regular kids. His conditioned, Harvard-bound brain told him to act like it was no big thing. His orphan's heart told him it was the only thing.

"Heteracyl-chloride," answered Goldsmith as he watched the rotating flash card image on the table between them. Camilla pursed her lips and hit the remote control one more time. Another shape popped up. It looked like jagged bits of orange pasta linked by pencils. "Amino six and trylo . . ." She dropped the remote to the table with a clatter and leaned over, flipping off the projector.

"That's three errors in a row, Mr. Goldsmith. You're not focused."

He looked at her. His heart started to beat up into his throat. Just tell her. "I quit today," he said.

"Quit what?"

"Valedictorian duties."

"*What?*"

"I guess . . . after twelve years I'm finally ready to leave this place."

"They're letting you quit?"

"I didn't give them much of a choice."

She fixed him with her patented cold gaze. "It's not going to be that easy, Mr. Goldsmith. Think about the consequences of your actions."

"You don't think I already have?"

"No."

"Well, Miss Moore, that's just—"

"Because if you had, you'd have realized that the entire structure of Stansbury society is predicated upon the existence of a valedictorian to inspire and lead four thousand specimens," she explained with all of the assurance of a true believer. As if what she was saying was the most obvious thing in the world. "The administration relies on that individual to instill order, to enforce policy. If that position is vacant— especially if it's rejected by the chosen specimen—it sends a signal to everyone inside this tower that there is something wrong with our way of life. It could indicate a fundamental problem with Stansbury itself." She paused to look at him, seeming to be searching for signs of waning belief in the gospel of Stansbury in his eyes. "It could also indicate a problem inherent in the method of selecting the top specimen, or, perhaps worse, a behavioral anomaly within the specimen himself, and, since all specimens are brought up and engineered by the same system, this would bring us back to the existence of a fundamental flaw in the institution. The only thing that can follow is chaos, anarchy, or both."

"It's been twelve hours since I informed the headmaster of my decision. Everything's normal."

"Because they haven't made that information public yet. The masses haven't had the opportunity to react. Or . . ." Camilla broke off eye contact with him and looked down at her feet.

"Or what?"

"Or they don't plan on allowing you to quit in the first place."

Goldsmith stared at her. It always struck him as funny that Camilla wanted to be a writer. Listening to her postulate and extrapolate logic so articulately always made him believe she'd be more suited for a position on the Supreme Court, or perhaps as a dictator of a third world nation. Didn't a photographic memory like hers get in the way of the imagination necessary to create the fantasies found in literature? To her, a horse would always be a horse. A vividly recalled, extremely detailed horse, no doubt, but ultimately realistic and based in fact. Goldsmith always thought a writer needed to have the capacity for error, to remember that horse well enough to craft a picture, but simultaneously forget just enough detail to be able to imagine it sprouting wings and soaring up into the sky of a world unlike our own. Sitting there listening to Miss Moore's parsing of his situation, he couldn't imagine her ever disassociating herself from practicality long enough to act on impulse, on feeling, and not pure utility. He glanced at the stack of books peeking out of her bag on the floor and smiled: dog-eared novels by John Grisham, Stephen King, Helen Fielding, and something by an author whose name actually seemed to be Plum Sykes.

"You're still reading that twentieth-century shlock?" he asked. She immediately grabbed the bag and zipped it up, blushing.

"It's none of your business what I'm reading."

"I've looked at that stuff before. Isn't the prose style a little banal? How can someone with your mind not find each chapter utterly predictable? Or maybe that's exactly *why* you like those books."

"I don't know what you're getting at."

"I'm just suggesting that maybe even Camilla 2.0 likes to escape her workload to have some mindless fun every now and then."

"I have my motives."

"What are you reading now?"

"Something called *Catcher in the Rye*. It's about a young man who runs away from home."

"Why?"

"Frankly, this is what I find so confusing. He seems upset about something, but never specifies what it might be. He harbors unexplained animosity toward the world despite his stable, nuclear family's comfortable economic status. He deems the people and institutions around him to be quote-unquote 'phony' when they are merely fulfilling the functions society has assigned them. This neurotic behavior is the central reason why I find the book, well, so implausible."

"Why?"

"Because neither I nor anyone I know of a similar age has ever felt anything remotely similar."

Goldsmith tried to suppress a smile. Angst. She's the smartest specimen he's ever met and she's got no idea what it means to be angst ridden. A petulant, angst-ridden teenager was as foreign to her as an extraterrestrial from another galaxy. "How are you ever going to be a writer?" he blurted. "You're too stuck on how things are. Not how they could be. Or ought to be."

"I fail to see how my being a writer has anything to do with the central point of our larger discussion, which would be the situation regarding your valedictorian's duties."

"But . . . what would you write about?"

"Does it matter?"

"I'm only asking."

"Specimens aren't exactly big on life experience," she said, glancing in the direction of her secret book stash.

"That's my point."

"I'll probably end up writing about this place, unfortunately." Camilla shifted her gaze downward, seemingly ashamed by this confession. "That's why they're so good at making us what we are, Mr. Goldsmith. They make us trade in all the stories we could've told for this one, long, twelve-year epic on their terms. And by the time we're finished, Stansbury is the only language we know how to speak."

He reached across the table and took her hand in his. It was cool and dry. He could see the red flashes of her fingernails in the gaps between his fingers. They looked like buried, shining jewels aching to be unearthed. Camilla looked up at him. For a moment, Goldsmith caught her—that dorky, giggling Athena in the holographic mirage of a field at night—and he smiled at the glimpse of this old friend. She did not smile back.

There was a knock at the door. Camilla pulled her hand back from his and stood up. He followed suit. After a single beep, the door opened and President Lang entered, her key card in hand. She looked at them standing at attention before her and smiled.

"Mr. Goldsmith and Miss Moore. Studying hard?" They nodded in unison. "For which progression?"

"Biochemical Compounds and Analysis," said Goldsmith. Lang smiled again, studying him. He glanced over at the Nature & Co. window that hung next to her on the wall. A cloud passed the moon, eating up an awkward ten seconds of silence.

"Miss Moore, would you mind excusing us?" she finally said.

"By all means, ma'am." Camilla picked up her books and headed for the door, not making eye contact with Goldsmith before she exited. Goldsmith looked at the president, watching her gaze as it passed over the contents of his room.

"Professor Harking showed us a clip of that talk show you did yesterday," he said, trying to keep the nerves out of his voice, "when you defended the school. Sometimes I feel like no one understands what this place is about—much less outsiders—and somehow, you made it seem so simple. Like good versus evil."

She gave him a warm smile, the kind she would never have betrayed before the cameras, lest it be interpreted as a sign of weakness or sentimentality. "I think she likes you, Mr. Goldsmith."

"Uh . . . beg your pardon?" Goldsmith felt his face erupting in a burning shade of red right before her very important, very official eyes. President Lang slowly raised her hand up toward his head. If Goldsmith did not know better, he would have thought she was about to stroke his hair or cheek. She stopped short and smoothed out her own hair instead, making it seem like the most natural motion in the world.

"Well, Miss Moore, of course," she smiled. "Time goes by so quickly around this place. Just when I get used to familiar faces on the young specimens it seems that they've suddenly become adults while I was occupied with some staff meeting."

"Um, yes, ma'am."

"But back to that broadcast you were shown. Yes, good and evil are precisely what we're dealing with. Progress versus stagnation." Her smile disappeared and she established eye contact, indicating that it was high time to get down to business. "Now, I am aware of the conversations you had today with Captain Gibson and the headmaster, but . . ." Her normally confident voice trailed off into an uncharacteristically stammering muck.

"Ma'am?"

"There's been an incident, Mr. Goldsmith."

"What kind of an incident?"

"A very grave one. Rest assured that I have no problem with the decision you have made and do not hold it against you. But nonetheless, as president of Stansbury, it is my responsibility to ask for your help." She turned toward the door.

"Can you elaborate?" He asked as he watched her hand on the doorknob. Just before she pulled it open, Lang looked back at him over her shoulder.

"Yes," she answered. "Mr. William Winston Cooley."

Goldsmith grabbed his blazer and followed her out the door toward the elevator bank. On the way it occurred to him that sacrificing all of the friendships he could have had over the years for this one shot at the punk hero of Guernica was a trade he was more than willing to make.

12

Pete's watch read five A.M. as he sat at his desk inside the spare guest suite on Level 7 provided to him by the Stansbury public affairs office and sipped a nutrient-enriched coffee from the cafeteria, wondering if it was really going to make him smarter like everyone said it would. The Nature & Co. window on the wall showed a broadcast of a sunny field of daisies in what looked like the Napa Valley. Pete grinned to himself and reckoned that the abnormal success of this strange school was maybe 25 percent actual genius and 75 percent the power of positive thinking. Something about the famed specimens—the focused stares plastered on their faces, perhaps—made his neck prickle. The way their uniforms were never dirty and how they always seemed to know when to applaud in the coliseum, before marching off like soldiers in unison down the tower's cold hallways, just plain freaked him out. He'd never seen so many tall, beautiful children in one place at one time. Twelve-year-old girls looked down on him in the hallways. Nerdy chemistry whizzes had the physiques to stand up to any number of bullies that ruled the parking lots of the proletarian public schools he had become familiar with over the years. But it was those weird gazes that stuck in his mind; they put the kids somewhere between the lifelike androids in campy sci-fi movies and the budding *ubermensch* youth of some fascist regime. And then they'd spring the cure for cancer on you. Say what you will about Stansbury, Pete mused, but they, like Mussolini, made the proverbial trains run on time.

Even his tour guide, Mr. Thomas Oliver Goldsmith, seemed a bit off, and he was the one the school chose specifically for the diplomat's job. If their hand-picked representative specimen couldn't even come off as normal and balanced, what did that say for the rest of them? Goldsmith struck him as a true believer, but Pete could tell the kid was smart enough—naturally smart, as opposed to medication-enhanced smart—to know there were chinks in the armor of this place. He scrolled through the digital windows of his Tabula 6000 to the files containing the first stages of the Stansbury story he planned to send to his editor in chief. The *San Angeles Times* would run it in three days, the same edition that would herald the likely victory of the school's bid for one trillion taxpayer dollars per annum. His shorthand notes read:

> Goldsmith (protective of school, but honest) . . . Headmaster = moral conscience & spiritual heir to Doc Stansbury . . . Security Detail/Capt. Gibson = ??? . . . Potential whistle-blowers/inside source/turncoat list pending . . .

A flip to another screen:

> Perhaps the only things more extraordinary than the achievements of Stansbury School are the souls who inhabit it. From the students—referred to within this literal ivory tower as "specimens"—to the administrators to even the jani-tors, the pursuit of excellence is the religion of this formidable utopia. But while religions have their deities, they also have their devils . . .

The words ended there. A bit dramatic, to be sure, but basically to the point. Now, about that devil . . . Pete had the perfect, yet surprisingly elusive candidate in front of him. He flipped open a blue folder and thumbed through several blurry color pictures shot with a telephoto lens: President Judith Lang in San Angeles exiting the Boeing building, Lang dining at a café with three congressmen, Lang exchanging documents with an unidentified man at Penn Station in New York City. Underneath the photos were logs of the phone calls she made during her stay at the Ritz-Carlton Hotel in Washington, D.C. just last week. His Tabula beeped. The caller identification display showed a Capitol Hill area code. It could only be him, Pete thought.

"Yes?"

"Is that fancy scrambler working?" came the voice of Senator Bloom. "Lord knows you invoiced my office enough for it." Pete glanced at the long, thin, silver attachment plugged into his Tabula. It had a small pea-size light that glowed green.

"I never said I was a cheap date, Senator. And the line's secure."

"How's my rascal on this fine mornin'?"

"Working hard as always."

"I believe it. You're the only one I know who's gotten inside that place."

"Just because reporters don't have any loyalty doesn't mean we're not resourceful. Besides, you're paying me too well to hit dead ends." He heard Bloom guffaw.

"Must be nice havin' two salaries."

"Hell of a way to keep your pool heated."

"Tell me what you've got on everyone's favorite ball buster. She was fixin' to tear me a new one yesterday and that was just over a simulcast."

Pete glanced through his Lang file. "She's pretty close to clean. I've had Harris tracking her for two months now and he's got zilch. This place is a monastery. No one comes or goes without the school's knowledge. There's not one vice available to anyone. The lady doesn't socialize outside of her job, and that's a twenty-four-hour gig as it is."

"I'm not writing checks to charity, damn it. I want dirt. Everyone's got a history, and—"

"You're right. So stop busting a gut and listen. My man Harris rounded up a couple of Stansbury alumni."

"He's not the only one."

"What's that supposed to mean?"

"You'll find out," said Bloom cryptically. "Pray continue, Pete."

"So Harris heard through the grapevine that Lang might've had a lover back when she was at Amherst. Nobody knew too much about it, because the guy was a professor and she was a student. Apparently Lang wanted to keep it hush-hush because it was against the school's policy, but she was also worried people might think he was going easy on her. See, the rumor is that her lover had graded her exams at one point."

"Do you have a name?"

"No."

"Get a list of the professors she had at Amherst. Get Harris to track them down before the vote. If he can weasel something out of the guy, we might be able to cause a stink."

"That was only the first part of the rumor, Senator. Second part is, the guy's dead." Pete listened to the ominous silence on the other end of the phone line and decided he'd better wrap this up sooner rather than later, to keep in the powerful man's good graces. "Here's another unsubstantiated Lang rumor: she got knocked up at some point by this mystery man but didn't have the kid."

"Nice start, but this whole business is coming a day late and a dollar short," said the Senator, his voice rising. "Time's running out. Frieda Mark's the chair of the committee, and what she says goes. And she wants us to vote on this tomorrow. I'm doing my best to buy us more time, but the president himself has let everyone in the party know—including yours truly—that he wants the Stansbury bill on his desk ASAP. I've got some tricks left in me, but I can't buck the democrats *and* my own people and get away with it for very long. You hear me?"

"Yes, sir."

"*Then get me more dirt.* I want enough ammo to start a goddamned muckraking war if I have to. Big guns, Pete, a nice mud bomb to sling at her or the school. You read me straight? Huh? You still there?"

Pete thought back to his notes on the school, recalling a single shorthand sentence: *Potential whistle-blowers/inside source/turncoat list pending . . .* "I'm cultivating a source. Someone inside that'll spill with something we can use."

"A specimen?"

"Yes."

"Cultivate faster."

"I'm on it."

"What are they like, Pete?"

"Who?"

"Those brilliant little boys and girls of hers."

"They're . . . they're really something else, Senator."

"When all the dust settles," Bloom said thoughtfully and slowly enough so that Pete could practically hear the gears turning in his old mind, "are they going to end up on the good side or the bad?"

His brain flashed back to his notes one more time: *Goldsmith (protective of school, but honest)* . . .

"I'm not sure, sir. I'm just not sure."

13

The first thing Cooley felt coming out of his druggy, sedated daze was thick wool covering his face. It smelled like disinfectant. Its elastic fabric jammed his nose to the side, causing an uncomfortable build up of snot. The tightly woven material pressed up against the pores of his cheeks, still half wet. Perhaps worst of all, a dense web of saliva gathered around his dry, cracked lips because the fit was so snug he found it difficult to close his mouth and swallow. Add to this the ocean of black caused by his eyes being pressed shut and one would start to understand the experience of wearing a Stansbury security detail hood while awaiting peer review in one of the disciplinary level's ten examination rooms.

Finally, Cooley regained his consciousness and, after deducing that his current situation was not a dream, tried to piece things together. He recalled Riley with a gun, followed by Riley on the floor. The security detail was in the bathroom. That officer went through the window. Cooley himself slid down an iron ladder five floors to the street. There was a monorail in the distance that seemed reachable, but a sharp, sudden burning sensation in the back of his neck cut the whole adventure short.

He flexed his wrists and felt the hard plastic of cable ties binding him to a chair. His ankles were bound to the chair's legs. No matter which direction he shifted, Cooley could not seem to get comfortable. He tried to relax his muscles and the chair's back dug into his spine. He slumped his body forward to take the pressure off and the cable ties dug into his wrists. The chair was not level. Someone had stuck very short legs in the front and long legs in the back so the person seated in it would be perpetually squirming.

"It was designed that way," came a young man's voice. The thick hood made it difficult for Cooley to tell which direction it was coming from. "Maximum discomfort." He heard leather soles scrape against the concrete floor, getting closer. The hood shifted half an inch and the friction was a welcome sensation against Cooley's stale, suffocated skin. Then the darkness rushed past like thick water, as the wool scratched against his face and he reflexively spit out the collected drool and sneezed, snot flying everywhere. Cooley could feel it sticking to his nostrils and chin. After a moment, his vision settled, focusing on the sight of Goldsmith standing on the opposite side of a bolted-down steel table. Goldsmith set the hood down. There was a box of tissues, but he did not offer him one.

He squinted at the valedictorian through the glare of no fewer than nine bright lights shining on him from different strategic points in the cold, spare room. Goldsmith loomed tall, almost larger than life. His eyes behind the lenses of his glasses came off as blank, almost clinical. His hands rested comfortably in his pockets. The emblem on his blazer gleamed so brightly that it seemed electrically powered. It was as if the nervous tics Cooley always saw on him in elevator pods, waiting in line for meds or shuffling through the atrium, never existed. The guy's face was a portrait of rectitude, a canvas empty of self-doubt or hesitation.

Cooley glanced around the room for a clock. He was dying to know what time it was and wondered for how long he was out, and thought of asking but didn't want to give Goldsmith the satisfaction or control of withholding an answer to such a simple question. Goldsmith sat down in a folding chair on the opposite side of the table and

Cooley was silently relieved. Gazing up at him with that yellow hair and all the spotlights was like staring at the sun.

"Look," Cooley began, working the grogginess from his vocal cords, "I don't know what happened back there. I don't want any trouble, all right? I just want to get through the next four . . . well, I guess it could be three now . . . four or three days and graduate, okay? I'll tell you everything I know."

Goldsmith shifted his gaze from Cooley to a manila folder on the table. He opened it and started to scan its contents.

"Hey!" said Cooley, raising his voice just a tad. "Where's Riley?"

Goldsmith didn't look up.

"Where am I?" Nothing. "What time is it?" Cooley's voice broke slightly and he knew it was audible, knew that Goldsmith heard. Goldsmith glanced up at him like he had been waiting his whole life to get the two of them in a room just like this, on his terms.

"In 1953, the CIA began a series of experiments for a top-secret program known as MK-ULTRA. The most famous of these involved sensory deprivation," he said, looking like a prissy tour guide but sounding like he was telling a ghost story around a campfire. "The lack of information initially caused stress in the men who volunteered. Simple things like date, time, and location were withheld from them. Soon, they found it unbearable, and their need for physical and emotional stimuli grew exponentially. Minutes began to feel like hours. They slowly lost touch with reality and started to focus inward, producing delusional fits, hallucinations." Goldsmith caught Cooley's eye and gave him a slight smile. "None of the volunteers lasted longer than three hours."

"I want a lawyer," said Cooley. How the hell am I gonna afford a lawyer, he thought. Bunson. Bunson's dad knows lawyers. And lawyers protect people's rights. "I've got rights," he said out loud.

"You don't. You're an orphan on a full-ride scholarship and the administrators of this school are your legal guardians."

"Just like you, right?"

"Like me. We owe this place everything—"

"Fuck that. *You* owe this place—"

"—and burnouts like you stand in the way of human progress."

Goldsmith's tone got a little bit sharper. Cooley decided to hit that nerve again just to mess with the officious little prick.

"Is it fucking progress if a cannibal uses a knife and fork? And when was the last time you saw the light? Real light from a blue sky that—"

"I'm asking the questions," said Goldsmith, having regained his cold, efficient delivery. Cooley watched him glance briefly at the mirrored wall over to the side and started to understand that the deck was stacked against him from the beginning.

"Fine. I did it. Okay?"

"Did what?" asked Goldsmith.

"I snuck off campus."

"Why?"

"Some specimens took . . . I mean, I took some dopazone hits and—"

"Which specimens?"

"Just me."

"Forgive me, Mr. Cooley. I was thinking that you might have been referring to the eleven specimens that were expelled this morning for drug use and possession. But please continue."

For the first time since the hood was removed Cooley was genuinely scared, and he knew it was showing clear as day. He thought of the looks on his friends' faces during their final gyrobus trip away from the tower, the yellow rain as it streamed down the windows, and the happy barking of Trigger when Bunson arrived home, juxtaposed with the hollow, sad stares of his once-proud mother and Bunson *pere*. Cooley thought of his departed friends, both hating and loving them for being so stupid. Why'd they have to do the things he did, say the words he said, think the way he suggested they should? "Why couldn't you have gone easy on them?" he asked Goldsmith. "Four days till commencement. Guys you grew up with—"

"You said you did 'it,' Mr. Cooley. Please elaborate."

"Fuck you!" He felt spit hanging from his trembling lips. The bindings around his wrists broke the skin and drew blood. Not that he cared at that point. "Just boot me. Get it over with. 'Cause I'm gonna be waiting the moment you set foot outside of the tower and—"

"You can elaborate for me or the police, Mr. Cooley."

"I needed purified urine samples for a drug test that I thought was going to happen tomorrow. Or today. I don't even know what fucking day it is . . . I went to Riley because he's sober and pays the bills by selling his piss."

"The security detail says they found you in his bathroom while he was in convulsions. There was a laser syringe on the scene, the type popular with users of drugs like—"

"Smack."

"You just said he was clean."

"He must've fallen off the wagon! He was acting like a . . . Look, anyone dumb enough to shoot up old-school street smack has an OD coming." Cooley went silent and studied the floor. "Is . . . is he okay?" he asked without looking up.

"Mr. Riley is dead." A moment passed. Goldsmith suddenly stood up and grabbed Cooley by the hair, yanking his face upward. Their eyes met. Goldsmith's were still calm despite what he was doing. Like he was a surgeon making an uncomfortable but routine exam. "It wasn't an OD and you know it," he said. "That syringe was filled with an unidentified poison and the entry mark shows it wasn't self-inflicted. Your prints were everywhere, all over the syringe and the body. You attacked a detail officer and fled the scene to—"

"I didn't kill him!" Cooley shouted. Goldsmith let go of his hair and held up the manila folder.

"Your blood tests don't show a trace of meds, and you've got a history of violence and delinquency."

"So?"

"You're a textbook unbalanced specimen, Mr. Cooley."

Goldsmith set down the folder and wiped off the hand he used to grab Cooley's hair on his trousers. Cooley could feel those ghoulish eyes roving over his sweaty face, looking for any trace of guilt or weakness his bodily functions might betray. It occurred to him that Bunson's Stansbury computer account had probably been terminated and he didn't have the Bunson family's home phone number or the faintest clue how to get in touch with him. Or how to get in touch with any of the other guys. Just like that. Twelve years of his buddies gone. Twelve years erased. Cooley was eighteen. Eighteen minus twelve equaled six. No family. No friends. He was six years old again. He thought about how long those twelve years felt and wondered if he was ready to go through another twelve to build a new life from scratch—but this time, without the full-ride scholarship to blow.

What was the point? Everything seemed inevitable, he thought. Like the story had already been written by the gods of Stansbury. No point in fighting it. But wait. Maybe that's how they wanted you to feel. Maybe they were assuming you'd quit. But what if you didn't? What if you screwed up their precisely laid chapters and disobeyed the careful instructions written on their pages? Sure, he thought, it'd be easier just to go along with everything, but two words raced through Cooley's mind over and over again: *fuck you fuck you fuck you fuck you . . .* Stick up for yourself, you pathetic bastard. Don't let them talk circles around you. Make it hard. Make it a bitch. Give them hell on behalf of Bunson and the guys. He was going to speak for all of them, look Stansbury's perfect theories and plans in the eye and say it loud: *fuck you fuck you fuck you fuck you . . .*

"I didn't do it," Cooley said, breaking the silence and matching Goldsmith's calm, controlled tone. "Strap me to the lie detector, the polygraph. Shoot me up with the truth juice and let me babble on record for hours. I didn't do it. I know you don't believe me, and you guys think you have this all figured out, but I dare you to do it. I fucking dare you."

Goldsmith stood there, his face blank. Cooley watched *his* face for a change, looking for the telltale signs in *his* eyes, on *his* skin. He saw a small, subtle vein on Goldsmith's temple start to throb gently. Cooley felt a smirk coming on but hid it. Goldsmith stiffened, like he knew what Cooley was thinking, and grabbed the manila folder before walking out of the examination room—fast. The click of the door closing behind him was the only good-bye that the great valedictorian offered.

"You heard him, sir," Goldsmith said to the headmaster as he entered the observation room on the other side of the mirrored wall. Something about that peer review session felt off kilter, he thought. He saw every color of Cooley's spectrum of emotions. Cooley was angry, scared, defiant, sad, defeated, guilty, innocent, thoughtful, and finally passionate, all within the course of fifteen minutes. Maybe it was because, having been used to the slow-building, controlled reactions of med cycle specimens all these years, Goldsmith wasn't accustomed to seeing such an unbridled display of feelings. Still, there was this nagging sensation in his gut—a close cousin of his inner bullshit detector, no doubt—that was telling him to get out of that room as soon as possible. Thank God he got the job done quickly. "Mr. Cooley consented to the polygraph and to Pentothal injection," he continued. "I suggest we—"

"No," said the headmaster. He was making eye contact with President Lang.

"Sir?"

"I say we shoot him up, strap him to the lie detector, and mix in some electroshock treatments just in case he starts getting mouthy again," said Captain Gibson.

"Categorically, no," said the headmaster.

Lang stood up from her chair and fixed Goldsmith with a look. "Stansbury is entering a new era, Mr. Goldsmith. Pentothal-based confessions aren't 100 percent reliable. We're capable of enforcing discipline without shooting specimens full of drugs." She beckoned him to the side, out of earshot of the others. "What does your instinct tell you?" she asked, lowering her voice.

"That there's more to the story than he's telling us. There's . . . there's a chance he might be innocent."

"And?"

"And if you lock him up and turn him over to the police, we may or may not discover the truth, but we *will* have a public relations catastrophe on our hands."

"An astute analysis." She beamed, delighted he was thinking on her level. "Go on, Mr. Goldsmith. Tell me what bold measure you propose."

"What was the name of the boy who led the specimens' bid for wider civil liberties all those years ago? The one who went to Dr. Stansbury and the trustees and made the case that the specimens had earned their trust, that the tower's security network should be reined in?"

"Peter Salazar, Class of 2019. He's now the president of the ACLU."

Goldsmith nodded and walked over to the headmaster, ignoring Captain Gibson's glare. Against his better judgment, Goldsmith just wanted another chance to talk to Cooley—but not in a peer review chamber. "Sir, I think the case against Cooley is incomplete. Since you are not opting for the Pentothal and polygraph test, I propose you release him back into the specimen pool and let me shadow him. If he's guilty, there's a good chance he'll run to someone and incriminate them as well. If he's innocent, he just might run to me."

"You got a death wish?" asked Gibson, jumping up to his feet. "The kid's got guilty written all over him! *Shadow* him? You're not gonna need to shadow anything because he'll be right in your face with a hand around your neck. You want to end up like Riley?"

"The tower is a controlled environment. I trust your men on the security detail—and my own training—to keep me safe." Goldsmith watched Lang shoot Gibson a look. Gibson sat back down and studied the floor.

"No," said the headmaster. "You're talking about letting a likely murderer into the tower."

"Reactivate the tower's security system. There's nowhere for him to run. If he did it, his actions will betray him. And I might be able to get him to confide in me. We're both scholarship orphans, sir. He knows I'm the one specimen who could help him. There's no adult in this school he trusts. And if you send him to the San Angeles Police Department, the media will grab this just in time to ruin the Senate committee vote." The headmaster looked at Goldsmith for a long moment. Goldsmith glanced at Lang and she nodded, giving him the silent signal to close the deal. "Sir, back in 2019, Peter Salazar convinced you and Dr. Stansbury that specimens were worthy of your trust. Think about what I could do for you—and Stansbury—if you extend this trust to me."

"What do you think, Madam President?"

"I think Mr. Goldsmith grasps the complexity of the issues at hand. I agree with his strategy." Silence filled the room as the old man considered his options. He looked at Goldsmith and smiled.

"Peter Salazar wasn't half the specimen you are, Mr. Goldsmith. I'm giving you until five o'clock today to secure proof of his innocence or guilt," he said. "Then we detain Mr. Cooley again and, if necessary, hold him until after the Senate committee vote before turning him over to the police."

"Thank you for performing your duty this final time," said President Lang. "That will be all."

Through the one-way mirror, Goldsmith watched a detail officer release the cables binding Cooley to the chair in the examination room. Out of his peripheral vision, he saw Lang and Gibson exchange eye contact across the room behind the headmaster's back. Goldsmith gently set down his manila Cooley file on the desk and headed for the exit. On the way out, Gibson gave him a warm smile as he wheeled his chair over to a computer terminal facing the door. Gibson's knee started to do this funny little bounce.

Goldsmith stood outside in the corridor and counted to ten. Then he opened the observation room door unannounced, striding in toward that manila Cooley file.

"Forgot my folder," he said, feigning annoyance at a mistake, the kind that he had never once made in his life, because he was not capable of such errors. The headmaster smiled, picked it up, and handed it to him. On his way out, Goldsmith caught a glimpse of the computer monitor behind the just-a-tad-too-casual Captain Gibson and saw a simulcast of a face so familiar that it didn't occur to him just who it was until he was outside of the room and headed for the elevator bank.

The image was digital and slightly static-ridden from the tower's heavy network server workload, but there she was, that stray strand of autumn hair and tortoiseshell eyeglass frames perched high upon delicate cheekbones: Camilla 2.0.

14

As Cooley made his way down the long hallway on Level 9, fatigue started to take hold; his feet went clumsy, his neck became a stiff, dead weight. It first kicked in when the security detail officers escorted him out of the disciplinary level and he saw the date and time on the elevator pod's display monitor. March 30, 2036. 6:15 A.M. The knowledge that he would not be able to sleep, that he had to figure out some way to beat Goldsmith, that he could not just call in sick and lie around all day only enhanced his exhaustion. One of the detail guys saw his eyelids getting heavy and offered to bring him to the med tech bay before it opened to get a Stimulum injection. As much as it sounded like a good idea, drinking the Kool-Aid at this point in the game seemed like a betrayal of Bunson and the guys.

Cooley swiped his key card and pushed open the door to his room, preparing himself for the depressing sight of the emptiness his friend had left behind. He was expecting a stripped bed, several discarded uniforms hanging in the solitude of a barren closet, perhaps Bunson's rusty brown stubble still clinging to the white basin of their sink as the only evidence of a past life. Did the school even give him enough time to leave a note before they sent him away? But Cooley walked in, looked around and . . . Everything was normal. Two unmade beds, two humming computer terminals, two messy closets occupied with dirty laundry just like he left them yesterday after his dopazone trip. But how . . .

"Hey!" called out Bunson in his baritone cadence. Cooley flinched and then felt his tired body lifted off the ground in a bear hug, his roommate's long, thick arms wrapping him up from behind. He looked at his grinning buddy as he towered over him in his triple-extra-large white robe.

"I thought—," Cooley started.

"Where the hell have you been? You got no idea what kind of shit went down while you were gone!" Bunson set him down and his face brimmed with nervous excitement, bearing the look of a giddy, shell-shocked soldier who had lost the rest of his platoon in battle. "The school searched the guys' dorm rooms, rounded everyone up— Mancuso, Oates, Sugiyama, the whole gang—and sprung a piss test on them. And then—"

"I know."

"You do? Maybe you should lie down, man. You look awful. I bet you spent the night in San Angeles, didn't you? At Riley's place?"

"Sort of."

"When the other guys didn't show up at lunch I knew something was up. Sadie was freaking out. She thought maybe you were down in the disciplinary level with them, but I told her where you really were. I was thinking I'd—"

"Why didn't you get busted along with the rest of them?" asked Cooley, blinking several times as if to make sure it really was Bunson and not some digitized replica.

Bunson's face went blank. "Well . . . I don't know. I figured we got lucky. Figured maybe you still had some good karma left over from Guernica and . . ."

Cooley closed his eyes and started shaking his head, trying to focus. The gears in his brain felt like jelly. Things weren't cohering the way they normally did. "No . . . no . . . ," he said. He opened his eyes and saw his buddy, this big, six-foot-nine oaf all confused about why he was not similarly ecstatic about their good fortune. "Think,

Bunson. Thirteen specimens tripped on dopazone two nights ago. Eleven of them had their rooms searched and got expelled. Our room wasn't searched, even though the evidence was out in the open for anyone to see. I didn't even lock down my computer terminal, I didn't think to delete the site history."

"So? Maybe they just took a quick look and didn't see anything that—"

"My goddamned dopazone cuff was sitting on the desk!"

Bunson shrugged his meaty shoulders. "So we got lucky," he said. "Why mess with that?" He reached into Cooley's closet and tossed him a white robe of his own. Cooley started peeling off his soiled uniform, changed into a clean pair of underwear, and pulled the robe on.

"There's no such thing as luck in this place," said Cooley as he splashed cold water on his face at the sink. "They let us off the hook for a reason."

"I love you to death, man, but you're being paranoid." Bunson headed for the door. "You coming to the solarium?"

Cooley followed him. "Yeah . . . I guess."

"Relax," Bunson said. "Just three more days. We dodged the silver bullet. Leave it at that." Cooley walked into the corridor outside. Bunson looked over his shoulder and smiled. "How's old man Riley holding up these days?"

Cooley thought of that tremor-ridden body, the severed tongue, and the red film of blood soaking Riley's white teeth. "Good," he said. "He's doing real good."

The corridor was packed with the flow of specimens all wearing identical white terry cloth robes and headed in the same direction. Cooley looked around at their distant gazes and noticed that their feet were unintentionally hitting the ground in unison, like they were solemn, monastic disciples marching in formation on their way to worship at an altar.

Cooley knew the administration was letting him back into the specimen population for a reason. The initial guess was that they assumed he'd freak out and drag someone else like Bunson down with him for some transgression or another. The headmaster probably wanted to reel in another fish before they had the polygraph session ready to go. Stansbury always liked making examples. They'd parade their captive in chains through the atrium and stick them in some gallows in the coliseum if they could get away with it. Cooley wanted desperately to tell his best friend about everything that happened last night—about Riley, about what Stansbury was trying to do to him—but he understood that Bunson was better off not knowing anything. Plausible deniability. He felt guilty enough about the other guys and wasn't going to risk the diploma of the last person he could count on.

Still, the fact that their room was conspicuously left out of the dopazone search gnawed at him. Why? He marched in time with the rest of the specimens and saw the entrance to the solarium appear in the distance. The answer to "why?" had to be a significant piece of this messed-up puzzle, he thought. Cooley tried analyzing the mystery the way a smart guy like Goldsmith would, logically, precisely.

The scenario: the security detail passed over the quarters of two of Stansbury School's most notorious unbalanced specimens during a search, the purpose of which was to locate and expel drug users.

Known fact: for the twelve years that Cooley had been schooled in the tower, he judged the detail's procedures to be nothing less than thorough and ruthlessly efficient.

Another known fact: Cooley admitted to dopazone use and possession less than an hour ago during his peer review in the disciplinary level and, despite the fact that this admission would normally warrant both immediate expulsion and a mandatory search of both his belongings and those of his roommate, no actions had been taken.

Postulation #1: contrary to his initial prognostications, the administration was not waiting for Cooley to incriminate his remaining associates. If that was their aim, they could have terminated Bunson's tenure yesterday or this morning.

Postulation #2: the fact that he and Bunson were not expelled with the rest of the specimens could lead one to believe that the two of them collaborated with the administration in order to save themselves.

Postulation #3: since Cooley did not collaborate, this left Bunson as a possible traitor.

Postulation #4: if Bunson was *not* a traitor, this indicated a strong likelihood that the school consciously spared them for a reason that had not yet been revealed.

Addendum: the concurrence of these events with the accusation of Riley's sudden death either meant it was: A) a strange coincidence; or B) a link somehow connected to a larger web of actions of which Cooley had no knowledge.

Final Conclusion: Bunson would never rat on his boys. Which meant the shit in which Cooley was swimming only got deeper.

Three hundred male specimens stood in the boys' solarium clad only in underwear. They were lined up in five perfectly straight, symmetrical rows of sixty specimens apiece, barefoot on the cold white marble floor and wearing darkened ergonomic lenses sealed tightly over their eyes. Hanging from the ceiling roughly one hundred feet above them were a series of ultraviolet Celestial Class spotlights positioned at varying angles. Each specimen was individually illuminated with his own halo of warm light that rendered his skin a healthy golden brown within fifteen minutes.

"*Sunlight shift,*" announced Mrs. InterAct over the loudspeaker. "*Please rotate ninety degrees east. Thank you.*"

The spotlights rattled and cranked as the machinery switched angles and, like a sternly choreographed dance company, the specimens made their turn in unison. Cooley saw Goldsmith standing in a neighboring row, five places down. He wondered if Goldsmith was helping the administration with whatever it was that was happening to him. If he was not, there was no doubt that the valedictorian had seen the same contradictions he had and started to put some theory together. He was too smart to overlook the clues. But then again, Goldsmith was the administration's personal attack dog. Which meant, if anything, he was in on it too.

Goldsmith knew exactly where Cooley stood, could feel him looking daggers into the bare skin of his back, shooting his glare through those smoke-colored ultraviolet lenses. The valedictorian preferred it this way, actually. He couldn't bear to look the kid in the eye. Goldsmith had always been more of a prosecutor than a defender, hence the pure animus that hung between him and just about everyone; and yet he couldn't help but feel as if he were letting Cooley down. Not because it was his job to protect him—it was not by any means, nor did he want such a hopeless task—but because he *knew* the bizarre manner in which events were transpiring. He had always done business the proper way, lived by the same absolute standards that he enforced. But now, after they had finally trapped Cooley after all these years, the administration went back on their standard procedure and, well . . . took a shortcut. It was almost no better than cheating. Here Goldsmith stood, officially retired from his duties, and full of the knowledge that he witnessed something that was, quite simply, wrong. He heard the cadence of specimens reciting the Stansbury Oath in his mind: *By virtue of the Gifts bestowed upon me, I swear my Eternal Duty to all those without such Gifts. For Power may point the way, but only Honor can lead it.* This is how they use their "power"? This is their version of "honor"?

Why didn't they just give Cooley the polygraph, he wondered. Did he know something that the headmaster and President Lang did not want coming out? They might have been protecting the school, a value with which Mr. Goldsmith could certainly empathize. Because without order there was no Stansbury, and with no Stansbury there was no AIDS vaccine, cancer cure, gyroengine or rescued orphans.

It also didn't help that the administration had gone behind his back by somehow bringing Camilla into it. Granted, they found themselves in an unusual situation—without a valedictorian with three days left in the semester—and it was only natural that they should seek the number-two specimen in the class as his replacement. But Goldsmith remembered what she'd said last night, how the very integrity of the school would crumble without a valedictorian, and it occurred to him that Camilla would probably not have the same issues with Cooley's treatment than he did. Perhaps it was all a bit too convenient.

"Sunlight shift. Please rotate ninety degrees east. Thank you."

Goldsmith rotated with the crowd and came face to face with Cooley, who had not budged an inch and stood there, out of sync with the rest of the rows of specimens, sending him the eerie, lonely stare of a condemned man.

15

The cafeteria was one of Stansbury's crowning achievements of industrial design: 25,000 square feet of polished, bone-colored marble tile fused into rising swaths of titanium that curled into booths and nooks for the specimens to sit and dine in. These metallic waves were crafted to look as if they were in a state of perpetual forward motion (like the surging waves of specimens, of course) and were intertwined with long sheets of crystal-clear glass walls. The architect had made it a point to ensure that every part of the dining area would be visible to all, so that meals would be an open, democratic experience. But grandiose design statements notwithstanding, specimens were still young adults as prone to congregate with their own cliques as much as students at any other school outside the tower. In fact, one quick glance at the dining area would have revealed a great deal of social anthropology at once.

The specimens filed in for breakfast hour, grabbed serving trays at the entrance, and waited in line for access to Stansbury's world-renowned nutrient diet. Against a wall were several large, floor-to-ceiling glass vats of liquid in a variety of aesthetically pleasing colors like beige, gray, and a tasteful shade of orange. The vats were labeled with the type of intravenous food they contained. Today, the menu included liquefied pancakes, croissants, and oatmeal, as well as mineral water and orange juice. Specimens brought their small glass jars for personal use to the vats and opened up the taps, letting the foodstuff aerate for a few minutes before consumption.

Mr. Hurley bounced around from table to table with his notebook, performing last-minute senior class interviews for the yearbook. He sat down at a table of three males and three females, looking at them eagerly.

"So today's yearbook question is, What Are You Going to Be When You Grow Up?"

"Stansbury's fifth Nobel Prize winner," said a boy.

"A pediatrician who works in third world countries," said a girl.

"Ambassador to the Middle East. For a Republican administration, of course."

"The first woman to throw a pitch in the World Series."

"I love you guys," said Hurley, scribbling everything down.

Cooley wasn't hungry at all, but went through the motions of picking up some pancake fluid anyway and walked over to Sadie and Bunson, who were sitting in their regular corner booth. Upon seeing him, Sadie jumped up and planted a kiss on his cheek.

"I was a wreck yesterday," she said, whispering over the din of hundreds of separate conversations. "No one knew where you were and then I heard that everyone else was getting—"

"It's cool. Everything's gonna be fine." He sat down with them. Sadie pulled a laser syringe from its sterility wrapper and filled its chamber with some gray liquid from her glass jar, the built-in centrifuge transferring nutrients. She rolled up her sleeve and tapped a vein before aiming the glowing beam and injecting herself with breakfast. Bunson followed the same routine, tapping the vein, but injected himself twice as fast as she did. Big guy must be hungry, Cooley thought.

"Man," Bunson said, grimacing, "they always put way too much starch in these pancakes." Cooley watched the gray liquid disappear through the laser and into Sadie's arm. With the exception of Stansbury's patented NutriTein bars (bland, dense blocks of solid nutrients that prevented the specimens' digestive systems from atrophying), the cafeteria served syringe food exclusively. The nutrient-rich formulas were actually vitamins and engineered chemicals designed to feed the bloodstream with essential materials with a minimum of excess fat, preservatives, or artificial additives. The pancakes weren't actually pancakes liquefied in a giant blender. They just tasted like pancakes because the laser-needles transmitted signals to the brain and taste buds that tricked them into thinking the body was feeding on the real thing. Another ancillary benefit was that these foodstuffs were specifically geared to maintain a certain blood sugar level, meaning there was no such thing as a specimen who overate into obesity. The cafeteria's menu had been adopted by several upscale health club chains and better spas around the world, providing yet another source of income for Stansbury. Cooley peeled open a NutriTein bar, bit into it, and choked back his usual gag reflex: it tasted like chewy clay sprinkled with a crunchy, powdered sugar substitute.

"Mmmm . . . The oatmeal's good," said Sadie. "Blueberry."

Bunson shot some up, tasting it for himself. "After graduation it's back to the outside world and all those working stiffs with their greasy hand-and-mouth junk food . . ."

"Tell me about it. I can't even remember the last time I used silverware. Might as well just dump the E. coli down our throats and get it over with quick, right?"

Cooley nodded, smiling halfheartedly. On the opposite side of the cafeteria, he watched Camilla set her tray down next to Goldsmith.

"Can I ask you something?" said Goldsmith. Camilla took a seat across from him and unwrapped a syringe.

"Sure."

"What did Captain Gibson say when he simulcasted you with the headmaster and President Lang this morning?" Now watch her face, Goldsmith thought. She looked at him, her features calm. Not even a furrowing of the brow.

"They put me on notice. They said you retired, I acted appropriately shocked, and they told me if there are any incidents between now and the end of the school year they might request my services." She filled up her syringe with oatmeal. "Not that it's any of your business."

Goldsmith studied her, wondering if she was trustworthy. Technically, he was bound by the honor code, which meant that all of the incidents between the valedictorian and specimens on the disciplinary level were to remain confidential. He was not supposed to divulge any information about what happened this morning. On the other hand, the penalty of violating this rule was stripping the valedictorian of his title, and Goldsmith had willingly given it up. He looked at Camilla, reading her for clues. She returned his gaze, reading him for the same. He remembered the promise he made her the night before Selmer-Dubonnet. Maybe they met during her once-in-a-lifetime moment of weakness. Perhaps it was just a coincidence that he ran into her that evening in the atrium and she would've opened up to anyone. But the fact was, he kept that promise ever since. She owed him one. Didn't she?

"I need your advice," he said.

"Are you asking Miss Moore or are you asking Camilla?"

"Camilla. Definitely Camilla." He leaned over the table and lowered his voice to a whisper. "Analyze the following scenario. The valedictorian is called in to interrogate a specimen. The specimen exhibits no signs of guilt regarding the charge and offers to submit to a polygraph test, with sodium Pentothal on hand. Yet the school refuses."

"For what reason?"

"Get this," Goldsmith said. "They don't want to inject the specimen with chemicals—even though they've done it to us every day for the past twelve years." Camilla glanced around at the glass walls surrounding them, wondering if any specimen out there was an expert lipreader.

"Graduation is imminent," she whispered, cupping her hand over her mouth. "You are three days away from completing one of the most remarkable twelve-year runs in the history of Stansbury, a career unprecedented for a full-ride orphan. I'd advise the valedictorian in question to obey orders and mind the honor code's confidentiality clause. And not to say anything that might incriminate himself in the presence of his replacement."

"That sounded a lot like Miss Moore to me. And don't hide behind the rule book. Each day since we've been here, you and I swore the oath, didn't we? The whole philosophy of this place is using our gifts to help other people, not suppress ugly questions about ourselves."

"Stability comes first. If Stansbury isn't secure, then the oath means nothing."

"I always thought it was the other way around." He paused, realizing they were speaking different languages, were living in different worlds. "Please, Camilla, I need your help. Tell me your theory on this."

"Fine." She leaned in close, lowering her voice to a barely audible murmur. "They won't inject the specimen because the truth is not what they want to hear. And it's none of your business why that—"

Someone set down a tray of intravenous food at the table. They both pulled back instantly and looked up. Pete smiled down at them.

"Mind if I join you?" he asked.

"By all means," said Goldsmith. Pete sat down at the table and held up a laser syringe.

"Can't I just use a straw?"

Cooley watched them from across the cafeteria, wondering who the outsider with the suit and the notepad might have been. The guy busted into a pretty interesting moment: whatever Goldsmith told Camilla 2.0 jacked up her blood pressure by about thirty points. He bet they weren't discussing cancer cures or progression work. He cut odds that Goldsmith was figuring things out like he was, rather than plotting his next peer review stratagem: fifty-fifty. Cooley decided to stick it out till the polygraph test he thought was waiting for him. Once he cleared himself of Riley's death he would sort out the contradictory mess of the dopazone bust and what connection there might have been, if any. But that was a tall order for one delinquent kid who was running on more than twenty-four hours with no sleep. He looked up at Sadie and Bunson and hoped he wasn't putting them at too much of a risk.

"Hey, guys," he began. They looked up from their meals. "Uh . . . what I'm about to tell you is gonna sound . . . insane, but I might be in a lot of trouble for . . ."

Sadie gave Bunson a glance. "Cooley," she said reaching across the table and taking his hand in hers, "I don't mean this in a bad way or anything but . . . I'd rather not know. I've got to focus on finals, and if I don't pass Wilton's progression I'm going to end up at . . ." She looked down in shame. "State college."

"Same boat," said Bunson. "I mean, we've had a blast all these years, but yesterday was a really close call. Freaked me out. Bad. Oates and Mancuso were my buddies and all, but I . . . I can't end up like them. You know?"

Cooley looked at him. Bunson stared off into the distance, avoiding eye contact. He pulled his hand away from Sadie, more hurt than pissed off. All he wanted to do was grab them both and shout that he was fucked and needed their help, or at least their advice. He felt like Sadie and Bunson were cheating on him, only it was not sex that they were having behind his back—it was the certainty of comfortable futures and college and nice apartments and jobs and white picket fences and glass doors that weren't shattered by chairs hurled from the fists of angry, violent men. But it was not where Cooley came from that held him back from sharing in the prospects of a future. After all, Goldsmith got with the program from the start and now he was in the driver's seat. Cooley had plenty of second, third, and fourth chances over the years. His more sympathetic professors always told him that he ended up in the tower for a reason, that the chances of him coming here were so statistically microscopic that it couldn't have been anything other than his destiny to be one of them, that God meant for it to happen.

Problem was, Cooley never believed in God in the first place. This he regretted now, too. Rumor had it that He was a pretty generous guy, that He loved everyone unconditionally and that faith in Him solved any number of life's fucked-up mysteries. Too bad he forgot to send up some stray prayers every now and then, Cooley thought. Was it too late to start? Because at the moment, he'd take any help he could get.

––––––––

Goldsmith watched his fellow specimens flow along the atrium's paths toward their morning progressions. He was able to pawn Pete off on Camilla for a couple of hours. He told her he needed to study, but knew that she knew he was lying. The crowds that passed through the holographic fields and meadows started to clear, and after a few moments Goldsmith saw him: Cooley sitting alone on a digitized rock overlooking a field of daisies. Goldsmith headed over.

"Nice view, isn't it Mr. Cooley?"

"Funny thing is, I never saw any of it," he said, not looking over. "All the hills and the flowers or whatever everyone always raves about. I just see a big white hall with a tall ceiling where the sun's supposed to be and black image projectors in the place of maple trees." Goldsmith nodded. He beckoned Cooley to follow him to a flowing stream a few feet away. "Where are we going?" asked Cooley.

"The water here is loud enough to cover up our voices. The security detail still operates the tower's surveillance system in public areas on an intermittent basis."

"I fucking knew it," Cooley laughed morbidly. "That's how you busted my guys."

"And given the trouble you're in, you need all the tips you can get."

"When's the polygraph and Pentothal session?"

"There's not going to be one," said Goldsmith.

"What? It'll clear everything—"

"I told them to put you under, but President Lang said she was hesitant to shoot a specimen full of drugs."

"*Lang* said that? Then what—"

"I want to help you."

"I'm honored."

"You're welcome," said Goldsmith.

"No, *you're* welcome. You think helping me is gonna get rid of the guilt from all that dirty work you've done for them, right?" Cooley stared Goldsmith down, inwardly relieved that someone gave a shit, but also feeling his anger bubbling up because he couldn't shake the feeling he was being used by this slick careerist punk. "It's not gonna make you a single friend, but if it means getting me cleared in time for graduation, by all means go ahead."

"I'm not using you."

"Yeah? Well, I'm using you."

"Is there anything you didn't tell me in the examination room this morning?"

"No, I told you everything I—"

"Think," interjected Goldsmith, sounding like he was training an animal not to piss inside the house. "Contradictions. You told me Mr. Riley was sober but he ended up with a laser in his arm. Were there any other details that didn't fit?"

"No."

"Think. Mr. Jonathan Clark Riley. A burnout Stansbury graduate . . ." He watched Cooley, who closed his eyes for a moment, searching, and then they snapped open.

"He had a gun," Cooley said. "A brand-new Glock 12. He was acting paranoid and kept waving it around, like he thought someone was coming to get him."

"But he never fired it while he was in the bathroom?"

"No. And when I found him there lying on the floor, I specifically looked around for it and didn't see it anywhere."

"Good. What else?" He watched Cooley glance downward, mulling something over.

"That's it." Cooley felt Goldsmith's eyes scan his face.

"You either don't know how good I am at what I do, or you think you can play me by holding something back."

"His coffee table . . . It was covered with stacks of yearbooks with pages ripped out. Photos of old specimens. I asked Riley about them and he freaked out. There was a hiding spot in the floor, a dummy wood plank underneath a rug, and he stuck the pages in there." Goldsmith watched his eyes carefully: they were glancing upward and to the left. Good. His brain was retrieving information, not making it up.

"That's a start," he said.

Without warning, the sun projected up in the atrium sky went gray and the clouds began to skip as the Nature & Co. system got caught in a glitch. Goldsmith glanced up, avoiding Cooley's eyes. For some reason he felt embarrassed by the technology's error, as if one of his houseguests had stumbled across a filthy bathroom during a dinner party.

"You ever wonder about your parents?" Cooley asked.

"At times."

"My dad beat my mom up. The orphanage said she ran away with me."

"And of course you think she's still out there somewhere."

"Maybe." Cooley looked at Goldsmith and smirked. "If only she could see me now, right?"

"What does your mother have to do with any of this?"

"Because I need your help. And I need you to see me as an eighteen-year-old kid who knows that shit happens just like you do. Not a specimen."

"There was this priest who helped run my orphanage, and he told me some things. My dad died of brain cancer," Goldsmith said. "My mother was too young, too broke to raise a son. The state took me away from her. That's how his story goes, anyway."

"Sorry, Thomas." He watched Goldsmith flinch at the sound of his own name without a "Mister" prefacing it. Casual talk made him squirm.

"How have you been getting from the tower to San Angeles?" Goldsmith asked, changing the subject.

"Universal Taxi service. But they charge an arm and a leg to—"

"Unlike you, Mr. Cooley, I've saved my allowance over the years, instead of blowing it on drugs to rot my brain." He pulled out his Tabula and ran a search, logging Universal's phone number. Cooley was surprised. He didn't think this priss had the balls to follow up on the new leads.

"Hey," he said. "Do you think I did it?"

"Things are . . . murky at the moment, Mr. Cooley. And sunlight is the best disinfectant. So said Justice Louis Brandeis."

Cooley looked up at the atrium's domed ceiling and saw the static lining the clouds, the strange, hollow-seeming light stretched far and wide over miles of open space that didn't really exist. "But the sun doesn't shine in this place," he mumbled, half to himself.

He watched that tall head of carefully groomed blond hair float off into the distance. A helping hand from Thomas Oliver Goldsmith was just about the last thing he expected. The guy had a calm serenity about him that rubbed off a little bit, like you just knew the ship was in good hands if he was the one steering. Cooley made Goldsmith for a smart guy with more of a conscience than he probably preferred. Probably had a good heart and wouldn't have minded making a friend or two before heading off to Harvard, or wherever it was specimens like him ended up. And he was probably lonely like nothing else, Cooley realized.

But if he didn't know what was coming next, twelve years of Stansbury progressions didn't teach him the most important lesson: the story of Goldsmith showing no mercy while booting eleven of Cooley's friends out into the street was not finished yet. As soon as Cooley got himself out of this Riley jam, the next job before commencement was something that came easy to the guy who made the name Guernica famous around this place. Revenge.

16

Inside the faculty conference room on the tower's fifty-second floor, the headmaster stood behind a podium at the head of a long white table shaped like an ellipse. Seventy-one administrators and professors were present, either in chairs around the table or simulcast via plasma screens hanging on the walls. The mood was typically solemn and serious, the faces of those good men and women long and grave with the rigors of duty, as if they were divine denizens of a modern-day Mount Olympus charged with overseeing the well-being of four thousand gifted but ultimately fragile mortals. For the past fifteen minutes, all eyes were on the headmaster, their Zeus in a slim black suit, as he summarized the events of the past twenty-four hours for them: a former specimen had died under as of yet unexplained circumstances and Mr. William Winston Cooley, the somewhat notorious specimen they were all familiar with, was being investigated by Mr. Thomas Oliver Goldsmith. At first the faculty thought they were being summoned for yet another tedious staff meeting; now each of them was riveted. Dozens of donut-flavored laser syringes were going stale at the table's center.

". . . And I can assure each of you that this matter will be resolved swiftly and—," said the headmaster as he tried (and succeeded, in his own experienced estimation) to project an air of reassuring authority and control in the face of danger.

"But sir!" All eyes shifted toward the image of Professor Partridge, who was being simulcast onto a screen at the far back wall. He sat in an office that had been overrun by dozens of congratulatory flower bouquets and bottles of Champagne sent from around the world after the previous day's announcement of Panacetix's government approval. The headmaster was not accustomed to being interrupted and wondered if young Partridge wasn't letting the good news go to his head. Partridge gulped and smoothed back what was clearly a toupee worthy of a game show host. The headmaster was tempted to ask him why finding a decent wig was more difficult than curing cancer, but the meds he took with breakfast helped him suppress the urge. "The Select Committee on Education is voting on the Stansbury grant proposal this evening!" Partridge said. "We're about to release Panacetix onto the market and we can ill afford a public scandal that—"

"There will be no scandal," said the headmaster. "The entire matter is being handled internally by Captain Gibson, the security detail, and the valedictorian." And don't worry about your stock options, Professor, he thought. They're in better shape than poor Mr. Cooley, not that you care about the young man's well-being.

The headmaster had always had a soft spot for Stansbury's orphans. He fancied himself a bit of a surrogate father to each of them, even the unbalanced ones like Cooley. And, contrary to the majority of his colleagues' tendencies, he did not judge a specimen solely on his or her academic achievements. The headmaster was the one who set forth the school's unspoken but widely understood hands-off policy toward Cooley following the Guernica incident four years ago. He would have called the young man into his office and thanked him personally for defending the Evans girl, but he did not want to give the impression that Cooley had carte blanche forever. Sure enough, Cooley proved to be more street-smart than his peers, and soon understood that the wide berth he was receiving from the security detail was a favor returned—as long as he did not cross certain lines. Stansbury, the headmaster had always privately believed, needed intellectuals like Goldsmith *and* those who instinctively understood the concept of honor and pride, like Cooley. It added to the diversity and character of the specimen body. But alas, Cooley crossed the proverbial Rubicon of the headmaster's goodwill after the dopazone and Riley incidents. There was no more he could do for the boy.

President Lang, seated at the table to the headmaster's right, cleared her throat. "Ladies and gentlemen," she said, "this crime involves current and former Stansbury specimens. Our security detail officers were the first ones on the scene and our relations with the San Angeles Police Department are cordial. They will hopefully understand that we retain jurisdiction over this matter."

The headmaster glanced around and detected a universal sigh of relief passing through Mount Olympus.

Goldsmith descended from the atrium in an elevator pod and thought about the future. His future. There would be harsh consequences if the administration discovered he had been communicating with Cooley without their knowledge. All it would take was a single phone call from President Lang or the headmaster to Harvard or any other university he would have considered attending and, number one specimen at Stansbury or not, he'd be blackballed. The pod's digital display lit up as floors shot past: *49, 48, 47* . . .

He was putting himself in an unacceptably vulnerable position. And for what? Doing the "right thing"? Goldsmith wasn't sure if he was undertaking this responsibility out of moral concern for a fellow human being or simply because he enjoyed solving puzzles and flexing his cerebral muscles. Camilla had a point: William Winston Cooley was not worth sacrificing everything he had worked for over the years. And where did Cooley figure into the larger scheme of things, anyway? No institution was perfect, but Stansbury was close. Its accomplishments and triumphs saved the lives of millions, perhaps billions of people, and kept the progress of human civilization pumping. Every endeavor of historical significance had its own collateral damage. Great societies had been built on the sweat and blood of slaves, wars regularly took the lives of women and children in the process of restoring liberty, captains of industry revolutionized our way of life and got rich while laying off thousands of employees. Wasn't the life of one unbalanced specimen a reasonable exchange for the cure for cancer?

Just minutes ago, Cooley admitted he was using him. Not that this was a problem for a valedictorian of Goldsmith's caliber, retired or not. He knew he could easily tap Cooley for his knowledge about the Riley situation, keep him at bay by threatening to follow through on his dopazone confession—an expellable offense to which he did admit—perhaps threaten to go after Bunson and maybe even Sadie, if Cooley started causing difficulties. If Goldsmith had to, he'd cooperate with the administration in building a case against him. Worst-case scenario, he could go around Stansbury entirely and inform the police of Cooley's narcotics use and possession. Either way, he would be protected from any vengeance attempts.

The elevator pod dinged and stopped on Level 34. The doors slid open. Pete stepped inside.

"Good morning, Mr. Goldsmith. Studying hard?"

"Just taking a quick break."

"Really? Me too."

The doors slid closed. Pete reached over and jabbed the Stop button. The pod remained stationary. "What kind of trouble is Mr. Cooley in?" asked Pete.

"I don't know what you're talking about," said Goldsmith, feeling his heart begin to race. If Pete knew even this much, that Cooley was under investigation at all (not to mention for *what*), the school's image and reputation would be at risk fewer than twelve hours before the Senate committee's vote that evening.

"No?" Pete gave him a smug grin. "You might be interested to know that a guard named Harvey, down on the registration and reception level has let him off campus five times in the past five months."

"Who told you that?" Goldsmith knew his face was betraying him, could feel his eyes getting wider against his wishes, the veins in his neck and temples throbbing.

"Journalist's Number-One Rule: Never divulge your sources. You're sweating, Mr. Goldsmith. Pressure of being the flagship model specimen getting to you?" Pete released the Stop button. The doors slid open. Goldsmith couldn't get out of there fast enough. The doors closed behind him and he stood by himself in an empty corridor on Level 34, his mind racing.

Get it together. You're a pro. Run through your options:

#1: Find Captain Gibson and get him to detain Pete before he finds out anything else about the Riley-Cooley affair that could incriminate Stansbury.

#2: Get the administration's permission to start yanking specimens out of progressions and start interrogating them with the aim of finding out who'd been giving Pete his inside info and why, starting with the probable cognoscenti: Cooley, Sadie, Bunson, and yes, Camilla.

#3: Get the security detail to detain and question the registration and reception guard that Pete mentioned in connection with the Cooley case.

#4: Find the headmaster, disclose everything he'd learned this morning and convince him to send the security detail to follow up on the torn-out yearbook pages and missing gun that Cooley claimed he saw in Riley's apartment.

#5: Forget the whole thing, go back to your room, lock the door, and wait out the three days left before commencement.

Goldsmith ran through the calculus of probable timetables and behavioral possibilities. Option #5 was out of the question; it left too much of a possibility that Pete could write and publish an exposé on Stansbury in time to ruin the school's reputation and sink the Senate committee's vote—whereby Goldsmith's diploma wouldn't be worth the sheepskin it was printed on, and his reputation would go down in flames along with everyone else's. Options 1–4 were methodically logical and in his and Stansbury's best interests, but in all cases he would be passing control of the situation back over to the administration. And he'd never solve the puzzle of *why* Stansbury was so dead set on placing Cooley and Riley in that bathroom together as murderer and victim.

Stop.

Pretend you're Cooley for a moment. Stop thinking so hard. Stop playing angles. For the first time in your award-winning life, stop thinking and just act. He hit keys on his Tabula, connecting him to Universal Taxi. A cheerful chirp of an outsider answered on the other end of the call.

Time to take a field trip.

Down on Level 1, Harvey leaned back in his chair and zoned out on the sports section of the *San Angeles Times*. The San Angeles Lakers defeated the Mexico City Aztecs 101–99 in overtime last night. Big deal, thought Harvey: the double doses of lithium and Equimodes he rationed himself from Cooley's meds pack had taken hold, and the frontal lobes of his brain pulsated gently, the edges of his vision smoothed flat into a two-dimensional haze. The powdered sugar on the donut next to the paper looked like it was breathing. Harvey was glad they didn't make the staff inject their food. Some, like President Lang, wanted to, because they were (in his opinion) fanatics. He glanced up and saw a gaunt archangel in a Stansbury blazer standing before him on the other side of the desk, his golden hair looking like a halo . . .

"Mr. Goldsmith!" Harvey stammered as he jumped up to his feet and tried to shake off the buzz. His blurry vision did not afford him the humiliation of seeing Goldsmith roll his eyes at this pathetic, roly-poly man who couldn't even conceal his altered state with the skill of the most delinquent specimen. "Don't see you down here much," Harvey found himself saying. "What can I do you for, son?"

"Open the front gates for me. Now."

"I, uh, can't do that. Even for the valedictorian . . . policy says—"

"I'll make it worth your while."

Harvey cracked a grin, feeling that the tables were slightly turning now that this goody-two-shoes nerd was veering into the kind of talk he was used to. "Now, what could you possibly have that I'd want?"

"Inside information."

"Do tell. Although I should warn you I don't get my rocks off on Stansbury gossip like everyone else."

"Open the gates." Something in Goldsmith's voice and the intensity of his gaze sent a nervous reflex down Harvey's arm. His hand hit the air lock switch. The large titanium door past the waiting lounge area started to hiss. Goldsmith turned and headed toward the exit.

"Uhhh . . . Mr. Goldsmith?"

"The security detail is coming for you," he said, not looking back. "You now have a three-minute head start."

Goldsmith disappeared into the desert rainstorm outside the tower. Harvey's stomach started to feel all ticklish and queasy. His legs went weak and he fell back into his chair before bouncing back up, glancing to his left and right. Around the corner, he heard an elevator pod ding, announcing its arrival, and several sets of footsteps. Then he heard another series of hisses as the front gates slid closed again behind Goldsmith. As much as the meds coursing through his veins told him to slow down, the fear in his heart told him to run. He took two steps, knocked the donut and newspaper to the floor, and moved away from the approaching rumbles of boots echoing against the marble floors as fast as his stubby feet and legs could carry him.

Up on Level 52, the headmaster glanced around at his fellow educators, letting the sure looks in their eyes feed his own confidence and authority, which in turn bounced back to them, creating a sense of unalterable destiny of purpose in the room. They were teachers, each and every last one of them, charged with the highest responsibility of all: the nurturing and care of this nation's youth. The headmaster was not so hubristic as to assume that the school created the prodigy in its population. He and his old friend Raymond Stansbury always believed that genius existed in the soul of each and every child born on the face of this planet. Some would be doctors, others sculptors, yet others would be warm, understanding mothers to a future generation of geniuses who would one day keep the human race alive and well with their efforts. No, Stansbury School did not create geniuses. It was merely a vessel the specimens rode on their journey to adulthood, a place where they could blossom and soar. Even at the age of seventy, this thought was still enough to bring tears to his eyes.

"Fellow teachers," he said, projecting his voice into a lush octave of beatitude, "in this time of adversity, let me remind you of Matthew 5:14. 'You are the light of the world. A city set on a mountain cannot be hidden. They do not light a lamp and then put it under a bushel basket. It is set on a lamp stand, where it gives light to all in the house. Your light must shine before others, that they may see your good deeds and glorify your heavenly Father.' Amen."

Across the room, the headmaster saw the image of Professor Partridge broadcast on a hanging plasma screen. Partridge rose up from his desk, the one cluttered with flowers and champagne, and stood at attention, bringing his hands together. His applause began slowly and then got faster. Then the claps became louder and louder, filling the entire room. Seventy-one pairs of strong hands—teachers' hands—came together in an ovation that restored the headmaster's faith in their mission and higher purpose.

Stansbury, he thought, will survive this. It will survive the passing of each and every one of the men and women in this room, himself included. Because it must. Because the world so desperately needs it.

In his dorm room on Level 9, Cooley sat at his work terminal and strapped his wrist cuff on after plugging it into the back of his computer. He was too proud to show it at the time, but Goldsmith's bombshell about there being no polygraph/Pentothal session hit him hard, tamping down the full-bore volume of his defiance into the kind of futile sensation common to those who do not control their own fate. Cooley navigated to the Dopazone domain site and transferred the last thirty-four dollars in this bank account so he could refill his stash. He didn't even bother locking the door. What was the point? Dopazone was small beans compared to killing a guy. He already admitted to doing drugs on the record, and Stansbury didn't seem to care. The only guys who did seem to give a shit about anything lately were Goldsmith and himself. And that was only because they were using each other out of selfish needs.

Cooley hit the familiar Return key and let the flood of narcotic ions take him away to another place. He leaned back in the chair and saw the long glass doors of that house in the distance, and Mom's frantic, shortened gasps punctuating the soundtrack. Everything cut to that window—golden sunlight pouring through—and then . . . wait. It was different. She was saying something. Talking to him. Her voice wasn't quivering anymore. He eased himself out of the trip just slightly, trying to take that bare big toe out of the warm pool of water and back up onto the cold, sterile deck under an artificial sky.

"Is it true?" she asked. No, Mommy. I didn't do it. Nobody understands . . . "I heard it's true. That it makes you see this beautiful light." What? Cooley forced his eyes open and blinked the luster away. The flashing spots cleared. There was Sadie, the door to his room closing behind her. Her hair looked just like that brightness squeezing through Mom's window. Cooley ripped off the cuff and tossed it to the side. It's not like Sadie never knew that he and the guys got high, but he still never liked getting caught in the act.

"I wasn't—" he started as she walked over to him as the circulation started to return to his legs.

"I heard it makes you see a beautiful light," she said. "Come on, tell me. What does it make you see?"

"It makes me see you."

She smiled and brushed the long ambrosial hair from her face. "Liar," she whispered into his ear. The way the word rolled off her lips let him know she was grinning. Sadie straddled him, wrapping her legs around his waist as his work terminal chair rolled them along the glimmering white marble tile across the room.

"I see . . . sunshine," he whispered back. He felt her lips against his neck, knew he smelled raw from the night and day, loved her even more because she knew too and didn't care.

"What else?"

"My mother's voice. It echoes."

She pulled back, loosened his tie and started to unbutton his white dress shirt. He looked over at the Nature & Co. window and saw a dirt road that wound through a forest. Cooley was certain it went on forever. His shirt fell to the floor, getting tangled in the wheels of the chair.

Cooley stared at her, taking in every detail of Sadie's face—the curl of the eyelashes, the perfect arc of the lips, the subtle curve of the neck—as if this would be the last time he ever made love to her. Looking at her like this was something he always did. He did it out of unabashed appreciation, and she always returned the favor. From the beginning, they never bothered switching off the lights or even closing their eyes because neither of them was interested in casting shadows on the presence of the other or cloaking any sort of bodily flaw out of teenage insecurity. When it came to sex, Cooley and Sadie preferred the experience pure and unadulterated, with everything— the wonderful and sensual as well as the damaged—bared for the other to see.

April 2, 2035, was the first time for either of them. They had been a couple for just about one month and, while they had not discussed openly the prospect of taking each other's virginity—as opposed to the rest of their prudish, gossipy peers, most of whom had already made informal wagers as to when Sadie would inevitably succumb to Cooley's charms—it was something they both wanted and decided that when it did happen, it would happen naturally.

April 2 was Sadie's birthday and that year she was turning seventeen. Cooley made certain that he would align as many stars as he could in order to provide her with the most special day possible. She woke up to a bouquet of while calla lilies, real ones he'd smuggled into the tower from the outside world just hours before. He loved the way their elegant bulbs, their scent, and even the occasional wrinkles of imperfection on their petals made a mockery of the picturesque scenery broadcast on the Nature & Co. window in her room. The flowers were accompanied by a data disk for her Tabula, which contained a dozen pieces of music that Cooley had uploaded; and each song— selections from his favorite old rock bands like the Cure, Interpol, and the Strokes—was prefaced by his recorded explanations for why a certain lyric made him think of her.

But the crowning gift he had procured would have to wait until dinner. Over the years, Sadie had taken to the intravenous food diet and actually quite liked it, but she always missed the raspberry tarts from Bubble Bakery that her mother bought for her when she was a little girl growing up in New York City. Ever since she started attending Stansbury, Sadie's brief trips home twice a year were so jam-packed with visits from extended family, along with the carefully engineered social and cultural event schedule her parents regularly laid out, that indulging in desserts—even those golden brown pastries topped with powdered sugar and filled with a warm, sweet berry filling—were the last thing for which she had time. But she always remembered those

Bubble Bakery tarts. She compared any tasty liquefied treat inside the tower to them and had a habit of describing them as "better than sex," even though she was, of course, a virgin. So in the days leading up to Sadie's seventeenth birthday, Cooley did everything in his power to get ahold of one for her. Since hand-and-mouth food was extremely difficult to come by inside the school, he offered two weeks' worth of meds to Harvey down in registration and reception if he would call Bubble Bakery in New York and ask them to overnight one of their famous tarts in time for April 2.

Harvey came through. He brought Cooley the parcel just before dinner hour, and inside was a beautiful, small yellow Bubble Bakery box wrapped with a beige bow. Cooley peeked inside and took a look at the prize for himself: a palm-size tart with a perfectly woven network of fresh pastry covering the glistening filling of dark red raspberry. He shaved, carefully combed his hair, straightened his tie, and discreetly brought the box into the cafeteria. Bunson was waiting for him, holding down the secluded table for two where Sadie had planned to meet him for the meal. He set the final gift of the day on the table and waited. Everything felt perfect and his heart throbbed, eager and warm, as the place started to fill up with specimens. He simply could not wait to see the look on her face and felt so lucky just to be a part of her life.

"Cooley," came a deep, scratchy voice. Cooley glanced up and saw Mr. Charles Lawrence Banks, a huge, and unbalanced, senior specimen, one of several for whom Cooley did the favor of serving as a cash-carrying middleman to drug dealers during his trips out to San Angeles. Banks and his buddies would give Cooley the money to make the illegal purchases and the dealers kicked ten percent back to him as a service fee.

"Yeah?" Cooley replied. Some of Banks's goons walked over.

"You look dapper. Special occasion?"

"Sadie's birthday." Banks set an envelope down on the table. Cooley knew there was money inside and felt a twinge of annoyance that these guys were ruining the gaiety of his special dinner. "Keep it," he said, sliding the envelope back toward Banks. "I was in San Angeles last night. I can't tap Harvey for favors every day. Someone's gonna notice. Come back next week. I'll make a run for you then."

Banks slammed a big palm against the table. Veins popped up in his neck and temples. His eyes were bloodshot. It's the BryleTran, Cooley thought: a snortable, powdery blend of opiates derived from crystal methamphetamine with strains of testosterone to keep the high going longer and prevent the muscles from getting strung out and weak. It was a great concept, except for the fact that it was as addictive as old-school crystal meth and the testosterone sent users into violent fits at the drop of a hat. Like the kind Cooley was witnessing at that moment.

"Bullshit," Banks hissed. "I was gonna make you go now, but since it's your girl's birthday, I'll make an exception and let you do it right after dinner." Cooley glanced around for Bunson, but the table he'd picked for Sadie's birthday was nestled in a corner, out of the sight of most of the cafeteria. "I'm a reasonable guy," said Banks. "So just do it, huh?"

Cooley simmered, pissed that Banks was talking to him like this and ordering him around like an errand boy, but he reminded himself that it was Sadie's day. He felt his forehead start to sweat from the simple exertion of restraining himself from opening his mouth. His carefully combed locks of hair began to fall, sliding down his forehead and into his face and eyes. Phys-D tactics automatically flashed through his mind. He could take these guys. But not today. Today was not about him. At this moment, his fury would stay pent up, under control, like he was just another obedient specimen.

Banks picked up the envelope of cash and leaned down, pressing it into Cooley's chest with his index finger. "There's enough in there for twenty-eight doses," said Banks, the drugs from his last fix giving him a bravado he didn't really possess. "Don't make me regret going easy on you." He sat himself down on the tabletop for emphasis. One of his big buttocks crushed the side of the Bubble Bakery box. Cooley looked down at Banks's finger, which was still jammed against his sternum. Banks's goons were all grinning. The BryleTran overrode their med cycle conditioning, nullified the beta blockers. If push came to shove, these guys weren't gonna hold back. And maybe, Cooley thought, that suited him just fine.

He locked eyes with Banks. "I'll go when I'm good and ready," he said, losing the control he had been telling himself to maintain but feeling an enormous wave of relief at the sensation of cutting loose. And then it bubbled over. "And get that fuckin' finger out of my face before I rip it off and shove it up your ass."

Banks's fat buttock crushed the box a little more. "Oh yeah? Well I—"

Cooley grabbed his finger and snapped it like a candy cane. Banks's eyes bulged. Cooley leaned back in his chair and kicked him in the face, catching his jaw and knocking him off the table. He felt a pair of hands grab him from behind and a fist slam against the side of his skull. One of Banks's BryleTran-juiced buddies yanked him up and threw him down against the table. Cooley felt the Bubble Bakery box smash under his body before Banks himself pinned him against the wall and started pummeling him with his uninjured left hand. Cooley crumpled to the floor, curling into a fetal position to shield himself from the shower of punches and kicks, and through eyes that were already close to being swollen shut he saw a team of detail officers shove gawking specimens aside in their rush to stop the brawl from getting any more gruesome.

By the time Sadie arrived, the only remnant of the incident that was left was the crushed Bubble Bakery box with a mutilated raspberry tart inside, its burgundy innards spilling forth and staining the white marble floor below, more collateral damage along the grim path of Cooley's life. She reached her fingertip toward the box, pulled away some of the golden crust and jam and brought it to her lips. Her heart flooded with warmth, both from the sweet taste and the knowledge that someone loved her so much.

She went to the infirmary and patiently waited the two hours it took for school medics to examine him. Bunson stopped by at one point and gave the news to Sadie to pass onto Cooley: the Class of 2035's valedictorian peer-reviewed the witnesses and promptly told Captain Gibson that Banks was a lunatic and Cooley acted in self-defense. Banks had already been removed from the tower and sent home.

After Cooley was ready to take visitors, Sadie walked into the room where he was being kept and stared. The left side of his face was purple and bruised. Both of his eyes were blackened. The head medic told her that three of his fingers were broken and that he had a cracked rib to go along with multiple contusions. He said Cooley refused all offers of painkillers and then the medic left them alone, shaking his head in resignation as he closed the door behind him. She walked over to Cooley's bed and touched his cheek.

"I'm so sorry," he mumbled through split, puffy lips.

"It's okay."

"It's not. No matter how hard I try to get things right, I always ruin them in the end. It makes me sick, but I can't help it."

Sadie held his hand, felt his puffy, purpled fingers and ran her palm against his smashed nails. She touched his swelled eyelids and smiled. "You're so beautiful," she said.

He watched as she locked the door to the room and walked back over to him, unbuttoning her white shirt as she stood there underneath the harsh fluorescent lighting. Cooley gazed at her. Her bra slid to the floor and she stepped out of her pleated gray skirt. He thought it was absurd, looking so monstrous and battered, reaching his arm out to this gloriously perfect naked girl, pulling her down on top of him, even though the pressure of her warm body made his bruises sting. The bedsheets slid to the side and he felt her hands on him, embarrassed that he roused so slowly for the first time they were going to make love, but then found himself relieved because the worst thing in the world would be for it to end too quickly. He wanted it to last forever: after it was over they would have to go back to their engineered lives in the tower. But for that series of moments, the taste and feel of Sadie's flesh made the pain racking his body subside—her taste and smells soothed those wounds both external and, perhaps more important, the ones lodged deep inside his mind and his heart.

Afterward, as Sadie lay next to him in that infirmary bed, she looked at the wounds that covered his slim frame. He shuddered and flinched in his sleep and each time he did, she stroked his head and whispered, "shhh . . ." in the hopes that he would rest peacefully, if only for a minute or two.

Cooley snapped back into the reality of his bedroom, of Riley's dead body, of Goldsmith, and glanced at his Nature & Co. window and the dirt path it displayed.

"What were you talking about with Goldsmith this morning?" she asked.

"When?" How did she know about that?

"In the atrium. After breakfast."

"Were you spying on me?"

"No. I was late to my progression and I saw you on my way there."

"It . . . it was nothing."

"It was a little strange, is what it was. I thought you two hated each other."

"The less you know, the better." She rolled away from him. "Look, Sadie, it's for your own good, okay?"

"I wouldn't trust him, if I were you," she said, not facing him.

"You don't even know him."

"Neither do you."

Cooley pulled her over on top of him, feeling the warm softness of her body against his. Her hair fell down around his face, tickling his cheeks. He ran his fingers down the ridge of her back and felt the tension leave her muscles. He looked her in the eye. "If I had to run, would you come with me?"

"Run where?" she asked, her cheek against the skin on his shoulder.

"Just say yes or no."

"Yes."

"Even if I was in a lot of trouble?" Fear made Cooley's voice crack just a little bit.

"Shhh," she whispered. "Yes." He pressed his face against Sadie's soft mane. It smelled like summer. His eyes welled up with tears and some spilled out, making stray hairs cling to his nose and chin. "Where would we go?" he heard her ask. He choked back a sob and focused on the winding, digitized forest path on the Nature & Co. window.

"Anywhere but here."

Way out in the D Sector of San Angeles, Goldsmith stood on the iron fire escape outside the late Riley's bathroom and watched the gyro-taxi that whisked him away from the tower disappear into the swarm of traffic high above. When the cabbie first picked him up, Goldsmith was almost certain they would fall off the end of a flat Earth, rather than cruise the hundred or so miles to San Angeles without incident. The school's constant warnings about leaving campus unsupervised

ran through his head the entire ride, despite the fact that those ad-
monitions were geared toward intimidating little boys, rather than
grown men on the verge of graduation: robbers and kidnappers were
waiting just outside the tower's walls; the impure city air would
cause tumors in specimens' healthy lungs; the countless tales of
specimens who left the tower and were never heard from again . . .
The silly list went on and on. And in spite of accepted wisdom, here
he was.

He was familiar enough with the apartment layout from the security detail's incident report. Cooley and Officer Jamison went through
the bathroom window right there. The wooden window frame was
still lined with shards of broken glass. A web of yellow plastic barriers
labeled DO NOT ENTER had been stretched across the window. Riley—
who Cooley said took the handgun inside the bathroom—was pro-
nounced dead right inside there, on the floor in front of the sink.
Cooley claimed the gun was nowhere to be seen upon his entry. That
hallway past the bathroom door led to the hovel's living room, where
the hiding spot and the yearbook pages that Cooley mentioned were
located. Goldsmith pulled off a few of the yellow banners and poked
his head inside the bathroom as the heavy storm outside soaked
through his blazer and shirt. It was quiet inside. His heart began to
pound and the rain on his palms mixed with clammy sweat. Right
now, you're not Mr. Goldsmith, he thought. You're brass-balled, unbalanced specimen Mr. Cooley. So cut the hemming and hawing.

He hopped through the window space, landing with a soft thud on
the tile next to the black outline of Riley's body drawn on the floor.
Except for the soft syncopation of the rain against the fire escape outside, it was silent. He glanced in the corners, behind the toilet, under
the sink, but did not find Riley's gun. File it away as a missing piece of
the evidence puzzle. Goldsmith eased open the bathroom door and
stepped through, taking in the combination living room and kitchen.
He had never been inside the apartment of a dead man before, and
imagined it would be eerie, dark, the air slightly stale. But it still
looked very much lived-in; the television was illuminated and muted,
and dirty clothes were strewn across an old sofa.

Two more steps inside the living room and he saw the coffee
table—there was nothing on its surface, because the detail probably

bagged whatever was there as evidence—and a red rug with brown stains on the floor. He kneeled down and pulled it up, tapping the wooden planks beneath. One of them sounded hollow. He lifted it up. Inside, he saw stacks of cash and, just like Cooley said, several torn-out sheets of yearbook photos with dozens of rows of black-and-white head shots of specimens.

Goldsmith grabbed them. The text in the bottom right-hand corner identified them as six pages from the 2033 edition. There: four red X's through faces he didn't recognize, along with two unmarked pages with circles around two more specimen faces. There was Riley on one and . . . Goldsmith looked closer, thinking it must have been a mistake: the other circled face belonged to none other than Miss Stella Saltzman.

Stella. She was four years older than him and the most accomplished valedictorian he'd seen during his twelve years in the tower. Being younger and a nobody for the majority of his time at Stansbury, Goldsmith always admired her from afar, but he would've been more than happy to kiss the hem of her top-ranked uniform had he been given the chance. After his Selmer-Dubonnet victory was announced in the school newsletter back in September, he was shocked to receive a short note in the mail from Miss Saltzman bearing her congratulations. He wasn't sure what she was doing now—she was probably twenty-one years old and maybe even a college graduate. What the hell did she have to do with a burnout like Riley?

Goldsmith stepped back and heard an alarm ring out. Damn. He froze, quickly realizing what had happened, and then grabbed the stacks of Riley's cash—a makeshift slush fund for the Free Cooley Movement, grand membership total of two specimens, which included Cooley himself—stuffing them along with the stray yearbook pages in his blazer's inside pockets. He shoved the wooden plank into its place and moved back the rug. Over the alarm, he heard the sound of heavy boots pounding down the hallway toward the apartment's front door. That was stupid, he thought. He knew security detail procedure and should've anticipated the trip wire laser. If they had ThermaGuns, he was finished . . . unless he could make it to the pedestrian traffic down on the sidewalk before they could lock onto his body's heat patterns: it was against policy to fire into a crowd of outsiders. The footsteps got closer. He could turn himself in, talk his way out of this, and knew he could convince Gibson that he was only trying to follow up on a lead and protect the school from Pete while procuring more evidence against Cooley.

But then he wouldn't know the answer to the only question he cared about: *Why?*

Come on. You're Mr. William Winston Cooley, bad-assed brawler, daredevil extraordinaire, man of action. What do you do? The answer to that question hit Goldsmith while he was already sprinting down the fire escape ladder, his long legs taking the steps three at a time.

You fucking run, of course.

17

Goldsmith's feet hit the pavement below the fire es-
cape. The fact that he was still up and running was his only indication
that the security detail had not gotten a ThermaGun lock on him yet.
It was not even worth worrying about. He could only keep going. If
they pulled the trigger, he wouldn't have more than two seconds to
consider the awful ramifications anyway. He sprinted down the alley,
instinctively dodging puddles to his left and right while covering forty
yards of pavement in roughly four and a half seconds (the agility and
hand–eye coordination training from that tenth grade Gymnastics
progression he hated was paying off, just like the school said it
would). He dashed into the crowds in the street around the corner
and looked back over his shoulder.

Three detail officers had him in their sights. Assume they've sent
word to their gyros to cut off all paths of flight in a ten-block radius.
Also assume they've made a positive identification of the fugitive,
namely him. And if that were the case, even if Goldsmith did escape
them and managed to get back to the tower, they would be waiting

when he arrived. He could maybe use up twelve years of goodwill and appeal directly to the headmaster . . . But at that moment, the priority was buying enough time to put together the mystery of these yearbook pages in his pocket. He squeezed his way into another heavy wave of pedestrian traffic on its way to lunch hour and ricocheted between strangers. They were still behind him: three officers in Tac IX utility vests moving fast, pulling off their black Nomex balaclavas (Goldsmith recognized them: Tannen, O'Shaunnessy, and Willets—nice guys, detail veterans) to ostensibly blend in with a packed street that didn't seem to pay them much heed in the first place. They were closing the gap. He ducked into another alley and sprinted for an alternate route that might be hidden between the huge D Sector towers. Twenty feet inside the alley, he froze. Two uniformed San Angeles cops were strolling toward him. One twirled a humming shock stick in his hand.

"Is everything all right, son?" asked the man on the left.

"You need some help?" inquired his partner.

Goldsmith realized they were just two police officers patrolling their beat, oblivious to the mess he was stuck in. His mind sped through the list of possible choices and probabilities given the addition of this new element to the equation of his perhaps ill-advised flight from the security detail. Asking for their help was not an option.

Goldsmith saw their badges. The one with the shock stick was Barnes and the other was named Morrison. "Hey kid, you okay?" asked Morrison.

"Yes, Officer, I just—" Goldsmith watched as Barnes caught sight of the Stansbury crest on his blazer.

"Morrison," hissed Barnes, turning pale, "he's a goddamned specimen. One of those Stansbury kids." He raised his shock stick and began circling Goldsmith, keeping him at arm's length. Morrison whipped out a pair of handcuffs, held one hand in front of him as if he was trying to placate a rabid dog, and inched closer. Goldsmith wasn't surprised. When it came to specimens, the SAPD trained their officers to subdue first and ask questions later.

"Here you go, kid . . . everything's gonna be just fine . . . you just stay right there," said Morrison, reaching out with the cuffs. "I'm just gonna slip these on you, and if you cooperate nobody's gonna get hurt."

Goldsmith's heart kept its slow, steady beat padding along. He was not nervous. He saw everything happening in slow motion. His mind was shouting *run run run* but his body was not responding. Med cycle conditioning. Beta blockers. Just like that day at Guernica; he felt the essence of his impulses—nothing less than his free will—tugging with all its might at this pharmaceutical leash that kept his body in check. He refused to let it end like this. The cop started to reach toward him.

"I'm sorry, gentlemen," Goldsmith heard himself say.

"Sorry for what?" said Morrison. An instant later, Goldsmith's right hand grabbed the cop's cuff-wielding arm and snapped it down. Morrison yelped in pain and reached for his gun. Goldsmith kept riding his Phys-D conditioning, surfing this wave of pure, concentrated, effortless action. He cracked Morrison in the face with his fist and swung him into the path of Barnes's woefully predictable shock stick swing. Barnes connected with his partner's body, knocking him out. Goldsmith let Morrison fall to the pavement but held onto the handcuffs. Barnes let out a primal holler of terror and rushed him with the shock stick. Goldsmith ducked a mighty swing—the electrically charged steel whizzing past his ear—and saw eight countermove variations flash before his eyes. He opted for number four, slipping a steel handcuff around his fist. He paused, saw the right opening, and let an uppercut fly into Barnes's jaw. He heard some of the cop's teeth crack and felt the man's blood spatter—warm and obscene—on his face. Both would-be captors lay prone before him. Goldsmith wiped Barnes's blood from himself and was ready to start feeling the gut grinding of fear any time now. It never came.

"I'm sorry I wasn't smart enough to figure out a better way than this," Goldsmith said as he ran toward the crowded street on the far end of the alley. And, he thought to himself, I'm sorry for breaking our oath, Dr. Stansbury. Forgive me, Doc. You always talked about honor with a capital H. And somehow I think losing it is a hell of a lot easier than getting it back.

Hit the street. Stick with the crowd. Go with the flow. Keep the obstacles between you and the detail as numerous as possible. He glanced back into the alley and saw officers Tannen, O'Shaunnessy, and Willets leaping over the injured SAPD guys he'd left in his wake. Suddenly, Goldsmith felt a hand grip his arm.

"Hey! You're one of those Stansbury kids!" came the voice to which the hand belonged. Goldsmith looked over and saw a toothless bum wearing a too-small suit that smelled like stale piss. His beard was missing chunks of hair, patches of smooth, dirty skin punctuating spots on his face, like he shaved his own personal crop circles. As soon as the word "Stansbury" lisped out of the guy's mouth, Goldsmith saw heads in the crowd around him turn to stare. A gang of kids—outsiders about his own age—looked over. A guide leading a group of tourists in track suits stopped in midsentence and discreetly motioned with his head for the group to catch a glimpse of this exotic creature before it got startled and flew away forever. The tourists closed in around Goldsmith, creating a traffic jam. The distance between him and the detail had suddenly gotten much more crowded, a mob of people packing the street full.

"Sir!" called out a tourist, grabbing Goldsmith by the arm and pulling him away from the bum like he was a coveted toy doll on a store shelf during the Christmas rush. "Can you sign this paper here? Do you mind? Make it out to my son . . . He just applied for the Stansbury admissions packet!" Goldsmith looked over the man's shoulder at the officers: they were pissed, stuck in gridlock and barking into microphones helplessly. Goldsmith took the paper and pen from the tourist, giving him his best Welcome to Stansbury Tower smile.

"Of course," he replied. "What's your son's name?"

The tourist smiled back, grateful. His group pressed in closer, surrounding Goldsmith and clutching their own pens and papers, waiting patiently in line. "Make it out to Billy," he said. Goldsmith started scribbling a message, slowly and surely moving toward the pedestrian traffic wranglers' batons he spied in the corner of his eye down the block in the direction of the San Angeles monorail track. There was a train in the station. Its doors slid open. He handed back the paper and pen, then took another paper and pen from a different tourist. He felt the masses obediently give way to his body move-ment and momen-tum, anything to keep this rare catch from getting irritated and running off. Leaning them slightly to the right, Goldsmith succeeded in shifting into the channel of pedestrians headed for the wranglers. The tour group followed. The detail officers were way back there now. Here came the wranglers, big, stocky guys. They slid Goldsmith past without even looking at him. He felt a fluorescent white baton against his ribs and waist as he was thrust inside the monorail car. It filled up to its 150-person capacity. The doors slid shut. Goldsmith kept on smiling and signing autographs as he watched Tannen, O'Shaunnessy, and Willets far off on the other side of the rain-streaked glass door. There was a soft beep and the monorail hummed to life. They got smaller and smaller in the distance.

Once the Universal Taxi ascended to cruising altitude and headed back toward the tower, Goldsmith carefully pulled out the yearbook pages and unfolded them. There was Stella Saltzman. There was Riley. Who else have we got? The faces crossed out with red X's in chronological order of pages: Mr. William Alvarez, Miss Monica Miller, Mr. Alberto Munoz Santana, and Mr. Daniel Ford Smith. None of them looked familiar. The only name on the six pages that had any academic distinction was Stella's. He studied the faces. Alvarez had curly dark hair and his eyes were opened extra-wide, like he was mugging for the camera. Miss Miller had pinned-back eyes, dilated pupils. She was tripping on something potent, maybe illicit drugs; whatever it was must have been stronger than regulation meds. Santana and Smith just looked plain thuggish. Smith's shoulders were huge. They took up the entire bottom part of the photograph. And then there was Riley: funny cowlicks in his hair, a skinny geek.

Goldsmith didn't need any fancy pills to help him figure out the most relevant thing they had in common: death. He closed his eyes and felt the gyrotaxi roll into a sudden sideways tilt, getting nauseous for a moment before he realized that gyroscopic engines didn't fail; it was just the sensation of his own mind going haywire. Goldsmith glanced down at the pages in his lap. His hands were clutching at them, the last remnants of a fairy tale he always loved but would never believe in again. Through the dark storm clouds, the tower rose in the distance.

———

It was quiet and calm inside the registration and reception lobby. Goldsmith walked through the air lock door expecting to see a phalanx of detail officers waiting for him, but there was only a uniformed guard—not Harvey. The guard saw him and jumped up from his seat, standing at attention.

"Mr. Goldsmith, sir!"

"Good afternoon." Keep on walking, he thought. Don't hesitate and arouse suspicion . . .

"Sir?"

"Yes?"

"You were . . . um, authorized to be off campus, right?"

"Yes." Just make it to the elevator pod. It was right there. Behind him, Goldsmith heard the guard rustling through papers at his desk. Goldsmith pressed the Up button and waited impatiently for the pod to arrive.

"Would you mind signing the entry log for . . ." The elevator dinged and the doors slid open. Goldsmith quickly stepped in and started to catch his breath.

"You're dripping wet, son," said Captain Gibson. Goldsmith didn't even notice him standing quietly in the corner of the pod. The doors slid closed but the pod remained stationary. He realized his shirt, pants, blazer, and hair were all still damp from his adventure in San Angeles.

"That guard at the desk spilled a glass of water on me," he responded, instantly realizing how absurd this sounded.

"Cut the shit. You were at Riley's pad. You went off campus without authorization, poked around a crime scene, and fled from the detail and—"

"Sir, I—," he began, but Gibson grabbed him by the neck and slammed him against the pod wall. Goldsmith started to choke under the pressure of his huge hand. Gibson got in his face.

"—and you coldcocked two San Angeles cops! Have you lost your fucking mind?" Goldsmith couldn't breathe. Gasps were coming out muted. He felt veins bulge in his neck beneath Gibson's palm. "They're both in the hospital, one with a broken nose and arm and the other with a fractured jaw, you dumb sonofabitch! You might've just set back specimen–outsider relations by ten years." Gibson finally let go. He gulped air back into his lungs. Gibson watched. "And you somehow overrode your med cycle conditioning to put that kind of hurt on those poor bastards. If your ass weren't graduating so soon, I'd probably give a shit." Goldsmith knew the relief was showing on his face. "Besides," said Gibson, picking up on it. "There's still the matter of Cooley."

"That's why I did all of this in the first place, sir," Goldsmith said, finally breathing regularly again. "I was following up on a lead."

Gibson studied him. "What lead?" he asked. Goldsmith ran through the scenario in his head and hoped his face didn't show the synapses firing in his brain. Don't flinch, he thought. Don't hesitate. Get your lies straight. Throw him some pure, unbridled rectitude.

"I confronted Mr. Cooley after our session this morning. I saw an opportunity and took it. There's too much at stake before the Senate committee's vote today for me to have gone by the book."

"More than you know," Gibson said.

"You need me. You need my brain. So please explain what you mean by that, sir."

"You're not crucial to anyone, Mr. Goldsmith. But I'll tell you anyway. Given the huge crime rate in San Angeles, the police department's overworked. Very badly. During periods where crime spikes, it can take them days to get to routine murder cases."

"Including Mr. Riley's."

"Yes. And even though the backlog is bad for the city, it happens to be good for us. We need to get this case solved, detailed, and delivered on a silver platter to the SAPD before they can get their people working on it and assume jurisdiction. After the stunt you pulled on those two cops today, the smart money says that time will come sooner than later. We've got nothing to hide, but the inevitable media frenzy will drag this school's name through the mud."

"And the Senate's trillion-dollar grant will be frozen."

"That's right. So why don't you tell me what Cooley said that got you riled to blatantly violate basic school policy."

"He said that Mr. Riley had a gun and was acting paranoid, like he was expecting a hostile visitor. Cooley claims that gun disappeared when he found Riley dead in the bathroom."

"Riley was killed with a laser syringe filled with a still-unidentified poison."

"I know. But the gun seemed like a missing link worth following up on. Firearms are traceable. Cooley intimated there was another murder suspect. And frankly, we haven't established what motive he may have had, if any." That's right, Goldsmith thought, lead him away from those yearbook pages in your pocket. Give up the evidence that you didn't find. Sit on your new lead and see what develops. Keep your control. "Riley had to have gotten the gun from someone," he continued. "That person might be able to give us evidence that incriminates Cooley or whoever else could be involved."

"Did you find the gun?"

"No."

"Cooley's guilty. He was just trying to buy himself time."

There went that air of zealous certainty again. Just like in the observation room following his peer review this morning. "Captain," Goldsmith began, "I understand that Mr. Cooley is the primary suspect, but—"

"Save your breath, son. We're about to take a little trip."

"A trip?"

Gibson swiped his key card against the pod's sensor and there was a beep. He pressed the disciplinary level's unmarked button. The pod hummed to life. Gibson gave him a thin smile. Goldsmith felt a plantation of tiny goose bumps explode across his body.

"And one more thing, kid."

"Yes, sir?"

"Keep your hands in your pockets. They're filthy."

Goldsmith flinched and looked down: his formerly pristine palms, knuckles, and fingertips were caked with dried, burnt red flakes of blood from men whose names he had already forgotten.

Goldsmith followed Gibson down the disciplinary level corridor in silence, passing one examination room after another. They came to a stop outside Observation Room #6. Gibson opened the door and nodded for him to enter. Goldsmith stepped inside and looked around: the gang was all here. President Lang, the headmaster, and detail officers Jackson and Jamison. Gibson shut the door behind him. Lang smiled at Goldsmith and the headmaster gave him a curt nod. Jackson and Jamison ignored him. Either Lang and the headmaster didn't know about his field trip to Riley's apartment or they didn't care. And besides, it wasn't Goldsmith who was in the hot seat.

Through the one-way glass inside the adjoining examination room stood Harvey in his black standard-issue underwear briefs and nothing else. He was soaking wet and shivering. Rolls of fat spilled over his elastic waistline. Goldsmith could see Harvey's chilly breath as it poured from his mouth in fits and starts. He glanced at the examination room's temperature display: forty-five degrees Fahrenheit. Through the one-way mirror a beep echoed, and the large circular showerhead above Harvey unleashed a stream of refrigerated water, which made his whole body tense up. He did not move from where he stood because someone had instructed him that if he stepped out of the water's path, moved even an inch, things would get much, much worse.

"Please!" Harvey cried to no one in particular. "Don't put me in here with one of the specimens!"

Goldsmith saw the door handle to the examination room turn and knew exactly what was coming next. A detail officer held open the door. Camilla stepped inside. She was wearing a navy blue Stansbury cloak over her shoulders cinched around her neck by a golden clasp in the shape of the school's emblem. It billowed around her long legs, coming to an end just above her knee socks. Her hair was pulled back as usual, but she was not wearing her glasses. For the first time, Goldsmith realized that they made her eyes softer. She walked up to Harvey and stopped about one foot away. At five feet and eleven inches, she easily towered over him. Camilla 2.0 looked at Harvey with her hard, icy eyes, affixing him with her gaze. It occurred to Goldsmith that Homer would have described it as "the terrible gaze of gray-eyed Athena."

"I . . . I still have to use the bathroom," Harvey said. "I asked out loud but nobody was here to—"

"That is not an option," said Camilla. Goldsmith noticed that her stage voice was a shade lower than normal. Her strategy was to reduce Harvey to a primal state, the kind where all of his worldly needs were reduced to basic impulses: he was either too hot or too cold, he needed to move his bowels but was not allowed, he could not sit down and make himself comfortable, he could not doze off, he could not eat, no one answered the questions he asked, even though he must have known he was under careful observation. The situation had been orchestrated so that there was only one person in his world, the valedictorian, and the only thing he could do to alleviate the discomfort of that world was to answer the questions she posed. She had done a splendid job of setting Harvey up, Goldsmith concluded. How long had she dreamed about this moment? How long had she waited to assume the responsibilities of being number one? Twelve years? Her whole life?

"As an employee of this institution," she began. "You were entrusted with the well-being of the specimens."

"I . . . I know."

"So why did you allow Mr. Cooley to leave campus?"

"He was . . . he was gonna pick up clean piss for me and him and a bunch of other specimens." Harvey paused, looking at her in unabashed fear. "Can I go now?" A large cloud of his frantic breath rose to the ceiling.

"Why did you need clean urine samples?"

"Cooley gave me meds and I had to pass the test, too."

"Jesus Christ," muttered Gibson in the observation room. "Med-addicted registration and reception guard allows dopazone-addicted specimen to travel off campus grounds . . ."

"And for the record," continued Camilla, "this was not the first time you allowed him to leave. There were also incidents on November 15 and December 9, 2035, and January 21 and February 17, 2036, leading up to the final transgression yesterday, on March 29, 2036."

"I was . . . just trying to help the kid out. What does it matter to you if—"

"Those dates correspond exactly with the unsolved deaths of five Stansbury graduates. The security detail and San Angeles Police Department have found samples of Mr. Cooley's hair, fingerprints, skin fragments, or DNA at each of the crime scenes."

Harvey's lips started to tremble. His eyes and his face began to twitch: the tears streamed down and tickled his skin, but he was too scared to use his hands to brush them away. "I don't know anything about that!" he sobbed.

"You know enough to testify in a court of law."

"*No! I said I don't know anything about that!* I'm not going to . . ." Harvey was teetering on the brink of hysteria. His body was already close to shock from the freezing water and air. His mind was about to fall apart. Careful, Camilla, thought Goldsmith. Soften up or you're going to lose him. The valedictorian's manual stated that the subject must always remain lucid and hence, useful.

"Yes, you are," said Camilla, stone-faced. "William Alvarez. Monica Miller. Alberto Munoz Santana. Daniel Ford Smith. And last night, Jonathan Clark Riley . . ."

Theory confirmed, thought Goldsmith. The red X's on the year-book pages signified dead alumni and Stella Saltzman's unmarked photo indicated that she was still alive. But where? Through the one-way, he saw Harvey breaking down. His knees were buckling. You're losing him, Camilla, you're . . .

She unleashed a wicked backhand slap that struck Harvey square in the mouth. The smacking blow of skin against skin echoed like a firecracker around the examination room and through the one-way glass.

Harvey wobbled slightly and then righted himself. He immediately stopped blubbering and stared at her like a hurt child. Goldsmith didn't move. He just kept his eyes on the two of them, this chubby guy in his forties cowering in front of a calm, collected eighteen-year-old girl. The observation room had gone pin-drop silent. Not even the headmaster dared to take a breath. Goldsmith glanced around Camilla's examination room. There was no electroshock machine around. He understood: she was avoiding the use of real physical pain, because any valedictorian worth his or her salt knew it was a shortcut that produced answers of questionable reliability. Subjects would say what they thought the valedictorian wanted to hear just to make the pain stop. And the top specimen in Stansbury should be able to use his or her mind to pry the information loose.

This was Camilla's debut. She didn't want anyone to think she was lazy. She knew the *threat* of pain was worse than pain itself. And the signal she sent Harvey was that the blow he just received was not pain.

It was a message that she was willing to do worse, that she had no problem crossing that line. She snapped him back into reality, derailed that train to a nervous breakdown. Now, like Goldsmith and the rest of the observation room, Harvey was riveted on her and only her.

"Blood on your hands, Harvey. You are going to testify."

"I don't—"

"Listen to me." She began to circle him slowly and methodically. Her heels clicked against the concrete floor. She stopped behind him and leaned in, practically whispering in his ear. "The word *torture* is derived from the Latin verb *torquere*, meaning 'to twist.' The dictionary defines it as 'the inflicting of severe pain to force information, confession, consent, et cetera.'

"I don't administer severe pain," she continued. "It's not civilized. I believe in moderation. Do you know how I define moderate physical pressure?" She walked around to Harvey's front side, standing face to face with him. He shook his head. "Severe pain that doesn't leave scars," she said.

"I'll . . . I'll do it."

In the observation room, Captain Gibson and Officers Jamison and Jackson whooped and cheered, exchanging backslaps. Someone turned down the volume on the speaker broadcasting from the examination room. Goldsmith watched Camilla pull up a chair in front of Harvey. She sat down and crossed her legs, for a moment looking like the innocent schoolgirl she was. Or used to be.

Goldsmith considered the new twists. The SAPD's imminent involvement, the impending Senate committee vote, and the discovery of Cooley's bodily traces at five different crime scenes made everything tidy. But perhaps too tidy: it still didn't explain Cooley's motives, the connection—if any—between the five dead former specimens, or Miss Stella Saltzman's involvement. Goldsmith had a hard time believing that an eighteen-year-old resourceful and determined enough to murder one person per month for five months straight would put himself at risk by running around San Angeles trying to get clean urine samples for twelve other specimens and one guard, and then, for no apparent reason, kill the man who was providing him with those very samples before he procured them in the first place.

Go back to the yearbook photos. Given Goldsmith's cursory analysis of the evidence, it seemed that the initial assumption ought to be that the killer had a deadly grudge against Stansbury School, in particular against this group of former specimens. No, strike the group grudge theory: Stella Saltzman's inclusion ruled out association with the other five. Goldsmith had studied her career closely while she was valedictorian and he remembered the specimens with whom she was friendly. They were overachievers like her, all far cries from unbalanced drug addicts like Jonathan Clark Riley. So assume the killer—or killers—harbored a deep resentment toward the institution of Stansbury itself. The culprit could be another former specimen, one deeply disgruntled. But this, Goldsmith realized, was practically impossible, because the med cycle didn't allow for violent psychological impulses of the sort required for the premeditation and murder of other human beings.

Impossible, that was, unless the murderer was a textbook unbalanced specimen who shunned the med cycle almost entirely during his time in the tower. A murderer with a propensity for savage fits of violence, but was savvy and gutsy enough to do something like . . . convince a weak-willed registration and reception guard to let him out of the tower. Goldsmith looked around at the others in the room. Camilla walked in. The headmaster shook her hand. Everyone rushed around, conferring with each other, flipping through files, typing at computers, but nonetheless sharing the same thought. Mr. William Winston Cooley, serial killer.

Headmaster Latimer looked from Camilla to Goldsmith, a grave, ashen look passing over his face as if his eyes were moving from a beautiful work of art to the still-smoldering ruins of a tragic train wreck. They held each other's gaze for a moment. "I assume there is a better explanation for your actions in San Angeles than the one with which you provided Captain Gibson," he said. Goldsmith looked down, suddenly ashamed, feeling Camilla's eyes on him, too. "That was not a rhetorical statement, Mr. Goldsmith. I know that you would not so egregiously abuse the power this school has given you without good reason. My office doors are open to you. I am expecting a visit before the end of the day, young man."

"Yes, sir."

President Lang caught Goldsmith's eyes and smiled. "Mr. Goldsmith? Let's take a walk, shall we?" He stood up and followed her to the door, making eye contact with Camilla on the way out. She looked right through him.

"Masterful performance," someone said to the valedictorian. Goldsmith stopped and whirled around for a moment before remembering that it was not him they were talking to anymore.

Lang and Goldsmith walked down the long disciplinary level corridor together. Even the harsh lights in these halls flattered her. The way her skin and hair glowed made her seem more like a perfect hologram in the atrium than a real, live human being.

"Don't worry, I'm not going to upbraid you for your actions this morning," she said. "Headmaster Latimer is much better than I am at that sort of thing."

"I deserve it, ma'am."

"You and I are not so different, Mr. Goldsmith. I've seen your work over this past year, both in your progressions and as valedictorian. You place a strong emphasis on getting the job done. As do I. In fact, neither of us would be standing in the favorable positions we are in right now if defying odds and expectations did not come as second nature to us."

"Thank you, ma'am."

"I presume you understand what is at stake here," she said. "The reputations of every single person associated with this school hang in the balance. Mr. Cooley is a tragic story. We'll never know what inner demons drove him to . . . murder. No institution is perfect, Stansbury included. But we're not going to let the mistakes of one specimen taint everything."

"Can I speak frankly?"

"Certainly."

"I don't know about Mr. Cooley. This whole situation might be about something . . . bigger."

"That will be sorted out in a court of law on a later date. Right now, time is not on our side. The SAPD will take over the case in the very near future, and soon the Senate Select Committee on Education will be casting its vote on our grant proposal. There is a senator who wants the debate to continue, but he doesn't have enough support from his party, not to mention the president. Things must and will be neutralized as fast as humanly possible. Having said that," she stopped and turned to face him. He returned her look. "I know you've got no more stomach for the valedictorian's duties, but—"

"With all due—"

"Right now we need both Miss Moore and yourself on our side. Help us wrap up the Cooley matter today and I'll turn over your file."

Goldsmith's heart began to pound. "My file?" he asked, failing to quell the tremor in his voice.

"The confidential file that contains information sealed by the orphanage when you enrolled here twelve years ago. Information regarding the whereabouts of your mother."

"She's . . . alive?"

President Lang smiled. "Remember what we said last night? Good versus evil? Right versus wrong?" Something inside her blazer beeped. She pulled out her Tabula. "Please excuse me, Mr. Goldsmith. I have a one-thirty lunch appointment." And with that, she headed for the elevator bank. Goldsmith watched her step into a pod. The doors slid shut, whisking her away.

Goldsmith stood there in the corridor, thinking of what that confidential file might reveal, while trying to suppress those nagging, dangling loose ends of the Cooley-Riley situation. And yet, despite his best efforts, he could not.

18

Murdered alumni, killer specimens, getting chased
down city streets, scary Camilla 2.0 smacking around grown men,
links to long-lost mothers . . . it was all speeding past into a blur, a bit
too fast even for a young man with a mind as sharp as Goldsmith's.
Feeling two steps behind everyone else was not something to which
he was accustomed. He checked his Tabula as the elevator pod
whisked him up the tower—12:39 P.M.—and e-mailed the assign-
ments that were due today to the appropriate professors, along with a
quick note apologizing for his absence. "On official Stansbury business," he told them. Yeah, right. But he couldn't exactly write "Chasing ghosts for clues." The only way to gain some leverage was to start
solving mysteries before everyone else. Fast. The mystery of the hour:
what was the connection between the five dead ex-specimens and
Miss Stella Saltzman?

The pod reached Level 41 and dinged. The doors slid open. Goldsmith headed for the yearbook office. It was time to chat with good
old Mr. Hurley and get an impromptu history lesson.

He knocked on the door. "Come in," Hurley called out.

Goldsmith entered and smiled. The walls were covered with years and years of black-and-white photos: candid specimen shots, sports teams, Latin clubs, the headmaster addressing the Class of 2028 on their commencement day. He stopped in front of the page proofs for this year's edition and saw a collage of photos of his own class taken over their twelve years in the tower. There was a shot of Cooley and Bunson snapped sometime back in the third grade, both of them grinning, Cooley reaching around Bunson's head to give him rabbit ears. There was one of Goldsmith himself, taken when he first arrived at the age of six. His hair was even blonder than it was today and his eyes were wide, eager to get on with this business of taking over the world sooner rather than later. For the first time in his life, he felt old.

"Mr. Goldsmith!" said Hurley as he walked out from his small office. "To what do I owe the honor of a visit from the valedictorian?"

Goldsmith shut the door to the hallway and pulled out a chair for him, nodding for Hurley to take a seat. Goldsmith grabbed another chair for himself and got comfortable. "You're here on official valedictorian business?" Hurley asked.

"I just have a few questions. About Stansbury history." Goldsmith jammed his blood-caked hands into his pockets, trying to be discreet.

"Shoot," he said. "You know that's my specialty."

"Names. William Alvarez, Monica Miller, Alberto Munoz Santana, Daniel Ford Smith, and Jonathan Clark Riley." Goldsmith watched Hurley's face closely for a reaction. Hurley twitched. The skin below his receding hairline started to glisten with sweat. Hurley whistled and shook his head.

"Déjà vu," he said.

"What?"

"What's the matter with that guy? I told him everything I knew, and he—"

"What guy?"

"That newspaper reporter from the outside. Pete? Is that his name?"

Goldsmith leaned in, getting in Hurley's face. "He was here? To see you?" Hurley edged away, getting nervous.

"Yeah . . . He gave me the same exact list of names and I . . ." Hurley looked down, ashamed. "Things get lonely in here, you know?

Just pictures of you specimens to keep me company. Pete's a nice guy. Didn't mind chatting . . . Didn't think I'd be getting myself into trouble—"

"You're not in trouble. Just tell me everything you told him."

"None of the kids you mentioned were friendly with each other except for Smith and Riley. The only thing they had in common was that they were Stansbury's most-wanted, Class of 2033. Losers and unbalanced specimens, every one of them. Even double med doses couldn't get them to shape up. You'd be hard-pressed to find a better lineup of kids this school couldn't help."

"And?"

"And . . ." Hurley lowered his voice to a whisper. "And between you and me, I think the Stansbury life just made 'em worse." Goldsmith nodded. Hurley looked at him, confused. "But didn't you already know all of that?" he asked.

"No. Why?"

"Because Pete told me *you* were the one who sent him here in the first place. I wouldn't have told him anything if—"

Goldsmith's stomach tightened. "What about Stella Saltzman?" he asked, watching Hurley's face. The man blinked a few times too many and started to squirm in his seat.

"Pete asked me about her, too. She was 2033's valedictorian. That's it." Hurley's hands went from his legs to the sides of his chair, gripping the steel hard enough for his knuckles to go white.

"But that's not it, is it?"

"Aw, hell . . . I didn't tell him the rest because he's not one of us, you know? I guess I'll tell you, though . . ."

"Spit it out."

"Okay, okay. I've worked here since Stansbury opened back in 2009, and in that time—twenty-seven years—Miss Stella Saltzman was the only valedictorian who asked to give up her title."

Goldsmith got chills. "Why?" he asked.

"She was a quiet girl. Bookworm, I guess. Kept to herself mostly. Rumor was she couldn't hack conducting peer reviews. She asked Headmaster Latimer and President Lang to give her title to the number-two specimen in her class, but they wouldn't do it. They probably figured being valedictorian wouldn't mean anything if everyone knew the top specimen didn't want to be one."

Goldsmith started to digest everything. Five delinquent specimens and a disillusioned valedictorian had only one probable thing in common: major-league chips on their shoulders when it came to Stansbury School. But this link aside, there was nothing indicating that they were friendly after graduation. Hurley's information took everything a step forward, but not enough to fill in gaping holes of the big picture or answer the question of Cooley's involvement. The only other source of information Goldsmith could think of tapping was taboo: the school's sealed file index, which contained detailed information on each and every specimen past and present. There was no way to get to it without the administration granting access.

But first things first. Pete running amuck inside the tower was unacceptable: the situation needed to be rectified and contained until after today's Senate committee vote. Goldsmith decided to contact President Lang, inform her that the reporter had violated the conditions of his guest status, and request that she have the security detail track the man down, rough him up, and toss him in an examination room immediately. And then he—not Camilla—would take Pete one-on-one and break him, find out what he knew and, how he knew it.

"Hey," said Hurley, oblivious. "Want to hear a funny story about that William Alvarez?" He was in his storytelling zone and didn't wait for Goldsmith to answer. "Back during his senior year in '33, he was in a language progression—conversational Spanish—and his professor was this real beauty, Señorita White. Mr. Alvarez bet the rest of the specimens ten dollars apiece that he'd plant a kiss on the señorita before the end of the semester. So she calls him up to the front of the room for the verbal portion of his final exam. She says, '*Hola*, Señor Alvarez.' And then he throws this sly grin over his shoulder and gives her a big old smooch with tongue and everything. She starts freaking out and Alvarez says, 'Hey, I thought you said this was an *oral examination!*'" Hurley started chortling uncontrollably at this punch line. Goldsmith thought of Alvarez with a red X over his grinning face of a class clown, the first of five to die, and decided not to rain on the yearbook editor's parade.

He headed for the door, thinking of those confidential records on the dead specimens locked inside the administration's computer network. Before he reached the yearbook office door, his Tabula beeped, announcing the arrival of a new e-mail. Goldsmith scrolled to the message. It read:

> I'm President Lang's 1:30 lunch appt.
> Will keep her occupied as long as possible.
> Remember:
> *All great truths begin as blasphemies.*
> Regards,
> P.

Goldsmith checked his watch: 12:47. He ran for the elevator bank.

Cooley sat on the edge of his bed, tying up the dog-eared laces on his black loafers. Sadie stood before the mirror in the bathroom, carefully reapplying her makeup. Cooley wondered if she was serious about running away with him despite her hear-no-evil-see-no-evil routine over breakfast, and thought it was strange she didn't even ask what kind of trouble he was in when he mentioned it half an hour ago. The door to his dorm room burst open. Goldsmith barged in, uncharacteristically frantic, unkempt. His carefully parted blond coif was askew, a golden lock hanging down over his forehead. Cooley jumped up.

"What—," he started to say, but Goldsmith grabbed him by the tie and threw him against the wall.

"William Alvarez, Monica Miller, Alberto Munoz Santana, Daniel Ford Smith," Goldsmith said, his eyes scanning Cooley's face. Cooley stared back at him, clueless.

"William who?" he said, wondering just what the hell had been happening to the course of his life over the past hour.

One thought ran through Goldsmith's mind: the bastard didn't flinch, didn't even blink, his eyes betrayed no recognition, he had no idea what the fuck these names meant or to whom they belonged. And for some reason the school wanted him to burn anyway.

Sadie stalked out of the bathroom and shoved Goldsmith away

from Cooley. "What the hell do you want with him?" she hissed, staring him down, resentment and hate in her eyes. She shoved Goldsmith one more time. He looked down at her, shocked. Twelve years of progressions with Sadie Sarah Chapman—a diligent med cycle adherent—and not once had he ever seen the universally acknowledged Hottest Girl at Stansbury this way.

Cooley stepped in between them, putting his hands on her shoulders. "Chill out, okay?" he said softly. "He's trying to help me get out of this."

She shrugged his hands away and stepped back, once again locking eyes with Goldsmith. "I'm not afraid of you," she said.

"I happen to be the only thing standing between your boyfriend and a multiple-homicide charge that everyone in this tower except for me believes he's guilty of," Goldsmith replied. "So maybe you should be."

Sadie looked away, back over at Cooley. Cooley grabbed Goldsmith and pulled him close.

"Now it's multiple homicides?" he said, trying to hide the tremor in his voice.

"Those names belong to four dead alumni of this school. Riley makes number five."

"But I never even fucking *heard* of those people before!"

"Calm down. Security detail says they've got physical evidence linking you to those deaths, they—"

Cooley brushed past Sadie and punched the wall. White chunks of plaster went flying. He pulled his hand away and saw that his knuckles were bleeding. He sucked the blood off and stretched his fingers out.

"Listen to me," said Goldsmith, calmly flicking a stray plaster chip from his shoulder. "I've got a plan. But we're running out of time. We've got to move now."

Cooley looked at Sadie. Goldsmith was waiting for her to burst out into tears at the first mention of dead people, but her eyes were dry. She just stared at Goldsmith, probably blaming everything on him. "I swear, I'm gonna get out of this," Cooley told her. "Go back to progressions and I'll—"

"No," Goldsmith cut in. "The plan, Cooley. We need to use her."

"Fuck you," said Sadie.

"No," said Cooley. "Don't get her involved."

Goldsmith looked at his watch, then back at Cooley. "I'm afraid it's too late for that."

"I'm not taking orders from you," she said.

"It's not me you'll be helping. It's him. You can save him."

"You're a fucking android," she said.

Goldsmith looked at her and saw Camilla's face. He blinked it away. He waited for his brain to formulate a suitable response. Sadie looked at Cooley. He shook his head and mouthed the words *I'm sorry*. It occurred to Goldsmith that silence was more appropriate. He walked over to Cooley's bathroom and flipped on the faucet, starting to scrub the blood from his hands. After a few moments Cooley stood in the doorway and watched as those horrible burgundy flakes stuck to the white porcelain sink under a cleansing stream of soap and water.

"What happened to you?" he asked.

"The security detail was chasing me in San Angeles. Two cops got in the way. I . . . I neutralized them."

"*You* beat up two *cops?*" Cooley looked shocked and amused.

"I'm not proud of it."

"But how? The med cycle's not supposed to—"

"I overrode the chemicals somehow." Goldsmith dried his hands. "It was like I'd always seen a glimpse of light behind two huge black curtains that were too heavy to move."

"And?"

"And today, I finally pulled the curtains down."

"Congratulations."

"For what?"

"Sounds to me like you just graduated." Sadie stood next to Cooley in the doorway.

"Fine," she said, looking at Goldsmith. "I'll do it."

Bunson reclined in the luxurious Aeron chair in Goldsmith's private suite. It seemed miniature beneath his considerable weight. Cooley pulled over a chair from the work terminal and sat next to him.

"This is insane," whispered Bunson.

"I don't have any other choice."

"You can't trust this guy. After the way he burned everyone yesterday and . . ."

"I'm fucked, Bunson. Plain and simple."

"That's the rumor."

"What are people saying?"

"No specifics. Just chatter that mighty Cooley might get the boot before commencement."

Cooley let out a morbid chuckle. "If only."

"What really happened in San Angeles?"

"I . . . I shouldn't tell you. I'd be putting you at risk."

"No offense, man, but I'm already risking everything just by being in this room with you. Not to mention the crazy shit you say Goldsmith's come up with. How do you know he's not just setting us up? Or that he'll back us up if we get busted?"

Cooley thought of Goldsmith in the same room with him and Sadie just a few minutes ago, disheveled, more than a little scared, desperate. "I trust him," Cooley said. "Like I said, I've got no other choice."

The door opened. Goldsmith walked in and pulled out a two-liter glass bottle of transparent liquid from a book bag. He set it on the table.

"The hell is that?" asked Bunson.

"Read the label," Goldsmith said.

Bunson looked at a white sticker on the bottle's side. Black letters spelled out the words: METHAMPHETAMINE CONCENTRATE, 100% UNDISTILLED, BATCH #424, STANSBURY SCHOOL MED TECH BAY. "How'd you get that?" he asked.

Goldsmith looked down at him, this Neanderthal about to snap the hinges off his fancy chair. "My reputation precedes me," he replied. "The tower is like anywhere else in the world. Holding a position of power smoothes over many otherwise troublesome things."

Bunson got up from the chair and his head seemed to skim the ceiling. He looked down at Goldsmith and cracked his knuckles. Goldsmith returned his gaze, smirking at the playground routine. Cooley watched them from his own chair—a six-foot-five nerd and a six-foot-nine bully—and thought they could be two huge pro wrestlers in an alternate reality. To his own surprise, he silently wagered a bet on the nerd.

"Hey, people are talking, and from what I hear, you're not so powerful these days," said Bunson. "What, Cooley? Smart guy here didn't tell you the news? The hot rumor is he's not valedictorian anymore. Golden boy quit."

Goldsmith glanced over at Cooley. His face was calm. He didn't betray any shock or surprise. He was smarter than everyone thought, Goldsmith realized. Smart enough to know that this was a minor pissing contest, compared to getting Bunson to do what they wanted. "You're right," Goldsmith said. "But, due to unusual circumstances, the administration has asked for my help."

"And you decide to backstab them and help Cooley instead?" Bunson headed for the door. "Sorry, I don't buy it. And even if I did, you don't have the clout anymore to square things with the school if something goes wrong. Word is, Camilla 2.0's running the show now and she's—"

Goldsmith followed him and grabbed him by the shoulder. Bunson whirled around and knocked his hand away like it was a mosquito.

"Miss Moore is good. I'm better."

Bunson looked over at Cooley. "Man, even if I did help you guys out, you'll never convince Sadie to go along with it."

"She already said she would," said Cooley.

"What?" Bunson's face went a shade whiter, like this news was heavier than a just-retired valedictorian stealing enough pure meth from the med tech bay to keep the whole school up for weeks on end. "No way." Cooley nodded in response. "Well, that's bullshit," Bunson muttered. "I just don't know why she'd . . ."

Goldsmith checked his watch. It was almost one P.M. "Are you in or out, Bunson?" Bunson didn't even look at him. He grabbed the glass bottle of methamphetamine concentrate, slid it into his book bag, and made for the door.

"Bunson," Cooley said. He turned around and looked back at him. "Thanks." The big guy nodded, a grimace on his face, and walked out.

"You could've mentioned the valedictorian thing," Cooley said.

"It was a news update I figured you could do without."

"Were you serious when you told Bunson that you were better than Camilla?"

"Yes."

"Do you really believe that? That if she's working against us you can beat her?" Goldsmith saw Selmer-Dubonnet flash past his eyes all over again. Cooley was scared of her—which just meant he was sane—and didn't know if Goldsmith could pull off another upset. "Goldsmith?"

"Yes, I do."

"But she's—"

"August 29, 2035. The day of the Selmer-Dubonnet exam. We—me, Camilla, and eight other specimens—had been going for almost four hours. Candidates were being eliminated one by one with each progressive stage. There were only three of us left—me, Gregory Marcus Garvin, and Camilla—when they dropped us in a sensory deprivation tank filled with eight hundred gallons of cold water. They strapped immobilizing braces on our limbs and made us wear headsets that ran loops of hallucinogenic video feeds over and over again. Weird stuff. Jackals feeding on human carcasses, these incredibly detailed and graphic animated sequences of invasive surgery . . . sometimes I'd just see blue and yellow patterns coiling around each other like snakes in front of a sunburst. The water around me became a kind of soundtrack. I replaced my fear with anger at what they were putting us through. It was the only way I'd last; I needed that burn to sustain me. Garvin went into a seizure forty-eight minutes in. He couldn't handle it. That left me and Camilla. The tank drained and the nurses came out to examine our vital signs. We both wanted to quit, that much I knew. I looked over at her. There was vomit—a morning's worth of NutriTein bars that cost enough to feed a family of outsiders for days—drying in her hair. We made eye contact. She looked like a stranger to me, which is exactly how I wanted it. I made her anonymous. Just another obstacle in my path, something to be dispensed with in short order. Neither of us knew what was coming next. But we looked each other in the eyes and I knew I had her beat. She wanted to win. I fucking *needed* it.

"They took us into another room for the final stage. On the way, I caught a glimpse of a recovery center that had been set up on the disciplinary level: the eight other specimens who didn't make it to the end were sedated in hospital beds, machines monitored their recovery. I didn't feel any pity for them. I'd already visualized that scene in

my head for months before the exam day: my competitors for the title laid before me, broken. Camilla and I were strapped down in
chairs. They attached electrodes to our temples and pressure points.
There was a control panel built into the arm of the chair and a plasma
screen on the wall. On the other end of the room was this huge mirror. I knew everyone was watching—Lang, Latimer, Gibson, probably
some team of shrinks and medics to make sure Selmer-Dubonnet
protocol was followed—and it fed my anger even more. A voice gave
us instructions. The screen would broadcast a selection of questions.
The peer reviewer would pick one, and if the reviewer's opponent did
not answer correctly, the reviewer would hit a switch on the chair's
panel, firing fifty thousand nonlethal volts into those electrodes. With
each incorrect answer the opponent would continue to be electrocuted. Upon a correct response, the roles would switch. This would
continue until one of us either gave up or was physically unable to
continue.

"I spoke up. Or at least I pretended to speak up. I said out loud that
I wouldn't agree to this, that I refused to be reduced to this behavior.
I didn't mean a goddamned word of it, Cooley. I was just saying it
for everyone else's benefit, so they'd think of me as a person with
morals, someone who believed in the Stansbury Oath, someone with
honor . . ." Goldsmith's voice tightened as he tried to choke back
tears. "I only protested because I wanted Camilla to be my friend
when it was all over. I wanted her to believe that I cared more about
her than winning the title. And I did care about her! But not so badly
that I wasn't prepared, right then and there, to do this awful thing. To
rip her fucking heart out in that room and crush it under my heel.
That's how I was built. That's what this place has made me, you see?
They trained me to be the best. She looked up and gave me this slight
smile. I smiled back and got on with the business of finishing her off.

"I picked question twenty-three. She had five seconds to answer.
'The day before yesterday is three days after Saturday. What day is today?' She stuttered, uncertain. Any other day, any other place,
Camilla 2.0 would've knocked that and every other question out of
the park. But four hours of testing, the high-pressure stakes, and this
fear jammed up that amazing brain of hers. She froze. She answered
'Friday.' I hit the button and watched the voltage turn her body into a

contorted, frozen figure of pain jerking so hard against the polymer bindings on her arms that they tore chunks out of that beautiful, perfect skin of hers. I repeated the question. She answered 'Wednesday.' I paused, my finger over the trigger, and made my face look hesitant, unsure. I glanced over at the mirror, like I couldn't go through with this anymore, like if I did, it wasn't my fault, but the fault of those hiding behind the glass. A look of hope passed across her face for a split second and I hit that switch again. It was the first time all day I'd heard her scream. I repeated the question: 'The day before yesterday is three days after Saturday. What day is today?' And then I leaned in and whispered to her.

"'I won't do it,' I said.

"'You have to do it,' she replied.

"'No, I won't.'

"'Yes, you will,' she said. 'I would. And I will, if you don't do it first.'

"'The answer is Thursday,' I whispered.

"'I don't believe you,' she said. 'You just want to win.'

"'Not this badly,' I told her. I was lying through my fucking teeth, Cooley. I hit the switch again. Her body gave out on her. She lost consciousness. I won. Lang and the headmaster rushed in and started congratulating me, but it was all coming too late. I had Selmer-Dubonnet won the moment I stepped in the room four hours earlier. Nobody else had a chance."

Cooley looked at Goldsmith. He no longer seemed upset. There were no tears to be seen. His voice had returned to normal. The med cycle pushed whatever ugly things he was hiding back to the dark place from where they came.

"Camilla and I are both smart, Cooley. But she's got a soul left. I don't." Goldsmith stood up. "Which one of us would you rather have on your side?" Cooley stood up and looked him in the eyes.

"You're still inside that last Selmer-Dubonnet room," he said. "Test hasn't ended yet, man. You can get your soul back. You can still walk out of there with your honor, Goldsmith."

"Second chances don't exist in this place."

"Yeah? Yours is standing right in front of you."

Goldsmith stared at Cooley for a long moment, studying his face, using all of his valedictorian's skills to check for any signs, tip-offs, or agendas, and not finding anything—just the unblinking face of an eighteen-year-old misfit orphan. After hundreds of peer reviews on the disciplinary level, that kind of face looked unfamiliar. It looked like a shot at redemption. Goldsmith glanced away to check his watch. "It's time," he said.

Cooley nodded. They stood up and headed for the door. A twinge of fear in Goldsmith's stomach brought him back to reality. He reminded himself that if Cooley tried to double-cross him, he could still turn him in and get his confidential file from President Lang. But he started to think that they might be able to pull this thing off. And if he cleared an innocent specimen of a multiple homicide rap and maybe even found out who really did it, Lang might give it to him anyway.

Two steps behind him, Cooley started to think that his new savior was a better guy than he would have ever given him credit for. Human. Just trying to make things work the same as anyone else.

19

In the girls' restroom on Level 82, Miss Caroline
Melissa Keating—a sophomore specimen—washed her hands before
her sixth-hour German Existentialist Literature progression. Miss Keating took her time because all she had to do was hand in a forty-page
final paper on the theme of death in Thomas Mann's *Magic Mountain*
(which, incidentally, she read in the original German). She reached
under her white dress shirt, adjusted her bra and frowned. No good.
She still had the figure of a lanky thirteen-year-old boy and thought it
was ironic that Stansbury could train her to crank out a stack of forty
publication-worthy pages filled with musings about death and angst
in a single evening, but they could not get her to grow a decent set of
boobs.

The door to the restroom swung open. In the mirror, Caroline saw
Miss Sadie Sarah Chapman walk in. Sadie glanced at her. Caroline
looked away out of deference. She'd kill for the kind of boobs that
Sadie had. It was so not fair. Why, just last week Caroline had finally
mustered up the courage to talk to Mr. Carl Maxwell Hainey and, five

minutes into their perfunctory small talk about the night's plane geometry homework, cute Mr. Hainey was glancing over her shoulder without any subtlety whatsoever. Caroline could practically *sense* Sadie Chapman and her perfect tits walking down the corridor behind her.

The door swung open again. Hey, thought Caroline. What's Cooley doing in here? Without even so much as apologizing for his intrusion, he grabbed Sadie by the arm and pulled her into a stall. Caroline heard a few whispers. She stood there drying her hands a bit longer than usual, straining to hear.

"Hey," came Cooley's voice echoing against the white tile walls. Caroline realized he was talking to her. "Can we get a minute alone?" Before she could even utter a subservient, obliging response, he cut her off. "Thanks." She packed up her things in a huff and headed for the door.

Inside the stall, Cooley took Sadie's face in his hands and gave her a kiss on the lips. She pulled back at first and then relented, kissing him back.

"You need to do this, okay?" he said.

"I just . . . I don't know why you're so trusting of Goldsmith all of a sudden."

"I don't have a choice."

"But I do."

"No, you don't," he said. "None of us do. Not inside this place."

"You look tired. You look so beautiful, but tired." Hearing her say this made him smile. "I know you didn't kill those people," she whispered, looking up into his eyes. "And if the school keeps on saying you did, I'm getting out of here with you. I won't have anything to do with this place."

"What about—"

"I don't care about anything else. That's why I'm about to do this."

"I love you so much."

"Not more than I love you." Sadie glanced at her watch: 1:08 P.M. "Let's go," she said. "We're almost ten minutes late. Just like he told us to be."

In Progression Room #231 on Level 52, Professor Jeffrey Nelson's image was broadcast onto a plasma screen hanging on the wall. His eyes scanned the area, always stopping on the two empty chairs smack dab in the middle of the room. It was the first time Miss Chapman had been late for his French Revolution progression. Mr. Cooley was regularly tardy, and since he was absent as well, this could only mean that he had gotten her involved in something unsavory. The professor had no idea what a beautiful girl from a prominent New York City family saw in a ragamuffin like William Winston Cooley.

Nelson was actually on campus at the moment, but was simulcasting from his private office on Level 29 because he had just wrapped up another simulcast address to certain members of the United States Senate, providing them with the philosophical justification—talking points, if you will—for the government bestowing Stansbury with a $1 trillion grant with the Select Committee on Education's big vote that evening. A vote that, if the grapevine was correct, was looking like more of a formality than the hotly contested debate that was anticipated. At the relatively tender age of thirty, Professor Nelson was the youngest faculty member at Stansbury and, as he was up for tenure the following fall, his consultation with the senators on such a crucial day could not have come at a better time for his career. He prided himself on relating to the specimens better than most of the stodgy old academics around this place, but still the sight of two empty desks at his final lecture before exams was a blemish he could not tolerate.

At that very moment, who entered but Mr. Cooley and Miss Chapman. They tried to be discreet while taking their seats, but with only fourteen other specimens in the room failed miserably. Sadie glanced up at Professor Nelson's image and gave him her best up-from-under-the-lashes smile. He tried to suppress the involuntary urge to smile back at her but only managed to turn it into a thinly disguised smirk. He felt himself blush. Get it together, he thought. Sure, he was only thirty—and single, at that—and finding this eighteen-year-old girl as attractive as he (and everyone else) did was not, on the face of it, a perverted embarrassment. But still, affairs between faculty and specimens were strictly prohibited and penalized by immediate dismissal of both parties involved. But he could look, couldn't he? She leaned back in her chair, crossing her legs as that gray pleated skirt rode up the thigh just a bit.

"What're you looking at?" snapped Cooley, glaring at Nelson's roving eyes. Nelson cast his sternest authoritarian look back at him and effortlessly summoned the condescending tone of all the teachers he hated while growing up.

"Mr. Cooley," he rumbled. "Now that we've been honored with your presence, please give us your thoughts on Montesquieu's themes of religious freedom in *The Persian Letters* and how they were embodied in Robespierre's speech before the Assembly." Take that, you little shit.

"Uh . . . well . . ." Cooley scratched his head, trying to buy himself some time. A specimen's hand shot up a few rows back. The professor saw who it was and smiled. If only they could clone that kid a thousand times over.

"Thank you, Mr. Goldsmith, for saving us once again."

"Given the fact that *The Persian Letters* were a metaphor for the French religious state," Goldsmith began with his trademark, crisp, controlled delivery, "one would postulate that . . ." His voice trailed off. "That . . . that . . ."

The other specimens in the room looked over. Goldsmith had his eyes fixed on Cooley, who was leaning back in his chair and staring holes through the valedictorian's head. Never breaking eye contact, Cooley snapped his pencil with one hand and the sound of wood and graphite splintering echoed around the silent room. Some of the girls gasped. Goldsmith shut up and looked over at Professor Nelson for some support, but Nelson was missing out on the whole thing. He had been watching Sadie the whole time.

"You finished?" Goldsmith asked Cooley, a slight quiver in his finest pseudo-tough-guy voice. Specimens stared in disbelief, like they were expecting him to spontaneously combust under Cooley's evil gaze. Cooley didn't smile, didn't blink.

"I haven't even gotten started."

A pregnant pause filled the progression room. Goldsmith ended the staring contest and looked down at the notebook on his desk, nervously doodling something in the margins. Cooley did not look away.

Professor Nelson finally broke off his appreciation of Miss Chapman's aesthetic qualities and looked over, realizing what had just transpired. Someone had better watch those two, he realized.

Bunson and Cooley sat with Sadie at their usual table in the cafeteria. They watched everyone around them inject lunch (grass-fed angus steak, organic greens, and spirulina protein smoothies). Their IV jars were full of nutrients, but they didn't touch them. Bunson looked at the table across from them and saw Mr. Ralph Owen Satterlee, John Jason Stevenson, and George Craig Jenkins set down their laser syringes and start to twitch. As if in synchronization, the noise level in the room rose and conversations took on a rattling staccato rhythm.

"Jesus, look at everyone," said Bunson. Jenkins's leg started to bounce uncontrollably, but his eyes were darting around too quickly for him to notice.

"It's working," said Sadie.

"Bunson emptied two liters of pure meth into the feeding vats," whispered Cooley. "Of course it's working. It throws the Normalcin doses out of whack . . . the med cycle can't keep up with that kind of pure chemical concentrate."

Sadie checked her watch. "It's time." She stood up.

"You don't have to—," started Cooley, but she was already walking off toward the exit.

"There he is," said Bunson, nodding in the direction of Goldsmith, who was walking from the food vats over to an empty table with a tray full of liquid nutrients. Cooley rose and cut into his path. He bumped him, throwing his shoulder into Goldsmith's chest and knocking the tray from his hands. Glass jars shattered on the marble floor. The cafeteria instantly went quiet, hundreds of pairs of unblinking eyes focused on the two of them in a standoff, everyone expecting Goldsmith to take the high road and let the janitors clean up the mess.

But he reared back and slammed a hard right hook against Cooley's jaw. Cooley stumbled back two steps and then threw his body into Goldsmith, taking him low and tossing him to the ground. The broken glass shards on the floor crunched beneath them. Every specimen in the cafeteria rushed over—adrenaline mixing in with the methamphetamine coursing through their veins—and gathered in a circle around the brawl. Cooley rolled on top of Goldsmith and smashed his head against the floor. Goldsmith reached a big hand over Cooley's face, raking his eyes until his fingers slid down to his neck. He started to squeeze. The crowd gasped.

"Security!" shouted Bunson from the doorway. Cooley and Goldsmith jumped up, brushing themselves off. The spectators dissolved and rushed back to their tables. A moment passed. "We're clear!" called out Bunson.

Cooley shoved Goldsmith one last time and headed for the cafeteria's exit. Goldsmith stalked after him. The specimens looked at each other and leaped up from their chairs, instinctively knowing what would follow. After all, there was only one thing that could come next. They rushed for the doors and filed out, sprinting for the elevator banks to catch up with the two nemeses.

Seventh grade specimen Mr. Joshua Calley had never seen anything like this before. It was the first real, live fight he'd ever witnessed, and between two of the most famous specimens in the whole tower, no less! His excitement made him forget all about the fact that his heart was racing at twice its normal speed and that he—like everyone else around him—seemed to be sweating and panting like an animal. Mr. Calley followed the flow of specimens toward the elevators and his curiosity got the best of him. He grabbed the arm of the closest upperclassman around, Mr. John Jason Stevenson, not caring in the least about coming off as naïve regarding the subtleties of Stansbury ritual.

"Hey! Mr. Stevenson!" chirped Calley. Stevenson looked down at him, annoyed.

"What?" he said, not breaking stride. Calley started jogging to keep up with him.

"Where's everyone going?"

Stevenson's eyes went into a shadowy squint. He cracked his knuckles. They popped, sounding just like the sound of glass crushed beneath Goldsmith's writhing, struggling body. "The warehouse," he answered. "Level 3."

———

The warehouse was a sprawling space that was rarely visited by spec-imens, except for occasions such as this. It was filled with row upon row of crates containing foodstuffs, school and office supplies, linens, uniforms, shipments of meds, spare Nature & Co. windows, discon-nected plasma simulcast screens, and just about any other material or infrastructure that was necessary to keep the tower running smoothly. The stacks of boxes reached almost all the way up to the eighty-foot-high ceiling. Forklifts weaved in and out of the industrial maze. Over the years the shippers, packagers, receivers, and other below-the-stairs folk who occupied this level learned that the specimens only came down here when something had gone awry upstairs and order needed to be restored. When there were scores that needed to be settled. So, on rare days like today these burly men parted ways in order to clear a path for the crowd that was following Cooley and Goldsmith toward the dark, dingy corner reserved for the most hallowed—and illegal—of all Stansbury traditions: the game known as dodgeball.

Up until 2012, dodgeball was played regularly in all levels of ath-letics progressions, just like any other school on the outside that needed to fill time during gym class. But, as Stansbury found out the hard way, the seemingly harmless game changed dramatically when played by beneficiaries of the med cycle: the IGF-1 protein had made male specimens so big and strong that the red rubber balls in their hands inadvertently became lethal weapons. The sight of several ag-ile, six-foot-four-inch, 220-pound teenagers whipping shots at each other at speeds of up to one hundred miles per hour was certainly something to see. The rubber balls became projectiles that whistled as they cut through the air, unleashing a grotesque, meaty smack when striking a participant's head or chest. An unintended consequence of the then-sanctioned dodgeball matches was that they provided the specimens with a type of raw, physical stress relief and primal excite-ment (for both the competitors and the audience) that meds and pro-gressions simply could not satisfy. But it all came to an abrupt halt one fateful day during the 2012 school year.

The names of those involved have since been forgotten, lending the story a feeling vaguely reminiscent of an urban legend, but still, the tale was passed on from year to year and dodgeball was no longer a part of the curriculum. During a match in an upper-level athletics progression—the rumor held that it was Practical Applications of Kinesiology, now considered a mundane gut course—a cuckolded male senior specimen found himself on the opposite side of the court from the young Casanova who stole his girlfriend's heart. While the med cycle had revolutionized the work ethic, physical prowess, and intellectual performance of thousands of young adults over the years, Dr. Stansbury's genius could not produce a pill to mend a broken heart. The match began and this sad, angry guy who only two days prior had lost the love of his life waited for the right moment and, when his rival left himself exposed, took advantage in the most brutal way. Some insisted that the professor supervising the progression—who also remained nameless—was said to have clocked the throw at 113 miles per hour. Others claimed that it was not the speed of the shot, but its placement that made it so deadly. Either way, the impact of the ball against Casanova's face was such that it shattered his nose and sent splinters of bone up into his brain, instantly rendering him a vegetable. His parents came to see him in the infirmary and held a week-long vigil before they consented to have the life support system's plug pulled. Casanova's assailant hung himself from a holographic projector in the atrium the very same day, his limp body swinging among the digitized branches and artificially green leaves. What happened to the tragic girl who came between them was anyone's guess. Following the two funerals, the headmaster laid down the decree: Dodgeball would never be played in the tower again.

Specimens were obedient and sensible, but they were still similar in many ways to their less-gifted counterparts in the outside world, despite the dignified mien they were given in the media and the school's glossy brochures. No kind of education could quench the taste of young people for dangerous, forbidden thrills. Almost immediately after the headmaster's proclamation, underground dodgeball matches began. They became a means to settle longtime grudges once and for all, on a field of battle that was storied and sought out by only the bravest specimens. The contest was governed by very few rules, acknowledged by a silent code of honor: matches were three-on-three; no female specimens were permitted to participate; the personal differences that brought on the match were permanently quashed following the conclusion; and, most important, no head-hunting was tolerated. Bored warehouse level employees helped clear enough room for a makeshift court in a particularly grimy corner of their space. Behind a crude sliding door made from scrap metal lay a concrete floor with a single yellow line painted across the middle, separating one side from the other. Three red balls remained placed along the line, glimmering like blood-red gems in the shadows. There was enough room around the court for roughly a hundred spectators, usually specimens and warehouse workers who wagered on the outcome of matches.

Today, there were closer to three hundred specimens filling the space, along with the school employees who were already jostling for prime viewing positions. Since the specimens generally tended to get along harmoniously, dodgeball matches were rare, perhaps only occurring once or twice per year and almost always involving older specimens who had learned to play by seeing the duels take place as they were growing up. Cooley, the veteran of an astounding five matches in which his team had never lost, had come to know and maybe even love the dynamics of the game: the raw energy that built on the court, the primal urge that was fulfilled both on the parts of the audience and the players, the comfortable, reassuring heft of the ball in his hand, and most of all, the knowledge that, win or lose, the conflict that brought everyone here in the first place would soon be over, most likely in his favor. Goldsmith, predictably, had never played the game before or even seen this illicit court in person. He had only heard the rumors.

The warehouse was chilly and smelled stale, a little like ammonia. Cooley stood on one side of the yellow line, joined by Bunson and his third teammate, an unbalanced specimen from the junior class named Mr. Jacob Scripps White. Goldsmith stood on the other side of the court. Misters Andrew Chang and Gregory Marcus Garvin, two straight-arrow, by-the-book seniors—both were part of the final ten top specimens who underwent the Selmer-Dubonnet exam along with him—stepped out from the crowd to join him.

"Someone's got to keep the thugs in line," said Chang. "Set an example for the younger specimens out there, let 'em know that they can't just lie down for punks like Cooley."

"It's an honor, Mr. Goldsmith," said Garvin.

Goldsmith nodded at them. After a series of shrill creaks, the scrap metal door slid closed and the audience started to hum with anticipation. He glanced around at the throngs of specimens surrounding the court. They were bouncing up and down already, nudging each other, pointing, making bets on how quickly Cooley was going to take them all out, whether he was going to abide by the headhunting ban or not. Cooley walked up to the line of red rubber balls and checked them all to make sure they were adequately filled with air. He squeezed them one by one, bouncing them against the floor. They were taut, hard, and packed plenty of spring. They left his hands and snapped against the concrete back into his grasp almost faster than the eye could see.

"Gentlemen," called out a warehouse worker, "take your places."

Cooley, Bunson, and White took ten paces back from the yellow line. Goldsmith, Chang, and Garvin followed suit. A nervous hush fell over the packed little arena. Goldsmith noticed the incessant scraping of leather shoe soles on the ground, the sound of jostling in the crowd, the frantic breathing of hundreds of kids jacked up on meth. Actually, that frantic breathing, he realized after a few moments, was his own. "Ready!" called out the warehouse guy. He held up three fingers high above his head and counted down. *Three, two, one . . .*

On Level 29, Professor Nelson watched the recorded broadcast of his earlier discussion with the senators. He knew President Lang saw the whole thing and figured she'd send it to the headmaster for his own personal review, but just in case she forgot during the course of her very busy day, Nelson attached a copy of the video file to an e-mail and sent it to the big man himself (the subject header read: "Monsieur Nelson Goes to Washington!☺") There was a knock at his office door.

"Yes?"

The door slid open. Wordlessly, Sadie sauntered in. Nelson noticed the way her hair fell down her shoulders and that the shade of blue in her eyes matched the idyllic image of the Rocky Mountain skyline broadcast on the Nature & Co. window on his wall. She slid the door shut and leaned her shoulders against it, her hips and legs arching toward him. All of a sudden, his office smelled like a musky bouquet of roses and lush pomegranate. The professor paused the image of his Senate meeting, wondering if she recognized any of the distinguished old politicos and also if she'd ask him what occasion he had to hold forth with them in such a personal, clearly prestigious manner.

"Miss Chapman! Did you, uh . . . want to schedule a review session before the . . . exam?"

"Yes, I'd like that very much." She walked toward him. Nelson leaned back in his desk chair and swallowed. Sadie held his face between her hands as she straddled him, feeling his palms slide against her thighs and up her skirt in that lewd, hungry way common to men of all ages. She noticed that he closed his eyes when she kissed him gently on the mouth, as if he was trying to make such a contrived encounter something even close to resembling romance. One of his hands remained up her skirt, pawing away, and the other moved clumsily to her chest, at first squeezing and then hurriedly unbuttoning her navy blue cardigan.

Her eyes quickly scanned the contents of his desk and just as he got to the final button, she saw it: a small, gleaming, black card with a silver cord strung through a hole near the top. It was the professor's faculty-clearance key card: the cord was common to the many faculty members who wore them around their necks so the cards didn't get lost. With one hand, she caressed the back of Nelson's neck. The other moved toward that Holy Grail.

A loud whistle rang through the air. Both dodgeball teams sprinted forward to reach the three balls in the middle of the court before their opposition. The shouts and cheers of three-hundred-plus specimens reverberated against the walls into a bona fide roar. Garvin went for the same ball as White. He got there first. The moment the rubber touched his hands, Bunson hurled a kill shot—the red ball a blur cutting through air—nailing Garvin in the stomach, knocking him back three feet and out of the game. Garvin wheezed, trying to cry out in pain, but couldn't because he'd gotten the wind knocked out of him and suffered three bruised ribs from the impact.

Cooley beat Goldsmith to the center ball. Relying solely on reflexes and adrenaline, Goldsmith leaped over Garvin's writhing body and narrowly dodged Cooley's first strike, the ball just missing his right shoulder. White grabbed the ball that fell out of Garvin's hands and tossed it across the court to Bunson, who winged it at Chang in a single, fluid, blink-of-an-eye motion. It sizzled through the air. Chang ducked and it nailed some poor freshman kid flush in the face. He went down gushing blood from the nose and mouth. The audience noise just kept building. Two sophomore girls stepped over the freshman's prone body and took his place. Some helpful warehouse guys dragged Garvin's body off the court.

Goldsmith grabbed a rolling ball at the far end of his team's side and hurled it as hard as he could at Cooley. Cooley dove to the ground, rolled, and grabbed it as it ricocheted against the back wall and moved along the floor. A pro-Goldsmith specimen in the crowd kicked a stray ball over to Chang. Chang passed it to Goldsmith. White flung a shot. Goldsmith deflected it high up in the air with his own ball, which he dropped, and then caught White's ball before it could hit the ground. The crowd went nuts. White was out. He trudged off to join the audience, his head hung in shame. Goldsmith tossed White's ball to Chang and picked up the one he was originally holding. Now they were both armed. They faced off against Bunson and Cooley. Cooley had a ball in his hands and looked focused, serene, in his element. Bunson bounced lightly on his feet from side to side, like a boxer. He had that playground bully's smirk on. Goldsmith made eye contact with Chang and glanced in Bunson's direction to signal that he would take him high, Chang should take him low. Chang nodded.

"One . . . two . . . ," Goldsmith counted under his breath, "three!" They let their shots fly. Goldsmith missed. Bunson dodged, leaping to his right and going horizontal in midair. Chang's shot nailed him in the shins, moving so hard and fast that it knocked all 250 pounds of Bunson into a 360-degree spin before his head smacked against the ground, causing a sickening cracking noise.

"One hundred five miles per hour!" shouted a warehouse guy standing high up on a ladder and holding an old, antiquated radar gun. The crowd cheered wildly. Bunson rose slowly, rubbing his skull, and limped off the court into the crowd. Cooley's eyes locked onto Goldsmith. He took aim.

"Watch out!" cried Chang.

Goldsmith watched Cooley's line of vision and picked a side to leap toward, figuring he had a fifty-fifty chance of dodging the shot. Cooley, watching Goldsmith the whole time, hurled a no-look missile at Chang, who stood there completely exposed. Goldsmith hit the ground and rolled. He saw Cooley's strike slam against Chang's groin. Chang let out a high-pitched cry and went down screaming, crumpled up. Two warehouse guys dragged him away.

"A hundred eight miles per hour!" shouted the man with the radar gun. The crowd let loose with a barrage of "oohs," "aahs," and "holy fucking shits."

Goldsmith picked himself up from the floor. It was down to just him and Cooley. The specimens that surrounded them started stomping a tribal beat against the ground. *Boom boom boom boom . . .* Goldsmith started to see things in slow motion. Cooley looked down. Goldsmith looked down. There was a single red ball rolling almost perfectly along the yellow line at the center of the court. At the same instant, they broke out into a sprint for it, two fierce gladiators speeding toward a head-on collision.

Sadie did her best to keep Professor Nelson's pants on without throwing cold water on the whole routine. She had reached for the key card several times but stopped short because he had this annoying habit of grabbing whichever stray hand of hers was available and thrusting it onto his crotch. Sadie jotted down a mental note: All men are boys. She checked the digital clock glowing in the bottom right-hand corner of the plasma screen on his desk. Time was running out. It was too late to turn back or, for that matter, come up short on her end of the plan.

She gritted her teeth and unbuckled Nelson's belt. He gasped as she grabbed him right about there with her left hand. Sadie yanked his pants and underwear down around his ankles and slid herself from his lap down to the ground. By the time the professor was mumbling some drivel about the color of her eyes (in *French,* no less), she had the key card in her right hand and was counting down the seconds until the next phase of Mr. Goldsmith's despicable, brilliant, far-fetched ploy.

Goldsmith sprinted. Cooley sprinted, but hesitated for one barely perceptible moment too long. That red ball rolled at an excruciatingly slow pace. The crowd was roaring around them, all eyes on the distance between each young man and that final weapon on the concrete floor. Goldsmith grabbed it and felt the pattern of ridges on its surface. He put on the brakes, his polished dress shoes sliding a few inches. Cooley froze, planting his feet for an extra half-second before moving to spring away to the side. Goldsmith got a bead on him and fired.

The impact of the ball snapped Cooley's head back and the hit echoed like a lone gunshot around the walls and high up to the warehouse's ceilings. Blood started flooding from his nose and mouth as he teetered on weak legs for a moment, his eyes rolling back into his head before he collapsed to the ground with an awful thud. Goldsmith stood above him. The court went silent. He glanced around at the specimens and saw hundreds of mouths gaping wide open. Flat-chested Miss Caroline Melissa Keating let out a horrified gasp that cut through the stunned hush.

"*Headhunter!*" shouted Bunson. Several other specimens yelled profanities in support. He lunged out from the crowd toward Goldsmith. Garvin jumped in between them.

"No! It's over! It's fucking over!" Garvin shouted back as he struggled with Bunson. Goldsmith looked down at Cooley's body. He heard Bunson scream something unintelligible before tossing Garvin to the side like a rag doll. Chang decked White, who fell into another specimen, whom White promptly punched out of his way in order to get back in Chang's face. Then the crowd exploded like a swarm of angry insects feeding on itself, as pro-Cooley factions pounced on pro-Goldsmith factions, girls at first jumping out of the way and then leaping onto other girls and smaller male specimens, kicking shins and pulling hair.

Bunson threw his huge frame onto Goldsmith, tackling him to the ground. Goldsmith felt the big man's hot, angry breath and lips pressed up against his ear.

"Now," Bunson whispered. "Do it now, you've got the cover."

Goldsmith reached into his blazer's inside pocket and discreetly pulled out his Tabula.

"And if Cooley's hurt bad," Bunson hissed, "I'll fucking eat you."

Not if I eat you first, Goldsmith thought. He scrolled to his Tabula's e-mail application and selected the draft he typed up not even twenty minutes ago. While the chaos of three-hundred-odd specimens brawling on methamphetamines erupted around them, he hit the Send button.

Captain Gibson sat in his office located up on the disciplinary level. His network console chimed and he glanced at a new e-mail from Mr. Goldsmith. The subject header read: *Urgent*. He double-clicked on it and read the message:

> Dodgeball match in progress.
> Warehouse level.
> Send team ASAP!

"Shit," muttered Gibson. He hit a red switch on the desk. A siren started ringing on the disciplinary level and began to spread through the rest of the tower. Footsteps rumbled toward his office. He jumped up to meet them, ready to start barking orders.

Sadie heard the alarm ring on Level 29 and felt relief flood through her body. Professor Nelson froze.

"Wait, wait . . . ," he said, easing her head away and rolling the chair toward his computer terminal. He read the bulletin: it was an illicit dodgeball game down on Level 3. So what? He had better things to worry about than . . .

Nelson looked back down at Sadie, but she was gone. The sliding door to his office was half-opened. He looked down at his desk and saw his key card missing. His face flushed with anger and he jumped up, ready to dash into the hallway and chase that bitch down before wringing her neck. Unfortunately for him, he tripped and fell gracelessly to the floor, twisting an ankle thanks to the tangle of underwear, trousers, and shoelaces that she'd bunched up and tied into knots around his feet.

Up in the Presidential Dining Suite on Level 121, Pete sat across a dark oak table from President Lang. He twirled up the last of his spaghetti (a sampling of Stansbury's gourmet hand-and-mouth food; rare, notoriously unhealthy nonintravenous food, cooked exclusively for important guests and visiting dignitaries) and wiped the brown sauce from his lips with a crisp white napkin. President Lang unwrapped a sterilized Handi Wipe and cleaned her shiny Mont Blanc laser syringe. It was a custom-made gift from the headmaster upon her appointment to the tower's executive office. She had not used a fork and knife for more than ten years now. The shiny black body sparkled. She placed it inside a sheath and slid the syringe into her blazer pocket.

". . . and so you see," she was saying to Pete, "despite all of this school's formal traditions, cutting-edge technology, and top-level professors, we're really just a tightly-knit community of friends and family like any other. I would hope that your article reflects this. Community and trust in one another are fundamental parts of what makes the Stansbury School so special."

"I'll be sure to mention that, ma'am." Pete took a sip of water. "Would you mind if I asked you some questions about your career? I mean, I'd like to be thorough, seeing as how I'm the only journalist the school has permitted on campus in almost five years. Come to think of it, I practically had to threaten you guys with some serious scandal-mongering just to—"

"Ask away to your heart's content. We've got nothing to hide."

"This might be from my own curiosity more than anything else, but you're a relatively young woman in a very powerful, time-consuming position. You work with all these great kids. Do you ever find yourself wanting a family, having children of your own?" Pete studied Lang's face. Her eyes stayed calm. She smiled.

"Perhaps one day. But for now, I am more than content to devote all of my time to this school and these wonderful specimens."

"So there's nothing to the rumor that you were in love with one of your Amherst professors many years ago but lost him due to a terminal illness?"

"No."

"Or that you may have been pregnant with his child?"

"Come now, Pete." She grinned gamely. "If you keep asking me such unfounded questions I might start firing some back at you."

"Oh? Such as?"

"Such as who has been paying you under the table to investigate my school? In large, weekly envelopes of cash that you haven't been reporting to the government as income."

Pete smiled. "I didn't come up with those questions on my own, Madam President. But I'll say, specimens sure do have wild imaginations, don't they?"

Before she could respond, the security detail's alarm echoed in the hallway outside.

"What's that?" he asked.

"Just a routine drill, I'm sure."

"Yeah," he grinned. "It's probably nothing. Tight ship you run, Madam President. Tight ship."

The dodgeball audience was so amped-up that they didn't even hear the blaring alarms reverberate throughout the warehouse. Some overly hyperactive senior specimen grabbed Bunson and hauled him off Goldsmith. Bunson shoved the senior to the ground and pinned him, the guy's arms and legs flailing around like an overturned turtle. Goldsmith got up and rushed over to Cooley as specimens freaked out around him, wrestling each other to the ground while the warehouse guys tried to break things up, hoping to save at least some face when the detail officers made their inevitable appearance.

"Cooley!" said Goldsmith. He lightly slapped Cooley's bloodied face. Cooley's eyes drifted open, dazed for a split second before focusing on him. "Are you okay?"

"Yeah, I'm fine . . . I'm fine."

Goldsmith nodded and extended his hand, helping him up from the ground. They opened the sliding scrap metal door and made their way through the warehouse, ducking behind a row of wooden crates near the entrance as a dozen detail officers stormed inside, headed toward the dodgeball court with cattle prods and bullhorns.

Cooley looked back at the riot. He saw Officer Jamison jab Bunson with an electric prod. He fell to the ground. Jamison kicked him in the head. Cooley's jaw clenched. He looked at Goldsmith.

"Ready?" Goldsmith asked.

"Yeah."

Goldsmith sprinted for the elevator banks. Cooley followed right after him, rubbing blood from his face and wiping it on the dark navy blue of his blazer so the stains didn't look too obvious.

20

Goldsmith and Cooley stood at the elevator bank on Level 3 trying to catch their breath. The din of cursing, hollering specimens echoed from the warehouse all the way to where they were waiting for a pod to arrive and whisk them to the next phase of their gambit. Cooley hit the Up button over and over again.

"What's taking so long?" he hissed. Goldsmith pointed to the tracking display above the sets of elevator doors: all of the pods (represented as green digitized lights) were zooming downward.

"There aren't any pods free," he said. "Everyone's responding to the alarm and headed down here. This diversion is part of the plan."

"But Sadie's waiting for us."

Goldsmith glanced at his watch. Time was running out. "I know. We're jumping in the next pod that arrives on this floor."

"And what if whoever's inside wants to bust us?"

"We neutralize him before he can."

"Meaning we kick his ass?"

"Yes," said Goldsmith.

Cooley looked at him and grinned. There was a ding. A set of elevator pod's doors slid open. They rushed inside to block the passenger in and commence with neutralizing, but stopped short.

"Get in," said Sadie.

They stepped inside. Goldsmith pressed the button marked "119" for the Office of Administration and Executive Suite. The three of them looked at each other in silence. Sadie looked at Cooley's face. Cooley self-consciously tried to wipe the remaining blood away.

Cooley stepped over toward Sadie. He tried to kiss her, but she pulled away.

"You don't want to kiss me right now," she said. "Trust me on this one."

"I'm . . . damn it, I'm so fucking sorry about this." Cooley looked down, his fists clenching over and over again. "Where'd you get the gum?" he asked.

"I had it," said Sadie.

"But it's against school rules to have it. How'd you get it?"

"I just did."

"Did you get it from Nelson?"

"No."

"It's not like you've been off campus. How'd you—"

"Here," Sadie said. She was holding out Professor Nelson's key card to Goldsmith. "You shouldn't have a hard time getting to Lang's office. Every adult and security detail officer in this place is falling all over themselves to get to the riot and help out."

He took it from her and tried to give her a friendly smile, like he had no idea what she had just been through. "Thanks," he said. "You don't know how important this is to us."

"Give me some fucking credit," she snapped. "Of course I do."

"How much time do we have?" Cooley asked Goldsmith, seeming somewhat cowed by Sadie's harsh tone.

"Their lunch can't go on much longer, despite Pete's best efforts. We've got five, maybe ten minutes at the most."

The elevator dinged. They arrived at Level 119. Goldsmith stepped out. Cooley stood there looking at Sadie. The security detail alarm still blared at an ear-splitting level. "Come on," Goldsmith said, raising his voice slightly. Cooley turned and exited, following him into the hallway.

"Be careful," he heard Sadie say as the doors closed behind him.

They jogged down the silent corridor past dozens of empty offices. Sadie was right: there were no guards, no bureaucrats manning cubicles or making Xerox copies. They turned a corner and reached a set of glass doors affixed with a sign that read EXECUTIVE OFFICE SUITES.

"Nelson is going to find Miss Chapman," Goldsmith said. "Can she handle him?"

"She knows what to do."

Goldsmith nodded and swiped the key card against a sensor on the wall to the left of the doors. It beeped, the light going from red to green. They entered an empty reception area. Cooley glanced behind the secretary's desk and saw a plasma screen simulcast of the warehouse level elevator bank. Administrators were pouring out from elevator pods and dashing toward the fray. Goldsmith headed for the office door marked PRESIDENT JUDITH LANG. He swiped the key card against the lock sensor. The light went green. He took a deep breath and pushed the door open.

Sadie rode down toward her dorm room on Level 11. She popped another red stick of cinnamon gum into her mouth and chewed voraciously. All she wanted to do was brush her teeth and take a long shower, but the elevator dinged and stopped on twenty-nine. The doors slid open. Professor Nelson stepped inside. His face was still flushed, but this time with anger. Sadie stepped backward, nervous. She bumped up against the hard wall. Nelson shoved her into the corner.

"You're in deep shit," he said, his voice shaking.

"Not as deep as you," she responded, calm.

"Give me the key card."

"I don't have it."

"It'll be worthless in a matter of minutes, you stupid bitch. You don't think I'll have it deactivated immediately?"

"I wouldn't do that, if I were you."

"*Where's the fucking card?*"

"Sitting on top of the sexual harassment suit I've typed up and am prepared to turn in to the headmaster if you take any action against me."

Nelson's face went pale. He reared his hand back. Sadie thought he was going to slap her, but his arm fell down to his side. The pod dinged and the doors slid open on Level 11. Sadie brushed past Nelson as he stood there, paralyzed. He wasn't really angry, she thought to herself as she walked down the hall toward her room. He wasn't blinded by the searing rage he must have hoped to convey. He was just plain heartbroken.

Inside President Lang's office, Goldsmith moved around the enormous eighteenth-century cherrywood desk and slid into the seat behind the computer terminal. He pulled out two pairs of skintight latex surgical gloves, more souvenirs from his pilfering of the med tech bay. He pulled them on and tossed Cooley the other pair. Just in case Lang got back here and found something amiss, he didn't plan on leaving his fingerprints everywhere.

The on-screen icon asked him for his password. He connected his Tabula to the system's hard drive and ran the cracking software he downloaded from the Web site that Cooley showed him. He watched as the small screen on the Tabula ran through the name of every person, place, and thing in the English language at lightning speed. If Lang's password was in Italian, they were screwed.

Cooley took a seat in front of the simulcast screen and started flipping channels to the tower's security camera broadcast. The screen showed dozens and dozens of angles from dozens of floors.

"Go to the Presidential Dining Suite on 121," Goldsmith called out. "When she appears at the elevator bank, we'll have approximately three minutes to get out of here." Cooley found the right channel. The bank was empty.

"How long before Nelson gets Captain Gibson to invalidate his key card?" Cooley asked.

Goldsmith tried to keep up with the cracking program's words as they blinked past. *Direful, dirge, dirham* . . . "I picked Nelson because he's up for tenure next fall. He's young and ambitious, so we've got more time than we'd have with anyone else. He'll dawdle for a while, think about his career, and probably spill his guts in about an hour, before begging for the school's forgiveness." *Henbane, henbit, hence, henceforth, henchman . . .*

"Shit," Cooley said. Goldsmith looked up at the simulcast monitor. Lang and Pete were standing at the elevator bank. The computer terminal chimed. Goldsmith looked down. The password was *Henry*.

"I'm in," he said. "Keep an eye on her. Give me five more minutes." He navigated Lang's desktop. He clicked on the folder labeled: Specimen Files—Alumni Database and started scrolling through thousands of names, finally locating the Class of 2033.

"We don't have five minutes!" said Cooley as he jumped up and rushed over to the desk. He leaned down, reaching below Goldsmith's legs and pulled out a navy blue steel trash bin with a gold Stansbury insignia on the side. Cooley grabbed it and leapt up onto the couch near the wall.

Goldsmith finally found the right names and highlighted them. Alvarez, Miller, Riley, Saltzman, Santana, Smith. The Tabula began its download of the files.

Goldsmith heard a metallic *ping* over in Cooley's direction. "What are you doing?" He glanced up and saw Cooley holding a silver lighter, reaching inside the trash bin and setting its contents aflame. Black smoke started to rise. Cooley held the bin up toward the fire sensors on the ceiling. And then something in Goldsmith's mind went *ping*. He navigated back through the specimen files and clicked on the folder labeled CLASS OF 2036. He scanned for two names. Cooley. Goldsmith. Two confidential files that represented two insurance policies against treachery from the school or—just maybe—future threats from Cooley himself. A shudder of paranoia ran through him. Don't leave leverage like this on a school-issued Tabula. The alumni files were now on its hard drive, but *these* . . .

"I'm buying us some more time," Cooley said, concentrating on the rising plumes of smoke. "The fire alarms shut down the elevator pods."

"Right," Goldsmith said, feigning interest. "Right." A honking noise went off. Along with the security detail's alarm, which had been ringing this whole time, it sounded disjointed, an almost maddening jungle of racket. Ceiling sprinklers sent a cold shower of water down, soaking the office. Cooley jumped off the couch and put the trash bin under the sink at the wet bar in the office's corner. The flames fizzled out.

"Look," Cooley said, pointing to the simulcast screen. Pete was looking up at the ceiling and covering his ears. Lang pressed the elevator bank's Down button again, checking her watch and shaking her head in frustration. Goldsmith's eyes were on the computer screen. He found their files: thousands of words of single-spaced text documenting twelve years of grades, behavioral analyses, medical reports . . . their family histories must be buried inside somewhere . . . He heard Cooley's footsteps pounding toward the desk. He needed a single set of hard copies to offset everyone's personal agendas. Goldsmith hit Print and closed the screens out, logging off from the system. Cooley reached down and replaced the trash bin under the desk.

"She might smell the burnt paper and figure things out," Cooley said. "But hopefully it'll be too late by then."

"She's taking the stairs," Goldsmith said, nodding at the simulcast screen as Lang left Pete and opened the door to the stairwell. He looked at the printer. It was still spitting out pages.

"We're only two floors below her," said Cooley, urgency creeping into his voice. "We've got to go now." Cooley grabbed Goldsmith by the arm and started to yank him out of the chair.

"If she catches us, the alumni files will be good for fuck-all," he said. "Come on!" He pulled Goldsmith up. The alumni pages were already stored on his Tabula, he was just waiting on those final bargaining chips . . . Cooley rushed over to the door. There was a mirror hanging on the wall adjacent. He reached up, took it off its hook, and crouched down, angling it on the floor so that he could see through the crack of the semiopened door and into the corridor without revealing himself to anyone outside. The printer spit out one final page and powered down. Goldsmith grabbed the pages and shoved them inside his other pocket.

"Shit," Cooley said. Goldsmith rushed over. Someone finally switched off the dueling alarms. The ensuing silence was thick, leaving a ringing in their ears. In the mirror's reflection, the door's slit revealed President Lang walking toward them.

Goldsmith started thinking of plans, options, some way out. He was positive he had enough information in his pockets to crack the mystery of the alumni deaths. He couldn't get caught now. There was only one feasible thing to do: turn Cooley in. He could say that he apprehended him following the dodgeball match and . . . Lang was getting closer. Think fast. He looked over at Cooley. If he turned him in, the whole thing was over. Covering for himself meant piling more guilt on top of a specimen innocent of the charges leveled against him. And if Goldsmith did that, wasn't he just as bad as everyone else? He would not do it. He stood up and decided he could handle whatever came next. He caught a glimpse of himself in the mirror in Cooley's hands. His face looked unfamiliar, different, vaguely proud, maybe coming up just short of heroic.

"Hang the mirror back up, Cooley."

"Shhh . . . No! We've got a few seconds. Just think of something to say to . . ." He leaned in, seeing something. His eyes went wide.

"What is it?" Goldsmith asked.

"Shhh . . . Listen." Goldsmith crouched down and looked at the reflection: Lang had been stopped by Captain Gibson in the hallway. He leaned toward the crack in the door, straining to hear what they were saying.

". . . IV food sabotaged with methamphetamine . . . ," came Gibson's voice. ". . . Riot on the warehouse level . . . adverse allergic reaction to specimens' med cycles . . . kids projectile-vomiting in the infirmary . . ."

"It makes no difference at all," rang out President Lang's voice, confident. "Come with me. Find the reporter and make sure he's contained until after the vote." Gibson nodded. They started heading back toward the elevator banks. A pod arrived. They stepped in and disappeared. For the first time since this whole insane plot began, Cooley and Goldsmith exhaled.

Cooley stood up and replaced the mirror on the wall. He looked at his face for a moment and shook his head at the sight of all the blood, watching a morbid smile form on his lips. His eyes went to Goldsmith. "Congratulations, Mr. Valedictorian," he said, and winked. "I finally believe the hype."

Goldsmith opened the office door and stepped out into the deserted hallway. He said nothing and made sure not to look back inside. He didn't want Cooley to see him grinning like a proud little boy.

Goldsmith and Cooley stepped out onto the eighth floor and headed for the room of Cooley's expelled pal, Nathan Donald Oates. They reasoned that anyone looking for them would look in their own rooms first. Hiding there just might buy them some extra time. Goldsmith speed-walked with his long legs, the alumni reports practically burning a hole in his blazer.

"Mr. Thomas Oliver Goldsmith!" rang out a man's voice. They stopped and turned. Pete walked up to them at a leisurely pace, grinning. "Don't ever let it be said that a Stansbury specimen won't make the most of an opportunity when it's offered to him." He approached them, walking up to Cooley and studying him. "You must be the famous Mr. Cooley. You've got some blood on your face, bud. I wonder how that came to be. Mind giving me a couple of comments on—"

"Yes," cut in Goldsmith. "He does mind."

"Well isn't that a shame," said Pete. "Journalist's Rule Number Two: always have *two* off-the-record sources."

"Who is he?"

"Whoever do you mean?"

"Your first off-the-record source. I'll provide you with information in exchange."

"See Rule Number One, Mr. Goldsmith: A journalist never divulges—"

"Let's go," Goldsmith said to Cooley. They turned and headed off down the hall.

"Even if *she* didn't ask for a confidentiality agreement," called out Pete behind them, "I wouldn't betray . . . *her.*"

Goldsmith whirled around. Cooley stopped, taking everything in.

"No quid pro quo necessary, young man," said Pete. He bowed his head and walked away, disappearing around a corner.

Pete slipped into the fire escape stairwell on Level 8, feeling a strange sense of comfort in the shadows. Those harsh, unforgiving xenon lights in the halls always made him feel like he was on display inside of a glass case. And the security detail didn't seem to patrol in here. Someone in the administration was going to wise up about his clandestine investigation sooner rather than later. He had to move faster than them. He dialed Senator Bloom's private number and felt his heart pound. He was on the verge of throwing a hell of a wrench into the school's grant proposal. He listened to the phone ring and thought about Stansbury's odd couple, Goldsmith and Cooley.

"Yes," answered Senator Bloom.

"It's me."

"Did Harris have any luck in tracking down Lang's former flame? Senator Mark's made up her mind. She's just itchin' to end debate. We're voting on the bill tonight and if it gets to the Senate floor it's gonna pass. I can't stop her. Mark's the committee chair, so she's got the numbers *and* goddamned parliamentary procedure on her side. If I'm gonna press her to keep the discussion going, you had better lob me a Hail Mary right about now."

"The former flame angle's a dead end," said Pete, who suddenly realized that his voice echoed up and down the solid concrete walls of the stairwell and lowered his tone to a frantic hiss. He thought he heard footsteps, but rang it up to his jangling nerves. "Listen to me. I'm positive I can help you sink this vote tonight."

"How?"

"I'm in a rush here, can't go into detail right now. I don't know how much longer I've got before Lang sends her goons after me, so just trust me."

"I do. Tell me what you need and you'll have it."

"Stella Saltzman, Class of 2033. She's the key. I need to get to her ay-sap. I'm betting you've got the address for her that no one else does." A long silence followed. Pete could hear Bloom breathing, contemplating, while he heard the sound of another set of breaths that sounded unfamiliar. They were probably his own. "Sir?"

"I'm not sure I'm ready to—"

"You've got to believe me," Pete interrupted loud enough for the echoes to return. "I need to get to her before they do. All I need to do is find her, and I guarantee the vote will be delayed, maybe even deep-sixed." Another long pause.

"She's at 565 West Miller Avenue, apartment 2309," said Bloom. "Southwest San Angeles."

"At 565 West Miller, apartment 2309," Pete repeated, writing it down on his notepad. "Got it." He checked his watch. "I've got a rendezvous with my inside source coming up in about twenty minutes. Then I'm paying Miss Saltzman a visit."

"Make it happen." Bloom clicked off the call. Pete put his phone back inside his jacket pocket and felt the wet sweat marks seeping through his button-down shirt. He moved for the door to the elevator bank, before deciding that he preferred the cover of darkness the stairwell afforded him.

He ran up the stairs, taking two at a time, missing the sight of Miss Camilla Moore II quietly lurking in the shadows just a few feet from where he was standing, her brain processing the wealth of information she had just received.

Goldsmith programmed his Tabula to broadcast the alumni files on the Nature & Co. window in Oates's room and took Cooley through the details. The names of the ex-specimens, their subpar careers at Stansbury, their lack of a truly common bond, and Miss Stella Saltzman, the distinguished, disillusioned non sequitur in the group. The non sequitur that also happened to be the only one still breathing. Goldsmith watched Cooley's eyes the whole time, observing him trying to keep up. As he suspected, Riley was the only dead alumnus that Cooley knew personally.

"The only place Saltzman would've met the rest is in an examination room," Cooley said.

"The same place where I met you." Goldsmith watched Cooley lean in and study the file photos. They matched the head shots in the yearbook, minus the red X's. "Riley knew they were all being targeted," Goldsmith continued. "Which leads me to believe they were killed by the same person. I've been trying to formulate a theory as to what would have gotten them in a room together in the first place, but this has proved difficult. I'm starting to think that Stella Saltzman isn't as connected to the others as I first thought. I've seen no evidence that the school is even aware that she's tied into this. Her name hasn't been mentioned once, while the others' have been. Riley wasn't the brightest guy, after all." Goldsmith looked over Stella's file. No listed phone number, no known address, no active e-mail accounts. If he could just get a word out to her.

"If she's the next to go—," Cooley said.

"It'll be my fault."

"It doesn't have to happen that way."

"Riley could have been wrong when he included her photo with the others," said Goldsmith.

Cooley glanced up from the photos and looked at Goldsmith. "He wasn't. She was recruiting a gang."

Goldsmith laughed out loud. "What?"

"Stella Saltzman went after these people specifically. Out of all the specimens she graduated with, she picked them."

"You think Miss Saltzman, a former valedictorian, is a *gang leader*?"

"Slow down. I'm not saying she was putting together a gang because she wanted to break the law. Look at these kids," he said, pointing to their photos. "They're not criminals. They're like any other delinquents. Scared, insecure . . . looking for someone to save them from . . . something, I don't know. They were all lost, just waiting to be taken in, waiting for someone to, like, convert them and make them believe. They look just like . . ."

"What?"

". . . like the kind of kids that've been following me ever since I got here." Goldsmith looked at Cooley in silence, knowing he wasn't finished yet. "Like the eleven friends of mine you expelled yesterday. These five," he said, pointing at the files, "they were all Indians looking for a chief."

"And you're saying that Miss Saltzman is it?"

"She's a valedictorian. She can't be anything else."

Goldsmith hit some buttons, flipping through the files. Each of them had a coroner's report attached at the end, which was not in itself unusual (Stansbury's estimable alumni office kept close tabs on all of its graduates), except for the fact that each of these reports bore the insignia of the San Angeles Police Department, since they were all murdered. Alvarez: electrocuted to death after being knocked unconscious and thrown into a bathtub along with a plugged-in radio.

Miller: bludgeoned to death in an alley, ruled by the coroner as a likely mugging victim. Riley: death by overdose, not self-inflicted. Santana: bled to death after suffering fatal stab wounds to the neck and chest. Smith: shot to death. Each report was filled with descriptions of wounds, the conditions of bodily organs, various foreign food and drink present in the body at the time of death. Reams of pages and information. Goldsmith pulled his favorite keepsake from his blazer's pocket and looked at it for comfort, for encouragement: his golden valedictorian's medal. Its surface was cold.

"That's what they gave you after you won Selmer-Dubonnet?" Cooley asked. Goldsmith nodded.

"Can I see it?"

He handed it to Cooley, who felt the weight of it in his palm and looked at the engraved lettering. "Nice," he said, handing it back.

Goldsmith brought it over to the bed and sat down, feeling the medal's ridges with his fingers, remembering how it felt when the headmaster placed it around his neck during a special assembly in the coliseum in front of the whole school. What seemed like hundreds of holographic renderers snapped around them, recording their images forever in a lifelike three dimensions. Goldsmith had wanted to wear the thing to sleep, and he almost did before realizing that he might smudge it in the middle of the night. His finger rubbed against the gold. It felt nice and solid. He rubbed it harder. And then harder. He dug the nail of his thumb into the metallic sheen and felt it give way without too much effort. He dragged his nail across the medal's face and saw the gold peel away, revealing an underbelly and insides made of dull, tinny steel. Goldsmith did a fine job of holding back the tears welling up in his eyes.

"I wasn't going to say anything," said Cooley, doing him the dignity of looking in another direction. "But I knew the moment I held it in my hands."

There was a knock at the door.

"Open the door, Mr. Goldsmith." It was Camilla.

Goldsmith shut off the Nature & Co. window. Cooley looked panicked, and in response Goldsmith gestured for him to sit down and relax, moving his hand down in a soothing motion. He opened the door.

"How did you find us?" asked Goldsmith.

"Simple strategic anticipation," she said. "You needed a place to hide, somewhere private, a place not equipped with surveillance. You were smart enough to know that your own suite wasn't safe, so you improvised, reasoning that no one would look in the rooms of one of the unbalanced specimens you had expelled just yesterday. I only had to search three other rooms before I found you."

"Did you tell the security detail?"

"No. But they'll figure it out soon enough, and then you'll be on the run." She glanced over at Cooley. "I'm here to take him into custody. I don't know what you're doing with him, but I don't know if I can trust you."

"President Lang personally asked me to join in the investigation. He's here with her sanction." Sure, it's bullshit, Goldsmith thought, but she's still green at this job and isn't going to go and ask Lang herself right now. He looked over at Cooley. The expression on his face said: *Do something, we're running out of time.*

He and Camilla locked eyes. Goldsmith felt like it was a high-noon showdown. She opened her mouth first. "I'd suggest that—"

"Tell me why you've been giving information to Pete."

She stopped short, her eyes filled with shock giving way to anger. "What?"

"I know you're his off-the-record source." He moved closer to her. "Tell me why the fuck you've been talking to him!" Her breath fogged up his glasses.

"I . . . I haven't said anything to him . . ."

"Then who—"

". . . *Because I've been spending all my time making excuses for you!*" she snapped.

He stepped back. "What?"

"Gibson told me about the police officers you assaulted in San Angeles. Half of the school's talking about some dodgeball match the two of you played. There was a fire alarm right afterward. The security detail's asking me what you're doing running around with a . . . serial killer."

"They could have arrested me hours ago."

"Headmaster Latimer won't let them do anything. He says . . . he says he trusts you."

"If he still does, can't you?" he asked, stepping back. Her eyes glanced downward, avoiding his gaze. It was obvious: she did still trust him, and there was something else she wanted to say. "I'm talking to Camilla right now," he said softly. "I'm done with Miss Moore. So tell me, okay? Just tell me what's going through your head."

"On my way here I overheard Pete. He was standing in the stairwell talking on his Tabula. I was there, too . . . I wanted to get here quickly, and the elevator pods were all packed in gridlock after the riot on the warehouse level and the fire alarm, so I took the stairs. Pete thought . . . he thought he was alone, but the echoes carried his voice and I heard him."

Goldsmith leaned closer, giving her a tender look to coax it out of her. "Please, Camilla, tell me."

"He was talking about Miss Stella Saltzman. She was valedictorian from—"

"I know who she is."

"The person on the other end of the phone call was giving him her address. Pete was saying that he needed to get to her before 'they' do. He never said who he was talking about."

Goldsmith's eyes darted to Cooley. "Saltzman's gonna be next," Cooley said.

Goldsmith looked Camilla in the eyes. "Did Pete mention the address out loud?"

"No."

"You might be a better valedictorian than me, but you're an awful liar."

She blinked, hesitating, not even bothering to come up with another denial, because she knew her face had already given her away.

"You've got to give it to me, Camilla." She looked away, like she was starting to realize whatever it was she was involved in had suddenly become bigger than she ever imagined. She shook her head. "Camilla, *please*."

"I'm sorry. I don't . . . remember."

Goldsmith slammed his palm against the wall just an inch away from her head. She flinched. "*The freak with the photographic memory doesn't remember?* Listen to me. If you don't tell me the address, Stella Saltzman will be dead like the rest of them! Okay?"

"But Mr. Cooley's—"

"Cooley's innocent, goddamn it!" He smacked the wall again. After a moment, she slowly opened her eyes.

"She's at 565 West Miller Avenue, apartment 2309."

"Southwest San Angeles. That's only twenty minutes from here," said Cooley. Goldsmith stepped back from Camilla.

"Thank you," he said to her. "I mean that." She just looked at him. He walked over and flipped the Nature & Co. window back to life. The five coroners' reports were scattered on the screen, an orgy of information. He took off his glasses and rubbed his eyes.

"I haven't slept in almost two days," Cooley yawned. "Sometimes I think that if I just took my meds like everyone else, I wouldn't be in this position. I'd be ready to go off to good schools in the outside world like you guys, you know?"

"You are who you are, Mr. Cooley," said Camilla.

"She's right," said Goldsmith. "Meds are just . . . chemical combinations with fancy names." Through the blur of his vision without glasses—orphans couldn't afford corrective eye surgery—he saw a black holographic flash card projector sitting on the floor. He smiled at it, remembering the study session he and Camilla had only last night. It felt so much longer than twelve hours ago. Then he put his glasses back on, stepped toward the files, and immediately saw it.

Amidst the overflow of coroner mumbo jumbo, he spied something that looked warm, familiar, and friendly. It was ADM+5, an abbreviation for a biochemical compound. It was rare and manmade—Goldsmith had no idea what properties it had, but there it was on Alvarez's and Miller's postmortem reports: ADM+5. Adamite-5. He scanned the other files. Riley: ADM+5. Santana: ADM+5. Smith: ADM+-fucking-5.

"What is it?" asked Cooley.

Goldsmith moved for the door, his heart pounding. "Camilla, please . . . stay here with him, don't let anyone take him anywhere. This will only take ten minutes, tops."

"Where are you—," she started.

"Please! Just do this for me. I swear I won't be long." Goldsmith grabbed the doorknob.

"Goldsmith!" Cooley said. "What is it? What did you see?"

Goldsmith opened the door and looked back at him. "Maybe everything."

Up on the disciplinary level several dozen specimens sat around in a cramped holding cell. Most were still jittery from the meth, and would be for the next day or so. Bunson sat by himself in a corner: nobody wanted to get in his space and face the consequences. His head was still throbbing from Officer Jamison's boot to the skull. Footsteps echoed past the cell's barred door down the corridor. They got closer and closer. Everyone looked over. It was Officer Tannen with a clipboard. He looked at it.

"Bunson, Thaddeus. Come with me." He unlocked the door.

Bunson stood and headed for the door.

"Be strong, man," called out White.

"You watch, everyone," said Stevenson to the younger specimens. "Bunson's not gonna tell them anything."

Bunson followed Tannen down the corridor and through another door. Tannen disappeared somewhere into the shadows. President Lang walked out from an observation room and stood before him. They were the only two people around. She gave him her best camera-ready smile.

"You've been a busy boy lately, Mr. Bunson."

"I've been doing what I have to do."

"Of course you have. Run along to progressions. I wouldn't want you to be tardy and put off those nice Princeton admissions officers who are watching."

Bunson walked past Lang without a word, heading for the elevator bank. When he turned around and looked back down the hall, she was gone.

On Level 11, Sadie stood in her bathroom wearing only a towel, gargling with mouthwash for the fifth time in ten minutes. Her hair was still wet and starting to feel cold against her bare shoulders. She leaned down and rinsed with water, taking it straight from the faucet. When Sadie stood up and examined her face in the mirror, she saw something sitting on her bed in the reflection. It looked like a medium-size white envelope, a touch thicker than an average letter. Somehow, someone placed it there while she was in the shower. She walked over and picked the envelope up. In its top, left-hand corner, she saw familiar shapes: a rising sun piercing clouds above a coat of arms bearing four open books separated by the stations of a reddish-orange cross. The insignia of Brown University. Her heart began to race. She sat down, hair still dripping, and sliced open the envelope with the nail on her index finger.

The first thing she saw were the words "Congratulations" and "your acceptance." She didn't get the chance to read the rest. The papers fell from her hands to the hard marble floor. Sadie's smile melted into a twisted expression of something less than the elation she was expecting to feel. The poking sensation welling up in her stomach moved into her chest and throat and shot up through her nose and into her eyes. At first, she choked, and then began to sob with abandon. Her lush, oft-admired lips trembled as she mouthed something over and over again. She tried to speak the words, but they struggled to come out.

"I'm sorry," those lips tried to say. "I'm sorry."

21

"Just one minute, Mr. Goldsmith," said Mrs. Elton, the headmaster's faithful secretary. She projected a round, healthy figure of seniority, and her motherly presence helped to calm Goldsmith's rattled nerves. She seemed to sense this effect on him and smiled. "Excited about graduation?" she asked.

"Yes, I am."

"I understand you're going to be a Harvard man."

"That's true."

"Congratulations, sweetheart. But remember," she said, leaning over her desk toward him as if revealing a secret, "you'll always be a Stansbury man first."

"I couldn't forget that even if I tried, Mrs. Elton."

She held up a finger, nodding in accordance with the instructions being passed through the small Tabula earpiece she wore around her ear. "The headmaster will see you now."

He walked down the hallway toward the headmaster's office suite. The white marble floor common to the rest of the school gave way to a thick maroon carpet, while Stansbury's trademark minimalist décor was replaced by walls carved of oak and the occasional cracked leather club chair placed along the corridor. As Goldsmith neared the office, he started to smell the familiar aroma of ten-year-old pipe smoke. Long before Goldsmith arrived at the tower, the headmaster and Dr. Stansbury were rarely seen without their matching mother-of-pearl pipes in hand, a plume of royal gray trailing behind them before disintegrating into the sterilized air. They were both very aware that it was a bad habit with potentially fatal consequences, but could not seem to bring themselves to quit. Stansbury, of course, died of old age, but the headmaster kept the tradition alive until 2026 on his sixtieth birthday, when an eleventh grade Pharmaceutical Engineering progression presented him with a fine gift indeed: a pill of their own creation that cured him of his tobacco addiction forever. Now, the headmaster's pipe sat inside a glass case on a shelf behind his desk, in retirement. But the smell of its smoke still lingered. He would not permit the custodial crews to fumigate his area, because he believed the residual scent was a tribute to the ghost of the man who founded the school in the first place.

Goldsmith stepped into the office. The headmaster sat in a large red leather chair behind a giant oak desk with piles of neatly arranged papers placed on top of it. He saw Goldsmith and smiled, gesturing for him to take a seat.

"Hello, Mr. Goldsmith. Has young Mr. Cooley confessed his guilt? Or have you come to explain your peculiar actions in San Angeles this morning?"

Goldsmith remained standing. "Sir, five alumni of this school are dead and Cooley's got nothing to do with it. There's a sixth who's next, and I—"

"Stop. Slow down and explain everything in a clear, concise manner. The way we taught you."

Goldsmith took a deep breath and tried to get his heart to stop racing before taking another step toward the desk. "The five alumni died in different ways," he said, reclaiming his methodical tone, "but according to their coroners' reports, each of them had the same foreign chemical in their bodies: the same unidentified foreign chemical in the syringe that caused Mr. Riley's death. It's a substance referred to as

ADM+5, or adamite-5. It's a man-made biochemical toxin with no practical applications. Feel free to look at the evidence yourself. It's all here in black and white." He plugged his Tabula into the headmaster's terminal and watched the screen broadcast the files, complete with Goldsmith's notations. He looked at Latimer, gauging his reaction.

"Where did you get these files?"

"The dead specimens' autopsies were performed by five different coroners, in five different districts of San Angeles," Goldsmith continued, ignoring the question. "They had no idea the corpse in front of them was linked to four other corpses, so they weren't looking for patterns. The mention of ADM+5 is buried deep in each file. They were drawn to the obvious physical trauma the victims suffered, and probably considered traces of an obscure chemical irrelevant. You see, sir, even in large doses, adamite-5 isn't enough to kill a normal, healthy human being, but it's rare enough for me to conclude that it's a clue connected to the person who killed them."

"For *you* to conclude? You're an eighteen-year-old boy. You're no biochemist, nor are you a police officer. Now, listen to me—"

"*No, you listen,*" Goldsmith said, recoiling a bit, as if he was ready to be struck down by lightning for interrupting the headmaster. "No cop—or security detail officer—would've recognized the significance of ADM+5 on a report. The violence is a cover-up, purposeful misdirection. I think the real cause of these deaths is somehow tied into the presence of ADM+5. I'm betting the killer put the corpses through that physical trauma postmortem in order to throw off the authorities. He wanted the murders to look brutal, not like the sophisticated killings they really were."

The headmaster took off his glasses and rubbed his eyes. The edges of his black suit were pristine, razor sharp. Goldsmith wondered how many dozens he had lined up in his wardrobe. He watched the old man's face as everything sunk in and decided the silence was a signal to keep on going. "Now do you see why I don't think Mr. Cooley is guilty? There's no denying that these files show his bodily traces at each of the scenes of death, but those could have been placed there by the murderer. He's the perfect fall guy to pin violent crimes like this on. He's got a known history of violent behavior and off-campus excursions. Of all the specimens in the tower, Cooley would seem to be the ideal candidate to commit these murders, except for one thing: he's not smart enough to turn a rare biochemical toxin into a deadly weapon. He just doesn't have the knowledge or resources. But with such a ripe, seemingly guilty suspect, the killer didn't think anyone would look closely enough at the details to come up with an alternate theory."

The headmaster put his glasses back on. They sat there as the office filled with a disconcerting silence until his desk phone beeped, yanking them back into reality. "It's President Lang and Captain Gibson on a conference call, sir," trilled Mrs. Elton's voice on the speaker.

"I'm occupied. Please hold all calls until I direct otherwise." He clicked off and looked at Goldsmith. Goldsmith could see it in his eyes: he was starting to believe. "My colleagues are anxious to have this matter resolved," said the headmaster. "Evidently Senator Arthur Bloom is hell-bent on seeing the Stansbury bill fail in committee before it gets a chance to reach the Senate floor. President Lang suspects—not unreasonably, I might add—that he would stop at nothing to make this happen. She's also worried about the news reporter. He threatened to publish an innuendo-laced exposé about us if we did not cooperate and grant him access, so we took a gamble and let him inside the tower. Now, the president is certain that he is on Bloom's payroll. She assigned you to be his tour guide because she thought you might pick up on this and find some evidence proving it." The headmaster paused for effect. Goldsmith felt his gut tighten. He suspected Pete might have wanted to manipulate him, but never thought he'd be tied to Stansbury's worst nemesis. "In fact," he resumed, "there's not one member of this school's administration who isn't concerned about the supposedly coincidental timing of the strange events of the past twenty-four hours somehow affecting the Senate committee's vote."

"Senate vote?" Goldsmith said, raising his voice. "Senate vote? We're talking about an innocent specimen—"

"Do not cut me off, young man," he rumbled. "I was about to agree with you. Now, tell me what you suggest as a next step."

"I'm positive that Miss Stella Saltzman is next on the killer's hit list."

"Why?"

"Her photo was included in a collection of yearbook pages found in Riley's apartment that showed each of the other dead alumni. Five of her possible known associates have been systematically killed off. She's the only one still alive. I don't know any more than that, but I'm positive she needs to be warned if she doesn't know already."

"And?"

"And I have her home address in San Angeles, twenty minutes away from here. I need to get to her before anyone else and make sure she's safe. I'm also betting that she has information that will fill in the missing pieces of the puzzle."

The headmaster shook his head, sighing in what sounded to Goldsmith like disbelief. "Your journey here is almost finished," he said. "The world will be yours after you graduate in just a few days. Why get tangled in this mess?"

"Because progress depends on the unreasonable man."

"Miss Saltzman is not like the others. How does she fit in?"

"That's what I need to find out. Sir, I'm requesting your authorization to leave campus and get to her before anyone else does."

"Oh, is that all?" he quipped. The headmaster gave him a wry smile.

"No. I also need you to ensure that the security detail won't interfere with my business." Goldsmith paused, taking a deep breath. "And I want to take Mr. Cooley with me. If my theory about the adamite-5 is correct, he's being framed by someone who has an intimate knowledge of Stansbury and its inner workings. It could be Senator Bloom, or it could be . . ." He stopped short, not wanting to vocalize any more sacrilegious thoughts than necessary. "Well . . . you can see why I don't think Cooley is safe inside the tower."

The headmaster fixed him with a stony gaze before turning around and grabbing the glass case that contained his old pipe. He set it on his desk, reached into a drawer and pulled out a key, which he used to unlock the box. He cradled the pipe like it was a small child and reached into another drawer, coming back with a bag of brown tobacco. He packed the pipe and struck a match, lighting it. Goldsmith watched the smoke billow up from the mother-of-pearl as if it were a chimney. He smelled something sweet, maybe nutmeg, and tried to read the headmaster's eyes through the fragrant fog, but the old man was nothing if not inscrutable.

Cooley leaned down and splashed warm water on his face, rinsing off the blood with the facial scrub Oates had left behind in his bathroom. He looked at his reflection: he didn't resemble a horror movie reject anymore, but his nose was swollen and bent just a tad to the left. It occurred to him that it would probably be like that for the rest of his life. His lips were still split open but no longer bleeding. He dried his face with a towel and glanced over toward the dorm room's living area. Right outside the bathroom was the steel study table. On the other side of it sitting in a chair with her legs crossed was Camilla, looking like Little Red Riding Hood's evil twin, with that dark blue Stansbury cloak wrapped around her. Cooley noticed that her back was to a corner, probably so he couldn't sneak up on her. She kept her eyes on him from that safe distance, as if she was worried close contact would infect her with whatever he had.

"So . . . looking forward to graduation?" he offered, standing in the bathroom's doorway. A silent gaze was her response. "I am, I guess. I'm not going to some fancy college or anything, though. I'm just gonna go find my mom." He looked at her and, sensing that she was listening to him, smiled. "I mean, she's probably dead, at least that's what I was told when I was a kid . . . but I've got find out for myself, you know?" Camilla 2.0 remained still, like she was just another inanimate object decorating the room. "Hey, Camilla," he said. "You always told great stories in creative writing progressions when we were kids. I remember the way your handwriting looked when we were young, like eight years old. It was . . . it was really beautiful, the way it looped and flowed so gracefully. Made everything you wrote look just like a fairy tale. I guess . . . I always just wanted to tell you that."

Camilla started to open her mouth to speak, but just as she did, the door to the room swung open. Two security detail officers stepped in, shutting the door behind them. One of them aimed a ThermaGun at Cooley. Cooley froze. Camilla jumped up, stepping in between them.

"Mr. Cooley is with me," she said. "State your business."

"Get out of the way, Miss Moore," responded the gunman. "Or face arrest for harboring a suspect. We're taking him to the disciplinary level. Captain's orders."

"I'm operating with President Lang's sanction in coordination with Mr. Goldsmith."

"The Captain told us you'd say that," said the other officer. "And he told us it don't mean a thing. Do what you want, but we're not leaving here without Cooley."

"Camilla, move!" shouted Cooley. He sprinted out of the bathroom and threw himself down onto the smooth marble floor, sliding across it toward the study table. Camilla leaped to the side. The gunman aimed at him and pulled the trigger. Cooley kicked the steel table up into the air in his direction and it took three bullets, leaving small indentations in its surface. The flying table knocked the officer backward and crashed against the wall, upended. Still on the floor, Cooley tripped up the gunman. He pulled him to his feet and kicked him in the groin before slinging him headfirst into Goldsmith's Nature & Co. window on the far wall. The officer's helmet slammed into the glass screen, shattering it, sending sparks flying. A couple stray ones burned holes in Cooley's blazer. He slammed his knee into the officer's face and bent him over, reaching for the arm that still held the ThermaGun. The other detail man grabbed Camilla and put a pistol to her head.

"Step away from the detail officer!" he yelled.

Cooley aimed the ThermaGun strapped to the gunman's limp arm and squeezed the trigger. The shot rang out loud, leaving Camilla standing over the crumpled body of her would-be assailant. She calmly stepped over him and brushed herself off. Cooley slammed the other detail officer's head against the wall one more time for good measure and let him fall to the floor, unconscious.

"Thanks for the helping hand," Cooley mumbled dryly, gasping for air.

"Did you kill him?" she asked, pointing to the man Cooley just shot.

"No. He got hit with a heavy-duty tranquilizer. They used the same thing on me last night. Look. He's still breathing. The wound's only superficial, just enough to pierce the skin and transfer the sedatives to the bloodstream." Camilla looked down and saw the man's chest moving up and down steadily. "Killing a Stansbury employee wouldn't help me prove my innocence, now would it?"

"How did you know the gun wasn't loaded with real bullets?"

"Because they need me alive. Otherwise, they couldn't pin Stella Saltzman's death on Mr. William Winston Cooley." Cooley collapsed into a chair, catching his breath. He felt his heart rate slow down and thought it must have been a trip to be on the med cycle and never have your pulse rise above one hundred. But it was a trade-off: trained detail officers got spoiled rotten keeping doped-up specimens in line. The kids' aggression got tamped down; their adrenaline never started flowing. When they had to deal with a real, live, scared-shitless guy like him, it was like they were bogged down, moving underwater, their reaction times dulled. "Goldsmith won't be gone long," he said to Camilla. She nodded in agreement. A moment passed. She pulled over the chair from her safe little corner and sat down next to him.

"What were you gonna say," he asked, "before they came in here?" Cooley looked at her and saw Camilla smile for the first time he could remember.

"I was going to thank you for what you said about my writing. It was the nicest thing anyone has ever said to me in my entire life."

Goldsmith remained standing before the headmaster at his desk, watching him puff away at his pipe, his eyes scanning the alumni files before him. Just as he was about to remind him that time was running out, the headmaster reached into a drawer and brought out a crisp sheet of Stansbury letterhead. The paper was slightly yellowed and heavy, crafted to seem like ancient parchment. At the top was the school's emblem in navy blue. The headmaster pulled a heavy black fountain pen from his inside pocket and began to write.

"I hated what Captain Gibson did to you in the elevator pod today," he said. "When you returned from San Angeles. The way he bullied and put his hands on you. He must have forgotten he ordered the surveillance system to be activated for the duration of the Cooley debacle. I saw the whole thing on the playback. This is the man I have entrusted with my specimens' security? Not when this is finished. Frankly, I trust you more than him and his security detail."

Goldsmith watched as he scrawled the words: "I hereby authorize Mr. Thomas Oliver Goldsmith, Valedictorian of 2036, and Mr. William

Winston Cooley (at Goldsmith's discretion) to come and go from the tower without impediment on this day, March 30, 2036. Mr. Goldsmith travels on Stansbury business of the highest order at my personal request. His actions and words are backed by the full faith and support of the headmaster of Stansbury School." He sheathed the fountain pen and engraved the document with his personalized seal. The headmaster handed him the paper and smiled. "He's in quite a bind at the moment," he said, "but I feel better knowing you'll be traveling amongst outsiders with Mr. Cooley by your side. Someday you must regale this old man with the tale of how the first specimen to befriend my lonely valedictorian was the last one anyone thought it would be. Be careful, son. And come home soon."

"I will, sir," Goldsmith responded, placing the parchment inside his blazer pocket. "It's been an honor serving you this year." He turned to leave.

"Mr. Goldsmith?" came the headmaster's voice. "Please send my best to Miss Saltzman when you find her. She was always one of my favorites."

"Of course, sir." Goldsmith disappeared down the corridor. The headmaster waited for a few moments before picking up his desk phone and dialing.

"Madam President?" he said. "Please come to my office immediately."

Goldsmith opened the door to his bedroom suite, saw the bodies of the two detail officers on the floor, the shattered Nature & Co. window, and put it all together, not even bothering to ask Camilla or Cooley what had transpired. "What did the headmaster say?" asked Cooley.

"He's on our side. He gave us his authorization to find Miss Saltzman and warn her. I just called Universal Taxi. There's a gyrocab waiting for us outside right now."

Cooley stood up and walked out of the dorm room and into the hall. "Go ahead," he said, nodding back in Camilla's direction, "say what you need to say."

Goldsmith looked at him for a moment and then walked into his room, closing the door behind him. Camilla stood up.

"What's your theory, Mr. Goldsmith?"

"I'm not sure. Things are . . . convoluted at the moment."

"You must have some educated guesses."

"How's this? The headmaster thinks Senator Arthur Bloom might be behind everything."

"That's not as far-fetched as it sounds," she said. "Bloom has had it in for Stansbury since day one. He thinks we're no different than doped-up Olympic athletes."

"I know. Apparently President Lang believes Pete is on his payroll."

"That could answer the question of how the killer knew so much about Stansbury history, wouldn't it?"

"Maybe," he said, looking down as his hands started to fret the edges of his tie. Camilla watched him fidget.

"You don't think the school could be—" She stopped when she felt his hand on her arm, clutching it softly.

"If for some reason we don't come back," he said, faltering, ". . . I know you'll give a beautiful speech on commencement day." He took a step closer and touched the stray lock of hair that hung down along the outline of her face, wishing he could bring it along as a good luck charm. He felt tears filling his eyes and a single drop rolled down his cheek. Camilla stopped its trail, gently pressing her index finger against his skin, and looked up at him.

"What's the matter?" she asked.

"This . . . this place means so much to me. It's . . . my home, and I don't want it to ever change. But the thing is . . ."

"What?"

". . . It already has." He stepped away from her and put his hand on the door handle. "I love you," he said, looking down at her reflection in the white marble floor. And then he walked out into the corridor to join Cooley without looking back.

Camilla walked back into Oates's room, her first-class mind wrestling with a flood of strange emotional sensations to which she was not accustomed. She felt the med cycle's chemicals push them away, far back into the hidden reaches of her psyche where they would not bother her again. But that was not what she wanted. Those sensations were strange, but . . . pleasant.

"Fr . . . freeze Miss Moore," came a dazed, pain-ridden voice behind her. One of the security detail officers—the one whose head Cooley used as a blunt instrument to ram against the Nature & Co. window—had regained consciousness. She whirled around and looked: he was holding a Colt M-8, aiming the pistol at her.

"Excuse me, officer?"

"I'm taking . . . taking you in . . . on charges of—" And like magic, Camilla somehow appeared right before him. She held his arm in a wrist lock and pain was shooting through his elbow. He dropped the gun. She kicked it across the floor and brought his face down into her knee. She heard cartilage pop. His body went limp.

Camilla glanced around, getting used to the new feeling of adrenaline flowing through her body. She saw the world without the haze. For the first time in twelve years, she was alive. Honestly, she admitted, she wasn't sure if she liked it, but her initial analysis of this altered state led one to postulate that—

"Mr. Goldsmith's in love with me," giggled Camilla 2.0 out loud and to no one in particular. She felt herself blush for the first time in her life.

Cooley and Goldsmith rode away from the tower in the back of a Universal Taxi gyro and watched the rain as it poured down from the clouds in the dark afternoon sky. Lightning bolts flashed to and fro. Thunder rumbled in the distance then got closer, the booms rattling the cab's windows.

"News report says there's a storm warning," called out the cabbie from the front of the gyro, looking back over his shoulder at them. The sky lit up with another bolt. "Hope you kids don't have a curfew. This mess keeps up, the S.A. transportation bureau's gonna shut down the flight paths 'til it passes, and who knows how long that could take."

"Figures," said Cooley. "They finally let you out of the tower and you don't even get to see the sun." Goldsmith stared out the window. "Bummer, isn't it, Thomas?" He watched as Goldsmith frowned. "How come you can't stand hearing the sound of your own name?" he asked.

"That's what my mom called me. I guess it just doesn't sound the same coming from someone else, that's all. It's like every time someone else says it I forget what it sounded like when she said my name in the first place. Like other people's mouths corrupt it."

"So, what's Camilla 2.0 gonna say when you guys are getting it on?" he asked, his voice creeping up into a girlish falsetto, " *'Oh yeah, Mr. Goldsmith! Do it to me just like that Mr. Goldsmith . . . '* " Goldsmith shot him an angry glare. Cooley started cracking up. "Hey, I'm sorry man . . . I just thought it'd be . . ." He stopped apologizing when he saw Goldsmith crack a smile.

"Hey," Goldsmith said after a moment, "do you ever think about what you're going to be when you grow up?"

"Sure," Cooley replied, trying to sound intelligent because he sensed Goldsmith wanted to have a meaningful chat. "I was thinking . . . um . . . ," he stammered, racking his brain for some made-up career goal that would sound suitably impressive to a straight-A Harvard-bound specimen. After a few awkward moments he gave up. "To be honest, man, I've got no fucking clue." Goldsmith started laughing. "Hey, what's so funny?" Cooley demanded. "Just because you've got it all figured out doesn't mean you can laugh at guys like me."

"I've got no fucking clue, either," said Goldsmith, the laughter beginning in small giggles, before erupting into big, infectious gales. Cooley cracked up.

"So what are you gonna do after graduation?" asked Cooley.

"Try to forget about the mess we're in."

"Meaning you're gonna get hammered and make a late-night Tabula call to Camilla?"

"Yeah," he grinned. "Pretty much." He burst out into laughter.

"Hey!" called out the cabbie. "Settle down back there! I'm trying to concentrate on the sky and not get us all killed!" But they kept on laughing and, from the sound of the thunder crashing outside, it seemed as if nature itself had joined in their brief moment of mirth.

On the twenty-third floor of the luxury condominium high-rise at 565 West Miller Avenue, Goldsmith and Cooley stood outside of door number 2309. "I guess this is it," Goldsmith said, raising his hand, getting ready to knock.

"What are you going to tell her?"

"I was going to start off by giving her the secret valedictorian hand shake."

"You guys have a hand shake?"

"That was a joke."

"Oh."

Suddenly, the door swung open and they came face-to-face with Miss Stella Saltzman. Even though she was only three years older than they were, she had the full, rounded figure of a woman. She wore a gray wool dress and a black shawl over her shoulders. To Cooley, she looked just like a nice librarian, and he had a hard time believing she could ever be tangled up in the business of dead former specimens or evil plots involving poisonous designer chemicals. He remembered telling Goldsmith his theory that she was starting a gang, recruiting all the other unbalanced kids for some unstated, perhaps sinister purpose, and started to feel more than a little foolish. An aroma wafted out from her apartment and into the hallway. She was baking banana bread.

"Look at what we have here," she said in a voice deeper than expected, as she looked Goldsmith up and down. "The little orphaned angel's all grown up. And you," she continued, shifting her gaze to Cooley, "must be the patsy."

"Miss Saltzman, are you aware that you might be in grave danger?" asked Goldsmith.

She studied them, sized them up, weighed probabilities in her head. Finally, she gestured for them to enter. "Come in," she said.

Back inside the tower, President Lang entered the headmaster's office. He gestured for her to take a seat across from him. She stared at the pipe in his hand. "If you're smoking again, I'm not expecting the news to be good."

"I just authorized Mr. Goldsmith to travel off campus," he said. "He has Mr. Cooley with him."

"*What?*"

"Mr. Goldsmith identified a foreign toxin present in each of the dead alumni."

"And how, may I ask, did he do that?"

"He said it was adamite-5." He watched the chagrin disappear from her face as she leaned forward in her plush leather club chair, stunned, her mouth hanging open. The headmaster waited for more of a reaction but did not get it. He decided to continue talking. "As you know, five years ago we began testing our Attention Deficit Disorder vaccine on lab animals and every mouse injected with it died of a massive brain seizure. When the scientists removed the ADM+5 element from the formula, the cure worked so well, the results were so effective, that it was distributed to every single specimen, faculty member, and employee at Stansbury, and still is to this day. It was a triumph. We single-handedly eradicated ADD—perhaps the most frequently diagnosed behavioral disorder of the last fifty years. But what the public does not know is that, because like all vaccines, the dosage permanently shifts our physiology and inoculates us from the disorder, an adamite-5 injection—as unlikely as that would be in a normal specimen's lifespan, given the rarity of that chemical—would be instantly fatal to anyone who was enrolled here. Judith, a human body cannot sustain even a small amount of ADM+5 and survive after they receive Stansbury's vaccination. The chemical combinations cause instantaneous death. Do you know what this means?"

"Well, it could mean that—"

"It means that whoever killed those five alumni had an intimate knowledge of this history. All of our meds have been billed as risk-free to the specimens, their parents, and the government—but as we both know, this isn't always the case. However, there is no way that Mr. Cooley would know this history, much less how to get enough pure ADM+5 doses to become a serial killer." He looked at Lang's face. She was pale. The Senate Select Committee on Education was voting in less than two hours and he imagined that she was seeing everything slip away right before her eyes. "A penny for your thoughts," he said, giving her what he hoped was a reassuring smile.

"That reporter from the *San Angeles Times* is still moving around the tower and the security detail has not been able to track him down. We had him contained with Mr. Goldsmith and then Miss Moore, but the Cooley situation diverted their attention, and now we have what could be a monumental public relations disaster on our hands."

The headmaster picked up the desk phone. "I'm calling the police. You were absolutely correct about not trusting Senator Bloom's intentions. I'm certain he's behind these crimes. No one else has the motive or the means to see that they happened. There is a sixth former specimen who might be in danger. Goldsmith and Cooley have gone to find her."

President Lang put her finger down on the phone's Off button, cutting off his connection. "Don't be rash," she said.

The headmaster pulled the phone away from her. "The silence you need to procure a one-trillion-dollar grant for the school is secondary to the purpose of the school itself, which is to nurture its specimens. I am going to do everything in my power to protect my children," he said, his voice rising. "I would think that you'd agree with me, given the . . . unique circumstances."

"Mr. Goldsmith and Mr. Cooley will be fine," she said. "And so will Miss Saltzman."

The headmaster looked at her, vaguely puzzled. "I never said the sixth former specimen was Miss Saltzman." They locked eyes. The Tabula inside Lang's blazer started to ring.

"Excuse me, it might be Senator Cass and—" She broke off her glance and reached inside her pocket, standing up from her chair. The headmaster watched her pull something out of her pocket—not a Tabula—and the next thing he saw was his right hand impaled against the wood of his desk by the laser needle of a Mont Blanc syringe, the very same one that he had bought for her as a congratulatory gift years ago. He felt something enter his bloodstream. His breaths got shorter and shorter before he started to gag. His mother-of-pearl pipe fell and hit the floor, breaking into two pieces. He tried to reach for the syringe to remove it from his hand but lacked the strength. The headmaster started to gag and felt himself vomit a mix of foamy bile and blood across the desk before collapsing, his head smacking against the blotter, blacking out for the last time in his life. He smelled the nutmeg of the still smoldering pipe at his feet, and in the endless haze of darkness he imagined that he was back at Dr. Stansbury's ranch, waiting for his old friend to open the door and greet him. But Mr. Goldsmith answered the door. He was tall as ever, grown into a man. The headmaster faded away, so glad that the boy made it home without a scratch on him. None that could be seen, anyway.

President Lang removed the syringe from the headmaster's hand and watched the final shudders of his corpse before it lapsed into rigor mortis as she quickly sterilized the chamber, cleaning away all the traces of the adamite-5 she had filled it with just minutes before she was summoned. Her Tabula was still beeping. She removed it from her pocket and answered the call.

"How was my timing?" asked Captain Gibson.

"Cooley and Goldsmith are at Saltzman's safe house."

"We looked for that address for the past five months and came up with zilch. How'd they get it?"

"It doesn't matter. Trace Goldsmith's Tabula and have the team intercept them. Now." Lang disconnected the call and ruffled her carefully arranged hair. She made herself weep, feeling the tears running down her face and rubbing them away so that they smudged her makeup in just the right manner. She made a mental note to call in her stylist no later than half an hour before she was scheduled to simulcast to the Senate Select Committee on Education once more before their scheduled vote on the Stansbury bill at 5 P.M. And then the president dashed down the corridor as fast as she could, shouting for Mrs. Elton to call the medics with a frantic hysteria that impressed even herself.

22

Cooley and Goldsmith followed Stella into her apartment past a mammoth antique mirror with a wooden frame and built-in candelabras of brass. Its long, thick white candles actually flickered with real, hot orange flames, as opposed to the digitized holographic light to which the young men had become accustomed. The soft light continued to stretch down a long hallway with soft Persian rugs on the floor. The syrupy scents of cinnamon and warm banana bread hung in the air. The lady of the manor seemed to glide just above the floor with a grace that did not seem possible, given her generous proportions.

The apartment seemed to go on forever, miles of dark wood; the only reminder that this was the year 2036 was the unending skyline of San Angeles outside the large wall-to-wall windows that unfolded as she led them into the living room. The long rows of tall jagged buildings and skyscrapers in the distance were punctuated by the intermittent bolt of lightning and seemed menacing, like a shark's grin. Cooley noticed that inside this home he felt safe for the first time in a long while. He and Goldsmith sat down on a plush purple couch of aged worn velvet. Stella sat in a mossy green chaise longue across from them.

"So tell me, Mr. Goldsmith," she said, the knowing smile audible in her voice. "Have the awards and the medals started to lose their shine?"

"I still believe in progress," he replied, his voice a bit shaky, like that of a shipwreck's lone, once-proud survivor who knew he was doomed but insisted on clinging to what remained of his dignity.

"Progress?" She laughed. "They're still selling the same bill of goods. 'City on a hill' and 'the elite.' Progress! Progress makes purses out of human skin, my friend." Cooley watched Goldsmith for a reaction and half expected him to stomp out of the room in disgust at her comments regarding his beloved school. Goldsmith maintained his poker face, but Cooley suspected he was burning up inside.

"Miss Saltzman, we're here to—"

"I know why you're here."

"I'm betting you knew the five dead alumni. Their files indicated—"

"They were killed with injections of adamite-5," she said in that clinical, no-frills valedictorian tone. "I'm certain you already knew this. What you probably did not know is that adamite-5 is a substance fatal only to Stansbury specimens who have taken the school's vaunted ADD vaccination. The ADM+5 creates an adverse reaction to the chemicals that the vaccination adds to the physiology, and produces an instantly fatal brain seizure." She paused, looking from Goldsmith to Cooley, and smiled at him. He felt a warm tingle pass through his chest. A handsome woman, he thought. She was a proud, handsome woman who makes me feel safe. "Those five dead specimens were similar to you, Mr. Cooley. Living, breathing proof that all the money and technology in the world can't teach a child how to grow up."

"I need to know if you think Senator Arthur Bloom is behind the murders," interjected Goldsmith.

Stella looked over at him. Cooley noticed that she and Goldsmith had the same sad expression on their faces: forlorn, resigned looks of dreamers recently shaken back into reality, only to find the wonderful world they thought they discovered after all this time was just a minutes-long illusion created by the combination of exhaustion, rapid eye movement, and foolish optimism. Goldsmith saw her face and looked out the window, knowing the answer would not be of the one-word or easily explained varieties. But Cooley felt as if he were being left out of an unspoken conversation. He was not intuitive like them. Silent explanations weren't enough and, unlike Goldsmith, he was not afraid of what the answers might have meant.

"Why would Senator Bloom do something like this?" Cooley asked her.

"Senator Bloom," she said, "is not only my employer. He is my mentor, my patron saint, and the only human being in this world that I trust." While the words came from her mouth, Stella was still looking at Goldsmith, as if she knew that her gaze was the only thing preventing him from falling apart into a million shattered pieces.

"But that guy hates specimens," said Cooley.

"And if you're working with him," Goldsmith said, "how can we trust you not to be involved in the crimes? You knew the others, didn't you?"

Stella reclined in her chaise longue as if she was preparing for a blow to strike her body, or perhaps about to embark on an epic journey back over some dark territory she had hoped never to see again. The kind smile left her face as she began to formulate her answer.

After winning the Selmer-Dubonnet test back in the autumn of 2033 (Cooley and Goldsmith were only fourteen years old), Miss Stella Saltzman did not look forward to the distractions and stress of the valedictorian's duties, but after twelve years of success at the school, she felt it was her obligation to fulfill them nonetheless. In fact, she began her tenure with the optimistic belief that her reign would be different: whereas her predecessors thrived on the inherently antagonistic relationship between their authority and the insubordination of those who violated policy, she would fashion herself as more of an advocate for them, a true diplomat shuttling back and forth between the delinquents and the administration. Stella did not make use of the traditional examination techniques detailed in the valedictorian's manual. She did not permit her suspects to be hooded and disoriented, and did not require the security detail to bind their hands or legs during questioning sessions. Perhaps most importantly, she did not use the arsenal of psychological pressure and trickery on the unbalanced specimens that had come to be routine in the preceding years.

After a few months of this strategy, she felt as if she were making progress. The problem students she confronted tended not to turn into repeat offenders, and even the most aggressive, violent specimens seemed to soften during peer reviews. Her presence around the tower and in progressions did not strike fear into the hearts of others, and, although she was regarded with a wary eye, the general sentiment was that she was a kind young woman merely putting in her time, paying her dues, not angling for prestige or the administration's favor at the expense of her peers.

The responses of the adults who ran Stansbury were varied. Due to her unconventional approach, Stella's questioning sessions lasted longer than any in recent memory, averaging more than sixty minutes per specimen. Members of the security detail believed she was letting offenders off easily and suspected that, while the occurrence of repeat offenders was going down, the general frequency of policy violations was rising because no one feared the consequences. Captain Gibson concurred, making the case (both to Stella herself and to his colleagues) that the most effective kind of policing was deterring misbehavior through the threat of uncomfortable punishment with severe consequences. President Lang remained silent on the issue. The headmaster insisted that Miss Saltzman be given a free hand to perform her tasks as she saw fit. He did not believe the school's top specimen should be deprived of the freedom of tailoring the valedictorian's duties to his or her own outlook on life, so long as they were effective in prosecuting wrongdoing.

And Stella was effective. In fact, following the winter holiday she took an unconventional step without the knowledge of the administration. She started to schedule unofficial, off-the-record sessions with unbalanced specimens that did not take place on the infamous disciplinary level. She offered to meet with various problem children and simply talk to them about anything they wanted—school, life, family, fears, or hopes. To her surprise, those invitations were accepted almost immediately by all to whom they were extended. After a few hours spent talking with unhappy delinquent specimens of all ages, she started to see more and more specimens on a one-on-one basis—not merely policy violators, but also children who were simply in need of an understanding ear and a good mind to provide them insight. Insight, Stella started to realize, that did not have to be especially profound, but merely sensible and human. It was something they were not receiving from anyone else.

Soon, she saw there were certain topics that kept coming up, the most frequent of which was a skepticism about life inside Stansbury, about having to give up one's freedom and childhood without their consent in order to become part of America's top 1 percent. Stella herself often debated this topic in her own mind, but she was shocked to find that it was a sentiment common to almost every specimen she met with, whether they were honor roll candidates or the latest suspects to be run down by the security detail. Word of mouth always spread very quickly in the tower, and soon she was spending so much time providing her makeshift advice and therapy sessions to specimens in need that her grades started to slip. She found herself increasingly uninterested by her progression work and uninspired by the four years of college (Georgetown University accepted her for their prestigious political affairs program) that awaited her after commencement day. And then she met Mr. Wayne Edward Haddon.

The first time they spoke was on the disciplinary level, in Examination Room #3. Mr. Haddon was there because, in addition to being tardy to progressions many times over, he had allowed a friend to cheat off him during a quantum physics exam. The security detail summary report billed him as an unbalanced case with a chronic disregard for authority, but Stella questioned him and saw a typical seventeen-year-old boy who didn't always do what he was supposed to do, but more often than not made the right decisions. Soon after their session, she ran into him in the cafeteria during dinner and they shared a table. Stella expected it to be just another hour of playing resident psychiatrist for a peer in need, but to her surprise they ended up talking about the theatre, in particular their shared love for a cult play of the late twentieth century called *This is Our Youth*, by Kenneth Lonergan. Of all the academics around the tower, Haddon was the only specimen she'd met who had read the play and loved it as much as she had: his older brother had given him a dog-eared copy a few years before on summer holiday, while she discovered it in a used bookstore the last time she was home in Cleveland over Christmas.

They fell in love. Consistent with her unorthodox approach toward being valedictorian, Stella wisely decided they should keep their relationship a secret from the administration and their fellow specimens. After a few weeks, Wayne revealed that he had stopped taking his meds months ago. He gave her vivid descriptions of feelings, surges of raw emotions that dragged him up and down without warning, daydreams of ideas, places, and marvelous, impractical goals, of which he previously had never dared to think. It was this new, unrestrained way of seeing life that allowed him to open up enough to Stella so that he was capable of truly loving her with all his heart. She was enthralled by the way he described his new world. The spontaneity and passion of it sounded foreign and irresistible to her. By the time Wayne summoned up the courage to ask if she would abstain from the med cycle with him, she had already decided that she would never take the school's pills again.

The weeks that followed were the most unusual and happy of Stella's young life. Her mind felt light without the burden of duty and restraint that she had grown up on. To be able to leave her textbooks and Tabula in her bedroom suite the night before a test and stroll hand in hand with Wayne through their favorite secluded, tree-lined path in the atrium seemed outrageous and yet completely natural. It felt as if they had begun constructing a home of their own inside the tower, one that was invisible but had sturdy, sheltering walls that could move along with them, protecting them inside their own personal world as long as they were together. Granted, it wasn't a completely idyllic life: often she found herself jealous for no good reason; he was concerned about her commitment to him after graduation; they would argue about the taste of intravenous chocolate soufflé after dinner, or the merits (or lack thereof, as far as Wayne was concerned) of *Franny and Zooey*. But these absurd, heated conflicts were what brought them closer. Soon Stella and Wayne found it hard to believe that their lives were ever governed by the med cycle, or much less, that they'd lived without each other.

After a routine physical exam, however, things became more complicated. The school medics discovered that Stella was two months pregnant. She was shocked and terrified. The administration was informed, but otherwise the incident was cloaked under a veil of the strictest secrecy. Even under normal circumstances Stansbury gossip tended to spread quickly, but in the case of arguably the most high-profile of all specimens, it would not only flood the halls but would irreparably damage Stella's image, permanently taint the office of the valedictorian, and, perhaps most destructively, set an exceedingly negative example for the thousands of young, impressionable minds in the tower (not to mention raise the ire of their tuition-paying parents, if and when they heard about the administration's failure to keep the children in line).

Stella immediately found Wayne and told him the news. Naturally, they were scared, but they were not naïve about the possible consequences when they began sleeping together. They were both well aware that their abstention from the med cycle was probably responsible for the sexual impulses they found impossible to repress, but once they had a chance to talk it over, neither of them viewed this unexpected pregnancy as the disaster the school seemed to think it was. From the start, the issue for Stella and Wayne was not whether she would bear the child, but whether they would raise it themselves or put it up to be adopted by parents who were more capable of providing it with the stable lifestyle it deserved. After much soul-searching and debate, they decided on the latter option.

"They didn't say whether it's a boy or girl?" asked Wayne.

"No."

"Well, I want to think of a name anyway."

"Like a name that will work for either one?" Stella asked.

"Right." They looked at each other for a few moments. Her top-notch brain was coming up with blanks, but Wayne got a peaceful look in his eye. "Evan," he said. "I like Evan. Makes for a cool girl or like, a really honorable guy. Like the kind of person I could trust, you know?"

"I like it, too," she said. Suddenly the news didn't feel as bad.

Later that same evening, Stella received a summons to President Lang's office. This much she expected. Headmaster Latimer, as universally loved as he was, knew better than to offer advice on a topic so sensitive to a young woman. What Stella did not expect was what the president had to say. From the moment she sat down, President Lang's point of view was obvious. She asserted that bearing the child was simply not a viable option. The president explained ("from one strong woman to another," was how she prefaced it) that she was once in a position very similar to Stella's. She started out as an ambitious young lady who had all the tools to succeed, if only those who could provide her with opportunities—men—would take her seriously as an equal. She asserted that the process of bearing a child out of wedlock would take its toll on her fledgling college career and leave irreparable psychological scars that could cripple her for the rest of her life. Lang finished by letting Stella know that she was committed to assisting her through this trauma, and had even taken the initiative of flying one of San Angeles's top surgeons to the tower to perform the abortion procedure as quickly and painlessly as possible. That was when Stella realized the president was not offering advice. She was dispensing orders. She politely declined Lang's assistance and promptly left her office without another word.

That night, the security detail came for Stella while she slept. They sedated her and brought her to the infirmary without the knowledge of any of the specimens. When she woke up the following morning, she was informed that the surgery had been completed. Stella tried to weep, out of sadness, anger, anything, but found she could not. She was numb. She also had yet to learn about another incident that happened the night before.

Another group of security detail officers came for Wayne. They took him to the disciplinary level and left him in an examination room with Captain Gibson. She had no conclusive evidence about what happened next, but Stella was familiar enough with Stansbury intricacies to put it together. Gibson had a conversation with Wayne, in which he probably told him about what had happened to unborn Evan and, she knew it deep in her heart even then, he must have lied to him about Stella's condition, which in reality was healthy, given the circumstances. The Captain left him in the room alone with two bottles: one of water, one of sedative pills. When he returned an hour later, Mr. Wayne Edward Haddon was lying on the room's cold concrete floor, dead from an overdose.

Stella, still bed-ridden when she heard, was shattered by the news. But when the president and the headmaster came to visit her she held it all in, feeding on the numbness that the doctor left inside of her in the place of her child. They brought their condolences, the gentle, kind, but ultimately clueless headmaster, and President Judith Lang, Stansbury's dissembling Machiavelli in a designer suit. There were countless things Stella wanted to shout out at her, innumerable accusations and threats, but she understood the dynamics of her situation very well: as a specimen she was at Lang's mercy, playing by her rules inside a castle over which she presided. The only thing Stella told them was that her valedictorian's career was over. She was retiring. The headmaster said he understood her position and was ready to relent. Lang said it wasn't an option, that it would destroy the stability upon which the entire school was based. That much Stella understood. She was dismayed to see that the president was shrewd enough to calculate the effects as well as she did. But the time would come, Stella vowed, that she would get her vengeance, and not just on Lang or Captain Gibson. She swore she would bring down the tower and, along with it, anyone who dared try to profit by associating themselves with the obscenity of the word "Stansbury."

Stella recovered and made it through the final months of her senior year. At commencement, she gave an uninspired speech plagiarized almost directly from some hackneyed book of toasts and bon mots she found in the school library. Everything passed without incident. On that huge platform in the center of the coliseum, she accepted her diploma and a firm handshake from President Lang in front of her beaming family and peers. Her move to Washington, D.C., followed, where Stella squeezed Georgetown's four-year political affairs program into three and immediately got a job as an aide to Senator Arthur Milford Bloom of California, a seventy-two-year-old curmudgeon who had a soft spot for bright young women who reminded him of his own daughter. More important, the distinguished Senator was known for his conservative skepticism regarding trendy new developments in education, in particular the increasing use of medical supplements. Because of its high profile—and because several of Bloom's rivals in the Senate were former specimens—Stansbury School was a particular point of interest for him. He immediately took a liking to

Miss Saltzman. What began as long dinner conversations about her insider's criticisms of Stansbury—during which she drew upon the hundreds of hours of her conversations with unbalanced specimens (never bringing up the story of Wayne and Evan)—evolved into briefings to Senator Bloom's staff and then talking points for the Senate Select Committee on Education, of which he was a member.

Roughly twelve months ago, President Lang began her own lobbying effort on Capitol Hill. Her goal was to facilitate the passing of a bill that would allocate $1 trillion annually to Stansbury, based on the importance of the school's contributions to American culture. But the benefits the school would receive were not solely financial. It would also effectively receive the imprimatur of the United States Government. The debate around Stansbury's methods and ethics would, for all intents and purposes, be rendered moot. The tower outside San Angeles might only be the beginning: Lang and her considerable number of backers in Congress envisioned towers all across the country, each serving as a factory of genius and progress that would eventually push the nation's already considerable achievements well past those of any rival.

Almost simultaneously, Senator Bloom began to organize an opposition to Lang's plans. He received support from a wide-ranging cast of civil rights groups and other nongovernmental organizations, but lacked the answer to the most convincing arguments in Stansbury's favor: the AIDS and cancer vaccines, the Nobel prizes, the college admissions numbers—the prestigious ends that justified their means. As he had already been doing with increasing frequency, the senator went to Stella for her insight and she confided to him an audacious plan. While the American public would undoubtedly support the school when confronted with its accomplishments, it might hesitate if shown the human cost involved. Literally, the faces and stories of those children whose freedom and lives were subjugated to both the med cycle and isolation from the outside world, in order to breed an engineered race to produce some miracle drug or masterpiece once every few years. Stella suggested what no outsider had the experience or knowledge to accomplish: she would locate and recruit a group of former specimens—a selection of the unbalanced misfits she came to know and love (and who loved her back) during her time as valedictorian—and convince them to testify before the committee. They could potentially kill the bill before it even got to the Senate floor for a vote. Senator Bloom deemed her stratagem brilliant. He gave her the full authority of his office to move forward.

Unfortunately for Stella, Stansbury's network was wide-ranging. By the time she had received her first dozen or so negative responses from the former specimens she was relying on, she understood that the school had gotten to them first. Through research and tracking, she discovered Stansbury was offering unemployed, underachieving alumni like Mr. Daniel Ford Smith jobs in a tight labor market. The ones who didn't accept them were intimidated with threatening visits to their homes. When she finally tracked down five who understood her vision and were willing to risk their lives by testifying about their shattered childhoods, one by one they paid the highest price. President Lang and her supporters manufactured their own convoluted murder mystery, complete with not-so-random victims who met apparently brutal ends, and a current, notoriously unbalanced orphaned specimen on whom to pin the blame, the school's calculated explanation being that one very bad apple in four thousand was the exception rather than the rule.

And now, with the committee's vote roughly one hour away, Stella knew that President Lang could feel the victory within her grasp. And yet, despite the somewhat daunting circumstances, the ghosts of sweet Wayne and little Evan would not allow her to fold her hand just yet.

Stella's story left in its wake a stunned silence. Cooley's first instinct was to question its veracity, but he understood that it was simply too incredible, the circumstances were too grave, and the look on Goldsmith's face was too horrified for it to be anything but the truth.

"But what about all the good the school's done for—," Goldsmith began.

"Is the cure for cancer worth a thousand childhoods?" Stella demanded. "It's a world where human connections are replaced by performance-enhancing pills. Criticism is silenced by peer reviews and shock therapy. And we were all locked up in the tower whether we agreed to be or not. An annual tuition payment of five hundred thousand dollars represented our consent. But not for me, Mr. Goldsmith. Not for any of us."

"What are you gonna do, now that everyone else is dead?" asked Cooley.

"I'm still going to simulcast to the committee during the debate this evening. I'm going to present them with the entire story behind the five alumni murders and connect the dots for everyone to see. It won't sink the bill immediately, but it will raise enough questions to at least delay the process and raise an investigation."

"Those are grave accusations to bring, Miss Saltzman," said Goldsmith. "Without the other five former specimens, Stansbury supporters will tar and feather you as a bitter alumna. The school will bring up your abortion and make it seem as if you have an ax to grind, which, frankly, you do."

"I won't be making my case alone, Mr. Goldsmith."

"Who are you going to find to . . ." Goldsmith's voice trailed off when he saw that Stella was smiling at him. And then he understood why she spent the past half hour bringing them up to speed. Cooley got it too, and it washed away all of his exhaustion and fatigue, gave him a rush that he might be able to clear his name and help Stella get her vengeance on the school at the same time. He started to feel giddy and knew he would do anything to help her. The normally selfish Riley probably got bowled over with the same zealousness back when she recruited him. For the first time in Cooley's life, he felt like he could be part of something great. He looked at Goldsmith, hoping to see the same fire, but there was nothing in the valedictorian's eyes. Just a hollow stare, like all of his theories and assessments were finally failing him. Cooley could practically hear his mind grind the question out: twelve years of busting my ass, and now this lady wants me to rip it all down?

He watched Stella lay a hand on Goldsmith's shoulder, like she was transferring strength and will to him. Outside the wall of windows, Cooley saw that beautiful, terrifying view of San Angeles from twenty-three floors up. A black cord swung past the glass outside. For a split-second flash, he caught a glimpse of what looked like the heel of a boot. He jumped up and grabbed Stella and Goldsmith by their arms.

"The kitchen," Cooley hissed.

"What?" Goldsmith said, suddenly snapped out of his trance, but Cooley was already hauling them across the living room and into the long hallway outside. There was a sudden explosion of glass and wind behind them, followed by the thumping of several sets of heavy feet landing on the wooden floor. Those digitized hums were now familiar to Cooley's ears as they fled: the sound of three ThermaGuns locking onto their targets' body heat patterns.

In the tower's boys' solarium on Level 9, Pete looked up at the vast array of Celestial Class spotlights that shone down on him and wondered if the artificial warmth on his face was going to give him the kind of golden tan the specimens all had. He heard a door open and close, followed by the clicking of footsteps getting closer: it was his coveted insider source. Instinctively, he moved out of the circle of light he was standing in and stepped into the dark shadows.

"That's one thing I love about you specimens," he called out. "You're always on time. They got pills for promptness?" The footsteps got closer, heels moving against marble. "This place is a trip. One huge tanning salon, right? I'd tell you these lights'll give you skin cancer, but hey, you whippersnappers sure licked that one, didn't you?" Pete watched Sadie step through the row of spotlights and into the shadow with him.

"Yeah, we did."

"Well, I'm a whippersnapper myself Sadie, 'cause I've got the whole thing put together. Dig it: A bunch of former specimens were lined up as whistle-blowers for the opposition to the Stansbury grant proposal in the Senate Select Committee on Education today. The school found out and started knocking them off one by one. They wanted to pin it all on your boyfriend, but that's not gonna happen, now that I'm . . ." He saw a single tear roll down Sadie's cheek and stopped. "Hey, I just said that he's gonna be all right, that I'm gonna—"

"You don't know what you're saying." Her voice trembled just slightly.

"I do. I'm right, sweetie. You know I am. That's why you're crying. Come on, I need your help. You said you'd give me a hand, right? I can't do it without my star insider source. I'll have you out of this place in half an hour and get you in touch with Senator Bloom and the cops. You'll be a hero and—"

"*You don't know what you're saying!*" she shouted so suddenly that Pete flinched, startled by the vehemence in her voice. It almost sounded like she was pleading with him to recant, like there was someone listening that she wanted him to make a good impression on. "Just say that I'm right, please! Please . . ."

A beep echoed. The Celestial Class lights shifted ninety degrees, illuminating the two of them.

"No, honey. I'm right. I know that for a fact, and I never even made—" A shot rang out, echoing in the chamber loud enough to make them both temporarily deaf. Pete looked at her hands, confused, but they were empty. He glanced up toward the ceiling but only saw the bright lights. He fell to the floor, a dark red hole in his chest that trickled at first and then poured forth into a stream of blood that formed a puddle around his crumpled body, inside the perfect circle of white illumination from above. ". . . the honor roll," he said with his last breath.

But Sadie didn't hear. Her ears were still ringing from the gunshot, and she was deaf even to the sound of her own screaming as she ran from the solarium as fast as she could.

Cooley threw on the switches of all six burners on Stella's industrial-grade gas-burning stove in her kitchen. The blue flames shot up fast, nearly singeing his eyebrows and sweaty locks of hair. He cranked the oven underneath up to 450 degrees. The smell of burnt banana bread that had been baking inside filled the room.

"The space heater," he shouted to Stella. "Turn it up all the way."

"What are you trying to . . . ," she started.

"Cooley—," Goldsmith cut in.

"Just do it now!" he snapped. "How'd they find us? I thought this address was a secret!"

Goldsmith realized something. "They traced my Tabula."

"Smash the fucking thing. Now."

"But Cooley—" Before he could finish, Cooley grabbed the Tabula from inside Goldsmith's blazer, threw it to the floor, and smashed it under his heel. It splintered into hundreds of small, jagged pieces. "You idiot!" shouted Goldsmith. "We needed that for—"

Cooley grabbed him by the tie and yanked him close. "Shut up," he hissed, "and whine at me after I get us out of here alive."

Stella rushed over to the heater and flipped the switch on. Rows of bright orange coils lit up. The sudden rush of gas into the gleaming silver stove made a hissing noise, swallowing up the eerie silence that followed after the wall of windows in the living room imploded just moments before. The footsteps of the detail officers pounded around the apartment as they secured rooms. Goldsmith listened, feeling his sweat in the increasingly hot kitchen soak through his dress shirt, the buttoned-up collar clinging to his neck. His mind raced, trying to formulate a plan to buy them some time, but failed: the bombshell Stella dropped on them just minutes ago still resonated. Everything Camilla said that the administration would be worried about if he retired— fundamental flaws in the system becoming apparent, shortcomings in the med cycle, the constant maintenance of a pristine public image at all costs—was true. They were never going to let him quit the valedictorian's job, any more than they let Stella quit when she was laid up in an infirmary bed. The compliments, the affirmation they showered down upon him that he needed in such a visceral way—it was that parental praise he always craved but never received—was all just lip service to keep him under their control. The whole time he was a pawn who mistook himself for a king. Stansbury hung that fake gold medal around his neck and played him for a fool.

"Cooley," he whispered. "I can talk to them. The headmaster said that—"

"They're not here to talk," whispered Stella.

"*Targets are in the kitchen!*" came a voice out in the corridor. Cooley, Stella, and Goldsmith crouched in the corner across from the flames of the stove. "*Activate your coolant vests!*" An earsplitting burst of noise cut through the apartment. An instant later sparks and flames flew, leaving the stove and space heater mangled, pierced with bullet holes. Smoke shot from the holes in the oven. The bullets missed: all of the burning-hot targets hid the body-heat patterns of three terrified human beings. The flames on the burner got irregular, rising up and down like the appliance was gasping for breath. The hissing sound got louder still. Goldsmith recognized the smell from chemistry labs over the years: propane.

"We've got to get out of here," he said, panic creeping into his medicated voice. "The stove is leaking gas and—"

"Stella, where can we go?" asked Cooley.

"We're twenty-three floors up," she said, calm. "The front door is the only point of exit." The hissing sound got stronger. One of the burners went out and the other flames rose higher still. Goldsmith stared at them, feeling paralyzed and terrified all at once, trying to muster up some of the bravery he felt earlier in the day. He tried to sound courageous, but knew his voice reeked of desperation.

"I'm not staying put and getting burned to death, I'm—"

"*Freeze!*" barked Officer Jackson from the kitchen's doorway. He stepped inside, pointing a pistol in their direction. Goldsmith jumped up. "Freeze, Mr. Goldsmith!"

Goldsmith pulled out the headmaster's piece of parchment from his blazer and held it up for Jackson to see. "Stand down! I've got the authorization of—"

"No!" shouted Cooley.

Goldsmith, still holding out his official document, wondered why Cooley's voice just went several octaves higher than he'd ever heard before. Then he saw Jackson aim the gun—at him. The barrel lit up and was followed by several thunderous claps along with the noise of shattering glass before he realized he was on the floor with a searing pain shooting through his left arm and shoulder. He looked up and saw the broken kitchen window and a hole in the wall where he once stood. It took him a moment to understand the pain was caused from bullets passing through his body. The surface of his skin flooded with warmth and he knew it was the feeling of his own blood.

From his vantage point down on the linoleum, Goldsmith saw Officer Jackson aim at Stella and fire three times. She was thrown back against the wall and then to the floor from the force of the impact, bleeding from her legs and torso, her gray dress staining in large black spots. Goldsmith tried to stand up and, through the haze of pain, saw Cooley reach for something shiny on the counter. His arm moved so fast it blurred. Jackson went down coughing up blood, neat little geysers of red erupting from his neck, the blade of a carving knife embedded so deep in his skin that its glint was now invisible, the dull black handle jutting out like a morbid piece of jewelry. Cooley rushed over and grabbed Jackson's gun from his shuddering hand before ripping the utility belt from his waist. He moved toward Stella. Goldsmith gritted his teeth together and helped him pull her to her feet, supporting her weight. Cooley pulled out two morphine Syrettes from Jackson's belt and jabbed them into the dark stains on Stella's dress.

"You've got to help me carry her," he said to Goldsmith. "I'll shoot you up with this stuff when we're out of here. Are you okay to move?"

Goldsmith nodded, knowing the only reason why the pain wasn't completely debilitating was because his body was still in shock. Footsteps pounded toward them over the sound of the stove's hissing. "Cooley," he whispered. "The stove . . . it's gonna—"

"I know." He pulled Goldsmith and Stella out of the kitchen, pushing them around the corner. Shots rang out from the corridor behind them, interspersed with the rhythmic percussion of running men. Cooley aimed the gun at the stove, fired, and dove out of the way. There was an explosive roar and an overwhelming wave of heat as the propane stove went up in flames right in the path of the detail officers. At first the rumble left an awful silence, then gave way to frantic, panicked shouts, with some officers calling for an extinguisher. Fire had begun to spread through the apartment.

The three of them reached the living room and saw the blown-out wall of windows as the high gusts rushed inside. The corridors from where they came were now makeshift wind tunnels that stoked the flames. Cooley left Goldsmith to support Stella and peered outside. He rushed back over and pulled them toward the edge. Another series of gunshots erupted, getting closer, a vase just a few feet away shattering, a line of holes appearing in the wall nearby. Cooley led Goldsmith and Stella to the window's edge. He found his left arm hurt too much to lift. Stella mumbled something, but he couldn't make it out.

"Don't look down," he heard Cooley say. He felt the dry skin of

Cooley's hand in his and let himself be pulled toward the cliff outside the living room. When Goldsmith took another step forward, there was nowhere to plant his foot. Cold air and hard yellow rain hit his face and he felt his body shudder from impact one more time, thinking he had been shot again, but found that there were no more burning holes in him, just a bit of wind knocked from his lungs, which was slowly making its return. He opened his eyes and saw a glorious, horrifying sight: the largest metropolis on the planet, from the roof of a Stansbury security gyromobile hovering twenty-odd floors in the sky. The gyro hurtled downward from the sudden force of three bodies landing against it, tipping just a bit, but they didn't tumble off—a practical application of centrifugal force, as taught in Stansbury's Principles of Physics progression, Goldsmith thought—and then he felt Cooley's hand pull him out into the thin air. He heard the crash of the gyro from which they had just leapt slam into the side of Stella's apartment building as they somehow landed on another Stansbury gyro, hovering a few floors below. Their impact sent this one sailing down as well. The driver tried to right the vehicle but could not. Cooley pulled Goldsmith and Stella off the gyro's roof and into the air once again and, although this time they were airborne for a few more seconds, they landed on something solid. Somewhere above them, the gyro smacked into a floating billboard that displayed the day's stock market gains (incidentally, Panacetix had sent Stansbury's publicly traded stock soaring up thirty-seven points in the day's trading).

The ground on which Goldsmith found himself lying was actually the artificial turf surface on the roof deck of one of San Angeles's public schools. Small children no older than eleven years old rushed around them, hurling small red dodgeballs at each other, screaming, terror in their eyes. Goldsmith tried to blink away the fever dream, but it remained. Bolts of lightning illuminated the sky.

"Y'all throw like girls!" shouted the children's gym teacher, a beefy lug with a crew cut and a bright red face. "Wing those balls harder! Hey!" Goldsmith could hear the teacher's voice more clearly now. The man must have been wondering why three bloodied bodies had just landed in the middle of his gym class. "Who do you people think you—"

Cooley grabbed a dodgeball from one of the boys and flung it at Mr. Crew Cut. It nailed him square in the face and he went down, stunned. The students cheered. Cooley hauled Goldsmith up. The rain on Goldsmith's face felt like the most refreshing shower he'd ever taken.

"Hold on," whispered Cooley, steadying him. "Just relax. You're gonna be fine." Goldsmith looked down at Cooley's hands and saw the silver needle of a morphine Syrette. He felt a couple of pinpricks. A glow flowed through him. "Good," he heard Cooley say. "The Stimulum you took yesterday for final exams is what's keeping you lucid." The pains in his arm and his side died down. Goldsmith's world started to get crisp and clear again. Thunder rumbled, sending a shiver through him. It sounded just like the noise of Stansbury gyros slamming against the steel and glass sidings of skyscrapers.

"What about . . . Stella?" he managed.

She was leaning against the wall, holding her hand over the hole in her side. The bleeding was not profuse, but still steady and wet. "I need the coroner's files . . . they were on my apartment's computer."

"We can't go back up there," Cooley said.

"And our only copies were on my Tabula, Cooley. The one you smashed. That's what I was trying to tell you back in the kitchen. Why can't you ever think things through? You always—"

"Fuck you," snapped Cooley. He shoved Goldsmith. "You'd be dead if I thought things through back there."

"Fuck *you!*" Goldsmith shoved him back, waiting for the med cycle to kick in and settle him down. "*You'd* be on your way to jail if I hadn't been thinking for both of us this whole time!" That calming sensation never came. He just felt anger. He wondered if he had outgrown his standard dosage, whether that was even possible.

"Please," said Stella, swaying on her feet, the painkillers letting some strength come back into her voice. "I can hack the files off a computer connected to Stansbury's network. One that's inside the tower." Goldsmith looked up and saw the gyros still hovering outside Stella's apartment way up in the sky, smoke billowing out from the broken windows.

Lighting cracked across the sky behind him. The detail gyros were starting to descend, getting closer, maybe drawing a bead on their location. "They're coming," Goldsmith said. "How are we going to get back to the tower in time?"

Cooley pulled out Jackson's Colt M-8 and cocked it. Steel grinded against steel as a bullet slid into the chamber.

23

Cooley led Goldsmith and Stella out of the service entrance of Public School # 239 and into the crowds and wranglers on West 465th Street. It was a nice part of town, with Starbucks outposts and Apple stores dotting every other block, along with plenty of families and strollers. To Goldsmith, the inside of the school looked strange, foreign, almost like a movie set. The hallways smelled thick, like several coats of soap were employed unsuccessfully in sterilizing the odor of all the grime and dirt tracked in from the city streets. He ran his fingers along the white brick walls as they jogged for the exit and saw large black and yellow block lettering that ran down the entire hallway that read (somewhat nonsensically, in Goldsmith's opinion) GO KNIGHTS! The lockers were a garish shade of pumpkin orange. Everything seemed haphazardly thrown together and anachronistic, almost primitive. That he would have ended up in a school like this if he was not selected in the Stansbury lottery was not lost on him and, despite everything he had learned today, Goldsmith still wasn't sure that he'd have given up the salvation he found inside the walls of the tower if someone offered him the choice.

As they stepped into the rainy street, Cooley took off his blazer, turned it inside out so the telltale Stansbury emblem was hidden and draped it over Stella's shoulders, hiding her wounds. Goldsmith knew he couldn't take his blazer off: the bloodstains on his white dress shirt would show. Cooley looked at him, understanding the dilemma. He reached over and, without a word, ripped the conspicuous gold patch from Goldsmith's chest and tossed it into a puddle. Adieu, Novus Ordo Seclorum, Goldsmith thought. He watched the stitched-in shape of the tower sink, disappearing into the wet muck on the pavement, dark and polluted precipitation swallowing that proud coat of arms whole. Still, he felt obligated to maintain the bearing of a valedictorian, even though he had been cast out of the Stansbury loop, clinging onto his past glory like a defrocked priest. Meanwhile, Cooley placed Jackson's gun into his waistband and untucked his dress shirt to conceal it. Thunder rumbled from above. A Stansbury security detail gyro sailed past, missing them in the crowd on the street.

"We're insane if we go back to the tower," Goldsmith said, feeling Stella's eyes on him.

"I've got to go back," said Cooley.

"She needs to get to a hospital. They'll get us if we go back, and even if they don't, she could die of her wounds anyway. If we get her to a doctor, she can still present the committee with evidence after they vote."

"The vote's not the only reason I'm going back there. Sadie and Bunson are still inside. Gibson and Lang are gonna go after them to get to me."

"Cooley, you can't—"

"And what about Camilla?" The sound of her name made Goldsmith's stomach drop and bounce back up. Camilla and her family were so tied to Stansbury that he wondered if she'd ever leave it, even if she knew what he knew now. "You think they don't know she means something to you?" Cooley continued. "You think they're gonna let you off the hook?"

"You're right." He watched Cooley help Stella down the street. More Stansbury gyros cruised in and out of aerial traffic lanes, looking for them. Lighting flung itself across the dark sky. "We can't risk flagging down a gyrocab," Goldsmith said, "they'd see us."

"I know," said Cooley, leading them through the throngs of pedestrian traffic past the monorail line to Old Sunset Boulevard. New Sunset Boulevard was several hundred feet above their heads and packed with bumper-to-bumper rush hour gyro traffic. Old Sunset was moving faster, a ghost of a once proud road bearing what few gasoline-powered automobiles were left in San Angeles. The antique cars rolled along belching fumes. They were either jalopies belonging to commuters who couldn't afford the newer, safer gyromobile technology, or handsome, well-preserved cars of the twentieth century, owned by the wealthy San Angelenos who could still pay the inflated price of petroleum gasoline following the destabilization of the oil market ushered in by the advent of Robert Cavil Moore's electric gyro engine. But Old Sunset was a throwback to a different era. Cars, even the beat-up clunkers, still had their fans among the nostalgic romantics who might have lived during their heyday, as well as among rebellious young thrill-seekers who ignored the warnings that riding in four-wheelers was a health hazard on par with Russian roulette or chain-smoking. Cooley walked over to a traffic light on a deserted stretch of Old Sunset far off from the densely populated sidewalk. A pair of headlights approached in the distance, winking through the gray fog. Cooley squinted at them and smiled.

"Man, look at that," he said, sounding as if they were in the midst of a leisurely scenic stroll. "Looks like a 1969 Shelby." The dark green car approached the light, slowing to a stop. "It's got a V-8. Does zero to sixty in six seconds flat, tops out around 115 miles an hour. You know, it went for only five grand when they put it on the market back in the day? I bet some rich old guy's behind the wheel."

"What's the big deal?" asked Goldsmith. "Even mediocre gyros hit two hundred and fifty."

"It's different when you don't have a cockpit computer and crash-motion sensors in the engine. Just you, the clutch, and the steering wheel."

"You've actually driven a car before?" Goldsmith saw Stella wince in pain. Cooley reached over and shot a few more drops of morphine into her.

"No," Cooley answered. "But I know guys who have." The Shelby rolled to a halt at the red light. Goldsmith had never seen a car in person before. The big, black rubber wheels shuddered from the vibrations of an almost offensively loud engine that seemed to snort and throb with a guttural rumble. From Cooley's description, he was expecting a sleek racing machine; but the wide blackness of its grille and its thick, rounded steel edges and stout, squat body that hugged the pavement looked almost too heavy to move anywhere efficiently, not to mention quickly. He tried to imagine what it was like living in a time when people rode around in machines like this on a regular basis, machines that were only a slight human error away from crushing or mangling living things that had the misfortune of straying into their paths. And what was to stop people from getting their feet smashed to bits by those clumsy wheels? Goldsmith instinctively took a step backward.

"I always wanted to drive one of these things someday. You know, before I died," grinned Cooley. He pulled out his gun and stepped in front of the Shelby, leaving Goldsmith to prop up Stella. "Get the fuck out of the car!" Cooley shouted, aiming the M-8.

The driver—a man in his forties wearing a sharply tailored suit—stared back at him, shock in his eyes. Cooley fired a bullet right above the car's roof. The man jumped out of the car instantly, stepping to the side, terrified. Cooley aimed at him. "Get down on the ground!"

The man obeyed. The antiquated street was empty, barren of any witnesses. Cooley looked over at Goldsmith. "Go. Squeeze into the passenger seat with her."

Goldsmith walked around, opened the door, and carefully laid Stella inside, sliding beside her. Cooley jumped in and got behind the wheel. He pushed his foot against some pedals below the dashboard, testing them out. When he hit one, the engine roared but the car stayed put. He eased the steering wheel from left to right and then grabbed the clutch, shifting the transmission around a bit. The engine screamed to life and then slowed down to a hum.

"Can you make it work?" asked Goldsmith. The Shelby slowly started rolling forward, then the engine stalled. Cooley turned a metal key in the ignition and it roared back to life.

A bright, whitish blue xenon light suddenly hit them. Goldsmith squinted and saw a Stansbury gyro hovering just twenty feet above. Officer O'Shaunnessy was aiming a ThermaGun at them. Cooley stuck the gun outside the window and fired twice. The gyro jerked. O'Shaunnessy ducked, losing his grip on the weapon. Cooley hit the gas and the car shot down Old Sunset, their heads snapping back against the cool leather seats. Goldsmith hung onto Stella, realizing that if Cooley crashed the car at this speed, they would all go flying through the windshield together. They should make people wear helmets in these things, he thought. He saw more xenon beams cut through the dark, rainy mist and turned around. Four more Stansbury gyros were speeding after them. Cooley yanked back on the transmission and the car hit a higher gear. Thunder from the storm exploded in the sky around them, creating a symphonic harmony of booms with the Shelby's engine. Rows of towering gray office buildings shot past through the windows like rungs on a ladder that never ended. They accelerated toward the few other cars ahead of them on Old Sunset at such a high speed that the other automobiles seemed as if they were actually hurtling backward in reverse. Cooley weaved in and out of them as they flew past. The even blips of the faded yellow line in the center of the road became one. Above them, the detail gyros descended, easily keeping up. Over the V-8 engine, a siren squealed. Red flashing lights mixed in with more xenon beams and bolts of lightning.

"The police," Goldsmith said. "Stansbury probably told them to shut down the road." He felt Cooley slow the car down, a defeated look on his face. Goldsmith glanced up at the gyros with the flashing lights. The words on their doors read: SAN ANGELES TRANSPORTATION BUREAU.

"All aerial traffic lanes are being shut down due to inclement weather conditions," came a digitized voice through a public address speaker. *"Please proceed to the designated docking bay at once."*

"They're stopping gyro traffic," Stella said. "The flying conditions are too risky." Another transportation bureau vehicle arrived. The Stansbury gyros slowed down and were escorted helplessly to a giant floating docking structure several hundred feet above, along with all of the other angry commuters who were more than willing to risk being struck out of the sky by lightning on their journeys home from the office. Cooley hit the gas.

"The highway's coming up," he said. "We've got maybe fifty miles to the desert exit, and we'll follow the Stansbury Tower signs from there. If I keep us going over a hundred we'll beat them back there. The administration will hear from them and have somebody waiting, but I'm betting they pulled out most of their guys to get to Stella before we could. There can't be that many officers left in the school."

"What if Gibson's there?" asked Goldsmith. A hush fell over the car. "He'll kill us if he thinks we're getting in the way."

"Relax. You've still got the headmaster in your pocket. He's got more juice than Gibson, and as much or more than Lang. He'll back us up."

"Cooley's right," said Stella. "The headmaster has always stayed above the political fray. If we can get to him, he'll listen to us make our case and provide the protection we need."

"He didn't stop the detail from coming after us," said Goldsmith. "If I've lost his support somehow, we'll be stuck inside the tower without a plan B."

"Here's plan B," cut in Cooley. "I've still got the gun. I'll find Bunson. He's a tough guy, bigger than any of those detail punks. He'll help us. We can take hostages."

"No. Nobody's taking hostages," said Goldsmith, sounding more than a little annoyed.

"Stop talking about Stansbury like it's some hallowed place!" shouted Cooley suddenly. He looked over at Goldsmith, taking his eyes off the road but, much to Goldsmith's amazement, somehow managed to keep driving in a straight line. "Their high-minded shit about morals and education is a fucking lie! Why can't you get that through your head? I don't want to hurt any specimens, but I'm moving my people out of there and getting Stella to a network terminal, and if things get ugly, then you know what Goldsmith? That's life. It's not some nice, tidy progression. They didn't have any problems killing people off and sticking it on me. Don't be so naïve. You think if I didn't kill Jackson back in that kitchen he'd have gone easy on us? You'd be dead. And if I've got to kill someone else to get myself out of this shit, you'd better believe I'm gonna do it." The veins in Cooley's temples throbbed. He took a deep breath and went back to focusing on the road ahead. Goldsmith felt Stella's hands on his wounds, pulling back his shirt so she could get a closer look.

"How badly does it hurt?" she asked.

"The morphine helped."

"They're both clean exit wounds. The bleeding has stopped for the most part. After some stitches and disinfection, you'll be fine."

Goldsmith nodded and looked down at the stains on her gray dress underneath Cooley's blazer. "What about you?" he asked.

She looked at him and forced out a smile. "Don't you worry."

Sooner than he expected, Goldsmith saw the tower looming in the distance.

The Shelby rolled to a halt on the rain-soaked desert surface at the tower, just outside of registration and reception. Cooley, Goldsmith, and Stella stepped out into the storm and walked up to the huge steel entrance door. Goldsmith buzzed the entry system. The video monitor broadcast the reception guard's face. It was a new, younger guy he didn't recognize who looked pretty wet behind the ears.

"Um, can I help you?" he said. Goldsmith got the authority back in his voice and held up the headmaster's parchment for the camera to see.

"I'm Mr. Thomas Oliver Goldsmith, valedictorian, returning from off-campus business. Here's my authorization. It comes straight from the headmaster's desk." A scratchy silence followed, dragging on a moment too long. "Is there a problem?"

"Uhhh . . . you'd better come inside, Mr. Goldsmith." The thick door started to hiss as it slid open. They walked inside the lobby, dripping water onto the clean marble floor. The reception guard stared at them. "Jesus," he said, his mouth agape as he took in their beaten appearance. "Should I call a medic?"

"No," said Goldsmith. "We're going straight to the headmaster's office. Please call ahead for me and inform him that I'm on the way with Mr. Cooley and Miss Saltzman. Tell him it's urgent." Goldsmith watched as the guard twitched and blinked, nervous about something. "What is it?" Tears filled the guard's eyes.

"I don't want to be the one to tell you," he managed, his voice cracking. "Just . . . just go to the coliseum. Everyone else is already there. I . . . I think you'll get the broadcast in the elevator pod on the way up."

Cooley grabbed the guard by the shoulders, reaching over the desk. "What the hell's going on?" he hissed. The guard just stared at him.

Goldsmith pulled Cooley away and they headed for the elevator bank down the hall. The doors to a pod slid open and they stepped inside. Goldsmith hit the button for Level 125 and glanced at Stella. It looked as if her wounds had stopped bleeding. He studied her face and it was focused, distant, no doubt cruising down memory lane after her three-year absence. He wondered if she was thinking of Wayne Edward Haddon. The elevator's plasma screen came to life, lighting up with an image of President Lang standing behind a podium in the coliseum. It looked like she was addressing a full house. She dabbed a tear from her cheek with a handkerchief.

". . . And it is tragic that a heart attack would rob us of the headmaster's learned guidance and gentle leadership so abruptly; but alas, there is no lab yet created that can cure the cruel hands of fate and nature . . ."

"Oh my God," muttered Stella. Goldsmith felt his knees buckle. Cooley steadied him. "It was her," she said. "I know it was her." Stella pointed at the clock on the plasma screen: 4:47 P.M. "This is it. The network server is on the atrium level. All the big machinery there is powered by the same generator, and it's inside that room. If I can get to that master terminal I can transfer the alumni files to the school's general server, get to a simulcast hookup, and be ready to present the information in time to address the committee. Mr. Goldsmith, you must know a safe place for me to simulcast, once I've got the data. Think. Somewhere obscure, where no one will find me."

"There's a progression room down on Level 4, inside the first grade housing space. I study there when I don't want to be bothered."

"I know that floor. Is it on the eastern side or western side?"

"Western."

"Perfect."

"Cooley," said Goldsmith. "I'm betting Bunson and Sadie are in the coliseum with everyone else. If you stand guard outside the network server room, you might see them file out after the assembly is finished.

The mainframe area is located near that small cluster of weeping willows by the river. Just be sure to tell your friends that they've got to move quickly."

"What about Camilla?"

"I don't . . . I don't think she'll come with us."

"Don't you want to try and change her mind?"

"No, Cooley." Goldsmith made certain his face remained impassive, businesslike. The pod dinged, stopping at the atrium level. The doors slid open and they exited, moving into the pale computerized sunshine. It was quiet, deserted. The river warbled away softly. A wind blew dead leaves up and they flickered, as if they were waving a welcome-home greeting to Stella. Goldsmith heard footsteps and saw a shadow approaching on the opposite side of a thick oak tree. Cooley was already aiming the M-8, moving toward the figure. He reached through the branches and yanked the person out into the open. It was Sadie with fresh tear streaks on her face, her eyes puffy. She stared at Cooley's gun blankly, like she was dazed. Cooley put it away and pulled her close.

"Honey, are you okay?" he whispered gently. "Tell me what—"

"They killed him," she said softly.

"Who? The headmaster?"

Goldsmith stepped between them, pulling Cooley aside. "Stop," he said. "Pete said his source was a female and implied we couldn't trust her. How do you know she's on our side?"

"What about Camilla?" snapped Sadie. "How can you be sure she's not the one who's been talking to the reporter?"

"Because you're the one who's standing in front of me after you just happened to come across us when everyone else in the school is mourning in the coliseum!" said Goldsmith, trying to keep his voice under control.

"But I helped you. I got the key card from Professor Nelson."

"She's right," said Cooley.

"She didn't have a choice. She would've exposed herself if she said no to us. That was one of the reasons I dragged her into this in the first place."

"What the hell would she be doing talking to Pete?" said Cooley, his voice rising.

"She could've been keeping an eye on him."

"For whom?"

"The administration." Upon hearing this, Cooley started laughing. Sadie started crying.

"We've got to move," said Goldsmith. "We're running out of time. If I find Pete before—"

"Pete's dead," croaked Sadie. "They shot him."

"Who?" asked Cooley.

"I don't know." Sadie glanced at Stella. "Who's this?"

"Just go," Cooley told Goldsmith and Stella. "Get the files onto the server now. I'll be waiting here with her. We'll get Bunson and then we're getting out of here." Cooley took Sadie by the hand. Goldsmith led Stella toward the digitized weeping willow grove in the distance.

"Cooley?" said Stella, looking back over her shoulder at him.

"Yeah?"

"I'm the best valedictorian this place ever saw. And her face says she's a liar." Cooley just stared as Stella and Goldsmith disappeared into the digital underbrush.

"What's happening? Why did she say that?" asked Sadie, pulling Cooley close.

"Everything . . . ," he started, the exhaustion catching up to him again, "everything's gone insane. I think the school's deep into this bad stuff. They've been trying to pin it on me."

"Who's been trying to pin it on you?"

"I'm not sure exactly." He stopped as Sadie pulled his head near, letting him rest on her soft shoulder.

"How do you know it isn't that senator who hates us?" she asked.

Cooley looked up at her, stepping back. "How do you know about him?"

"I just . . . I do read the newspaper, you know. I'm not totally sheltered."

"It's not him."

"Shhh . . . I love you," Sadie said, pulling him closer.

"I love you, too."

"Promise?"

"Yeah, I promise."

"Tell me who you think is trying to nail you."

"It must be Lang."

"What?"

"I'm sure, all right? I'm sure. I don't have the time to explain everything right now. You've got to get out of here with me. Help me find Bunson and we'll—"

Cooley felt a sharp pain in the back of his neck. It pushed his skull forward, jamming his chin against his sternum, forcing him down to his knees, like gravity was caving in on him. He reached back to somehow get rid of it, but could not. He strained to look up at Sadie and saw her staring at him, her lips shaking and her blue eyes watery. He finally managed to twist his head around and saw good old Thaddeus Bunson—his face tight with concentration, the same way it looked when he was polishing the sink in their bathroom before room inspections—pressing him down with his huge hands, jamming some kind of laser into him. Cooley felt something being injected into his body and understood that Bunson stabbed him with a laser syringe. He tried to stand up, but the big man's weight was too much for him to bear. Sadie let out a sob and knocked Bunson's hand away. Cooley collapsed to the floor, writhing in pain.

Their voices faded into flickering whispers, faint and distant as Cooley reached back and yanked the syringe out of his neck. The label read: ADM+5.

Goldsmith helped Stella into a chair, placing her before the simulcast terminal in an empty first grade progression room on Level 4. Her eyebrows were furrowed, giving the impression of serious contemplation. Her wounds were deep, red, and wet. Stella's head nodded to an unseen rhythm, like her gifted brain had already calculated the precise number of seconds that were left to her in life and she was counting them down, rationing them out so that she could complete this final task. Goldsmith had so many questions he wanted to ask her. Feeling his gaze on her, Stella looked over.

"I enjoyed it," said Goldsmith. "Everything. Selmer-Dubonnet. The peer reviews. The power. Truthfully? I can't imagine life without those things."

"It's not an easy thing, is it?" she grinned. "Tearing down everything that's made us who we are." For a moment she looked exactly like what she was: twenty-two years old and unsure of what she would be when she finally grew up. "Without this place, I don't even know who I am."

"I don't know who I am, either," he said.

"Sure feels like something else, doesn't it?"

Bunson stepped over Cooley's body and slapped Sadie, his huge hand drawing blood. She stopped crying.

"Get a grip," he hissed. "We had to do it."

"I . . . I know."

"Lang said if he specifically named her, we had to go through with it." From the floor, Cooley heard Bunson's baritone voice crack the way it always did when he was scared. Bunson took a big gulp of air to force the fear away. "Just get out of my way and let me finish this."

"I never would've gone through with everything if I knew it meant doing this!"

"Sadie, get the fuck out of my way!" Cooley saw the ADM+5 syringe was still half full. Lying prone, he spied Bunson's and Sadie's feet shuffling as they argued: Sadie's knee socks and Bunson's trousers above two pairs of polished black shoes from the uniform department. He watched Bunson's legs and thought of all the different ways that two friends could say good-bye. After racking his brain for a few moments he only came up with one thing: Sorry, buddy. I'm sorry you bought into whatever they were selling. I'm sorry I didn't notice sooner. I'm sorry I didn't rescue you. Most of all, I'm sorry we both ended up at a place like this. I blame them, not you. Really, my friend, I do.

Cooley had tears hanging in his eyes when he slammed the syringe into Bunson's ankle and pressed down, injecting the remainder of the chemical into his bloodstream. At first, Bunson swatted at his leg the same way one would brush away an insect. By the time he saw what had happened, his knees went dead on him and he collapsed to the floor, almost on top of Cooley. Cooley jumped up, watching as Bunson started to lose his breath and gag, a sickeningly rough grinding noise coming up from his throat. Blood began to pour out of his nose as he reached into his blazer, pulled out a gun— a Glock 12—and aimed at Cooley. Cooley drew his M-8, but saw that it was only a cursory move on Bunson's part: his eyes were darting back and forth, unfocused because something in that brain seizure adamite-5 caused had irrevocably damaged his vision and depth perception. The Glock fell from his hands, making an anomalous metallic clatter against the ground, which was meant to look like a soft dirt path. As his best friend fell forward, his huge body shuddering a few more times before finally coming to a permanent rest, Cooley was grateful he could not see his face, that he would never know if it ended up this contorted, bloody, foamy mess without a tongue like Riley's did.

Cooley could feel Sadie's eyes on him. He looked over and saw they were wide with shock because he was not dead despite the ADM+5 injection. He remembered the day his class received the ADD vaccine, way back when they were eight, maybe nine years old. Laser needles terrified him back then, too. He skipped the whole day of progressions just to avoid getting shot up by the med techs and hid far off in the outskirts of the atrium's forest, counting fake leaves fall from silvery beech trees as they spun to the ground.

He aimed his gun at Sadie and tears blurred his vision before he could see the look on her face. The chokes and sobs (his first since this whole ordeal began, he realized) came from his mouth as if they were sharp emotive projectiles because each time they did, Sadie shuddered and sobbed herself. After a moment, he wiped his face off and picked up the gun lying next to Bunson's dead hand. That Glock 12. It looked eerily familiar.

"This is Riley's gun," he said. "He took it from him that night in the bathroom." Sadie nodded her head. "And I'm betting Bunson used it to kill Pete." She nodded again. "Bunson . . . you and Bunson killed Riley."

"In the beginning Lang said . . . she said she could get us into àny school we wanted . . . even Brown or Princeton and—"

"I don't buy it. No one cares about getting into college that badly. Not even in this place. And why wouldn't she hire professionals?"

"She secretly doctored our med cycle doses, Cooley! Added drugs that made us more malleable, clouded our judgment, chemicals that aren't even legal, okay? Lang had us on it for weeks before she even approached us with the offer. She could control us . . . blackmail us. And professionals couldn't spy on you like we could. She needed us to make sure you'd leave campus on the same dates the murders were scheduled. She needed us to spy on you and Goldsmith. Only specimens, friends of yours, could do that for her." Cooley remembered favors done for Sadie and Bunson over the past six months—runs to San Angeles for cigarettes for her and the girls . . . most recently, his disastrous journey to Riley's two days ago for clean piss for his boys. He just stared at her, numbing over. "In the beginning, it was simple," she said. "All we had to do was stick a laser syringe into this foul homeless man who slept on the street. Somewhere in E Sector out in San Angeles."

"Because laser syringes don't leave any traceable evidence." She nodded. "Keep going."

"He . . . he smelled like some filthy bathroom, and she was right, he was just taking up space. We injected him while he was passed out in an alley and watched him die . . . he opened his eyes at one point after the chemical kicked in and had this look of disbelief, like it had to have been a bad dream. He probably was hoping for a good dream when he fell asleep that night. You know, some way to escape things. He died, and then the real work started. We . . ." She started to become unhinged. Cooley waited for her to slip up in the retelling somehow so he could convince himself that she wasn't really involved. "We stabbed him with a rusted knife Captain Gibson gave us, plunged it into his neck . . . right into his carotid artery. Gibson showed that artery to Bunson in an anatomy textbook, so he'd know exactly which one to sever . . . it started gushing blood and then we stabbed his chest over and over again until his body was . . . mutilated and . . . we told ourselves—I told myself, anyway—that no one would miss him."

"Mr. Alberto Munoz Santana," said Cooley, not capable of looking her in the eye, relieved to find his voice wasn't shaky anymore. "That was his name."

"We freaked out afterward. I . . . I wanted to go to the police, you have to believe me. I did. I wanted to do it and told Bunson I would, like right after it happened. But he said he'd kill me if I did. And then Lang told us that she lied, that it didn't end with one person, and if we didn't do it again she'd expose us, turn us in."

"And what did you two say?"

"Bunson was the one who spoke up."

"He stood up to her?"

"No." She started weeping. "He just asked her to give him more of the drugs." Cooley looked away. "The next one—"

"Miss Monica Miller," said Goldsmith, stepping out from around some trees. He crouched down and took a look at Bunson's corpse. Sadie looked at him.

"Just listen to me! She was worse than worthless . . . her little boy was born addicted to some street drug, and she hit him when—"

"She didn't deserve to die," interrupted Cooley.

"If we didn't do it she would have sent us to jail!"

"So you thought it would be better if I went instead? Who placed my hair and skin fragments at the crime scenes?" Cooley grabbed her shoulders, yanking her close.

Sadie just looked at him. Her big, beautiful eyes were all cried out. "The paper they send in the mail to tell you that you're accepted is so beautiful," she said. "Expensive, heavy stock in this milky, ivory color. Even the creases from the folding are perfectly symmetrical. Their coat of arms at the top is so bright with color that it practically jumps out at you and dances right before your eyes. It's a funny thing, opening an envelope and finding the validation of your entire life inside on a single sheet of that wonderful paper. It felt so heavy . . . so heavy in my hand."

Goldsmith stood there, looking at her. If they were in an examination room and this were a peer review, he'd have had some pithy remark to offer, something about how he received dozens of those love letters from places she could only dream of, and how he too hoped to find the kind of validation she mentioned upon opening the envelope. But he never got it. Never really felt it in his heart, anyway, and that's what was most important. Not with the first one (Harvard) or the last (Stanford, for those keeping score).

Suddenly, he felt her eyes on him. "Don't look at me like that!"

shouted Sadie, snapped out of her trance. "Not everyone's as smart as you! I took the same meds my whole life, the same progressions! Why didn't I know the answers?"

"Let's go, Cooley," he said, breaking off her gaze. He put his hand on Cooley's shoulder and gently began to pull him away from her. "It's almost time."

Sadie stared at Cooley as he moved away. Cooley took one last look at Bunson's crumpled body, the syringe still jutting out from his ankle. Compared to his thick leg, it looked almost comically small, the tiny laser needle that felled a giant of Goliath proportions.

"She made me do it," she said to Cooley. "We never had a choice, remember? You told me that yourself. I said that I'd stick by you if you were in trouble. I told you that, and . . ." Her voice disappeared into the wind and running water as Cooley and Goldsmith walked away through the atrium space. They made their way down another winding path.

"Stella's about to begin her simulcast," said Goldsmith.

"What do we need to do?"

"She told me to find a phone and call the police." He looked at Cooley as he stared off into the distance, his eyes hollow. "Cooley, I'm sorry about Sadie."

"What about Bunson?" he asked, his voice wavering slightly. "Are you sorry about him, too?"

"Yes."

"Part of me was doing all of this for them. I was fighting for my life because I loved being with them so much I didn't ever want the ride to end. And now . . . I've got to admit I'm searching for reasons to keep on giving a shit."

"How about me and Stella?"

Just as Cooley was about to answer, he stopped short. Goldsmith looked at him. The atrium began to fill with the slowly building din of specimens pouring out of the coliseum on their way to the last progressions of the day. "Cooley," Goldsmith said.

"Shhh . . . ." And then Cooley heard it. A barely perceptible, slightly high-pitched hum that could be just another holographic hummingbird flittering around from digitized branch to digitized branch underneath the high hanging, washed-out sun. But it was not.

Goldsmith instantly recognized it, too. And with every moment that passed, that sweetly deceptive hum of a security detail ThermaGun locking onto its target got louder and louder. They broke into a sprint, Cooley running directly through the illusions of this paradise of Nature & Co. technology, passing through trees, rocks, and whole mountains while Goldsmith's long legs kept him just a few steps behind.

24

It was a strange sensation for Goldsmith, running directly through apparently solid, massive objects like age-old maple trees, boulders, even that big red barn that was near the meadow, the whole time not incurring any damage to his person. They seemed realistic enough, absorbed light and cast shadows perfectly (the barn even smelled a tad raw, like manure), and had remained standing in the same place for the twelve years of his time there, these immovable landmarks of Goldsmith's childhood; and yet, now he found himself able to pass through them with ease. Running a few steps ahead of him, Cooley came to the riverbank and did not slow down. He simply ran across the surface of the water without getting a drop on him. Goldsmith followed, not sure where he was being led, but getting to like this feeling of invincibility. They reached the opposite side of the river. Cooley sped up. Goldsmith did the same and crashed into a disconcertingly solid object at full speed. The flock of specimens walking to their next progressions, unfortunately was not a hologram. The legs that Goldsmith found himself tangled in on the floor belonged to Mr. Ravi Chandrashaker, a sophomore who Stansbury rumor held had found a viable, improved alternative to the Mandelbrot Set equation.

"Hey!" Chandrashaker shouted, grabbing at stray papers that were knocked loose from the impact. "Watch where you're going!" The boy froze upon seeing at whom he was yelling. "Uh, I mean I'm sorry to be in your way, Mr. Goldsmith, sir."

The collision seemed to jar the painkillers flowing through Goldsmith's body and his bullet wounds started to throb. As he picked himself up, he saw Camilla staring at him from the crowd, the only stationary specimen among dozens of others as they swarmed around her to their destinations.

"Camilla," Goldsmith began to say, watching her eyes as they glanced inside his blazer and focused on the half-wet bloodstains on his shirt. "I'm . . ."

"Goldsmith!" came Cooley's voice. Goldsmith looked over and saw Cooley beckoning to him, frantic.

He knew they had a few seconds. The detail's ThermaGuns couldn't fire into a space with this many warm-blooded targets, so Goldsmith searched for something meaningful to say. Not wanting to repeat the "I love you" statement in front of all these other people, some of whom were now gawking at him as he stood up from the floor, he tried to think of something appropriate, another sincere declaration, an explanation, maybe even a warning for her not to trust anyone inside this place.

"I'm sorry," was all he could manage. She blinked some tears back, probably wondering when the world she knew started to go insane. Goldsmith ran off toward Cooley and saw Officers Tannen and Willets headed toward them. Tannen had his ThermaGun out. Willets wielded an electrified shock stick, specifically made for close-quarters specimen control. Some specimens saw their ordnance and, since they were med cycle adherents, did not scream or panic, but rather turned and walked off in another direction like businessmen studiously avoiding a minor car accident that might have made them late for work. Goldsmith saw Cooley's hand go for the Colt M-8 in his waistband.

"No," he said. "If you miss and hit one of the specimens, you're finished."

"I'm finished anyway."

The clearing looked familiar to Goldsmith. Just yesterday he and the headmaster strolled through here, right after he busted eleven of Cooley's closest friends for dopazone possession. He dashed over to the hidden control panel that he watched the headmaster use just yesterday to fix the atrium's glitched gray sun and beige sky, during their stroll together following Goldsmith's dopazone peer reviews. He waved his hand wildly over some strangely tall dandelions before he heard an infrared sensor chime. A white display and keyboard emerged from thin air. Goldsmith started typing while the officers cut the distance between them in half. He watched as Willets headed cautiously toward Cooley, holding the shock stick in front of him.

"He's armed," called out Tannen. "Move in, let me get locked." He peered through the scope of his gun and blinked, confused. "Wait, Willets, that's not . . ."

Willets swung the stick at Cooley and caught thin air as it passed right through his upper body, humming with its electrical charge. He glanced around, puzzled, and saw dozens of holographic Cooley replicas swarming around him. One of them snuck up behind Officer Tannen and clubbed him in the back of the skull with the butt of his pistol. Tannen went down, out cold. Willets rushed over, running through fake Cooleys and swung blindly. He caught the genuine article on the back of the leg and Cooley went down, thousands of volts paralyzing his muscles. Goldsmith ran over from the atrium control panel and dove for Tannen's ThermaGun. He aimed and pulled the trigger, plugging Willets in the chest with a shot. He wasn't sure whether the bullet was a lethal one or just a sedative round. Goldsmith took a moment to catch his breath and found his head clearing for the first time in a while. He started to play the current scenario out in his mind, factoring in possibilities and likely outcomes . . .

He grabbed Tannen's limp body, unzipped his Tac IX utility gear, and pulled off his regulation coolant vest. He unbuttoned Cooley's shirt and strapped on the thin, almost skintight vest underneath, and activated it before buttoning him back up again. He grabbed Willets's body and went to pull another vest off for himself, but saw the gaping hole in his chest, blood and coolant fluid mixing together into a shallow pool and realized that not only was the equipment useless, but he had killed a man. Goldsmith tried to keep it all down, but could not. He started dry heaving over Willets's wounds. Cooley stirred. Goldsmith choked everything back and pulled Cooley to his feet. The atrium was quiet, eerie. Everyone else was in progressions.

"We don't have time to call the police," Goldsmith said. "Stella's about to go on the air. Let's get out of here. If we can make it out of the tower we'll bring the authorities back here to get her."

"What . . . ," started Cooley, still dazed from the blow he took, "what if they find her?"

"Once she simulcasts, the school can't kill her. They'd have the whole Senate committee as witnesses."

"That's a big chance to take, man."

"I know." Goldsmith hefted the ThermaGun in his hand. "But if she comes up short, somehow I'll find Senator Bloom and finish the job." The weapon felt weighty, a terrible burden. Cooley grinned at Goldsmith like he was a youngster who had just learned to tie his own shoes. "They'll have the elevator pods and the main entrance on registration and reception monitored."

"The stairs," said Cooley. "There are too many floors for them to guard at once. You still have Nelson's key card?"

Goldsmith nodded.

"There's a chance they didn't deactivate it yet. If we can get down the stairwell to the loading entrance, the key card will let us out."

Goldsmith considered it. They didn't have any other options. He nodded again and followed Cooley to the stairwell entrance. Cooley pulled the door open and they took in the aroma of ammonia and chemicals floating up from the bowels of the tower. The odors were stinging and sharp, a far cry from the lilacs and lilies of the atrium. They sprinted down the stairs, taking three at a time. The door swung shut above their heads as they started their descent, the echoes sounding grave and final.

Down on Level 4, Stella sat in a small wooden chair constructed for use by seven year olds and arranged her array of data along the computer terminal's desktop, ready for transmittal to Senator Bloom and the Senate Select Committee on Education's office on Capitol Hill. Under other circumstances, she might have felt ridiculous occupying this space, channeling the precocious little schoolgirl she was so many years ago, but the morphine that cloaked the pain (and critical nature, of this she was well aware) of her wounds also happened to cast a cozy glow around the room. The bright colors of the blue-and-yellow plastic slide, and the brown-and-green playhouse sitting in the corner seemed fantastical, the cubbyholes where the little specimens stored their shoes and rainbow colored schoolbags for athletics progressions—schoolbags being among the few gifts from the outside world permitted in the tower—appeared to Stella as gateways to a special place where dragons existed, along with large, furry creatures who spoke in plummy English accents, that lurked about, just waiting to befriend small boys and girls. She swore she saw Curious George in a red shirt swing by above her head on an invisible vine. Her eyelids drifted shut and then popped open. Stella reached inside Cooley's blazer and removed the Stimulum laser syringe Goldsmith secured for her. She tapped a vein in her arm and injected herself.

Her wounds almost felt welcome—sharp sensations of repentance for leading five of her former classmates to violent, painful deaths. She understood they weren't the brightest specimens, but their eyes all lit up with glimmers when they grasped the enormity of the larger plan. Stella wondered if they held all of this against her. She glanced around the room, at the other tiny desks and chairs, and it occurred to her that Evan would have been almost old enough to occupy one of them if he (or she) had made it into this world.

The simulcast screen whirred to life, presenting the image of Senator Arthur Bloom. His balding scalp looked tan and healthy despite his advanced age, and he instinctively smiled when he saw her face broadcast back to him.

"Good afternoon, Stella!" his image said. "Big day's here, isn't it?"

"Yes, it is."

He peered a bit closer, leaning in. He donned the pair of glasses that hung around his neck, examining her face through his screen. "Are you . . . all right?"

"Of course, Senator."

"Where are you, girl?" He glanced to her left, probably seeing the colored plastic of the playhouse in the corner. "You're not in your office."

"I'm in Stansbury Tower."

Shock spread across his face. "What? It's too dangerous! I won't put you in harm's way."

"It's too late for this, sir. I'm ready. When do we go live?"

"In two . . . in two minutes."

Stella nodded weakly and felt her body sway a bit before she righted herself against the edge of the table. The walls of the progression room melted into that magical forest she had always dreamed about when she was younger. Curious George climbed up on top of the absent teacher's desk and winked at her. The muscles in her back began to tremble from the strain of merely sitting upright. The senator seemed to be saying something, but Stella only saw his mouth move. She fell to the side and Curious George caught her just in the nick of time, standing on the floor next to her miniature chair, holding up her body with his long, furry arms, that perpetual smile on his face. He doesn't speak, Stella thought. In all of the books that ever bore his name, this monkey never once spoke. He never asked any questions. That must be why he was so curious. An old flash ran through her head, chasing the years and finally catching up to her. *George was curious. He opened a box and peeked inside. The box was empty. (That was not a good surprise!) George opened another box. And another. They were all empty! Suddenly the store clerk came running. "Stop! Please!" he cried. "You are ruining my display!" But George did not want to stop. He wanted to go . . .*

"Thirty seconds," Stella heard the senator say. Stella took a deep breath and focused on the two screens before her: one with the alumni file data and the other showing the committee's members waiting for her to begin. She executed a final set of keystrokes on the computer—programming her simulcast to be transmitted to all public screens throughout the tower—and prepared her best Judith Lang smile. Then she winked at little George, getting ready to open up those boxes for all to see.

———

Cooley and Goldsmith ran down the stairs, which bent around in ninety-degree angles over and over again, in a seemingly endless descent. They ran past a door marked LEVEL 61. Everything had passed by much more quickly than Goldsmith thought it would. His well-conditioned heart started to pound harder than he'd ever felt before. They darted past floors . . . 50 . . . 33 . . . 19 . . . Cooley's breaths had gone from controlled, determined hisses to frantic pants. They passed Level 4. Goldsmith sent up a silent prayer for Stella Saltzman, wondering if she'd stay alive long enough for the old valedictorian to make the hardest speech of her life. Part of him considered the possibility that she would not, and he wondered which outcome would be worse for him, if his fate were sealed more ominously whether Stansbury School stood or crumbled in the public eye. He reached into his pocket and pulled out Professor Nelson's key card, ready to swipe it against the security sensor waiting for them at the loading entrance door.

They passed Floor 2. The big titanium sliding door gleamed in their line of vision, the sheen of it almost otherworldly. Cooley leaped down the last flight of stairs, flying through the air over eight steps and landing right before it. Goldsmith followed suit, reaching out and swiping the card in one clean motion. The sensor beeped and a red light shined. Cooley yanked the door handle, but it remained electromagnetically sealed. He aimed his gun at the sensor in a frenzy of futility.

"Don't," whispered Goldsmith. "The bullet will ricochet against the titanium and kill us both." They stared at each other for a long moment. Goldsmith knew Cooley was waiting for him to come up with one last move.

"Professor Nelson confessed everything to me," echoed President Lang's voice. Goldsmith whirled around, peering into the darkness. "You were gambling that he wouldn't, but his loyalty is impeccable." She walked out from the shadows at the stairwell's base and stood before them, aiming a security detail–issued M-8 at Goldsmith. "Professor Nelson knows what Stansbury means to this country. Do you, Mr. Goldsmith?" She stepped closer, flipping the safety off the pistol, cocking it. Lang was now within arm's reach.

Goldsmith felt adrenaline flow through his body. He got that Phys-D déjà vu. His brain willed off the counteractive surge of med cycle beta blockers like it was nothing. He saw eighteen different ways to disarm her from where he stood. A new sensation overwhelmed him at the sight of the president. Outrage. Hurt. That pure, grade-A *Catcher in the Rye* angst that Camilla found so implausible. Where was she now? Goldsmith could tell her all about it. Lang advanced closer. Twenty-nine ways. Fuck each and every one of them. Fuck Phys-D. And fuck Stansbury.

"Shoot me," he said, calm.

"Goldsmith!" he heard Cooley shout.

Goldsmith stepped forward in her direction. No shot came.

"Go on. Shoot." She just looked at him, frozen.

He took another step forward. He easily batted the gun from her hand. She yelped in shock. It sailed through the air and clattered to the floor. Lang gawked at him. He reared back a fist and swung. Her eyes went wide with fear.

"Mr. Gold—" The blow cut her off in midsentence. She crumpled to the ground and stared up at him, speechless, her beautiful whitened teeth stained with blood pouring from big gashes in her lips and nose. The drops looked black when they hit the floor, like she was an Armani suit–wearing cyborg leaking oil.

"Murderer!" He spat the word at her in a hybrid of anger, frustration, and disappointment. He tried to keep his voice under control, but it was no match for twelve years of pent-up fury at this woman kneeling before him. Angst. He stared Lang down, watching her kneeling and trembling before him, her eyes on his black loafers, like she knew she didn't deserve to gaze up at him. "You puny woman," he hissed, disgust in his voice. "You think you control me? You think you can use specimens however you want?"

"Listen to me," she sputtered. "I—"

"Don't you get it? *I could kill you a hundred different ways right now!* You're worthless!" Goldsmith took a breath and worked himself back under control. "Tell me you were behind everything. I want to hear you say it out loud."

"This . . . this was all my plan. I take the responsibility."

"Goldsmith," said Cooley. "We've got to call the cops." Goldsmith studied Lang's face, her eyes, watched her the way he watched hundreds of guilty specimens under peer review on the disciplinary level over the past year. She kept glancing down, focusing on the puddle of her blood forming on the floor. And then she looked up at him. A thin smile passed over her torn-up lips.

"Not yet," Goldsmith said. "There's something she's not telling us."

"Like what?" asked Cooley.

"There's someone else involved, isn't there?"

"No," she replied. Eyes up and to the right. She was lying. Goldsmith cut loose with a backhand. Her skin sounded like a balloon popping against the force of his blow. It knocked her onto her side. Goldsmith heard Cooley gasp, but never took his eyes from her. He pulled Lang up to her knees, setting her up like some breathing, bleeding bowling pin.

"One more time. Is there someone else involved?"

"No!" Goldsmith raised his hand again. She flinched. "Yes!"

"Who?"

"You . . . you don't want to know." Goldsmith let fly. He used his other hand this time. Her head smacked against the concrete floor. He pulled her back up yet again and watched Lang sway as her eyes got refocused.

"Goldsmith," said Cooley, his voice softened, as if trying to soothe. He placed a hand on Goldsmith's shoulder. Goldsmith batted it away and got back in Lang's face.

"I want a name."

"No . . . ," she murmured. Goldsmith reared back again—this time with a fist. Cooley grabbed his arm and spun him around.

"You're gonna kill her!" he shouted. Goldsmith shoved him out of the way.

"You can't beat me," he said to President Lang in that cold, terrifying examination room tone that still made Cooley's skin crawl. "You could never beat any specimen. You're not smart enough. You're not strong enough. You're too slow. You can only dream of having our gifts. You're practically fucking handicapped. All of you people. The whole world gets off on thinking we're your little pet army of prodigies . . . keep us doped up, prod us with shock sticks and we'll turn out acts of genius for you, right? Listen to me, *ma'am*." He bent down and grabbed Lang by her bloodied lip, pinching it. She wheezed in pain. "You're like any other outsider: an evolutionary liability. What is there to stop me from eliminating you from the food chain at this very moment?" Lang stared back at him in silence. "There's nothing stopping me. Tell me who else is tied into this, goddamn it."

"Your mother," she breathed, a barely audible whisper.

"*Liar!*" Goldsmith grabbed her by the neck, cocked back his fist, and lined up a coup de grace. Cooley bear-hugged him, easing him away from Lang. Goldsmith struggled beneath his grasp. "Get out of my way, Cooley . . . she has to pay the price."

"No!" Cooley hissed in his ear. "Stop! We swore an oath, remember?" He felt Goldsmith ease up. Cooley slowly let him free. "We swore an oath." Goldsmith stepped back and looked at him.

"The oath never meant anything to her," Goldsmith said, pointing at Lang. "You know that. It was just another lie they fed us. It was all a lie. This place, these people, everything. Don't you get it? You won, Cooley. From the very beginning, you hated this place. All these years, you were right and I was wrong."

"I never hated the oath. I hated their interpretation of it."

"Why shouldn't I make her pay? Why shouldn't they all pay? They don't believe in it!"

"It's too late for her to start believing, Goldsmith. It's not too late for us." Goldsmith stared at him, taking everything in. Cooley grinned at him like it was the simplest thing in the world. "Look at me. I'm eighteen. You think I'm gonna spend the rest of my life hung up on this place? It's high school, man. You get through it."

"That's wishful thinking."

"Yeah." Cooley paused, trying to think of something eloquent. "But I got nothing else," was all he could manage.

Goldsmith looked over at Lang. She slowly rose to her feet. "What do you know about my mother?" he asked. And then there were footsteps, rubber soles of boots pounding against concrete steps. Figures of men descended the stairwell toward them. Goldsmith flipped the safety off his ThermaGun, getting ready to fire. Cooley aimed at the stairs.

Captain Gibson, flanked by Officers Jamison, O'Shaunnessy, and Tannen, appeared, all aiming guns at Cooley and Goldsmith. Lang picked up her own gun and walked over toward the detail men. "More than you could ever dream," she said, looking directly at Goldsmith. From his peripheral vision, he saw Cooley watching him. "My offer still stands, valedictorian. But the stakes are now raised. I'll extend to you an unconditional pardon. I know Stella Saltzman is somewhere inside this building. All you have to do is give me her location. And then aim at Mr. Cooley and pull the trigger."

"Do what you've always done," said Captain Gibson. "Use your brain."

"It will be reported as self-defense," said Lang.

Goldsmith pointed the ThermaGun in her direction and moved his finger to the trigger. "No," he said, trying with all of his strength to stop his hand from shaking.

"You were impressive," she said, smiling through her wounds. "You put the whole thing together yourself. Exactly the way I thought you would. This wasn't the deal we agreed to earlier, but finish this matter once and for all and I'll turn over your confidential file."

"She's lying," muttered Cooley.

Goldsmith felt as if Lang's voice was easing his aim over toward Cooley.

"Isn't the death of one unbalanced specimen, a good-for-nothing delinquent, worth ridding the world of cancer?" she asked. "Of AIDS? Isn't it worth the discovery of the next Beethoven?"

Goldsmith glanced at her. Even in the foul darkness of the stairwell, she shimmered beautifully.

"Remember progress, Mr. Goldsmith. More progress would have saved your father's life. It would have saved him and his young, pregnant wife-to-be the pain of him . . . withering away like a dry, cracked leaf in summer." She paused, her voice just barely catching before getting her timbre back. "Progress would have saved that young girl who never had a chance to see the inside of a school like this . . . she was too young, too poor to be a mother to her baby boy. She wouldn't have had to give him away."

"Don't listen to her . . . ," said Cooley, his voice rising, just short of pleading, but Goldsmith didn't hear it because he was too busy watching the pieces fall together right before his very eyes, every word that flowed from Lang's mouth a new part of the one puzzle that always eluded him. She must finish telling him. He needed to hear it, and then they could do what they liked to him, to Cooley, to Stella, to Camilla, to anyone they wanted.

"Stella's in an empty first grade progression room on Level 4. The western side," he said in his familiar examination room voice. Gibson turned around and ran up the stairs.

"I backed the full-ride scholarship program from the start," President Lang said slowly, calmly, like she was recounting a fairy tale. Her eyes would not leave his. He began to realize why they looked as familiar as long-lost friends. "I always knew where you were. I was too young to have a child; it would have ruined my career. The whole time I kept track of you. I made sure you'd win the lottery. And look how far you've come, sweetheart. You did so well . . . my Thomas. But schooling isn't everything." She smiled through the blood glistening from her mouth and nose. "You always had good genes."

Goldsmith's eyes overflowed with tears and they spilled out, getting trapped beneath the rims of his eyeglasses. His vision blurred behind them, but he knew it didn't matter. The ThermaGun in his hand hummed. Cutting-edge technology made using these things easy. He looked at Cooley and watched, seemingly drop by drop, as the life drained out of his face.

"No . . . ," was all William Winston Cooley could manage before Goldsmith gritted his teeth and squeezed the trigger. The barrel of the gun lit up into a white flame, releasing a burst of hollow point bullets in a rattling hail. They whipped about in precisely programmed ellipses, first around Cooley's body and then back past Goldsmith. He knew it was impossible, but was nonetheless certain he could feel them cut through the air around his ears as they flew past. President Lang and Officers Jamison, O'Shaunnessy, and Tannen didn't have the chance to even gasp in shock as the bullets cut through their flesh and erupted inside their bodies. A mere moment after the burst of the gun, the dull sound of four limp bodies thumping to the concrete floor followed.

Goldsmith watched as Cooley slowly opened his eyes and felt his own chest and torso. He flinched and then unbuttoned his shirt, touching the cold surface of Tannen's coolant vest that he received as a far-sighted gift back in the atrium. "You . . . ," he managed to breathe.

"I set the ThermaGun to its automatic burst setting," Goldsmith said. "I suspected it would nail anyone other than the person who was holding the weapon itself—or someone who was wearing an activated coolant vest." He paused, as if to admire the cool logic of his strategy. Then a look of panic came over his face. "Oh my God," he said, suddenly frantic. "Stella."

Cooley grabbed the ThermaGun from Goldsmith. "Relax," he said. "What are you—" He watched Cooley look through the gun's large scope, gauging a shot.

"You've got this rep," Cooley said, concentrating on the task at hand. "Rags-to-riches orphan, prodigy of the prodigies. Well, I got a rep, too." Cooley looked from the scope to Goldsmith and grinned. "I'm the baddest fucking specimen who ever lived." He squeezed the trigger. A single bullet flew from the barrel upward, having locked onto a breathing man's body heat signature, and sailed through a steel door three floors above them without losing any of its terrible velocity.

Captain Gibson jogged through the brightly lit, unpopulated corridor on Level 4, his pistol out, following the sound of a young woman— one far too old to be a first grade specimen—who seemed to be talking to herself. He hadn't seen Stella Saltzman since commencement day years ago. And before he could lay eyes on her today, he heard the clean smack of steel being punctured by a sharp object moving fast enough to displace its own density. The ThermaGun bullet that Cooley fired just a few seconds earlier hurtled through the corridor and embedded itself in his chest, entering his body from behind, just below the aorta, ripping it apart. Gibson died facedown on the hallway floor of the school whose policies and laws he upheld for twenty-odd years, the sound of Miss Saltzman's voice from a monitor carrying him off with a final lullaby.

Goldsmith leaned down toward Jamison's bullet-riddled body, the corpse's eyes still opened wide in shock, and pulled the security detail key card from around his neck. He wanted to leave this place forever. The antiseptic smell of the stairwell blending with burnt flesh singed his nostrils and seemed to cling to his body. He walked over to the titanium door's card sensor and glanced at Cooley as if to say, *now, finally—are you ready?* Cooley instinctively understood, giving him a nod. Goldsmith swiped the card. A soft beep echoed against the dark brick and industrial concrete surrounding them. The thick silver door hissed, letting in foreign air from the desert outside and slowly began to slide open.

"You let me down," came President Lang's voice up from the stairs where she fell, sounding strong and alive. They whirled around and looked up at her. She pushed O'Shaunnessy's mangled body away. He was noticeably more mutilated than the others: Goldsmith realized that she managed to dash behind him during the volley of fire, using him as a makeshift shield. She aimed her pistol at Goldsmith, her hand steady. He looked at Cooley, nodding for him to step outside into the safety of the desert. Cooley did.

A bright light streamed into the stairwell from the outside, casting a golden path on the floor for him to follow. He heard another set of footsteps slowly descend the hard stairs. President Lang's hand fell to her side as if she was hiding her weapon from whoever was approaching. She stared helplessly at some spot on the wall behind him, her once ethereal eyes dulled. Camilla appeared behind her. She walked down and stood before him, perhaps subconsciously avoiding setting foot in that path of light, as if she might melt if it touched her. Goldsmith heard Lang's gun clatter to the floor. Camilla stepped toward her and Stansbury's president shrunk backward into the darkness, bumping into the wall behind her. The young lady cast her hard, Athenian gaze upon the broken woman, daring her to run, plead, or explain. Lang did not.

"I can't go, Mr. Goldsmith," Camilla said, looking over at Goldsmith. "I contacted the police. Someone needs to stay here. To see things through."

"I know." He smiled at her and turned toward the exit. "The thing is, Camilla," he said, looking over his shoulder at her, "I just wish I could remember all of the good things I ever told you and say them all over again, so you'll never forget."

"Don't worry," she said, failing to hold back a young schoolgirl's mischievous smile, perhaps not even trying to do so in the first place. "I've got a great memory."

Goldsmith walked out into the fresh air and felt his breath get swept away. Some time during all of this, that long, epic rainstorm stopped as suddenly as it began. All that remained in the sky was a warm, setting, orange sun—just another star, really, but one that happened to be just the perfect size for a world such as this—and it hung large enough for a hopeful young man to honestly believe that one day he could stretch out a hand and touch the brightness if he really wanted. Goldsmith took a step toward it. And then another.

25

"... Ladies and gentlemen of the committee, the education of youth is not about plaudits. It is not about headlines. Nor is it about ensuring the future's progress by any means necessary. You have seen the evidence of Stansbury's crimes, and now I pose this question to each and every one of you: Are you willing to explain to the families of these murdered twenty-one-year-olds that the lives of their children were taken in order to improve the quality of life of those who never knew them?"

The words flowed from Stella's lips exactly the way she knew they would. She just needed to keep up the strength to finish. She could see the audience of the committee's senators on the simulcast screen clearly. Stella imagined them as small children who would be heartbroken if her story was cut short before its ending, an ending that could have been interpreted as happy or sad—that was out of her control—but nothing was as disappointing as a tale left unfinished, once it had begun. She had thought she was losing consciousness perhaps ten minutes ago, but the photos of Alvarez, Miller, Santana,

Smith, and Riley in the alumni files came to life, whispering words of encouragement to keep her going. Obliging them was the very least she could do. While speaking, Stella pinched her left arm hard enough to break the skin and draw blood. Her body had numbed to the point where she could not feel whether it dripped across her arm or just stayed inside the canyon of the gash. All she cared about was whether the pain would keep her awake long enough to finish the task at hand.

Several hundred specimens were gathered in the atrium and had been watching the Senate committee broadcast since it began. This was not what they were expecting after President Lang regaled them with promises of publicly acknowledged glory yesterday morning. They all stood very still, their heads cocked upward, looking at the extra-large plasma screen hanging, seemingly, in midair. The brightness of the artificial sun had been dialed down so that Miss Stella Saltzman's pallid complexion was the sole beacon floating in space. Many of the older specimens recognized her and shushed the younger ones who nervously nudged one another and started asking questions, confused about the scandalous things this distinguished alumnus was saying about their school.

". . . Education is about caring and nurturing youth in all its shapes and forms, its ups and downs, its genius and its quirks," rang out Stella's voice, loud and clear. "It is about teaching children that they can stay young forever. After all, what does it mean to hold an unchanging youth? It is to reach, at the end, the vision with which one started . . ."

"She's actually saying all of this on television?" shouted out a girl from the junior class. "Is she nuts?"

"What does this mean?" said someone else.

"She's presenting all of this to the senators?"

"Do you think the administration really did it?"

"I mean, doesn't she know that college admissions officers are watching?"

"Chill out. Your SAT scores are good enough to get you in."

"Does anyone have a Xanax?"

"If we keep standing here we're all gonna be late for progression."

"Yeah, I've got a final exam tomorrow."

The loud smack of a thick textbook falling from a specimen's hands and hitting the solid floor echoed across the atrium's walls and roof, cutting the voices short. The noise was repeated a few more times as others allowed their academic artifacts to fall from their hands as well, and then over and over again, sounding like code being passed throughout the tower. Mr. Gregory Marcus Garvin (sporting an impressive black eye from the dodgeball altercation earlier in the day) and Mr. Andrew Chang were the first to turn from the broadcast and head for the elevators. Shannon Louise Evans and Katherine Mary Lewis were not too far behind. The shuffling of many more pairs of feet followed them.

Just outside the loading dock entrance, Cooley and Goldsmith stood for a moment in the rapidly drying desert and squinted into the warmth of the setting sun. Goldsmith started to perspire a bit and took off his blazer, setting it on the cracked ground. He undid his tie and unbuttoned his dress shirt, tossing both to the side, leaving him in his trousers and white undershirt. He stretched, his skin soaking up all the natural light. And then he remembered some papers printed out from President Lang's computer that he had stashed inside his blazer earlier in the day and pulled them out, holding them tightly in his hand.

"What now?" asked Cooley.

"I don't know," said Goldsmith, mesmerized by the sight of the sunset in the distance.

"I've still got the keys to the Shelby. We can drive it into San Angeles and figure things out from there."

"Okay." They walked around the base of the tower, a task that, due to the building's enormous size, took about ten minutes. They finally came upon the blazing carcass of the car, which someone (most likely the security detail before the stairwell incident) had set on fire with the intent of depriving them of their means of escape. The formerly glorious dark green machine roasted, flames curling upward from the windows, giving off too much heat to approach any closer than fifteen or twenty feet. Cooley tossed the keys to the ground.

"I'm not going back into the tower," he said.

"Neither am I."

"I guess we're walking, then."

"I guess so."

They walked for a few moments in silence, Goldsmith's long legs taking him a few steps ahead of Cooley toward the civilization that waited for them far off in the distance. He wondered if they'd make it there before nightfall. Then he realized that Cooley was letting himself lag behind on purpose. He stopped and turned to look at him. Cooley was standing still, the gun in his hand at his side.

"Did you want your revenge?" Goldsmith asked. "For those friends of yours I prosecuted?"

Cooley studied him for a long moment, feeling the reassuring weight of the pistol. He thought about all of the dead bodies they were leaving behind in the tower—the headmaster, Captain Gibson, Officers Jamison, O'Shaunnessy, Tannen, and Willets; Pete, Bunson (especially Bunson), maybe—probably, Miss Stella Saltzman, not to mention the murdered alumni—and felt tears stream down his face. He remembered the way that Sadie held him close and touched his cheek so that she could ease the pain of her knife piercing every dream and memory he held dear. What a waste, he thought. Duties were forsaken. Futures were shattered. Good people were corrupted and died because of it. And for what, Goldsmith? So you and I could ruin the lives of four thousand specimens and tear down the walls of Dr. Stansbury's noble dream, all because we yearned to reach some bogus stage of life called "adulthood"? Cooley jammed the gun into his waistband. He had never wanted a magic batch of meds to make him feel instantaneously better more than at this moment. He wiped the tears away with the back of his hand.

"I'd say we're even, Mr. Goldsmith."

"Good."

"We could go back. Well, you could. They'll end up having graduation. You can still go back."

"Please, Cooley. I've lost my faith. I haven't lost my mind." He watched Cooley look down at his shoes, observing him trying to gather up the gall to ask the question that had been tugging at both of them since they stepped outside of Stansbury and saw the first glimpse of red chasing the blue up in that early evening sky.

"Do you think Lang was telling the truth?" Cooley began to ask, but stopped when he saw Goldsmith give him a look that said, *hush, please.* The valedictorian reached inside his blazer and handed him a small stack of beaten-up pages folded lengthwise. Cooley opened them and looked at a cover sheet that bore the Stansbury emblem and the words: Confidential File History—William Winston Cooley. A jolt raced through his stomach up to his chest and he felt the pages cling to his already-sweating fingers.

"Maybe she was," Goldsmith said as he held out his own stack of confidential pages at arm's length. The cool desert wind picked up as he released them. They immediately scattered into the distance, white sheets snapping in the breeze, swirling and dancing a giddy, discordant rhythm as they disappeared into specks, and then nothing at all. "But maybe she wasn't." He watched Cooley stare at the cover sheet of his own file, and then started off on the long walk to San Angeles. Soon he heard his friend's footsteps moving close behind.

On Level 41, Mr. Hurley sat on the edge of his work terminal chair and watched his plasma screen as it broadcast Stella Saltzman's testimony to the committee. His mouth was agape and his heart raced.

". . . My words may sound harsh," she said, her tone indicating that she was headed for her big finish, "but they are no less harsh than Stansbury's betrayal of those it has sworn to nurture. Ladies and gentlemen, senators, children, let me remind you: All great truths begin as blasphemies." The data feed cut to a shot of the committee's chamber as a din started to rise. Whispers gave way to scattered applause that built into a crescendo. Hurley heard crowds of specimens swarming past the open door of the yearbook office and glanced at his watch. Progressions didn't end for another twenty minutes he realized, and wondered where everyone was headed. He poked his head out the doorway and watched scores of uniformed children of all ages headed toward the elevator banks and the stairwells, as if drawn by some invisible pied piper that was only audible to those under the age of eighteen.

"Hey!" he called out to them. "Where are you going?" He did not receive an answer. Young Mr. Joshua Calley was also wondering the same thing, however. He watched the broadcast from the strange woman like everyone else, and didn't quite understand what the other specimens were up to, but he did not want to be left alone inside this big, all too frequently scary place. He saw his older specimen friend, Mr. John Jason Stevenson, and tugged at his blazer. Stevenson stopped.

"Hey, Mr. Stevenson! Where are we going now?"

Stevenson looked down at Calley and smiled warmly. "Recess."

"Stella?" said Senator Bloom over the simulcast system on Level 4. "Are you there?" He did not receive an answer, because the progression room had become a different world. The red sun outside poured in through the windows that Stella's mind had created inside the thick concrete walls, illuminating birds and trees that seemed to reach up forever. The fragrance of a steaming supper filled every living thing around with a voracious appetite, which was fine, Stella thought to herself, because there was more than enough to go around. She floated about behind the stove, watching fresh food in large ceramic pots simmer as she took in the view through those huge windows that overlooked the world from a perch high up in the sky. She felt two strong hands on her waist, wrapping around her in a soft embrace, and she leaned her head back a bit, just enough to feel the day-old stubble on Wayne's cheek and the cursive smirk of his lips as he whispered yet another secret that would be heard by her ears only. He reached over and held up a crystal goblet of dark red wine for her and she took a sip from it, feeling a warm tingle spread throughout her whole body. She accepted the goblet from Wayne and he pointed off into the distance where two small figures ran into the tall grass holding hands. Stella could only see their silhouettes, but she knew it was Curious George leading small Evan into a soft meadow, because all of the meadows in their neighborhood were soft. That, after all, was why they moved here in the first place. Evan wanted to keep on going, but George would not allow it. He saw the color and height of the sun and knew the hour drew near. Dinner was approaching, and when mother called out they would go to her as fast as their little legs could carry them.

"Stella," came the senator's voice one final time. "Are you out there?"

"You can't let them all go!" pleaded Mr. Hurley to President Lang as she stood there leaning against the brick down near the loading entrance, watching the steady stream of specimens flow past them and out of the loading dock into the desert beyond. "Why aren't you stopping them?"

Camilla watched as scores of familiar faces passed her by. Lang had not uttered a word since Goldsmith walked out into the light. Camilla had determined that she must stay behind. It was her duty. She had become the captain of this ship by default, and she intended to remain there to gather up the few specimens who were not ready to walk out on their world. But, she thought as they kept walking by her, ignoring her presence, soon there might be none left. Even if one of them stopped and invited her to join them, she would politely decline. Her honor—her family's honor—would simply not allow it. But that path of light streaming in past the titanium door was almost hypnotic to her medicated eyes, as it slowly morphed from gold to orange to a startling shade of red. Against her better judgment, Camilla 2.0 decided to steal a look. She would most assuredly not walk outside, but would take a quick peek from the safety of the doorway. It occurred to her that it might be courteous to inform the president and Mr. Hurley that she was not going to leave them like all the others, but she did not want to make these adults feel any more foolish or worried than they already were. The flow of specimens had slowed to a trickle, just single exits now, rather than large groups all trying to squeeze through the small opening at once.

Camilla walked over and stepped into the brightness, the warmth sending a wave of goose bumps up under her knee socks where they popped through her pale skin, running all the way up to her scalp.

She carefully leaned her head outside and took in the sight of scores of specimens—boys and girls who looked just like her—filling what seemed to be the entire horizon of the desert. The world had gone silent. The only sound she could hear was the soft dry breeze blowing up dust against the hard steel edges of the tower itself. She scanned far and wide for a glimpse of Goldsmith, but only saw all of the shapes of the other young boys who were following in his footsteps. She stood there as the sun went dark and night fell before her, bidding a silent good-bye to the last specimen to fade into the distance as he slipped from her sight. And then Camilla turned around and closed the sliding door, sealed it tightly, and slowly began her long walk up the stairs to the solitary desk where the meticulous study sheets she had arranged for her final exams awaited.

EPILOGUE

"Don't worry. I've got a great memory."

Those really were the last words I ever said to Thomas Oliver Goldsmith. And maybe they were more appropriate than I could have known at the time, because it's this memory of mine that has in many ways kept me locked inside that school even after we all graduated. The last thing I wanted to do was put the story of Stansbury down on paper. From the first moment of my first creative writing seminar at Yale, my new classmates stole looks at me, because the rumors had already started: I was one of *them*, one of the kids who was at *that* school when it all happened. And in all of the courses that followed, every teacher and student was waiting for me to finally break down and write that story they all knew I had inside, but I never gave in. It would have been too easy, too cynical for me to re-create all the sordid details and watch as my audience used it to nourish their curiosities, turning my personal recollections into literary pornography.

But here I am a senior in college, and I've spent the past four years telling mediocre stories about everything else in the world but

Stansbury. I imagined all of the things a normal girl my age would find inspiring, and handed in short story after short story on eating disorders (literal ones and allegories), forbidden love (both interracial and intergenerational), satires on upper-class manners (some witty, some subversive, some plainly awful homages to Fitzgerald), childhood loss of innocence (boring ones filled with far too much animal imagery), a woman's right to choose (spare me, I know) and even dabbled in science fiction (my easily injured pride will not allow any more detailed a mention than this). While some of them earned me above-average grades, none won any awards, or even publication in the most pedestrian of campus literary magazines. Submitting them for group critique every other week eventually became unbearable. I would sit there in an old musty room with my peers, these unkempt retro-hippie pot smokers stuffing their faces with rancid vegetarian burritos as they mercilessly tore apart every sentence I'd written in between chomps and swallows. "Insincere," "stylish, but lacking true feeling," and "characters too emotionally guarded to resonate" were the most frequent thrusts of their comments. And the whole time, whichever professor presided over the seminar that particular semester would sit in the corner nodding along with the jury, and when they had finished picking the carcass of my latest work dry, he or she would inevitably hand down a nugget of wisdom along the lines of: "I think we're all still waiting for that one story, Camilla, where you really let go and show us what keeps you up at night, the one that may embarrass you, but will bring a surge of life to your carefully constructed use of language. Now, on the other hand, Teresa's delightful musings on her summer spent as an intern to the editor of the world's most powerful fashion magazine . . ." But every teacher and every class was really saying the same thing: Stop dillydallying with these little yarns about your feminine alienation, and start writing about all of the insanity that happened inside Stansbury Tower, the stuff that didn't get printed in the newspapers after the Senate committee testimony back in the spring of 2036. Take the gloves off and give us the real, uncensored version, so we can turn your adolescence into juicy dinner conversation.

Stansbury School's Class of 2036 ended up graduating on time that spring. The seventy or so of the three hundred and fifty seniors who remained after the tragic revelations that came to light on the day of Stella Saltzman's testimony to the United States Senate Select Committee on Education went through their final exams. The San Angeles police blocked off the majority of high-trafficked floors inside the tower for their investigation, so the tests were held in makeshift progression rooms on lower levels; but we were able to have commencement inside the coliseum as planned. Of course, it felt strange and empty. Without the headmaster or President Lang around to conduct the ceremony, a team of junior level administrators and professors— lead among them was Professor Jeffrey Nelson—stood in with predictably clumsy results. As promised to Mr. Goldsmith, I delivered the valedictorian's speech to the few who stuck around. I neglected the usual exhortation to, basically, take over the world in time for our fifth-year reunion, in favor of eulogizing the departed headmaster and encouraging my fellow specimens to one day affect someone as much as he had affected us. Not so surprisingly, the usual talk of conquest and domination of years past went over much better than what I had to say. My father and mother seemed to be the only ones in the audience who applauded. There were, however, quite a few TV crews and reporters who were in attendance. The school's trustees thought it would make for good PR to balance out everything else for which Stansbury was making news. Unfortunately, it didn't even come close.

You see, the next time I saw Mr. Goldsmith was the following day on a plasma-screen broadcast in an elevator pod, after his departure from the tower along with 1,875 specimens. He was being introduced to the public at a press conference held at the San Angeles Police Department's central offices, and was flanked by the noted Stansbury critic Senator Arthur Milford Bloom on one side and the chief of police with his district attorney on the other. The news anchors and writers labeled him a noble whistle-blower, the perfect witness, who was willing to sacrifice all of the benefits the corrupt institution of Stansbury conferred upon him in order to bring justice to those who deserved it. His voice sounded much older when he spoke into the assembled microphones and tape recorders. His shoulders were held high. His beautiful blond crown of hair seemed to have gone several shades darker overnight. He looked, well, like a grown-up. Standing there alone inside that elevator pod, I could imagine all of America swooning over him. I wondered who coached him to radiate that kind of authority, and then remembered: Stansbury did.

Before a national television audience, Mr. Goldsmith calmly named President Judith Lang as the mastermind of a criminal conspiracy aimed at procuring a $1 trillion annual government grant for the school at any cost. He accused her of premeditating and orchestrating the murders of six Stansbury alumni, the school's headmaster, and a reporter for the *San Angeles Times*, as well as devising a complex plot to frame an innocent eighteen-year-old orphan named William Winston Cooley for the crimes. The following week, Goldsmith enumerated the intricacies of this plot in a lengthy testimony to a grand jury.

President Judith Lang, the ringleader of the Stansbury conspiracy, was charged with eight counts of first-degree murder. Due to California's progressive stance regarding the death penalty, she is currently serving consecutive life sentences in a maximum security penitentiary. Miss Sadie Sarah Chapman, of the New York City Chapmans, was tried as an adult, but was able—through a top-notch criminal defense lawyer her father hired—to successfully plead guilty by reason of insanity brought on by the large amounts of behavior-altering drugs with which the school supplied its specimens with on a daily basis. She is in the midst of a ten-year sentence at a San Angeles prison known for its exceptional mental health facilities, and is eligible for parole in 2043. During the Stansbury trial—dubbed "The Preppie Massacre" by the *San Angeles Times*—neither the prosecution nor the defense made mention of the popular tabloid rumor that Judith Lang was actually Thomas Oliver Goldsmith's biological mother.

After the criminal phase of the trial the civil charges commenced. Multiple families of past and present specimens brought a multibillion dollar class-action suit against the school's trustees, charging them with violating dozens of child labor laws in the production of Stansbury's famed, hugely profitable pharmaceutical advances, as well transgressing multiple child abuse statutes by providing specimens with drugs they falsely claimed were approved by the Food and Drug Administration (such as the ADD vaccine, among others) and forcing delinquents to undergo the sort of incarceration and peer review that qualified as cruel and unusual punishment in the eyes of the law (Mr. Goldsmith was an especially enthusiastic witness during this phase of the trial). The charges were devastating. The board of trustees was ordered to pay out packages of compensation in the hundreds of millions. Coming on the heels of the Preppie Massacre Trial, the once proud name of Stansbury was forever tarnished.

The school did, however, survive. With strict government oversight, the trustees appointed an interim administration, mixing Stansbury veterans with eager volunteers from outside schools and universities to keep the place going. The med cycle was eliminated. The trustees had windows—real windows—installed in the tower over the summer holiday. Enrollment dropped by some fifty percent, but the administrators and professors who remained—most of them chose to stay, surprisingly enough—have been very vocal about keeping the good things about Dr. Stansbury's dream alive.

The fate of Panacetix, Professor Alan Partridge's heralded cure for cancer, remains unresolved. Despite its obvious allure, production of the medication was frozen during the months of legal and political drama involving the school in which it was created. Although there have been outcries for the government to nationalize his patented formula, the country's leaders have been averse to doing so. Meanwhile, the Professor has been in long negotiations to enter into a business deal with one of several pharmaceutical giants, but the talks stall on a regular basis due to one rather unconventional demand: Partridge is adamant that portions of what will surely be gargantuan profits go toward the families of each and every specimen over the years that had enrolled in his progressions, as well as the families of the six murdered alumni.

The Stansbury courtroom drama that gripped much of the nation and provoked passionate public debate over the direction of education and America's continued obsession with academic excellence ended nearly a year after it began. It made temporary stars of Mr. Goldsmith and Mr. Cooley, but neither took the bait of book offers, made-for-TV movie deals, or prime-time interviews. When their testimony ended, they disappeared completely from the public eye. In this, they were, I suppose, just like the rest of us. After everything that had happened, it was rare to come across a former specimen who would admit they were educated at Stansbury. Nobody wanted to be perceived as if they had benefited from a corrupt, murderous regime, even if there was no way they could have known about it while it existed. Everyone—the ones who left with Cooley and Goldsmith that day, and the few who left with me following commencement—bid each other silent good-byes and tried their best to melt into society unnoticed, to pursue their dreams and goals without the golden emblems on their chests or the once proud declaration of having been raised inside the tower.

I saw the transformation before my eyes during my freshman year of college, as I watched the television broadcasts from inside the courtroom, quickly switching channels to some ridiculous soap opera if anyone ever came knocking at my door. I'd walk out into the center of campus, into the dining rooms, into local bars and house parties, and see those familiar faces, and they, of course, would see me. There were twenty-eight other specimens in my graduating class who matriculated along with me at Yale, and I am certain that not once have any of us admitted where we were formed. Other students talk about us in hushed tones, knowing that the spaces left empty next to the *High School* query in our class's face book were full of meaning. I've heard naïve freshmen ask former specimens where they attended high school—sometimes they asked to make routine small talk, and other times on a bet or a dare—and heard the response that, while it sounded strange at first, is now my own standard answer: "Oh, just a little school out West. Nowhere you'd have heard of. What about you?"

Walk through this country's cities and sometimes you might catch a glimpse of one of us; those unusually tall, calm-faced men and women on the street pushing strollers, speed walking to catch the monorail to the office, or even putting out the garbage on Wednesdays and Fridays on tree-lined suburban streets. Shortly after the press revealed that close to two thousand specimens walked out into the desert that day and that many are still unaccounted for, it was speculated in workplaces, on street corners, in restaurants, who might be one of *them*. I will say this: I know them when I see them. They're the ones who stand out in the crowds, who always seem to laugh at jokes a moment too late, the ones who—like anyone else, I guess—wonder why the world didn't end up as perfectly as they were told it would. Sometimes I see them and they see me. We exchange curt nods and walk along, keeping the secrets only for those who understand.

An encounter like this is how I finally came to write this story, actually. A few months ago, during winter break, I was visiting my family in San Angeles and had stopped inside a department store for some last-minute Christmas shopping. One thing that most assuredly has not changed over the years is the overcrowding. The place was packed full of people dashing around frantically, acting more or less like animals.

"Camilla?" came the voice of a young man behind me. Somehow I just knew it had to be a specimen. Forgetting all about the rigors of anonymity, silent repentance, and curt, meaning-filled nods, I turned around and came face to face with Mr. Cooley. The last time I saw him was on television during the trials three years ago. His eyes still had that unmistakably defiant energy simmering inside of them. He had a coat of brown stubble covering his face and an inviting smile. I wanted it to be an inviting one, anyway, and made it that, whether he intended it as such or not.

"Mr. Cooley," I stammered, cringing at the officious sound of my own voice as soon as it left my lips.

"Hey," he said, that grin still on his face, "it's Will now, okay? Just Will." The years had done good things for him. His body had filled out from skinny to firm. He might have even grown an inch or two.

"Squeezing that shopping in before the big day, right?"

"Yeah." He held up a bag with an enormous brown stuffed monkey inside. "For my daughter." I remembered the look on his face when it was just the two of us waiting in an expelled specimen's bedroom suite that one day, bloody and scared, the way he stumbled over his words trying to extend an olive branch to me by complimenting, of all things, my writing. I could see the look in his eye. He was back in that room too, probably amazed that I ever terrified him, that any of us ever terrified him.

"What's her name?" I asked.

"Evan."

We left the department store and headed to a deserted stretch of C Sector, where we sat down and had an early dinner together inside some shabby diner. To my surprise, he asked me about Goldsmith before I could ask him. Cooley—I mean Will—told me he disappeared right after the trial and didn't leave a forwarding address or phone number. He told me he was surprised to hear that Goldsmith didn't get in touch, because of how much he talked about me after they left the school, how he called me the only real thing about the whole place. I started to cry. And then Will started to cry too.

He asked how my writing was coming along and I told him the truth, that all of it was fake, lies told in flowery prose, that our story was the only one anyone wanted to hear—including, probably, myself—and that despite my integrity, I, the once proud purebred ice princess of Stansbury, was now going to take a stab at it only because I was scared of flunking out. Something about this idea appealed to the punk rebel that was still inside of him, most likely the delicious irony of a former highly-touted specimen selling out her memories of the school—photographic memories, no less—in order to pass out of a course and avoid the real work of creating something from scratch. So we sat there at that chipped Formica table for hours, well into the evening, and we put the pieces of this story back together. I loved hearing about the adventures of he and Goldsmith venturing away from the tower's walls and sleuthing-out an impossible mystery; he loved hearing about the valedictorian's clumsy romantic missteps. Tiny bells would jingle whenever the diner's door swung open and we both looked at it each time it happened like we were expecting Goldsmith to rush in, apologize for his tardiness, and sit down for a piece of warm apple pie. I told Will that I'd send him a copy when it was finished. He recited his address, smiling because I never had to write stuff down to remember it. He said he'd read my story to Evan every night before bedtime. I don't think he was kidding.

We paid the bill and stood up to go. He had a wife and little girl waiting for him. And I, as usual, had homework to complete. We stepped out into the street and I watched Will Cooley as he disappeared into the throngs of pedestrians on the sidewalk, that big shopping bag in his hand, a stuffed animal's face peeking out of the top, looking back at me, smiling a silent good-bye. Then I went on my own way, blending into the masses of people happy just because it was a beautiful night during that special time of year. And I was glad to find that, despite the story I was finally prepared to tell, I felt the exact same way.

—Miss Camilla Moore II (Stansbury School, Class of 2036)
New Haven, Connecticut
April 21, 2040